That Summer In Eagle Street

Harry Bowling

HEADLINE

First published in 1995
by HEADLINE BOOK PUBLISHING

First published in paperback in 1996
by HEADLINE BOOK PUBLISHING

10 9 8 7 6 5 4 3 2

ISBN 0 7472 5196 7

Typeset by
Letterpart Limited, Reigate, Surrey

Printed and bound in Great Britain by
BPC Paperbacks Ltd

HEADLINE BOOK PUBLISHING
A division of Hodder Headline PLC
338 Euston Road
London NW1 3BH

Harry Bowling was born in Bermondsey, London, and left school at fourteen to supplement the family income as an office boy in a riverside provisions' merchant. Called up for National Service in the 1950s, he has since been variously employed as lorry driver, milkman, meat cutter, carpenter and decorator, and community worker. He now writes full time. He is the author of ten previous novels: *Waggoner's Way*, *The Farrans of Fellmonger Street*, *Pedlar's Row*, *Backstreet Child*, *The Girl from Cotton Lane*, *Gaslight in Page Street*, *Paragon Place*, *Ironmonger's Daughter*, *Tuppence to Tooley Street* and *Conner Street's War*. He is married and lives with his family, dividing his time between Lancashire and Deptford.

'What makes Harry's novels work is their warmth and authenticity. Their spirit comes from the author himself and his abiding memories of family life as it was once lived in the slums of southeast London'   *Today*

To Edna
with love

Prologue

September 1940

It was a warm and sunny Saturday, and the country had been at war for exactly one year and four days. In the North Atlantic the conflict was raging and the toll in human lives and shipping had risen alarmingly; in France two massed armies faced each other across the Maginot Line; and in Bermondsey, on that balmy Saturday afternoon, the Eagle Street women went shopping.

The stalls that stretched in a long ragged line along Tower Bridge Road were piled high with fruit and vegetables, and there was wet fish fresh from Billingsgate Market. Cheap Jack's stall was heaped up too with his usual paraphernalia, and next to it a haberdashery stall was decked out with cottons and ribbons, frills and lace in a colourful display. The war seemed to have wrought no changes here in the market, except for one thing: there were no bananas to be seen anywhere.

The women shopped as usual, traipsing from one end of the market to the other, buying from the stalls and squeezing in and out of the neighbouring shops, stopping briefly to hear from one stallholder that Godfrey's Tonic was the

1

answer to practically all their problems, and a bargain at one shilling and sixpence a bottle. They smiled cynically and walked on, and gradually shopping bags became heavier and ration books were marked, ticked and stamped for the week. Some of them stopped at the sarsaparilla stall and sipped the hot concoction, which according to the costermonger, 'Looks good, tastes good, an' what's more it does yer good.'

On that warm, sunny Saturday afternoon the children of Eagle Street played in their small turning off the Tower Bridge Road, happy, innocent and unaffected as yet by the war, except that they were missing their friends who had been evacuated, and there were no bananas to eat. They played at the bone-dry kerbside, rolling glass marbles and scraping cryptic messages in the dust, constantly being warned to keep away from the smelly drains for fear of scarlet fever and worse. They sat on their doorsteps exchanging cigarette cards, parading lead soldiers and cuddling tatty dolls, and on the doorstep of number 6 the street's newest arrival was being discussed.

'Well, she is very pretty, but she's all crinkly an' sort o' red,' Linda Weston told her best friend.

'I fink all babies look really ugly at first,' Kate Selby replied. 'My sister looked like a little pig when she was born.'

Linda pulled a face. 'My little baby bruvver's got ginger 'air an' a screwed-up nose, but 'e's very pretty.'

The two eight-year-olds lapsed into silence and then Kate popped the question, 'Can I see 'er?'

Linda looked thoughtful for a while. 'I s'pect yer can, but not terday. You can be the first one ter see 'er though, 'cos you're my best friend.'

They looked along the turning and saw a large woman approaching. She wore a long black coat and hat and carried a small, oblong leather bag. Her feet sounded loudly on the pavement, and as she drew near the two children made way for her to enter the house. She gave them a brief smile and Linda saw that her forehead was covered in sweat.

'Is she gonna barf the baby?' Kate asked in a low voice.

Linda nodded. 'She 'as ter come every day till Mum's better.'

Her friend glanced furtively along the dark passage and watched the large woman moving about the scullery, then she turned to Linda. 'My mum said it's dangerous to 'ave too many children, 'specially when yer not very young.'

'My mum's not old,' Linda told her sharply.

'Yeah, I know, but six is a lot o' children to 'ave.'

Linda's father came to the front door and smiled weakly at his eldest child. He was a big, stocky man with dark hair greying at the sides and soft brown eyes. He wore a collarless, blue-striped shirt with the sleeves rolled up over his elbows and a thick leather belt around his waist. His heavy boots were covered in dust and his thick trousers stained with grease.

'As soon as the midwife's finished I'll be doin' the tea, so don't go wanderin' too far away,' he warned her. 'I'll want yer ter collect the little ones.'

Linda nodded obediently and watched him hurry back down the passage. 'I better not go down the market, Kate,' she said, and seeing the look of disappointment on her friend's face, 'but we could go up on the roof.'

Kate shook her head. 'My mum said I mustn't go up there, in case I fall.'

'Yer can't fall unless yer climb up on the wall,' Linda told her.

'Yeah, but the porter might catch us, an' 'e'll tell us off 'cos we don't live there,' Kate replied, looking apprehensive.

'C'mon, the porter won't know we're there if we're very quiet,' Linda pressed her. 'Besides, 'e's always up the pub on Saturdays. It'll be nice up there an' we can see fer miles. Yer can even see St Paul's an' lots of ovver places.'

'Oh, all right then,' Kate sighed.

Linda stood up and brushed her hand down her shabby cotton dress, the mischievous look in her pale blue eyes lighting up her pretty face. 'Charlie Bradley goes up there sometimes,' she said.

The two held hands as they walked across the street and slipped into the block entrance facing number 6, with Linda urging her reluctant friend on. They climbed the creaking wooden stairs of Sunlight Buildings to the first landing and walked on tiptoe past the front doors to the next flight of stairs. As they walked quietly along the second landing a door opened and an old lady came out carrying a shopping basket.

'You gels aren't s'posed ter be up 'ere,' she growled at them.

'We promise we won't make a noise, Mrs Brown,' Linda told her.

They reached the top landing and Kate looked frightened as she stared up at the short flight of stairs which led out on to the flat roof. 'The door's locked,' she whispered.

'No, it's not. C'mon, scaredy-cat,' Linda urged her.

'I'm not scared, but I'm goin' down though. I gotta be 'ome early fer tea,' Kate told her, glancing up nervously at the roof door whose ancient coating of brown paint was peeling away.

'Well, I'm goin' up,' Linda said firmly. 'I'll see yer termorrer then.'

The asphalted roof was soft underfoot as the young girl stepped out through the doorway and walked quietly towards the balustrade. It was chest high to her and she reached up on her toes to peer down into the street below. She could see the Colton children by the lamppost and then her friend Kate walking quickly along to the end house. The sun beat down from a cloudless afternoon sky and there was just a hint of a breeze. Linda stood staring out into the distance, her fair hair barely stirring. She could see the tops of the riverside cranes and the tall factory chimneys and smell tar and woodsmoke, and as she sauntered round to the other side she saw the golden-tipped dome of St Paul's glistening in the sunlight. Here at the back of the roof Bill Simpson kept his pigeons in a ramshackle lean-to, which was enclosed with a wood framework of wire mesh. The old man never seemed to mind who went on the roof provided they gave his beloved pigeons a wide berth. In his seventies now, Bill lived with his wife in the top flat just below the roost, and flying his birds and getting his pint of beer were all he cared about. Today he was sitting comfortably in the Beehive on the corner of Eagle Street, and Linda Weston was left alone with the whole roof to herself.

Another baby in the family had been quite an upheaval so far. Her dad was pleased, but her mother had had a hard time with the birth and was still confined to bed so he was rushed off his feet and sometimes shouted at them all. The midwife was nice but she had a loud voice and made everyone feel a little frightened. Tommy, Linda's three-year-old brother, cried every time he saw her and four-year-old Pamela looked very frightened too. Six-year-old James did not seem to mind too much and his usually dirty face took on a curious look whenever she arrived. Frankie was the most daring of the Weston children and he made the rest of them giggle with his antics behind the big woman's back.

Linda stared out over the rooftops to the far patch of green. It would be lovely to live in a nice house in the country, she thought. They could have a swing in the garden and play in the fields. The war would be over and they could grow potatoes and cabbages and carrots. Maybe they could have pet rabbits and a puppy dog that didn't bark very much. When the winter came they could all build a big snowman with coke for its eyes and it could have a pipe and a scarf. Their father would get a job on a farm and take them all to see the animals. He would earn lots of money and not have to work nights in the factory any more.

The distant hum grew slowly louder and Linda stared into the sky, suddenly becoming frightened as she spotted the planes. They were getting nearer, flying together like a swarm of bees and she heard the terrible wailing noise of the siren start up nearby. Thuds reverberated, dull at first but then louder and louder. She could see the small white puffs of cloud around the planes as they grew larger in the blue sky. There was a flash of fire and immediately after a loud crash sounded. Black smoke and flames rose upwards and it seemed as if the whole world was on fire. The noise was deafening and the petrified eight-year-old slid down against the balustrade and pressed her hands hard over her ears. She was too frightened to move, too terrified to look out at the carnage being wrought and she huddled against the warm brickwork, tears beginning to fall.

She heard him gasp before she saw him and then he was kneeling down in front of her.

'It's all right. They're bombin' the Surrey Docks,' he said knowledgeably. 'We'll be OK. They're not bombin' us.'

Linda looked up at him and through her tears she could see his large brown eyes wide with excitement. His black curly hair was unkempt and his grubby face flushed. He had a grey pullover over his dirty white shirt and grey trousers, and his socks were hanging down over his dusty shoes.

'I'm frightened,' she said tearfully.

'C'mon, I'll see yer down,' he told her confidently.

'Fanks, Charlie,' she mumbled in a tiny voice.

The eleven-year-old boy stood up and reached out his hands and when she clasped them he pulled her up. She leaned against him as the noise increased to a crescendo and he put his arm around her. 'It's our guns firin' at 'em,' he told her reassuringly. 'Look, yer can see the bursts comin' from the park.'

Linda shook her head. 'I can't look. Take me down, Charlie, please,' she implored him.

The lad laughed, made to feel like a knight in shining armour as she nestled closer against him. He led her down to the street below and the terrified faces of the Eagle Street folk. Her father was out on the street, his face chalk white, and when he saw her he stretched his arms out.

'Fanks, Charlie,' she said quickly, before she ran into her father's arms.

'It was nuffink,' Charlie said, walking away calmly with an exaggerated swagger.

Chapter One

The warm June evening sky was full of fire; molten reds and gold shifting and blending into deep purple as the night came down. On Eagle Street the children were waiting, knowing that soon the clanging bell would herald the arrival of the toffee-apple man. Pennies rattled and grew hot in clenched fists as anxious faces looked towards the Tower Bridge Road.

'I'm gettin' two, one fer me an' one fer me bruvver,' one child announced to all and sundry.

'Yer gotta be careful they ain't got worms in 'em,' another young lad said. 'Worms can grow ter be snakes if yer eat 'em.'

'Who wants to eat snakes?' the first lad replied.

'There 'e is!' they cried out as a bell sounded loudly and the tall, ungainly toffee-apple man pedalled his rusty bicycle into the small turning. The large wicker basket on the handlebar disappeared beneath a seething mass of heads and arms and outstretched hands. More children came flowing out from the little houses, pennies clasped tightly in their hands as they joined the throng around the bicycle.

'Now, don't push an' shove. There's enough ter go round,' the vendor told them sternly.

The children stood wide-eyed as the man separated the sticky toffee-apples and passed them out.

'Two, mister.'

'Me first.'

'I want two as well.'

'Now, don't push an' shove, I told yer. There's plenty left.'

'Where's me penny?! I've dropped me penny,' one small lad shouted out.

'There it is, on the kerb,' his friend told him.

The children of Eagle Street were joined by those from the neighbouring backstreet and the growing rumpus around the bicycle was duly noted and frowned upon by the two hawks, Mrs Harriman and Mrs Chaplin.

'I fink they should stop it this time o' night,' Doris Harriman remarked.

'I make yer right,' Phyllis Chaplin said. 'Kids should be in bed by now. I dunno where their muvvers are to allow it.'

'I'd never let a kid o' mine out this late,' Doris went on.

'Me neivver. They just don't care,' Phyllis remarked, her arms folded over her apron.

The two thin-faced middle-aged women were never apart and were often taken for sisters. They might as well have been, for their views on everything and everybody seemed to coincide to an unnatural degree.

'Did yer 'ear that Dopey Dick's bin banned from the pub?' Phyllis asked.

''As 'e?' Doris said, looking surprised.

''E was blasphemin' in front o' some priests who were in there 'avin' a drink an' the guv'nor chucked 'im out,' Phyllis went on. 'I mean, 'ow could yer?'

''E could.'

''E should be locked up. Fancy swearin' at priests.'

The frenzy at the kerbside had abated and the toffee-apple man was catching his breath. He served the last of his impatient customers and then decided to pedal home for another supply before it got dark. The two viragos had run out of breath themselves and decided to retire to their respective parlours, but not before Doris had given her friend an update on the medical condition of one of their near neighbours.

''E's bad again, by all accounts.'

Phyllis followed the direction of her friend's jerking head. 'Who, John Weston?'

'Yeah. Dora's bin ter the doctor's fer some more jollop. I don't fink it does 'im any good, but there you are. If 'e finks it does, what can yer say?'

'Oh well. Night, Doris.'

'G'night, Phyllis.'

John Weston leaned back in his chair and grunted as the sharp pain in his side stabbed like a knife. 'It's easin' up but it still catches me now an' then,' he said.

'Well, you just take it easy, an' don't start worryin' about gettin' back before yer feel prop'ly fit again,' Dora told him firmly. 'We can manage.'

John frowned as he looked at his devoted wife. 'Yer gonna be short o' Frankie's money soon,' he said in a worried voice. ''E'll be called up any time now. Then there's James. 'E'll be eighteen next year. We'll 'ave two of 'em away tergevver.'

'Well, it can't be 'elped,' she replied cheerfully. 'Pam's

11

leavin' school this September an' Tommy next year. They'll balance it out.'

John moved his heavy frame in the chair to ease the dull ache and picked up the glass of barley water. 'This stuff's fillin' me up like a bleedin' balloon,' he grumbled.

'That's as it may be, but yer gotta take notice o' the doctor. 'E said it's the finest fing ter take when yer got kidney trouble,' Dora reminded him.

'It's only a cold in me kidneys, it's not exactly kidney trouble,' John demurred.

'Doctor Sweetley said it's a kidney infection an' the only way ter clear it is ter do as 'e ses an' drink gallons o' that. Bloody 'ell, John, it's cheap enough, pearl barley, an' it's no 'ardship boilin' it up. An' while we're on about yer kidneys, take my advice an' see if yer can get a dry job. Standin' in all that wet's brought yer trouble on, mark my words.'

'Yeah, it's all right you sayin' that but the steam room pays the best wages,' John told her. 'If I went anywhere else in the factory I'd 'ave ter take a drop in pay.'

'Well, sod it. Take a drop,' Dora replied angrily. 'Yer gotta look after yerself now. You ain't a spring chicken remember.'

John gave his wife a warm smile. 'Yer right, luv. I got you an' the kids ter fink about,' he said quietly.

Linda Weston walked along Eagle Street and entered Sunlight Buildings. She climbed the three flights of stairs to the top landing and then the short flight that led out on to the roof. They were all there. Kate Selby was standing some way apart from the others, talking intimately with Peter Ridley who lived in the Buildings. Kate was dark and shapely, with full lips and eyes that teased and tempted the young men, but those who knew her well enough realised that Kate Selby was no siren, although she flirted with such enthusiasm. In fact she was still a child at heart.

The rest of the young people stood in a group, drawn up on to the roof away from the street below by the quietness and intimacy of the place. It was their domain, a place to plan, plot and scheme, and a place to weave dreams.

The old Buildings had been erected way back in 1876, a time when the borough was developing as an industrial area. Docks, wharves, food factories and tanneries, sheet-metal firms and the growing railway network were all attracting a large workforce, and enterprising businessmen saw the sense in buying up the available land that was already occupied by stinking insanitary hovels. They put up new tenement blocks with inside toilets and running water, and rows of terraced houses for the rapidly growing population. Some of the large tenement blocks had flat roofs, accessible from adjoining blocks, which afforded alternative means of escape from the buildings; thus the new safety law was satisfied without proper fire escapes being installed, and money was saved. The flat roof idea was also convenient for the tenants. It was a good place to put the washing out, instead of stringing it across the living room or hanging it over the fire and the gas stove, and risking setting the whole place alight.

The big disadvantage with the flat-roof tenement, however, was that rainwater tended to puddle and eventually penetrate the roof, seeping down through the walls. Sunlight Buildings had suffered in that way and was now a damp, unhealthy place to live in the winter, and even in the summer was not much better. The smell from the communal rubbish tip at one end of the tenement caused more than just discomfort. Flies and bluebottles swarmed into the flats, and Cheap Jack found it necessary to order ever-increasing stocks of flypapers to meet the growing demand. The young people of Eagle Street enjoyed using the roof, nevertheless, and on such nights as this it was never deserted.

Linda Weston waved a greeting to her best friend and left her and Peter Ridley on their own. The main group of young people was sitting around on planks stretched between upturned buckets or standing by the balustrade, and she went over to stand with Jenny Jordan, a girl of her own age who lived in the Buildings. The sky was darkening now, with the last tinge of gold and red fading rapidly.

'I love Friday nights,' Jenny sighed. 'There's the weekend ter look forward to. Two whole days away from that bloody thumpin' machinery.'

'Yeah, I like Friday nights too,' Linda told her with a sigh. 'It's bin bleedin' murder at the vaults this week. We 'ad a big contract ter finish an' we were on target fer our bonus, an' what d'yer fink?'

'Tell me,' Jenny said smiling.

'We run out o' labels, so we ended up on flat rate.'

'Oh dear. Never mind, it's Saturday termorrer.'

Linda was quiet for a while, her mind going back to the early days of the war, as it invariably did on nights like this. She had been standing almost on the same spot eleven years ago, when the roar got louder and the docks started to burn. She could see Charlie Bradley's face clearly and she smiled to herself as she recalled how grown up he had seemed that terrible afternoon. She had fallen in love with him that September day when he led her safely down into the arms of her father. It was an innocent puppy love that had stayed with her and grown; and despite the fact that he was three years older than her and never chatted her up the way he did other girls in the neighbourhood she still loved him, but now it was an adult love, and there was a desire inside her that frightened her sometimes with its intensity.

'Look at Kate Selby,' Jenny grumbled. 'Don't it make yer sick? She's all over 'im. I feel like goin' over an' tellin' 'im 'e's wastin' 'is time. 'E'll never get 'is 'and up 'er skirt.'

Linda laughed as she saw the look on Jenny's face. She was a plain girl in comparison with the voluptuous Kate. Her dark hair was thick and unruly and her mouth was small, with thin lips in an oval face. She was inclined to chubbiness too, but Linda suspected that underneath she had a passion and fire that would put Kate Selby in the shade.

'Seen anyfing o' Charlie Bradley?' Linda asked her.

'Only once since 'e got demobbed,' Jenny replied. 'I saw 'im goin' in the Bee'ive. 'E was wiv those Carter boys. I don't like them, they're right dirty gits. It was Nick Carter who got Beryl Page pregnant, an' that bruvver of 'is makes me shiver every time I see 'im. Boy-boy Carter's definitely the worst o' the two.'

Linda looked out over the rooftops of the houses opposite and saw the distant City buildings, some bathed in light and others grey and shrouded beneath a velvet blanket of dark sky. A gentle breeze touched her face and she sighed. 'It's a lovely night, Jenny,' she said quietly, her mind conjuring up the young man of her dreams, the brave knight who had rescued her from terrible danger and had later ridden to her rescue and saved her from a fate worse than death. Well, maybe not, she smiled to herself, but it was a long while ago and she had been very young. Tonight though, in the balmy, calm twilight, she felt tempted to share her childhood secret.

'We used ter meet up 'ere, me an' Charlie Bradley,' she told Jenny.

'Did yer?'

'Well, it wasn't planned. Nuffink like that,' Linda said smiling. 'But 'e always seemed ter be around when me an' Kate came up 'ere. I remember one day. It was school 'olidays durin' the doodlebug time, an' I was sittin' over there by the stairs talkin' ter Kate. I remember 'er gettin' upset over somefing or the ovver an' she stormed off. Yer know 'ow she was.'

''Ow she is,' Jenny corrected her.

'Yeah, well anyway I stayed up there by the stairs, leanin' against the slope. It was very warm an' then those Carter boys came up wiv a few o' their mates. They saw me an' started showin' off. Yer know what I mean. I 'ad me slippers off an' they nicked 'em. It was all fun ter them. They was passin' 'em to each ovver an' then Boy-boy Carter said 'e was gonna chuck 'em over the roof. I started cryin' I was so upset. But then I saw Charlie Bradley come up an' 'e grabbed the slippers an' brought 'em over ter me. The Carters started takin' the rise out o' me 'cos I was cryin', an' Charlie got really angry. 'E challenged Boy-boy to a fight, but it never came ter that. They all run off an' then Charlie sat wiv me fer a while. 'E was smashin'. 'E showed me this knife 'e'd found. It was one o' those Tarzan knives the lads used ter wear in their belts. Charlie sharpened it up on the concrete an' while we was chattin' away 'e cut a love-'eart in the washin' post. It's still there, let me show yer.'

Jenny followed her over to the stair doorway and Linda pointed to an adjacent post. 'There it is,' she said.

The post had been ravaged by the weather but the small neat heart shape could still clearly be seen in the light by the door. The initial 'C' had been cut inside the heart and below it at an angle there was a deep scratch mark.

'Charlie never finished it then,' Jenny remarked smiling. 'Was it meant ter be your initial?'

Linda nodded. 'There was an air raid an' before we could move this flyin' bomb came over. We both stood transfixed. It looked like it was comin' directly at us. Suddenly the engine stopped an' we saw it start ter dive. Charlie grabbed me an' we both crouched down by the stairs. It ended up on the factory in the street. Twenty people were killed that day.'

'Yeah, I remember me mum an' dad talkin' about it,' Jenny replied. 'I was evacuated at the time.'

Linda walked over to the balustrade and leaned on the high wall. That was the second time Charlie had been there when she needed him, she thought; then she had needed him as a child, seeking comfort and protection, but now she needed him in the way a grown woman would.

'Well, I'd better get in, it's gettin' late,' Jenny sighed. 'See yer around, Lin.'

'Yeah, see yer around, Jen.'

Night had settled down now, with a pale moon rising and stars beginning to dot the deepening sky. The breeze strengthened, moving Linda's soft fair hair, and she shivered as she reluctantly turned towards the stairway, away from the twinkling lights and the place that haunted her dreams.

Chapter Two

The warm June weather seemed to have settled in and the rays of the morning sun struck Sunlight Buildings, highlighting the old brickwork and the neglected window frames. The little row of houses facing the tenement block was still in shadow and folk enjoyed the cool air as they stood chatting at their front doors.

Eagle Street led off from the centre of Tower Bridge Road, from the middle of the market, and when entering the small turning from that end the Beehive public house was on the left-hand corner. Beyond the pub was a yard protected by a pair of stout wooden gates, and past the gates were the terraced houses. At the end of the row there was a cleared, open bombsite, where the leather factory had once been. On the right-hand side of the turning, Sunlight Buildings followed on from the corner bakery and took up the whole length of the street, and at the far end of the tenement block there was an alleyway where the huge communal bins were placed. Gale Street led away at right angles at the far end, and its twin rows of terraced houses stretched the whole length of the road.

Eagle Street's closeness to the market meant shopping

could be done in a relaxed way. The Eagle Street women tended to shop as they saw fit and as the need arose, rather than try to do all their shopping in one trip. While the market was set up and the shops were open there was a continual coming and going in Eagle Street. The women of Gale Street used it as a route to the market, and a rapport grew up between the denizens of the respective streets. Everyone in Gale Street knew what was going on in Eagle Street, and nothing in Gale Street could ever be kept from the inquiring Eagle Street folk.

At number 6 Eagle Street, John Weston was feeling better and his complaint was yielding favourably to gallons of barley water. At number 10 Gale Street, Mrs Watson was feeling a little more sprightly too; her arthritic hip was always easier in the summer. They and their ailments were being discussed and exaggerated by interested neighbours, as was everyone else who purposely or otherwise put themselves in the limelight.

Dora Weston usually made two trips to the Tower Bridge Road market on Saturdays if the weather was kind, and today it was warm and sunny. First she bought her vegetables and fruit from the stalls, calling in at Cohen's grocery store on her way home. The next visit was more leisurely. She strolled along the line of stalls, idly looking at what was on offer, and as she stopped at Cheap Jack's stall she felt a tug on her arm.

''Ello, luv. I 'ear John's not too good then.'

Dora turned to see Phyllis Chaplin, her neighbour from number 2. She was a slightly-built woman in her mid-fifties, hawk-faced and with her brown hair scooped up into a bright blue hairnet. She was with Mrs Harriman from number 1. Like Mrs Chaplin, Doris Harriman was small and thin. She had piercing brown eyes and a headful of curlers. Dick Conners, the street's drunk, had named them the hawks, and as she faced the two women that morning Dora had to admit that it was an inspired description.

'As a matter o' fact, 'e's a lot better terday,' she said, smiling at them both.

'I'm glad to 'ear it,' Phyllis replied.

'It just shows yer can't believe all yer told, can yer?' Doris added.

'It's funny 'ow bad news gets round quicker than good news,' Dora said stiffly.

'We've just bin talkin' ter Mrs Watson. 'Er wiv the bad 'ip. Terrible pain she's in,' Phyllis said, pinching her chin between thumb and forefinger. 'She was sayin' she might 'ave ter go in again.'

Dora could not help feeling somewhat sorry for the two hawks. Phyllis Chaplin's husband had left her for a younger woman a few years ago and Doris Harriman's husband had been killed while firefighting during the Blitz. They were both lonely souls who found comfort in sharing their time with each other, and they took pleasure in gleaning all the information they could and then spreading the news far and wide.

Feeling sorry for the two was one thing, but to stop and trade the current local gossip, unreliable or not, was a different matter, Dora thought. 'Well, I better get 'ome. John might be needin' me fer somefing,' she told them.

The two hawks moved off and Dora continued her stroll, hoping to avoid any more confabulations. She passed the clothes shops at the end of the market and turned back towards Eagle Street, reminding herself to get some shoe-laces from the haberdashery stall. The sun was high in a clear blue sky and she strolled along leisurely, enjoying the afternoon jaunt. As she reached the haberdashery stall she met up with her next-door neighbour, Maggie Gainsford. Maggie had five children, the eldest nine, and she was too busy to stand chatting to the likes of Doris and Phyllis. She had been caught on the hop today, however, but had managed to make a quick getaway.

Dora turned quickly as Maggie touched her arm. ''Ello, luv, I didn't see you there,' she said, smiling.

'I've just seen the ugly sisters,' Maggie told her, smiling wickedly. 'They started ter tell me all the tales o' the old iron pot but I wasn't 'avin' any of it.'

'I 'ad the pleasure just a little while ago,' Dora told her. 'Still, they're ter be pitied.'

'Yeah, I s'pose so,' Maggie replied grudgingly.

Dora bought shoelaces and some white cotton and then the two women walked home together.

'I must say you're lookin' more cheerful this mornin',' Maggie remarked.

'Yeah, I feel it,' Dora said. 'My John's a lot better. It's bin a worry.'

'I was the same when my Wally got that back trouble. Off fer weeks 'e was. I was gettin' really worried in case 'e could never work again. Fortunately 'e made a good recovery.'

'I wish my John didn't 'ave ter do that night work,' Dora said sighing. 'It's a killer. 'E ain't bin really right since 'e started it.'

'I know what yer mean,' Maggie replied. 'When my Wally was at the gasworks 'e done a lot o' shift work. I couldn't sleep prop'ly on me own, even though the kids were there. It sounds funny but it's true.'

They turned into Eagle Street past the Beehive just as the public-bar door opened and Dopey Dick Conners staggered out into the turning. 'All right! All right! I know where I'm not wanted. In future you can stuff yer bloody pub right up— sorry gels, I didn't see yer there,' he said, raising his cap in an exaggerated gesture as he reeled backwards on the pavement.

'I thought 'e was barred from the pub,' Maggie said quickly, looking puzzled.

'Only the saloon bar, so I was told,' Dora replied, before turning to the drunk. 'Now what's the trouble wiv you, Dick?' she said sharply. 'I 'ope you ain't bin makin' a nuisance o' yerself again after what yer promised.'

Dick Conners stood up straight with an effort and put his cap back on his wiry fair hair. 'I wasn't causin' any trouble, gel, as the good Lord's my judge,' he said slurring. 'I was just – just 'avin' a quiet pint when that load o' camel shit came in. They fink they own the bloody pub.'

'Who's they?' Dora asked him, hiding a smile.

'Why, those bookies. Fink they know everyfing they do,' Dick grumbled. 'I foxed 'em though. I asked 'em who won the Lord Derby Gold Cup in nineteen 'undred an' frozen ter death. None of 'em knew the answer. I told 'em though. I told 'em it was Charlie Peace the burglar when the ole boy was out. Ha ha.'

'Yer better get 'ome an' sleep it off,' Maggie advised him.

'It's all right, darlin', I'm fine. The guv'nor chucked me out the pub 'e did. Bloody rabble,' the inebriate went on, trying hard to keep his balance. 'We used ter shoot the likes of 'im when I was in India. Bloody punkah wallah, that's all 'e is.'

The two women tried hard not to laugh at the unfortunate drunk, not wanting him to feel humiliated. During the twenties and thirties Dick Conners had been a proud soldier in the British Army, serving in India, Africa and the Middle East, and had retired on a small pension just before the Second World War. He volunteered as an air-raid warden when war broke out and was dug out from beneath a pile of rubble when part of Long Lane was flattened by a high-explosive bomb at the height of the Blitz. Dick had never been the same afterwards and as time went on he became more and more dependent on drink. He was merely an object of ridicule to many who did not understand or did not want to, but there were some kind souls who still had a high regard for Dick Conners and sympathised with him, tolerating his foibles.

'Come on, Dick, I'll see yer ter yer door,' Dora said, attempting to take him by the arm. The drunk was too quick for her however, and he staggered back alarmingly.

'I'm all right, gel,' he slurred. 'I'm gonna take a nice steady stroll down ter Manzies an' get meself a nice pie an' mash.'

Maggie and Dora looked at each other in resignation. There was nothing more they could do, though they both remembered the incident a few weeks ago when they passed the pie shop together in Tower Bridge Road and saw the crowd gathered. A policeman was trying to revive Dopey Dick after he had fallen asleep in the shop, snoring loudly with his head resting in a plate of fresh pie, mash and liquor.

'Mind 'ow yer go then,' Dora warned him. 'An' no fallin' asleep.'

'Bloody shame,' Maggie said sadly.

'Yeah it is,' Dora replied. 'Anyway come in fer a cuppa. I wanna ask yer somefing.'

Mr and Mrs Coombes were the elderly occupants of number 9, the last house but one in Eagle Street, where Dick Conners lodged. Ginny and Albert Coombes had heard the news from Lucy Perry, who had popped in during the late afternoon. Enjoying a cup of tea with Ginny, she had voiced her concern for John Weston before going home to dust and polish her house ready for her husband Bernie when he got back from watching Surrey play at the Oval.

Albert Coombes was very deaf and did not hear a word but Ginny listened to it all, not that she was all that interested. The elderly lady felt that she had enough on her plate to contend with, what with Albert's deafness and contrariness, not to mention that drunken cowson Conners who lived upstairs, without concerning herself too much with the neighbours' business. She did feel sorry for Dora though and she nodded her head, pulled a face and left it at that. She paid Lucy for the shopping, saw her to the door, then prepared herself for the usual grilling.

'What she want?' Albert asked.

'She brought me the shoppin',' Ginny shouted, pointing at the bits and pieces lying on the table.

'I know that, but what was that she was tellin' yer?'

'Mr Weston's not too good. It's 'is kidney.'

'Sidney? Sidney who?'

'I said kidney.'

'What about the kidney?'

'Mr Weston's. It's packed up,' Ginny yelled even louder.

'All right, there's no need ter shout,' Albert moaned.

'Oh sod yer,' Ginny growled. 'I'm gonna put the kettle on.'

Albert smiled and picked up the paper. 'Go on then.'

Ginny could never understand how Albert always seemed to hear quite clearly whenever she mentioned putting the kettle on. It wasn't as though he could read her lips, because if he had he would have walked out on her long ago.

26

Chapter Three

The Westons were gathered around the table for their Sunday lunch; for Dora it was the one day in the week when she was able to lavish time on the meal and her family. John worked nights and ate at different times to the rest of them. The two eldest boys, Frankie and James, both worked as labourers on building sites and during the favourable weather they did all the overtime available. Meals in the Weston household were always difficult to organise but on Sundays Dora insisted on propriety. The table flaps were pulled out, four fold-up chairs were brought out from under the stairs to accommodate the large family and Dora usually had a few words to say to her two eldest sons. 'We'll all sit down tergevver, an' I don't want you two comin' in after 'avin' a skinful o' beer an' settin' a bad example round the table,' she told them. 'What's more, I want yer both 'ome early, not when the pub turns out at two. Anyway, you're not s'posed ter go in a pub, James.'

The two young men considered themselves to be hard-working adults and quite able to hold their beer, but their mother's word was law and they respected it. Nevertheless they did manage to get a few pints down them at the

27

Beehive, with one eye on the clock.

Frankie and James were both stocky like their father. Frankie also had his colouring and mannerisms, while James favoured his mother, with fair wavy hair and pale blue eyes. The Weston boys drank in the saloon bar on Sunday lunch times and they always dressed for the occasion, feeling that after wearing boiler suits or thick cord trousers and heavy working boots all week it was nice to be well booted and suited on Sundays.

Linda enjoyed the Sunday get-together. She helped her mother prepare the meal and was allowed to take a lot of credit for the crisp batter pudding and perfectly cooked roast potatoes, as well as the cabbage and brussels sprouts, all covered with thick meat-stock gravy. She usually made the apple pie too, but she had to admit that no one could make creamy, lump-free custard better than her mother.

Pamela, Tommy and Ben helped by laying the Sunday table. Pamela at fifteen was leggy and beginning to fill out, and like the rest of the womenfolk she was fair-haired and blue-eyed. Tommy was fourteen and of dark complexion like his father, but eleven-year-old Ben, the youngest of the Westons, was ginger-haired, with a cheeky, freckled face.

'The Carters were in the pub terday,' Frankie said to his father as they tucked into piled-up plates of food.

'Oh yeah?' John replied. 'They seem ter be makin' the Bee'ive their local these days.'

'They got chucked out o' the Risin' Sun, that's why,' James cut in.

'They didn't exactly get barred,' Frankie told him. 'They got warned off by the Kerrigans. They was gettin' a bit too flash wiv their money an' Tommy Kerrigan didn't want any rozzers sniffin' round an' queerin' 'is patch.'

'The way you boys talk, anyone would fink they're Chicago gangsters,' Dora remarked. 'Now stop talkin' an' get on wiv yer dinner.'

Linda was listening to the conversation with interest. She had heard from Jenny Jordan that Charlie Bradley was often in the Carters' company and she was eager to find out if he had been at the pub that day. 'Were there ovver fellers wiv 'em?' she asked casually.

'The Carters usually drink mob-'anded,' Frankie told her. 'They was on their own terday though.'

'I don't fink Bert Warner was all that 'appy ter see 'em,' James remarked. ''Im an' Gladys like ter keep it a family pub.'

'Well, they won't if they let the Carter boys an' their cronies make it their local,' John Weston said, cutting his slice of beef with precision. 'They're trouble, that lot.'

'Yeah, an' if they upset the Kerrigans an' they come lookin' for 'em the Bee'ive'll turn into a battleground,' Frankie remarked. 'It'll be just like the Crown was when the Fisher boys upset the Malts.'

'I'm gettin' a little tired o' this,' Dora growled. 'Now shut up an' finish yer dinner, or I'll stop yer afters.'

John caught his wife's eye and they exchanged smiles, while Frankie and James pulled long faces. Pamela, Tommy and Ben had been listening avidly at the crowded table but they looked at each other with serious expressions on their faces when their mother made the ultimate threat.

Once the plates had been scraped clean, Dora looked round the table. 'Now listen, you lot. I'm gonna serve the afters up, an' if I 'ear any more about the Kerrigans an' the

Carters, an' all that stupid talk about gang fights, it'll go straight in the dustbin,' she warned them.

A dutiful silence reigned and the Weston children were able to enjoy the hot, sugary apple pie, dripping in creamy, lump-free custard.

Bill Simpson, now a frail eighty-four-year-old widower, still managed to climb up to the roof of Sunlight Buildings from his top-floor flat to see his beloved pigeons, but he now had a young helper, Jack Marchant, who lived in the flat below. Jack was a mere baby at seventy-six and he argued all the time with his mentor.

'What you should do is say to 'em, "Now, look you lot. I'm not 'avin' yer come up 'ere frightenin' my birds." That's what you should say,' Jack told him as the two old men sat together on the roof.

'Cobblers! Why should I go gettin' meself in 'ot water over the birds when they ain't frightened?' Bill replied derisively.

'Yeah, but they shouldn't be up 'ere anyway,' Jack persisted.

'What, the birds or the kids?'

'The kids.'

'Who ses?'

'I say.'

'Who are you?'

'I'm a tenant.'

'So am I.'

'Well, yer should keep 'em in check.'

'It ain't my job ter be a nose-wiper.'

'Nah, but it might teach some o' them saucy gits a lesson.'

'They never sauce me.'

'Well, they did me.'

'P'raps it's yer attitude,' Bill Simpson told him sharply as he reached down beside him for his bottle of brown ale.

'S'posin' they started larkin' about an' one of 'em fell over the top?' Jack Marchant pressed him.

Bill filled his empty glass with a surprisingly steady hand. 'They don't lark about, at least not ter my knowledge,' he replied.

'Ah now, there you are. You ain't always 'ere, are yer?'

'Well, I don't exactly live up 'ere.'

'But don't yer see, if one o' those little monkeys fell off the roof you'd be the one who'd take the can back fer allowin' 'em up 'ere in the first place,' the younger man went on.

'Cobblers! 'Ow can they blame me?'

'Well, I still say you should put yer foot down.'

Bill Simpson took a long swig from his glass then he wiped a gnarled hand over his froth-covered whiskers. 'Now, you listen ter me,' he said with authority. 'I've kept pigeons on this roof fer over fifteen years, an' in all that time I've seen plenty o' youngsters come up 'ere. They stand about an' chat, just like we do. Sometimes they joke an' get a bit excited, but in all that time I've bin comin' up 'ere they've never given me one minute's grief. They're good kids fer the best part, an' when yer fink of it, what else is there fer 'em ter do? The pub? The dance 'alls? It strikes me they're more likely ter get in trouble at those places than sittin' up 'ere in the fresh air. I love it up 'ere, Jack, an' I expect they do too. I've come ter terms wiv a lot o' fings up on this roof. It's quiet an' yer got time ter fink clearly. In the warm weavver like we're 'avin' now it's pleasant ter feel the breeze what you ain't got down below. An' in the cold weavver I come out 'ere all wrapped up an' look up at the stars. I've even spoke ter my ole dutch while I've bin up 'ere on me own. She can 'ear me too, I'm sure of it. She's up there somewhere an' she's waitin' patiently fer the day I go up an' join 'er.'

Bill took another long swig from his glass and then his rheumy old eyes twinkled. 'When I do get up there I might just come down an' haunt yer one stormy night; if yer don't get a bit more charity in yer soul, that is. Yer a bloody ole moaner, that's what you are.'

Jack Marchant drank his own glass down to the dregs and passed it over for a refill. 'What makes yer fink yer goin' up there?' he said, a wicked glint in his eyes.

'Now, don't get all upset,' Bill told him. 'When me time comes I'm gonna 'ave it out straight away wiv Peter or Moses, or whoever else is givin' out the weekend passes. I gotta 'ave a regular pass fer the over place, I'll say to 'im, ovverwise my ole pal Jack Marchant is gonna fret.'

Down below in the sun-baked street, as the evening shadows lengthened and a gentle breeze stirred, the two hawks stood together at Doris's front door. They were discussing their neighbour from the last but one house.

'I fink it's a bloody disgrace,' Doris was going on. 'D'you know, I was in me front room fixin' me curtains when I saw 'im walk by terday. Stagger by, I should say. Just after two o'clock it was, an' 'e was pissed out of 'is brains.'

'Disgustin',' Phyllis agreed with a shake of her head. 'Go on, luv.'

'Well, far be it fer me ter stand spyin' on me neighbours,' Doris continued, 'but I couldn't 'elp noticin' 'im. 'E was all undone.'

'What, yer mean . . .'

'All 'is buttons were undone down the front.'

'Good Gawd!'

'I gotta tell yer, luv. 'E banged inter that lamppost an' 'ow 'e didn't do 'imself a mischief, I'll never know.'

Further along the turning Maggie Gainsford was sitting dreamily in an old wicker chair at her front door, humming gently to her youngest lad who was slumped against her with his head in her lap as she scratched his tousled hair. She looked up to see the tall, lean figure of Dick Conners standing watching her.

'I wish I 'ad a camera right now,' he said with a smile.

'You gave me a scare,' she said quickly.

'Sorry, luv,' Dick replied. 'I was just takin' a stroll down ter the pub fer a pint an' I said ter meself, what a lovely picture that is.'

Maggie's son Michael looked up at the street's drunk and yawned widely, and Dick jerked his thumb in the direction of the corner pub. 'I see the ugly sisters are at it,' he remarked. 'I wonder who them two ole biddies are slaggin' off now.'

'Me, you, maybe both of us, I shouldn't be at all surprised,' Maggie told him.

Dick Conners scratched his dishevelled mop of sandy hair, an amused look on his thin face. 'D'yer know somefing,' he said, narrowing his eyes. 'Those two just reminded me of Ali Jaffa's women, the way they're gabbin' away.'

'Who the bloody 'ell's Ali Jaffa?' Maggie Gainsford said as she got to her feet with a grunt.

'Ali Jaffa was a Bedouin chief,' Dick told her. 'Bedouins are like our Gipsies, always on the move, but they set up bloody great tents in the desert an' they 'ave harems.'

'Nice if yer can get it,' Maggie remarked.

'No listen, Maggie,' the drunk urged her. 'While I was in the army I done some time in the Middle East an' I got ter know ole Ali Jaffa. 'E 'ad loads o' wives an' some of 'em were really ugly. Anyway there were two who looked somefing like them two standin' down there. They was always gabbin' tergevver an' old Ali got the 'ump wiv 'em. 'E was always usin' the whip on 'em but they still kept on rabbitin', so one day when Ali was breakin' camp an' movin' off frew the desert 'e broke the Arab code. Instead o' the women followin' after the men 'e let these two women walk in front.'

Maggie was perplexed and she shook her head. 'I dunno what yer talkin' about, Dick,' she sighed.

'Well yer see, Ali Jaffa an' 'is tribe were goin' frew a dangerous part o' the desert. It was sown wiv mines an' nobody seemed ter know where the minefield was. Ali found it, or should I say Ali's two wives found it. 'E told us all about it when 'e passed frew our area again. 'E wasn't a bit concerned. In fact 'e told us that 'e was only too glad it was them an' not two of 'is camels what stepped on the mine.'

'It sounds like 'e was a charmin' sort o' cowson, this Ali what's-'is-name,' Maggie replied.

Dick Conners' blue eyes were twinkling as he looked down the street and saw the two hawks approaching them. 'Look out, Maggie, they're comin' this way,' he warned her.

'They're off on their usual evenin' stroll,' she groaned aloud.

'Nice evenin', Mrs Gainsford,' the two chorused as they

34

passed by, ignoring Dick Conners completely.

'I wonder where they go every evenin'?' Maggie said to him once they were out of earshot.

Dick watched them disappear round the corner, then he turned to Maggie. 'I dunno, but ole Ali Jaffa would 'ave 'ad a few suggestions ter make, given the chance,' he told her, grinning evilly.

Chapter Four

Early on Monday morning the dustcart drove into Eagle Street and pulled up at the end of Sunlight Buildings. The dustmen called twice a week, now that the weather was warm, and on Mondays the weekend collection of rubbish was overspilling the two bottomless cylindrical bins. The dustmen worked at a fast rate, upturning the bins and shovelling the refuse into wicker baskets which were humped out from the alleyway into the covered dustcart. As they worked, a fetid smell grew in the turning and people shut their front doors and closed their windows until the dustcart pulled away. Once the job was done the porter swilled down the yard and sprinkled a copious amount of disinfectant powder around the bins, and slowly the stench drifted away and the street returned to normal.

Just as the dustcart pulled up Linda Weston left for work. It was a fine day and she walked out into Tower Bridge Road past the stalls and shops, exchanging pleasantries with the costermongers she knew, and then crossed the end of the market into Bermondsey Street which ran down the side of the Trocette cinema. The long stretch of road led to the wine vaults in Tooley Street where she worked, and as she passed a lorry that was being loaded with empty wine barrels she heard a sharp wolf whistle. 'Dirty gits,' she muttered, grinning to herself as she carried on.

She walked briskly through the long railway arch at the end of Bermondsey Street and turned into Tooley Street at five minutes to eight. The familiar vinegary smell greeted her as she walked into the wine vaults, took her time card from the rack and slipped it into the machine. The air was cool beneath the huge brick arch of the railway viaduct, and the women assembled round a long wooden bench as their forelady Irene Cutler came up hugging a clipboard to her bosom.

'Right, gels. We got anuvver bonus job,' she announced cheerfully. Then, seeing the looks on her team's faces, 'It's OK, I've already warned ole Wilson I don't want any balls-up wiv this one.'

The women quickly set to work and very soon they had slipped into their accustomed efficient routine. Linda hummed quietly to herself as she expertly rolled the freshly labelled bottles of Algerian white wine into tissue sheets and twirled the paper at the top before slipping them into cardboard cartons for each specific order. The team made good progress, with Kate Madigan running the labels through the roller and spreading them out on a large square of plywood, while Doll Williams stuck them on to the bottles and lined them up for the forelady to wipe clean and pass along to Linda. While they worked at the bench another woman was busy making up the cartons and inserting the partitions, and one of the young lads hurried back and forth from the bottling chamber with fresh supplies of the newly bottled wine. The filled cartons were finally sealed with a strip of gum paper by another young lad and stacked on a pallet board ready to be hauled away to the loading area.

It was mundane work, but the bonus was a good incentive and the women rallied, chatting, singing together and giving the young lads a hard time if the supply of bottles dwindled. Irene ran the team well. She was middle-aged, small and wiry and her sharp eyes missed very little.

'Oi, Freddie, when yer gonna move that pallet, it's in the way,' she shouted to the hard-pressed young lad with a mop of ginger hair.

'Gis a chance, Irene, fer Gawd sake,' Freddie moaned. 'I've only got one pair of 'ands.'

'Get that lazy bleeder Colin ter move it then,' the forelady grumbled.

''E's out in the chamber 'elpin' the foreman fill the boxes,' Freddie told her.

Irene gave him a hard look. 'Well, go an' tell 'im,' she ordered him.

The women smiled at each other, knowing that an argument was in the offing, and they did not have long to wait.

A large, red-faced foreman came hurrying out from the bottling chamber to confront his opposite number. 'What's all this about gettin' be'ind, Irene?' he shouted as he came up to the workbench. 'Yer got a table full o' bottles.'

'Yeah, an' my gels ain't 'angin' about, Jim,' she replied quickly. 'We got a target ter reach.'

'Yeah, so 'ave I,' Jim Watson growled.

'Well, get this pallet moved so we can get on,' Irene insisted.

'I'll get Freddie ter stick anuvver one beside it,' the foreman said in a conciliatory manner.

'Oh no, you won't,' Irene said sharply. 'Yer'll block us right in.'

Freddie came hurrying up. 'There's a lorry just pulled up outside wiv wine drums on,' he told Jim.

The forelady gave the women a quick look. ''E'll 'ave ter wait till yer sort us out, Jim,' she told the harassed foreman.

'Don't you start givin' me orders,' he retorted angrily.

'I wouldn't dream of it,' Irene went on at him. 'All I'm sayin' is that yer'll 'ave ter get that pallet moved right away or I'm gonna go an' see Mr Norman.'

'Don't you start stirrin' up trouble, luv. I got enough ter worry about wivout 'im givin' me a bad time,' Jim told her.

The women listened in silence, trying to hide their amusement. They knew that when Irene Cutler got her teeth into anything she would not let go until she got her way.

'Look, I know yer very busy, but surely it won't take five minutes ter get that board moved,' she said in a slightly less bullying tone.

Jim Watson's face became even more red. 'I'm just about sick of it,' he raved. 'It's do this, do that. Don't you lot ever stop ter fink I've got ovver fings ter do? There's the bottlin' team moanin' about the shortage o' bottles, there's corks ter soak, loadin' an' unloadin' ter see to, an' you want me ter stop everyfing ter get that poxy pallet moved. I'm runnin' around like a blue-arsed fly. Give us a chance fer Gawd sake.'

Irene knew just how far to go in dealing with her opposite number and she switched her attack. 'Look, Jim, I know yer under the cosh, an' no one knows more than I do 'ow 'ard you work,' she said quietly. 'Trouble is I gotta fink o' my gels, an' it don't become yer ter start swearin' at me, just 'cos I'm lookin' after their interests. If it was just fer me I'd say shift the pallet when yer can.'

Jim sighed and shook his head slowly. 'All right, luv, I'm sorry if I got a bit carried away, but you know 'ow it is.'

'Yeah, I do, an' I appreciate what yer do fer us, Jim. You always do what yer can. Nobody can say yer don't earn yer wages.'

The foreman looked around the workbench and caught sight of the amused expressions on the women's faces. 'Freddie!' he called out loudly.

The young lad came out from behind a stack of crates where he was sitting comfortably on a large bag of corks. 'Yeah?'

'Move that pallet,' he told him.

'Jim, yer a diamond,' Irene declared with a big smile.

The large man looked a little abashed. 'I'm gonna see ole Norman about gettin' anuvver loader,' he said firmly as he turned away. 'We need an extra man badly.'

Doll Williams sniffed loudly and arched her back to ease her aching muscles. She was a buxom woman, with a large moon face that always looked glum. 'My friend's feller came up 'ere fer a job but that boss-eyed git Norman turned 'im away,' she remarked. 'Apparently 'e'd done time an' Norman found out over 'is cards not bein' stamped.'

'I don't fink the pay's all that good 'ere,' Kate Madigan cut in. 'Yer wanna tell yer friend ter tell 'im 'e should try Fry's the furniture removers down the Elephant. My bloke got a start there on the lorries a couple o' weeks ago an' 'e likes it. The pay's pretty good an' they get tips as well.'

'The problem wiv this job is, it's a bonded ware'ouse,' Doll said, 'an' they gotta be careful who they take on.'

41

'That's why my bloke couldn't get a start 'ere,' Kate replied. ''E'd done two years fer nickin'.'

The women continued to chat together as they worked, and far from merely tolerating it the forelady encouraged them, knowing from experience that, unlike men, women worked more efficiently when they were able to natter amongst themselves. There was a bonus to be earned every week and it was very rare that the targets were not met.

''Ere, Irene, our Kate's got a new lodger who looks like Tyrone Power,' one of the women said.

Kate nudged her in the ribs. 'Shut up, yer silly mare,' she growled.

'Tell us about 'im, Kate,' the forelady said, pouring a new batch of glue into the roller.

'There's nuffink ter tell,' Kate replied.

'I wouldn't tell neivver,' a buxom woman said. 'I'd just feed 'im up, do 'is dirty washin' an' then drop a few 'ints before I went ter bed.'

'Like what, Mary?' Kate asked.

'Well, I'd say I wasn't sleepin' too good 'cos I couldn't get warm in bed, an' I'd tell 'im I sometimes got frightened o' sleepin' alone on stormy nights,' Fat Mary said grinning.

'While yer piss-ballin' about like that, yer might just as well come out wiv it an' tell 'im yer'd like 'im ter pay yer a visit one night,' Irene remarked.

'What I'd do is lock me bedroom door every night fer a week an' I'd do it loudly so 'e 'ears me,' Doll cut in. 'Then after a week I'd give 'im the ole come-on an' that night I'd leave me door unlocked. If 'e didn't get the message then 'e'd be a right prawn an' I wouldn't be missin' much, would I?'

'I knew somebody who used ter take in lodgers,' Irene told them. 'She 'ad a large room wiv four beds in it. She used ter take in lorry drivers. Anyway, there was a regular lot o' fellers stayed every Monday night an' one o' these blokes who was called Chunky used ter sleep in the nude.'

''Ow did she know that?' Doll asked.

''Ow the bloody 'ell do I know?' Irene replied quickly. 'I s'pose she peeked. Anyway, ter get back ter the story. One mornin' this woman came in the bedroom where these fellers were, an' she saw this bloke who slept in the nude doin' 'is exercises.'

'Exercises?' Doll queried.

'Yeah, apparently 'e used ter do arms-up, arms-out, an' then 'e'd grab 'is ole bill an' give it a couple o' shakes fer good measure. It must 'ave bin good measure 'cos the next time the fellers all met on Monday night they could see that there was only three beds in the room. "Who's missin'?" they asked. "Chunky's sleepin' in anuvver room," the land-lady told 'em. "'E's bin complainin' about you lot snorin".'

'An' did they snore?' Doll asked.

'Doll, you are a dozy cow at times,' Irene told her amidst loud laughter.

The women enjoyed the banter and good-humoured chafing and it made for a good atmosphere. The work was hard at times and almost always tedious, but the chatter helped to make the day pass quickly and today it seemed to be flying by. Their forelady hurried off after the next pallet board had been filled and came back smiling. 'I just offered ole Jim a quick feel if 'e got that pallet shifted,' she joked.

Laughter filled the arch, and as the banter went on Irene had another story to relate. ''Ere, gels, talkin' about lodgers,

I knew a woman called Florrie Batley who took a lodger in, an' 'e was a real cracker,' she began. 'A real charmer 'e was. Anyway, one night 'e come 'ome wiv this dog, a little mongrel who looked 'alf starved. Now Florrie didn't like dogs. She wouldn't 'ave one in the 'ouse normally, but like I said, 'er lodger was such a charmer 'e managed ter talk 'er into it. She fancied this bloke like crazy. 'E could do nuffink wrong. Anyway, 'e started takin' the dog out for a walk every night wivout fail. Never missed. Now one night Florrie's 'usband 'ad ter go an' visit 'is sick muvver who lived in Brighton. 'E'd arranged ter stay down in Brighton fer the night so she saw 'er chance. She did 'erself up ter the eyeballs an' put a bit o' scent in the important places all ready fer when the lodger got in. She cooked 'im a nice meal an' fed the dog wiv chunks o' best meat instead o' scraps to impress 'im. The lodger, not the dog. She done everyfing she could fink of. When 'e finally arrived 'ome that night Florrie was all over 'im. She told 'im 'ow good an' kind 'e was ter care fer a poor little doggie an' 'ow impressed she was. She told 'im that 'e only 'ad to ask an' 'e could 'ave anyfing 'e wanted. Well, Florrie thought she was 'ome an' dry when 'e knelt down an' took 'er 'ands in 'is an' told 'er 'ow much 'e'd admired 'er from afar an' 'ow 'e'd bin taken by 'er warm an' tender feelings fer 'im an' the dog. Then 'e said that as they were alone 'e wanted to ask 'er somefing really darin', but 'e didn't know 'ow ter say it. "Ask me, just ask me, Clarence, I'm yours ter command," she told 'im.'

Irene paused and stifled a chuckle. 'Anyway, while Clarence is divverin' she goes upstairs an' comes back wearin' a dainty nightdress that was so skimpy it barely covered Paris. Clarence looked at 'er in amazement. "Command me. Anyfing," Florrie whispered. "I can't," Clarence groaned. "Why not?" Florrie said. Clarence moved nearer. "I'm feelin' tired an' I was gonna ask if yer'd mind takin' the dog fer a walk," he told her, "but yer'd catch yer death o' cold in that outfit".'

The laughter finally subsided but the chatter went on. The day turned out to be a good one, with a bonus comfortably earned, and when Linda left the vaults that evening she hurried home feeling tired but contented.

The evening sun was an orange-red disc low in the sky as Bill Simpson plodded wearily up the short flight of stairs on to the roof. He unlocked the small padlock on his pigeon-shed compound and went in to inspect his charges. The small bird he was particularly interested in was a comparative newcomer. It had been there only two weeks and had arrived exhausted. Bill had examined it and seen that there was no tag attached to its leg. It had not appeared to be harmed in any way and looked able to fly away once it had recovered, but it seemed reluctant to do so. Sometimes it fluttered up to the balustrade and just perched there as though trying to make up its mind, but it invariably went back to the compound.

The old man opened the loft and let the flock fly off into the evening sky, then he stood with his hand cupped to his forehead as he observed them circle the buildings, high up and in close formation. Finally they swooped down in a group and settled themselves back in the roost, and the newcomer was with them. Bill scratched his head as he stood alone on the cool roof. Jack Marchant would be up the next morning to clean the loft and he would have to talk to him about that bird. It should be encouraged to leave, he thought.

The sun was going down now, like a huge red coin sliding very slowly into a giant stone money-box. Splashes of purple and ash-grey cloud changed colour subtly as the fiery orb slipped away out of sight, and as he leaned his elbows on the stonework and watched, Bill felt a sense of contentment. His life had been a full one. He had sailed the oceans as a young man in the old tea clippers on their fast runs to China and back, and then he had tasted life as a stoker on the coal burners. He had seen the world and its wonders and watched the sun dip into the Pacific, fall in icy splendour behind the high, snow-tipped mountains, and set beyond the steamy tangled jungles of the tropics, and never had he thought to worry that he might not live long enough to see it rise again. It was different now though; he was an old man, to whom every day was a gift to savour. Still, it did not seem to matter all that much that he might lay his head on the pillow and never wake up again. He trusted that he would meet Tessie again in the hereafter, and his sailor son, who had not survived the war. He would miss the sunsets, true, but maybe he would see far better ones. He was content, and hopeful, and he thought that he understood what Lord Tennyson seemed to be saying in the tattered little book of poems that he kept beside his bed:

Twilight and evening bell,
And after that the dark!
And may there be no sadness of farewell
When I embark.

Chapter Five

On Wednesday it rained, a soft summer rain from a fitful, unsure sky, but on Thursday the sun was out early. The day turned out to be hot and sultry, and in the evening after tea Linda met Kate Selby and they walked out together and talked. Once it had been club night at St Mary's Church that brought them together, but they had outgrown that. Now they met on Thursday evenings to talk about themselves, their hopes and aspirations, and the young men who took their fancy. They paraded themselves, coyly but proudly, linking arms and often strolling out to where the young men would be. If the weather was nice they walked as far as Southwark Park and sauntered along to the rose gardens or the bandstand where young men congregated to brag about their conquests and puff on cigarettes while they ogled the girls who walked by.

Tonight the air remained close and it was Linda who suggested that for a change they might take a stroll over the river to the Tower Gardens.

'Peter Ridley asked me out,' Kate revealed, trying to appear casual.

'Will yer?' Linda asked her.

'Will I what?' Kate queried with a look of mock horror.

'Go out wiv 'im,' Linda replied smiling.

'I dunno. 'E wants me ter be 'is steady but I just dunno.'

''E's a nice feller, an' a nice-looker,' Linda remarked.

'Yeah, but 'e's so juvenile,' her friend sighed.

Linda hid a smile as they crossed over the centre span of the high, white stone bridge. She had known Kate for as long as she could remember and the girl was incorrigible. She had walked out with quite a few lads and there was always a postmortem at the end, but it seemed that she was jumping the gun a bit this time.

'Pete's a nice feller but 'e talks so much rubbish,' Kate told her. ''E wants four kids, two of each, an' 'e reckons that women shouldn't 'ave ter go out ter work once they're married.'

''Ave yer snogged wiv 'im then?' Linda asked her.

'We did 'ave a kiss, an' 'e put 'is arms round me when he was up on the roof one night, but it wasn't anyfing special,' Kate explained matter-of-factly.

'So yer told 'im no,' Linda said.

'I told 'im I'll fink about it,' Kate corrected her.

As they drew near the Tower of London, two young men came towards them. They were smartly dressed in light suits and crepe-soled shoes and they glanced nervously at the young women as they passed by.

'I fink they're gonna foller us,' Kate remarked, pulling a face.

'They've stopped,' Linda said, looking over her shoulder.

'I don't fancy 'em,' her friend replied, walking on with an exaggerated sway of her hips.

The young men seemed to be having a difference of opinion, then they walked on.

'Are they still follerin' us?' Kate asked.

Linda looked over her shoulder again. 'Nah, they've carried on walkin',' she replied.

Kate looked disappointed. 'What about you?' she inquired after a while.

'What about me?' Linda said, brushing a wisp of fair hair back from her forehead.

'Are you still carryin' a torch fer Charlie Bradley?'

Linda smiled and shook her head. 'I've always liked Charlie but there was never anyfing between us,' she replied. 'Besides, Charlie's bin in the army fer eighteen months an' most o' that time 'e was in Germany. I only saw 'im once when 'e came 'ome on leave, an' that was only fer a few minutes.'

'Yeah, but 'e's demobbed now an' I've seen 'im about,' Kate told her. 'I thought yer might 'ave bumped into 'im. Everyone used ter fink you was 'is gel. You was always wiv 'im when you was younger.'

'Yeah, but we was always in a crowd. I was never on me own wiv Charlie; well, not on a date or anyfing,' Linda reminded her.

The two young women followed the line of railings and passed through the gate of Tower Gardens. Flower beds flanked the narrow pathway that skirted the moat, now a dry area that had been lawned and rolled, and here and there a few wooden benches were set back amongst the flowers. One or two old folk sat on the seats, their eyes staring out at the strong white walls of the Tower, and a young couple came towards them, the woman pushing a pram and the young man carrying a small canvas bag. The baby was crying loudly and as they passed by Kate glanced at her friend.

'Four kids 'e wants. Bloody 'ell, Lin, one would be more than enough fer me,' she growled. 'I can't stand all that screamin'. When me sister brings 'er kid round an' it 'as a tantrum I feel like shakin' it.'

'So yer don't plan on 'avin' any then?' Linda said, her eyes straying to the smooth green lawn below them.

'Not right away at any price,' her friend said quickly. 'I wanna see a bit o' life first. I wanna get tied up wiv a feller who can show me a good time. I wanna go places, see fings. I wanna move away from that dump we live in. That street drives me mad at times.'

Linda tugged on her friend's arm and they stopped to look down at two large ravens which were strutting towards a flock of sparrows feeding on the lawn. 'I 'eard once that if those ravens leave the Tower the monarchy'll fall,' she said.

Kate shrugged her shoulders. 'C'mon, let's move on. It's too quiet 'ere,' she said irritably.

They walked along to the far gate and out on to Tower Hill.

'I used ter bring Pam an' Tommy up 'ere when they were little,' Linda told Kate. 'Ben as well sometimes. This is where they be'eaded the traitors.'

'Oh yeah?' Kate replied in a bored voice.

'C'mon, let's walk along by the cannons,' Linda suggested. 'We can get back on ter the bridge that way.'

They entered the wide gates and carried on along a cobbled riverside path. Across the quiet river the cranes and the ships berthed at the wharves were lying idle. On either side of the path, cold iron cannons of various shapes and sizes were positioned at regular intervals on stone bases, and a beefeater was standing with his hands clasped behind his back and a benign look on his ruddy face. Some children were clambering over a large cannon, and up ahead an old man held a camera up to his face and pointed it towards an old lady who was smiling widely at him as she stood with her back to the river.

'I dunno why yer suggested we come 'ere,' Kate Selby moaned. 'It's dead as a doornail. We should'a gone up the park.'

'C'mon then, let's go,' Linda sighed, beginning to grow a little tired of her friend's attitude.

'I fink I might go out wiv Peter after all,' Kate announced as they made their way back to Bermondsey.

'Yeah, why not?' Linda replied, suddenly feeling miserable.

The light was failing by the time they reached Eagle Street and Kate sighed as they walked into the quiet turning. 'That place should be condemned,' she growled, staring at Sunlight Buildings. 'It's a bloody eyesore.'

The two youngsters parted at Linda's front door and as Kate walked to her house at the end of the street she turned and waved. Linda let herself into the house and found her mother standing by the gas stove in the scullery.

'I'm boilin' up some more barley, but it don't seem ter be doin' much good,' Dora sighed. 'Yer dad's bin in pain all day. I've told 'im 'e should go back an' see the doctor.'

Linda nodded, a worried look appearing on her face. 'Is 'e still up?'

'No, 'e's gone ter bed.'

The chimer on the mantelshelf struck ten as mother and daughter sat sipping tea in the parlour. Frankie and James were at the cinema and the younger children, Tommy,

Pamela and Ben, had gone off to bed.

'Yer dad's worried about 'avin' so much time off work,' Dora was saying. 'I told 'im not ter worry. We can manage. There's the sick pay, an' your money. 'E's worried about losin' Frankie's money now 'e's due fer call-up, but I told 'im it don't matter. Anyway, Tommy'll be startin' work this September.'

'I could give yer a few extra shillin's,' Linda offered. 'We've bin doin' all right lately on bonus.'

'I wouldn't dream of it while we can manage,' Dora told her. 'Yer give up most of yer money as it is. Yer gotta try an' save a few shillin's fer later. When yer start courtin', yer'll need fings fer yer bottom drawer.'

'There's plenty o' time fer that, Mum,' Linda replied, looking up at the clock again and wanting nothing more than to get to bed and let the night carry away the inexplicable sadness that was welling up inside her.

Sunlight Buildings was made up of four blocks, and above the entrance to each one the flat numbers were marked up on a board. Gaslit wooden stairs led up to three floors with two flats on each, and there were two flats on the ground floor. At number 3, the first-floor flat in the block nearest to Tower Bridge Road, a heated discussion was going on.

'Yer've bin 'ome now fer two weeks an' yer still 'aven't sorted yerself out,' May Bradley said sharply. 'Yer gotta fink o' the future. That job was a good one an' why yer won't consider goin' back there beats me. After all, they're obliged ter take yer back on.'

Charlie Bradley sighed irritably as he sat back in the armchair facing his mother. 'Look, Ma. I know it was a good job an' there's prospects, but it's not fer me,' he said quietly. 'I don't wanna go back workin' me way up ter be a chief clerk or whatever. I wanna get a job workin' out in the open air. It'd drive me round the twist workin' inside again.'

May Bradley gave him a hard look. She was a tall lean figure with short grey hair neatly set and arranged in waves around her head, and she had grey eyes and thin lips that very rarely relaxed into a smile. Her neighbours felt that she was stuck-up and not very approachable, and they were right. May Bradley had been widowed for five years, her husband Norman having died suddenly from a heart attack. He had been employed as a roofer and tiler and had made some provision for his family, so that May now enjoyed a small pension which supplemented her widow's pension. Her daughter Sara had married a man a few years older than her who had inherited a grocery business from his father. They lived with their two-year-old son in a smart house in leafy Chislehurst, and May was grateful that her daughter at least had done well for herself. Her concern now was for her son Charlie, who she felt had been ruined by eighteen months in uniform. She dearly wanted him to make something of himself and marry into a respectable family, buy a nice house in the suburbs and live a comfortable life.

'You talk about workin' in the open air,' she went on. 'What does that mean, a labourin' job on a buildin' site? Workin' up on roofs in all weavvers like yer dad did?'

'I'd sooner do that than sit at a desk all day long sayin' yes, sir, no, sir, three bags full, sir, ter some jumped-up squirt of an office manager,' Charlie replied angrily.

May Bradley shook her head sadly. 'I dunno what's got inter yer,' she said sighing. 'It's the army, that's what it is.

Yer've not bin the same since yer come 'ome.'

Charlie stared up at the ceiling as he thought about it. The army did change people, and everyone he had spoken to since getting demobbed who had done national service felt the same as him. Opinions and attitudes had changed, and it was no bad thing.

'Look, Ma, I'm not gonna argue wiv yer, but I've gotta do what I wanna do from now on, not what you want me ter do,' he said quietly.

'I want the best for yer,' she responded sharply. 'I don't wanna see yer end up workin' as a common labourer an' livin' in a place like this wiv a tribe o' kids runnin' round yer feet.'

Charlie got out of his chair and stood looking down at his mother. 'I've gotta earn a livin', I know that,' he told her, 'an' if it means ditch-diggin' or climbin' up on roofs ter get money so be it. One day I'll 'ave me own business, 'cos I'm not intendin' ter work fer a guv'nor all me life. Fer the time bein' though, yer gotta let me do fings my way. After all I'm not a kid anymore, Ma.'

May stared moodily into the empty grate with her chin resting on her closed hand. He was just like his father, she thought. Norman could have done much better for himself, if he had not been so pigheaded at times. Charlie was much the same, too bigheaded to knuckle down in a job that offered good prospects.

'I'm off ter bed, Ma,' he told her. 'Don't sit there broodin' all night. I'm gonna do OK. Yer'll see.'

At the end of Eagle Street, in the little corner pub, Bert Warner the landlord slid the bolts over and looked around the bar. 'That's about it then,' he said with a sigh, rubbing his hand over his large bald head.

Gladys Warner threw the barcloth into an empty bucket and slumped down on a barstool. 'Feeling like a nightcap?' she asked him.

Bert nodded and walked round the counter. 'That mob was in 'ere again ternight then,' he said, pushing a glass under an optic.

Gladys watched while her husband poured a large measure of lime into her gin. 'Nick Carter can be a nasty cowson but that Boy-boy unnerves me,' she remarked. 'There's somefing about 'is eyes. Did you see the way 'e was lookin' at that young woman who was wiv Johnny Adams the docker? 'E never stopped staring at 'er. I was worried in case the feller spotted 'im.'

'We're gonna 'ave ter seriously fink o' what we're gonna do about those Carters,' Bert told her as he put another glass under the optic. 'I don't want this pub turnin' into a meetin' place fer the likes o' them. The Risin' Sun was a decent pub till them an' the Kerrigans started usin' it. There's bin two landlords come an' gone there in the past three years. I ain't bein' forced out of 'ere by the likes o' those monkeys.'

Gladys sipped her drink thoughtfully. She was a buxom woman, with pale blue eyes and blonde hair that was piled up on top of her head and fixed with a large tortoiseshell comb. Her cream silk blouse fitted high in the neck and she wore a knee-length brown gaberdine skirt with silk stockings and dark brown high-heeled shoes. Together with her husband of thirty years she had managed several pubs, and they had been in the Beehive for seven years. She had seen her share of villains and aggravators and she rated Boy-boy

Carter one of the worst. 'Do they live round 'ere?' she asked.

'Bermon'sey Street, so I bin told,' Bert replied. 'Their ole man was a bit loopy when 'e was younger. Like farvver like son, I s'pose.'

'You mentioned the Kerrigans,' Gladys said. 'Do they mix wiv the Carter boys?'

Bert laughed aloud. 'Yeah, like fire an' water does. They can't stand the sight of each ovver. The Kerrigans told 'em they're not welcome in the Risin' Sun an' that's why we got 'em 'ere. Ter be perfectly honest, I don't fink there's much ter choose between the lot of 'em. The only fing I'd say in Tommy Kerrigan's favour is that 'e don't stand fer any ole nonsense in the Sun.'

Gladys finished her drink. 'Well, I'm off ter bed, I dunno about you,' she said yawning.

Bert drained his glass and then turned the bar lights out. It had been a busy evening for a Thursday and tomorrow would no doubt be even busier, but he realised that it probably wouldn't stay that way if he continued to welcome the Carters as customers.

Chapter Six

Dick Conners had never married, although he had enjoyed the company of women throughout his younger days. He had been a fine figure of a man in his military uniform and he had photographs to prove it. The one he kept on the mantelshelf in his room was his favourite. Whenever he showed it to people they were invariably impressed and usually said so. Dick was in his fifties now, aware that the bloom of youth had long gone, but he still had his pride and regretted the fact that he had become a drunkard. Every so often he tried to cast out John Barleycorn, but the spirit of strong drink was not easily sent packing.

Ginny Coombes understood his problem, and when Dick had found himself without a home after his landlady in Gale Street died right at the end of the war Ginny came to his aid. She had good reason to, for Dick had saved her life one cold winter's night at the height of the Blitz when she was ill in bed and an incendiary bomb crashed through the roof. It had landed by her bedside and started to burn, filling the room with phosphorus fumes, and Ginny thought she was going to die. Albert her husband was in hospital at the time, after being injured while serving with the heavy rescue squad. Dick had visited him only that afternoon and promised him he would keep an eye on his sick wife. True to his word, he was on hand and actually letting himself into the house to check on Ginny when the incendiary fell. He managed to smother the fire with a pail of sand and drag her out of the fume-filled bedroom before she was overcome.

Ginny was advised of Dick's growing dependence on drink by certain people and warned that taking him in as a lodger was a step she would live to regret. She ignored them, however, and let him use the back bedroom. Dick kept his room clean and tidy, and often helped her prepare the meals, when he was sober. He peeled potatoes, cut the meat and watched the gas while Ginny did other things about the house. He changed light bulbs, fixed doors that got stuck and one time he put a new pane of glass in the parlour window after one of Maggie Gainsford's children kicked a ball through it. Dick was a man of many talents; he also wrote letters for his landlady, mended her old chimer and fixed up her damaged rocking chair, when he was sober.

When he was drunk Dick seemed to have an inbuilt safety valve, as far as the Coombes were concerned. Many got the sharp end of his tongue on those occasions but never Ginny or Albert. He would come home, stagger into the house and somehow manage to negotiate the stairs. He stomped about in his room, fell against the washstand or the bedside chair, and then tumbled into his bed, or rather on to his bed, where he slept like a baby until morning. Ginny cursed him, swore at him and often called him a no-good drunken whoreson when he came home the worse for wear and fell over in the passage, but she would never tolerate anyone else having one bad word to say about him. She loved him like a brother and felt that his drinking problem was a direct result of the war. Dick loved her and Albert too. They were his family as far as he was concerned, and after heavy drinking bouts when he crashed about the house and upset the applecart, as he put it, he felt remorseful.

On Friday morning Dick Conners was feeling remorseful for the usual reason, and he looked around the house for something he could do that would be appreciated by his long-suffering landlady.

On a warm, sunny afternoon, with time on their hands, it was inevitable that Doris and Phyllis should be at one or the other's front door discussing current events. For the two hawks of Eagle Street the prime current concern was very near to home, at number 6 to be exact.

'Like we was sayin' only the ovver day, Doris, yer can't neglect fings like that,' Phyllis reiterated. 'I mean ter say, yer kidneys are funny fings.'

'It's what I've always said,' Doris replied. 'Yer gotta be so careful.'

'I told 'er straight ter make sure 'e gets ter the doctor's again. It could be a stone, or it might be infected,' Phyllis went on. 'Look at ole Mrs Sanford. Look 'ow she went. Come up like a balloon she did.'

'I remember it well,' Doris told her. 'They 'ad ter take the water off. Gallons they drew off 'er.'

'That's 'ow ole Dopey Dick Conners is gonna end up,' Phyllis said, slipping her hands inside her floral pinafore.

'That man's gonna kill 'imself wiv the drink before long,' Doris remarked. ''E's often got a black eye or a fick lip, an' yer can't tell me it's all down ter bumpin' inter somefing or slippin' over when 'e's pissed.'

'I fink 'e gets 'alf o' those lumps an' bumps frew gettin' stroppy. 'E's very nasty in drink an' people ain't gonna take it, are they?' Phyllis said.

'I dunno what this street's comin' to. Mind yer, I blame Ginny Coombes,' Doris told her. 'Yer'd fink she'd 'ave learnt 'er lesson when she took that piss artist Paddy in. D'yer remember? Always pissed 'e was, an' then she takes anuvver one in. As if we didn't 'ave enough ter put up wiv.'

'Did you 'ear 'im last night?' Phyllis asked.

'Nah, I 'ad the wireless on,' Doris replied.

'I 'eard this noise an' when I looked frew me curtains I saw it was 'im,' Phyllis went on. 'Right in the middle o' the street singin' 'is 'ead off 'e was.'

'Good Gawd.'

'Then yer never guess what 'e did.'

'What did 'e do?'

''E staggered over ter the factory wall an' relieved 'imself,' Phyllis told her. 'I was watchin' 'im. Well, I didn't exactly watch 'im do it, but I see 'im lean wiv one 'and on the wall an' 'e was fiddlin' around like 'e was tryin' ter get 'is fing out. I could see it plainly. I pulled the curtains to in disgust. S'posin' one o' the kids 'ad come past while 'e was pissin' up the wall?'

'Gawd knows 'ow the Coombes put up wiv 'im. The 'ouse must suffer. Mind yer, some don't care if the place is a shit-tip.'

'Yeah, yer right,' Doris replied, nodding towards the empty number 3. 'Take that Mrs Campbell who used ter live next door ter you. That place was an absolute pigsty. Ten kids she 'ad but yer'd always find 'er chattin' at the front door.

My ole man used ter drink wiv 'er ole man up the Roebuck. George Campbell was always moanin' about the kids. "Why d'yer 'ave so many then?" my old man asked 'im once. "I love my wife," George said, all shirty like. "I love my pipe but I take it out occasionally," my bloke told 'im.'

Phyllis chuckled and slapped her friend's arm playfully. 'You are a one,' she said, between coughs.

Freda Colton from number 4 came hurrying into the street and stopped as she reached the two hawks. ''E's orf work again,' she said sighing. 'I just bin up the chemist fer some o' that Wintergreen ointment. It's about the only fing that does 'im any good.'

'I fink they play up wiv their ailments 'alf the time,' Phyllis remarked, putting her hand up to pat her blue hairnet. 'It's a good job we don't take to our beds every time we get a pain.'

Freda was a timid woman and loath to upset the two viragos but she felt bound to defend her husband against their remarks. 'I make yer right, but my old man is in real pain wiv this turn-out,' she told them. ''E wanted ter crawl out o' bed this mornin' ter go ter work but I wouldn't 'ave none of it. "You stay there, Sid, an' I'll get the doctor 'ome," I told 'im, but 'e wouldn't 'ear of it. 'E said 'e didn't wanna go on the panel. Our doctor puts yer on the panel fer the least little fing.'

'Who's your doctor Shipley?' Phyllis asked her.

'Yeah. 'E's gettin' past it, if you ask me,' Freda replied.

''E come 'ome ter me the ovver week,' Phyllis told her. 'Doris 'ere sent fer 'im. I was in a state, wasn't I, luv.'

'Yeah, I remember that,' Freda said. 'It was yer waterworks, wasn't it?'

Phyllis nodded. 'I was in agony. Stones, 'e told me. Anyway

61

'e give me some jollop an' said I'd pass 'em frew me. Bloody stuff was useless. Doris got me some stuff off Cheap Jack's stall. Marvellous it was. Varley's iron tonic fer women it was called. Only a small bottle. I took a couple o' doses an' I was right as ninepence the next day. Nah, I got no faith in Shipley. Too old fer the job.'

'Well, I'd better get in an' give my ole man a good rub in,' Freda told them.

As soon as she had closed the front door Doris was hard at it again. 'She's too bloody soft wiv 'im,' she remarked. 'Plays on it 'e does. 'E's bin like that as long as I've known 'im, lazy bleeder.'

Maggie Gainsford was the next to put in an appearance but unlike Freda she did not worry about what the two hawks might be thinking. ''Ello, ladies,' she said as she hurried by.

Once again Doris plunged the figurative knife into Maggie's back. 'Never got time fer anyfing, that one,' she said. 'Just a skivvy fer 'er lot she is. If it was me I'd put me foot down once an' fer all.'

'Yer know, I fink yer right, luv,' Phyllis said. 'She's carryin' again too, I'd take a bet on it.'

They watched their neighbour go into her house and then suddenly Doris spotted Dick Conners coming towards them. 'There 'e is, pissy Dick. Just look at 'im. Don't it make yer sick?' she growled.

'What's that 'e's got in 'is 'and?' Phyllis asked.

'It's a bleedin' chopper,' Doris said fearfully.

Dick Conners caught sight of the frightened look on the women's faces and he purposely flexed the chopper and scowled at them as he drew near. Doris and her friend Phyllis hurried into their homes as quickly as they could, and the inebriate smiled to himself as he walked up to the corner pub and entered the public bar. The two old crones would no doubt have heard that he had been barred from the saloon bar and they would be standing behind their lace curtains expecting a terrible murder to take place any second.

'Watch'er, Dick. Yer finished then?' the landlord said as he took the chopper from him.

'Yeah, I'm much obliged, John,' the drunk said smiling. 'Their bloody chopper's as blunt as old 'Arry. Anyway I chopped the lot up. Those apple boxes burn lovely. The poor ole sods feel the cold an' they need a fire at night, even in this weavver. Those poxy little bundles o' firewood they buy at the oil shop don't last 'em five minutes.'

It had not been a good day, and as Linda Weston walked home she was thankful that it was over. The morning had started well, with a good bonus job to complete and the target well within their reach, but soon things started to go wrong. A fresh cask of Algerian wine was tapped ready for the bottling team but found to be tainted. Jim Watson began running around in a panic and his flushed face went even redder and looked set to explode when Irene Cutler cornered him.

'I don't care if someone's pissed in the cask, Jim, I gotta 'ave work fer my gels,' she growled at him.

'What am I s'posed ter do, wave a magic wand an' make it all better?' he snarled.

'Yer can wave yer plonker fer all I care, as long as yer sort us out,' she responded angrily. 'Surely there's anuvver order we can start on?'

'There would be, if we 'ad the poxy labels for it, but we ain't,' he told her, equally angry. 'Yer'll 'ave ter tell yer gels they've gotta wait patiently till the manager comes back wiv 'em.'

'Where's 'e gone for 'em, Timbuktu?' the forelady growled back.

'Look, I ain't got no time ter stand 'ere arguin', woman,' he raved. 'Tell 'em from me that I'll do me best ter get some work for 'em by this afternoon.'

Irene was forced to retreat and she got the women to scrub down the pasting boards and the workbench and just tidy up in general. The afternoon dragged on, with little to do, and Jim Watson seemed to be hiding out somewhere in the depths of the arches for fear of the forelady's wrath.

Linda smiled to herself as she recalled how Irene had berated the foreman and she felt sorry for him. Irene could go on at times, though she knew just how far to go. She was loyal to her women and fought tenaciously on their behalf.

Anyway it was Friday, Linda thought. She had her wages in her handbag and a weekend to look forward to.

At seven o'clock on Friday evening the Carter boys and two of their associates were sitting in the saloon bar of the Beehive. They were gathered around a table in the far corner talking quietly, and the worried landlord gave his wife a meaningful look. It was one thing to bar undesirables when they were standing at the counter ranting, but it was another matter when they were sitting quietly in a corner and not disturbing other customers.

'I wonder what they're schemin',' Bert grumbled to Gladys.

'I dunno an' I don't wanna know,' she replied. 'As long as

they don't upset anybody 'ere we'll 'ave ter suffer 'em, I s'pose.'

Nick Carter was doing the talking. He was smartly dressed in grey suit, collar and tie. His light-weight black patent shoes looked expensive and he had a confident air about him. Six feet in height, with broad shoulders and narrow hips, dark wavy hair, deep-set dark eyes and a square chin, Nick Carter could have walked into films. His younger brother Tony did not resemble him in any way. He was slightly built, with a thin, baby face and fair lank hair. His grey eyes were piercing and he moved with nervous jerks, never still and always glancing around him as though he was expecting trouble to come his way at any moment. His baby face had earned him the nickname Boy-boy, but he took offence if he was not addressed as Tony.

'I'm gonna give 'im the opportunity an' then it's up to 'im,' Nick was saying. 'Charlie can be an aggravatin' bastard at times, but yer can trust 'im. If 'e decides ter come in wiv us 'e'll pull 'is weight, that's fer sure.'

'I dunno why yer wanna involve 'im,' Tony remarked.

'We've all known Charlie Bradley since we run the streets tergevver as kids,' Nick replied. ''E's just out o' the Kate Carney an' lookin' fer a job, an' we can use 'im. What's more, Charlie can supply a bit of extra muscle if needed. We've got a very good fing goin' 'ere an' we're gonna earn a packet, but we gotta protect our interests. If Charlie decides ter come in we can split the area up inter five sections, each of us responsible fer our own bit. It's the way the Chicago mobs used ter do it in the pro'ibition days.'

Tony's baby face broke into a grin as he toyed with his glass. 'This is Bermon'sey, not Chicago,' he said derisively.

'Yeah, but I've read a lot about the roarin' twenties,' Nick told him. 'Those geezers was well organised. They earned millions wiv their booze 'cos they 'ad their areas sowed up. That's what we're gonna do.'

The other two at the table had been listening intently and they nodded their heads at Nick Carter's plan.

'It sounds good ter me,' George Morrison said, his wide flat face breaking into a smile.

'Yeah, it's a good set-up as far as I'm concerned,' Don Jacobs added.

Nick saw the look of agreement on the pugilistic features of his associate and grinned. 'Right then, let's get a refill an' we'll wait an' see if Charlie's gonna join the business,' he said, draining his glass.

Chapter Seven

Linda stepped out of her house into the warm evening air and looked up at the roof opposite. It was nearly nine o'clock and they would all be gathered up there, she thought. Kate would no doubt be flirting with Peter Ridley, unless she had had a change of heart since last night. The old man would be there too in his pigeon loft with his friend, and Jenny would be standing with the others, glancing over at Kate and making catty comments about her. It was Friday night and the only place to be, she thought as she crossed the street. Suddenly she saw him. He had just stepped out of the Beehive pub and looked as though he was going home. He spotted her and started walking towards her.

''Ello, Lin,' he said, giving her a warm smile. 'I was beginnin' ter wonder when I'd bump inter yer. I've bin 'ome two weeks now.'

'So I 'eard, Charlie,' she replied, her face reddening slightly.

'Where are you off to? Up on the roof?' he asked her, his grin widening.

'Yeah, I usually go up there on Friday nights,' she told him. 'Fings 'aven't changed much.'

'D'yer mind if I join yer?' he asked. 'I'd like a chat.'

'I'd like it too,' she said.

They entered the block and climbed the stairs together, their footsteps sounding hollow on the boards. As they passed one front door an old woman came out to put an empty milk bottle down at the doorstep and she gave them a stern look, mumbling to herself as she went back in.

'I remember durin' the war we used ter creep up on this roof an' that ole lady came out then an' told us off,' Linda said smiling.

'That's ole Mrs Brown,' Charlie told her. 'She must be turned eighty an' she still goes out every day.'

They walked out on to the roof and saw the little group chatting amongst themselves. As Linda had guessed, Kate saw her friend with Charlie and she made a little expressive movement with her eyes. Linda smiled back and walked over to the balustrade.

'The weavver's bin lovely this past two weeks,' she said, breathing deeply and releasing the fresh air slowly from her lungs.

'Yeah, I fink it's settled now,' Charlie said, leaning on the stonework and looking down into the street below. 'Well, 'ow's fings?' he asked her suddenly, swinging round to face her.

The young woman shrugged her shoulders and gave him a shy look. 'Dad's not too well. It's 'is kidneys. It could be an infection.'

'I'm sorry to 'ear it,' he replied. ''Ow about you?'

'I'm fine. I'm still at the wine vaults. What about you?'

Charlie turned and stared out over the rooftops, his eyes taking in the view. 'I just bin in the pub. That's where I was comin' from when I spotted you,' he told her. 'I've just 'ad a proposition put ter me. The Carter boys. They want me ter go in wiv 'em.'

'Are yer goin' to?' Linda asked him.

Charlie shook his head. 'They've rented one o' the railway arches in Abbey Street. They're in the perfume business, would yer believe?'

Linda smiled at his expression. 'It sounds good,' she said.

'Yeah, it does,' he replied, glancing at her briefly. 'They've got a good set-up there. They've got 'old o' these special base oils that go inter the expensive scents an' they're mixin' 'em wiv spirit an' knockin' 'em out all over the place. They've got labels printed an' boxes ter put 'em in as well. They can bottle an' pack the stuff fer a couple o' bob an' they're chargin' 'alf the retail price.'

'An' they wanted you ter go in wiv 'em?' Linda said.

Charlie nodded and then looked down at his clasped hands thoughtfully. 'I was offered a patch ter work on,' he explained. 'What 'appens is they go in pubs an' clubs an' build up contacts, sayin' the stuff's knocked off an' bein' sold at a bargain price. Yer know yerself 'ow people jump at a bargain, 'specially expensive perfume that they couldn't afford at the full price. They're not worried about it bein' dodgy gear, as long as they fink they're gettin' a good deal.'

'It's a bit risky, I would 'ave thought,' Linda remarked.

'Yeah, it can be, but it depends on 'ow yer go about it,' Charlie told her. 'I was offered the Dock'ead area 'cos I know a few o' the pubs down there. It was very temptin' but I 'ad ter say no.'

'It was prob'ly the right decision,' Linda said, looking at him and noticing his serious expression.

'I 'ope so, but there yer go,' Charlie sighed. 'The trouble is, when yer get involved wiv the likes o' the Carters yer sell yer soul to 'em. Yer see there could be some bovver. When they go knockin' out dodgy gear on ovver gangs' manors there's bound ter be trouble o' some sort, an' everyone gets pulled in on it. Besides, there's always somebody who wants ter muscle in on the business. I'm not lookin' fer trouble, not that sort o' trouble.'

''Ave yer got fixed up wiv anuvver job then?' Linda asked him.

Charlie laughed and shook his head. 'I've bin told there's labourin' work goin' down at Dock'ead so I'm gonna give it a try on Monday,' he replied.

They stood together looking out at the night sky and Linda shivered.

'Are yer cold?' Charlie asked her.

'No, it's just someone walkin' over me grave,' she joked.

Charlie looked at her for a few moments, noticing how her fine fair hair was cut and set around her head, and how it moved in the light breeze. He thought of how she looked when she smiled at him, and how she listened to him with interest, and he was intrigued. Linda had grown into a very attractive young woman, he thought. She was tall and slim, with nice legs and a firm bust. Her eyes too were warm and friendly, and he saw something else there too, something he could not quite understand, and it excited him.

The sun had gone and the smouldering miracle of colours had faded too, leaving the dusk to settle and thicken into a deep velvet night, and Linda felt as safe and secure as she had that day during the war when she leaned against Charlie and he led her away from the roof. She sighed, a deep contented sigh, as she looked up at the pinpoints of light high in the heavens. Tonight felt special, as if a sort of magic was in the air. Charlie was there with her, just a foot away, and she could almost feel the heat of his body. He was quiet, leaning forward on the stonework as he stared out at the City lights, and she studied him surreptitiously. He had filled out and grown taller. He looked lean yet powerful, and she noticed how he had swept his dark wavy hair back from his forehead. His brown eyes were brooding and full of expression and she traced the line of his straight nose and square chin with her eyes. He was not particularly handsome, she thought, but there was something about him, something that pleased her, made her want to be with him, and she wished she knew how to tell him so.

'Linda.'

'Yeah?'

'I was just finkin'. Do yer remember that time when the Carters were givin' yer a bad time over those slippers an' I got 'em back for yer?'

'I've never fergot it,' she said softly. 'Whenever I'm up 'ere I fink about that day.'

'I remember challengin' Boy-boy Carter to a fight over those slippers of yours an' 'e wouldn't 'ave none of it,' he told her. 'Boy-boy mentioned it ternight while we were talkin' about when we were kids.'

'I still go an' look at that carvin' yer did that day. Do yer remember doin' it?'

Charlie looked surprised. 'No, I don't.'

'C'mon, I'll show yer,' Linda told him with a big grin.

They skirted the stairway and she pointed at the post.

'There, look,' she said, running the tips of her fingers over the old markings.

'Did I do that?' he said, smiling at her.

'That's your initial inside the 'eart an' yer never got time ter finish it.'

'Charlie loves who?' he said, laughing aloud, and then stopped suddenly as he saw the serious look on Linda's face.

'I was eleven then an' I was 'opin' you were gonna finish it some time,' she told him. 'I used ter come up 'ere quite a lot as a kid, an' I always went ter look at this. I used ter wish that one day I'd see my initial carved in there wiv yours.'

'Yer gotta remember that I was fourteen at the time an' you were just a baby ter me then,' he explained.

Linda saw the humorous look on his face and smiled. 'I was a very grown-up eleven,' she said.

'Yer've certainly grown up now,' he told her, his voice sounding hoarse as he moved a little closer to her.

Linda's stomach tightened as she looked into his eyes. She sensed it happening and as his arms went out and his hands closed over her shoulders, she moved forward. His lips touched hers, softly at first and then harder in a full kiss. She closed her eyes, her arms hugging his waist and she felt him clutching her to him, gently but firmly. She could smell his aftershave and feel the smoothness of his face against hers, then she felt his body tense and they moved apart. He looked embarrassed but Linda felt happy and self-possessed. It was not her first grown-up kiss, after all. She had dated young men before and sampled their goodnight kisses, but this kiss was special. It was her first kiss with the man who had stolen her heart all those years ago.

'I'm sorry, I couldn't resist it,' Charlie said, giving her a sheepish grin.

'I'm not. I wanted yer to,' she told him familiarly.

They heard voices and giggling as two of the group came round by the stairway. The couple were surprised to find anyone there and the young man gave Charlie an apologetic look before they disappeared back where they had come from.

'I bet 'e was gonna steal a kiss too,' Charlie laughed as he took Linda's hand. 'We better go back inter view or they'll all be comin' spyin' on us.'

They walked hand in hand to the balustrade and leaned against it, still holding hands.

'Will you walk out wiv me?' Charlie asked.

'I'd love to,' Linda replied, her eyes going up to meet his, and she felt his hand tighten over hers.

'Would yer like ter go ter the flicks termorrer?' he asked.

She nodded with a smile and then moved close to him as he put his arm around her shoulders. 'I feel so happy,' she said in a soft voice.

'I do too,' he told her.

Jack Marchant climbed the last flight of stairs on to the roof and went to the pigeon shed. It was late but Bill Simpson was worried about Monty and he had nagged his friend into checking the loft. Bill had named the bird after Montgomery because he said it reminded him of the field marshal inspecting his troops when it strutted past the other birds.

Jack could see that all was well and he went back down to Bill Simpson's flat for a nightcap. 'It looks fine,' he told him.

'I'm glad. It looked a bit peaky this mornin',' Bill told him.

'Yeah, so yer said,' his friend replied. 'Anyway if yer feelin' better termorrer yer can see fer yerself.'

'I dunno what came over me,' Bill said. 'One minute I'm right as ninepence an' the next I come over all giddy.'

'I told yer before. It's those bloody stairs,' Jack said sharply. 'I told yer enough times ter go an' see ole Parker. 'E'll get yer moved into a lower flat soon as one's available. After all, you ain't no chicken. Yer can't be expected ter keep on up an' down them bloody stairs.'

'I gotta 'ave me stout,' Bill told him. 'I can't do wivout me stout.'

'Now yer just makin' excuses, yer silly ole sod,' Jack replied with a ghost of a smile on his gaunt features. 'I told yer I'll bring yer a couple o' bottles o' stout from the jug side. Mrs Toomey can get yer all the bits o' shoppin' yer need. She's offered. She can't do no more than that.'

'I don't want ole Muvver Toomey comin' in 'ere,' Bill said firmly. 'She's a nosy ole bastard. 'Er eyes are everywhere. Besides, I fink she fancies me.'

'Yer gotta be round the twist,' Jack told him, shaking his head slowly. 'Fancies you? I should fink so! She must be seventy-five if she's a day.'

'What bloody difference does age make?' Bill said quickly. 'I still get the urge sometimes. Well, not all that often, but I do occasionally. I s'pose she does too, sometimes. She's bin on 'er own fer years.'

'Women ain't like men. They go orf it quicker than we do,' Jack said with authority.

'Don't you believe it,' Bill growled. 'Mrs What's-'er-name's still at it an' she's turned seventy.'

'Who yer talkin' about?'

'Why, 'er wiv the ginger 'air who lives on the first floor.'

'She's different. She's bin 'avin' it orf wiv old Wallace the fishmonger ever since 'is ole woman pissed orf,' Jack told him. 'They're like man an' wife.'

''E's always in 'er place. I've seen 'im go in meself,' Bill replied.

'That don't mean 'e's 'avin' it orf wiv 'er. 'E just goes ter see 'er, that's all,' Jack said, catching the smile on Bill's face. ''Ere, you ain't bin listenin' at 'er door, 'ave yer?' he asked quickly.

Bill grinned. 'All I'm sayin' is, I don't want that interferin' ole cow Toomey comin' in my place. I know fings about 'er.'

'Fings? What fings?'

'Just fings.'

'Well come on then, tell me.'

Bill remained silent and Jack got even more curious.

'Why won't yer tell me? I'm yer ole pal, ain't I?' he pressed him.

''Cos I don't want you puttin' it about at the pub, that's why,' Bill said finally.

Jack Marchant looked peeved. 'D'yer fink I go spoutin' orf at the boozer?' he said sharply.

'Nah, I know yer can keep fings ter yerself if yer told to,' Bill said in a conciliatory tone, 'so if I tell yer, yer gotta promise me ter keep it under yer 'at, 'cos ovverwise Jumbo Bennett's gonna know where it's come from. Apart from 'im, an' Alice Toomey, I'm the only one who knows about it.'

'About what?' Jack almost shouted in his impatience.

Bill put his glass of stout down on the table beside his armchair and drew a deep breath. 'It was like this,' he began. 'As yer know, Jumbo Bennett lost 'is wife a few years ago, an'' yer know that 'e ain't very good on 'is legs after that accident 'e 'ad on the ice last year when 'e broke 'is 'ip. Now Jumbo's gettin' on a bit, like we all are, but 'e 'as to 'ave his regular pint, come rain, come shine.'

'Yeah, I'm listenin',' Jack said impatiently.

'Well, one day Jumbo went inter the Crown fer a drink,' Bill went on, 'an' 'e met Alice Toomey in there. She was on the ole muvver's ruin an' gettin' all upset. Yer know 'ow they get on the gin.'

Jack tutted. 'Yeah, yeah. Go on,' he pressed him.

'Now Jumbo puts 'is arm round 'er all neighbourly like an' tries ter comfort 'er,' Bill continued. 'She's bubblin' away, ain't she, goin' on about missin' 'er ole man. That's a laugh on its own. She never 'ad a good word fer the poor bastard when 'e was alive. But anyway, one fing leads to anuvver an' Jumbo walks 'ome wiv Alice, arms round each ovver. Mind you, I dunno who was 'oldin' who up, what wiv Jumbo's bad 'ip an' 'er pissed as a newt. Now yer know ole Jumbo lives wiv 'is eldest daughter. Well, she was out fer the day so the dirty ole bastard seizes 'is chance. When they gets ter the block Jumbo invites 'er in fer a drop o' tiddly. One fing leads to anuvver an' they start kissin' an' canoodlin'. Jumbo tells 'er 'e ain't felt this way fer years an' she said 'ow much she was missin' the old 'ow's-yer-farvver, so they decide ter go ter bed. She 'ad to 'elp Jumbo get undressed 'cos of 'is 'ip. Anyway they do the business an' then Alice is up an' got 'er corsets back on before Jumbo 'ad 'is feet on the oilcloth. Then she sees this ole coat 'angin' be'ind the bedroom door. It's Jumbo's daughter's winter coat that she used ter chuck on 'is bed when it got really parky. So she tries it on an' asks 'im 'ow she looks in it. Jumbo tells 'er ter take it off but she wasn't 'avin' any of it. Out she goes wearin' the bloody fing, would yer believe? Now poor Jumbo can't get up ter stop 'er an' 'e sits there rantin' an' ravin', swearin' ter choke the fievin' cow when 'e does catch up wiv 'er. Anyway, ter cut a long story short, Jumbo did see 'er in the Crown a few days later an' she was still wearin' the coat. They 'ad a big row an' she told 'im that if 'e didn't let 'er keep it she'd say that 'e'd raped 'er. Can you imagine?'

'What did 'is daughter say when she found the coat was missin'?' Jack asked him.

Bill took another long sip from his stout. 'Jumbo told 'er she'd given it ter the rag man when 'e called. She couldn't remember it an' Jumbo told 'er it was when she 'ad one of 'er blindin' 'eadaches an' 'e'd queried it wiv 'er but she'd told 'im ter piss orf an' mind 'is own business.'

'Bloody 'ell, who'd 'a' guessed it about Alice Toomey,' Jack said, shaking his head slowly.

'Now yer know why I don't want that nosy ole cow in my place,' Bill told him.

Ten minutes later Jack Marchant left his old friend's flat and as he walked down to his flat below he saw Alice Toomey coming up the stairs looking the worse for drink.

''Ello, dear,' she slurred as she reached the landing. 'I got a nice drop o' special indoors. Fancy a snort?'

'No fanks, luv,' Jack said nervously, going in and closing his door tight before Alice could grab him.

take it off but she wasn't havin' any of it. Out she goes swearin',
the bloody thing, would yer believe? Now poor Jumbo can't
get up ter shut 'er an', 'e sits there rantin', an' ravin', swearin'
ter choke the flamin' cow when 'e does catch up wiv 'er.
Anyway, ter cut a long story short, Jumbo did see 'er in the
Crown a few days later an' she was still wearin' the coat.
They 'ad a big row an' she told 'im that if 'e didn't let 'er
keep it she'd say that 'e'd raped 'er. Can you imagine?'

'What did 'er daughter say when she found the coat was
missing?' Jack asked him.

Bill took another long sip from his stout. 'Jumbo told 'er
she'd given it ter the rag man when 'e called. She couldn't
remember it an', Jumbo told 'er it was when she 'ad one of 'er
bindin', headaches an', 'e'd queried it wiv 'er but she'd told 'im
ter piss off an', mind 'is own business.'

'Bloody 'ell, who'd 'a' guessed it about Alice Thorne?' Jack
said, shaking his head slowly.

'Now yer know why I didn't want that nosy cow in my
place,' Bill told him.

Ten minutes later Jack Marchant left his old friend's flat
and as he walked down to his flat below he saw why Thorney
counting up the stairs looking the worse for drink.

'Here, love,' she slurred as she reached the landing, 'I got a
nice drop of special tiddows. Fancy a story?'

'No fanks, luv,' Jack said nervously, going in and closing
his door tight before Alice could grab him.

Chapter Eight

Charlie Bradley was out early on Monday morning. He wore an old pair of cord trousers and carried a brown paper parcel under his arm, and as he reached the large stretch of wasteground at Dockhead he spotted a wooden hut with a few men milling around outside. He guessed that they too were hoping for a start and as he walked up to the group one of them turned to him.

'They're takin' a few on this mornin',' he said cheerfully.

Charlie gave him a smile. 'We might be lucky then,' he replied.

The man looked him up and down curiously. 'Are you a tradesman?' he asked. 'Chippies an' pipelayers 'ave ter go over there.'

'No, I'm after labourin',' he told him.

'Ever done any trench diggin'?' the man went on.

Charlie shook his head, aware that the rest of the men were eyeing him with some amusement.

'They won't last yer five minutes,' one of them said, pointing to Charlie's shoes. 'Yer'll be up ter yer arse in clay.'

The young man bit back on a smart reply. They were older men, used to labouring by the look of them, and they were only trying to warn him. 'I got me boots 'ere,' he replied casually, nodding to the bag he had under his arm.

The man who had first spoken to him grinned and held out his hand. 'Sid's the name, son. Sid Green. You stick wiv me. I'll soon put yer straight.'

'Charlie Bradley,' he answered, gripping the outstretched hand.

'Yeah, I can see by yer mitt you ain't done much diggin',' Sid remarked. 'Yer've bin away, ain't yer? Army or nick?'

'Army,' Charlie replied. 'I only got demobbed two weeks ago.'

'Not ter worry. This firm ain't worried who you are or where yer bin, long as yer can 'andle a pick an' shovel. They gave me a start when I got out the nick a couple o' years back an' I've worked fer 'em on an' off ever since.'

A man came out of the hut holding a clipboard. 'We've got a few problems so yer'll 'ave ter come back at nine sharp,' he told the men. 'Give us yer names then yer won't miss yer turn.'

Charlie added his name to the list and then as he walked away Sid came up to him. 'I'm goin' fer a bacon sandwich an' a cuppa,' Sid said.

The young man glanced up at the church clock away in the distance. 'I fink I'll take a stroll,' he replied.

A stream of trams, buses, horsecarts and lorries flowed along Jamaica Road and workers hurried by as Charlie made his way along the thoroughfare to the gardens at St James's Church. He passed through the ornamental iron gates and walked along a path of yellow stone chippings, and almost immediately he smelt the freshly mown grass and the scent coming from the flower beds which were still damp from the morning watering. The early sun lit up the church facade and the gilt dial of the clock, and it felt warm on Charlie's face. He breathed deeply as he sat down on a bench facing the Doric columns at the top of the wide stone stairs to the church.

He wanted time to dwell, to put his thoughts in order and think about Linda and the brief time he had spent with her. It had been a nice weekend. He had taken her to the Trocadera on Saturday night and they had sat in the back row holding hands. Afterwards they strolled home talking about themselves, and Charlie recalled how easily they had got on together. Linda had been very interested when he chatted to her about his army service in Hamburg and he understood why when she told him later that her brother Frankie was due to go in at any time. She had talked to him about her family and told him how worried she was about her father, and they had lingered for a while in the darkness of the block entrance and kissed shyly.

They had seen each other again on Sunday evening and taken a long stroll along the quiet riverside, and he had coaxed her into the Anchor, an ancient pub which looked out on St Paul's Cathedral across the Thames. Charlie smiled as he remembered the anxious look on her face when he suggested a drink and his surprise at learning that Linda had never been in a pub before. They had taken their drinks on to a raised veranda over the river and sat talking nonstop as they enjoyed the coolness of the evening, and later they looked up at the stars from the roof of the building and sought out a shadowy spot behind the stairway to kiss goodnight.

The church clock showed ten minutes to nine o'clock

81

when he got up and walked swiftly back to the Carmody office at Dockhead.

'Right, next one.'

Charlie glanced quickly at Sid Green who was coming out of the office and got a thumbs-up sign. He stepped into the cramped room and saw a heavily built man with a mop of unruly grey hair staring up at him. 'Let's 'ave yer cards,' he demanded.

The young man took his insurance cards from his reefer jacket pocket and handed them over. The site foreman glanced at them and then looked up at him.

''Ave yer done any ditch diggin' before? We want experienced ditch diggers,' he said, looking him up and down.

'I done lots o' different jobs before I went in the Kate,' Charlie told him.

The big man folded his arms and leaned back in his chair. 'I asked if yer'd done any ditch diggin'.'

Charlie straightened up and threw out his chest. 'No, but I can work wiv the best,' he replied with spirit. 'I'm not scared of 'ard work. I need a job.'

'Right then, I'll give yer a start. The wages are four pounds seventeen an' six an' there's a chance to earn bonuses,' the site foreman informed him. 'Yer gotta work 'ard fer 'em, mind. I'm gonna warn yer straight off. If yer not up to it yer'll soon be told ter piss off. We don't give a week's notice on this sort o' work. Understood?'

Charlie nodded, his face brightening. 'Yer won't 'ave no reason ter get shot o' me,' he told him. 'Fanks fer the start.'

'Right then, go an' report ter the ganger. Yer'll find 'im outside.'

The young man stepped out into the sunshine feeling

pleased with himself, but when he crossed over to where Sid and the rest of the men were standing he realised that there were likely to be problems. They were listening to a huge man who stood with his feet apart, his large belly hanging over a wide leather belt. He had a bald head and a ruddy complexion, and he scowled at Charlie as he came up. 'Right, fer 'is benefit I'll start again,' he growled, jerking his thumb at him. 'Sid 'ere knows the drill so yer'll be known as Sid Green's crew. We got targets ter meet an' yer gonna sweat. Joe Brody's crew are good an' yer gonna 'ave ter go some ter stay wiv 'em. Joe's the diggers' foreman, so yer'll take yer orders from 'im. 'E's an 'ard taskmaster but if yer pull yer weight yer'll keep on the right side of 'im. OK then?'

The men nodded dutifully and the foreman beckoned them to follow him, leading the way across the wasteground to another hut. 'Get yer waterproofs an' then report over there,' he told them, pointing to where a brick building was springing up.

Along with the rest of the men Charlie was handed a pair of waterproof trousers, and a few minutes later the novice ditch diggers marched over to the building area looking a little apprehensive. Charlie carried his shoes in the paper bag, and he knew that he was going to ache in every muscle before the day was out.

'Oi, you lot. Over 'ere.'

They tramped over to the huge man who was standing beside a coke brazier set outside a black tarpaulin tent. He was all of six feet six and wide-shouldered, making the previous foreman look small in comparison. His face was covered in stubble and his dark eyes stared out from deep sockets. 'Right, I'm Joe Brody,' he said in a deep voice that seemed to come from his boots. 'The mechanical digger's marked out yer trench. Get yer tools an' get ter work. I'll be over in a while ter see 'ow yer gettin' on.'

'Right'o, cocker,' one of the men said, making a stab at humour.

Brody's face grew dark as he ambled over. 'We got a joker in the pack, I see,' he growled, his eyes boring into the inoffensive novice. 'Well, let me tell you, sonny boy, there's only one joker round 'ere an' that's me. Now get ter work. I'll be watchin' you very carefully, so be warned.'

The crew took their guidance from Sid, who hustled them into the tent to collect their picks and shovels. 'Take no notice o' that poxy gorilla,' he advised them.

'Yer never warned us about 'im,' one of the men said to the dapper ganger.

''E left the job when I was 'ere last,' Sid told him. 'I didn't fink 'e'd be back.'

'Are we expected ter dig wiv these?' a voice called out. 'The poxy tools are useless. Just look at this pick. The bloody 'andle's all loose.'

'So's this shovel. It's all bent as well,' another said.

Charlie began to feel deflated. He realised that digging a deep trench was hard enough, even if equipped with good tools, but with this collection of antiques the chance of earning a bonus was less than nil. Sid on the other hand seemed calm and resigned to it. 'It's no good complainin'. Brody makes sure 'is crew get the pick o' the tools,' he told them. 'We'll just 'ave ter manage wiv what we've got. Come on, lads, let's get to it.'

The sun was climbing high in a clear sky and it looked like it was going to be a hot day as Sid Green's crew began cutting down into the dry earth. The six-man team worked hard and were soon making good progress despite the sorry state of their equipment. After a while Sid decided to switch the jobs round and Charlie immediately understood why. His hands were already becoming sore from handling the rough shovel and it was a relief to wield a pickaxe for a spell. Sid organised them well and soon they were down to waist level along the marked-out length.

The men broke off at ten o'clock for a mug of tea and cheese rolls that were brought up to the job by an elderly looking workman on a bogie-truck. After they had finished eating, Charlie sprawled out on the warm earth along with the others to ease his aching back muscles, and all too soon the whistle sounded. The men jumped down into the trench once more and worked hard trying to earn their bonus, prompted and encouraged by their slightly-built ganger who never seemed to tire. They had reached solid clay now and found it more difficult to make progress, and when the midday whistle shrilled out Charlie hauled himself out of the trench and saw that the palms of both his hands were rubbed raw.

'I'm goin' fer a pint. Who's joinin' me?' Sid said, licking his lips.

Charlie and the rest of the crew followed him over to a little pub on the edge of the site. It was full of dockers and building labourers and pints were flowing as the men jostled to get served. Carmody's trench diggers found space in a corner once they had finally got their drinks and Sid smiled as he looked at their solemn faces. 'Don't look so bloody miserable,' he told them. 'We ain't doin' too bad. We should be able ter step it up this afternoon.'

Charlie took a sip from his pint of bitter, the palms of his hands now beginning to look like raw meat. Sid noticed them and pulled a face. 'Yer better soak 'em in brine ternight,' he said. 'It'll 'arden 'em up, an' stop 'em goin' septic.'

One of the crew, a broad-shouldered young man with a mop of fair curly hair, turned to the man next to him. 'I was surprised I got a start this mornin',' he said. 'I ain't got no stamps on me card. I bin away, yer see.'

'In the nick?' the other asked.

'Yeah. I got eighteen months fer receivin',' he replied.

'Where d'yer do yer porridge?' Sid asked him.

'Wormwood Scrubs.'

'I done a spell there,' Sid said. 'They moved me there from Wandsworth.'

'What was you done for, Sid?' the fair-haired man asked him.

'Yer'd never believe it, son,' the ganger said, shaking his head slowly.

'Try me.'

'I got four years fer bigamy,' Sid told him, and, seeing the look of disbelief on his face, 'Yeah, that's right. Me first ole woman was a right miserable ole mare. Nuffink I could do would please 'er. I worked me fingers ter the bone fer that bitch an' shit was me fanks. Anyway, I stood it as long as I could, then one night I just pissed orf,' he chuckled. 'I was livin' over Shoreditch at the time an' I come over this side o' the water. The war 'ad just ended an' I got a job on the demolition. Good money it was. One night I was in this pub at the Elephant an' I saw this woman. Bit older than me it turned out, but what a stunner. She was wiv this great big tub o' lard an' it looked like 'e was givin' 'er an 'ard time. So when this geezer went outside fer a slash I went over an' introduced meself. I asked if she was all right an' if she wanted me ter sort 'im out. She got all frightened an' told me ter leave 'er before 'e come back or 'e'd kill me. It turned out 'e was Charlie Kovacs, the European 'eavyweight wrestlin' champion.'

'So what did yer do?' the man asked, intrigued.

'I was full o' meself at the time,' Sid continued. 'I said to 'er, I don't care if 'e's Charlie Chaplin, and then suddenly out 'e comes. I'm not kiddin' you, 'e must 'a' stood six foot fifteen in 'is socks, an' 'e looked as strong as a brick-built shit'ouse. 'E came up an' stood over me an' then roared out at me ter piss orf. So I rolled me shoulders like yer do when yer warmin' before a fight, an' then before I could do anyfing 'e picked me up an' chucked me across the pub just like I was a rag doll. Anyway I shook me barnet once or twice ter gavver me thoughts then I waited me chance. I saw 'im turn an' lean on the counter an' I picked up this iron table. I could barely lift it but I managed ter raise it up an' I brought it down on the back of 'is 'ead. Out like a light 'e went. "C'mon," I said ter this woman. "Yer can't stop 'ere now." So off we went.'

'An' yer married 'er?'

'A few weeks later,' Sid replied. 'She wouldn't let me get near 'er till we got married.'

'So yer lived 'appily ever after, till yer got caught,' Charlie said grinning.

'We was married six months before it all come a tumble, but by that time she'd pissed orf,' Sid said sadly. 'She said she couldn't stand bein' married to a demolition worker.

She said she preferred the artistic type. Marvellous, ain't it? When I first met 'er she was wiv a demolition expert.'

The crew grinned, amused by the look of disgust on Sid's face as he picked up his pint of beer and drained the glass in one gulp.

'It's ten minutes ter one,' one of them said, glancing up at the clock over the counter.

The men trooped back to work and stripped to the waist before clambering back into the trench. Sweat dripped from them and ran into their eyes as the hours passed and they toiled on under the hot sun. At four o'clock Brody came over to inspect their progress. 'Yer'll 'ave ter do better than that if yer wanna earn the bonus,' he growled.

'Piss orf, you ugly-lookin' git,' one of the men said under his breath.

Charlie leaned on his shovel as he watched the big man amble away. 'I wonder 'ow 'is crew would do wiv the crap tools we've got ter work wiv,' he said to Sid.

When the whistle sounded to end the day the diggers climbed thankfully out of the trench and made their way over to the tarpaulin tent. Brody's crew were already there and they looked across with crafty smiles on their faces as Sid and his crew flopped down on the wooden benches.

Charlie scraped a clod of clay from his boots and picked up the paper bag his shoes were in. 'I'm too tired ter change. I'm goin' 'ome like this,' he said.

'Don't ferget what I told yer about those 'ands,' Sid reminded him.

Charlie nodded and waved goodnight to the rest of the crew as he left the tent and set off home through Abbey Street, feeling as though he had been kicked all over. His hands were sore and bleeding and his dark hair lank and sticking to his forehead. The day was not over yet, he told himself as he turned wearily into Eagle Street and entered the first block of Sunlight Buildings. He still had his mother to face.

Chapter Nine

Linda walked to work on Tuesday morning feeling troubled. Her father was no better and the doctor had arranged for him to see a specialist at Guy's Hospital. Frankie had got his call-up papers, and as if that wasn't enough Jamie had squashed a finger at work and was off sick.

Linda hurried into the wine vaults with a serious look on her face, and as she clocked on the forelady was waiting. She gathered the women together as they came in and told them the news.

'There's no work fer us this mornin', ladies,' she said. 'Some bloody fool's ballsed up that order an' poor ole Watson's runnin' around like a chicken wiv no 'ead. We've gotta wait till they can sort it out, but in the meantime I'm goin' up ter see the manager. This bloody place is gettin' above a joke. We missed our bonus last week an' it looks as though we're gonna miss out again this week.'

The women sat around chatting while Irene was away and Linda let the conversation flow over her. She thought about her father who was at the hospital that morning, and her mother, who was putting on a brave face in front of the family but was obviously very worried.

'Are you all right?' Doll asked her. 'You look like yer lost a pound an' found a tanner.'

Linda shrugged her shoulders. 'I was miles away then,' she said, forcing a smile.

'That's where I'd like ter be now,' Kate Madigan cut in. 'Miles away from this bloody 'ole.'

'I fink they're doin' this on purpose ter stop us earnin' a bonus,' Doll remarked. 'That's what they did when I worked at the sausage factory. They kept on piss-ballin' wiv the bonuses till the gels on the machines got fed up wiv it an' started ter leave. They never bovvered ter replace 'em an' we found ourselves doin' two people's jobs.'

'What, work two machines at once?' Fat Mary queried.

'No, yer dopey mare. They shut some o' the sausage machines down an' us that was left was expected ter turn out the same amount,' Doll explained. 'I stood it fer a couple o' weeks an' then my ole man copped the needle 'cos I was gettin' so miserable. 'E told me ter pack the job up or 'e'd pack me up.'

'So yer left,' Fat Mary said.

'Nah, I let 'im leave,' Doll replied grinning. 'The no-good whoreson was leadin' me a dog's life anyway. I was gettin' so I couldn't trust meself wiv a sharp knife when 'e was around. I used ter get this terrible urge ter cut 'is froat when 'e was snorin' in the armchair.'

The chatting went on and Linda thought about Charlie. She had not seen him since Sunday and she wondered how he was getting on at work. She recalled the intimacy of their goodnight kiss and cuddle on Sunday night and wondered if it meant as much to him as it did to her. Charlie made her feel special, and she hoped she had made a good enough impression on him.

Irene came hurrying along the vault. 'C'mon, gels, get yerself sorted out, I've got us a job,' she said rousingly. 'Top-rate bonus if we can get the Dorchester order out by ternight.'

'Bloody 'ell, Irene, that's a day an' a 'alf's job,' Fat Mary cut in.

'What yer want, a quiet life, Mary, or d'yer wanna earn a few bob?' the forelady asked her.

'All right, luv, don't get yer knickers in a twist,' Mary said, rolling up her sleeves.

On the building site at Dockhead the trench diggers were getting ready for another hard day. Charlie slipped on a pair of waterproof trousers over his own and laced up his boots with sore hands that were bandaged round the palms.

'Did yer soak them 'ands like I told yer to?' Sid asked him.

'Yeah. They'll be all right,' he replied, doubting that they would last out the week.

Sid peeled a large clod of dried clay from the sole of his boot as he sat with his crew waiting for the whistle to blow.

'I feel like bustin' the lock on that chest an' takin' the best o' the tools before that ugly git arrives,' one growled.

Sid nodded. ''Ere 'e comes.'

Brody walked into the tarpaulin-covered shed without a word, went straight to the large chest at the far end and proceeded to unlock it. The rest of his gang followed him, eyeing the novice crew with disdain.

'Are you gonna last the day out?' one said leering as he spotted Charlie's bandaged hands.

'I should fink so,' Charlie replied calmly, which seemed to irritate him.

'C'mon then, you lot, there's a bonus ter be earnt,' Brody called out.

The man gave Charlie a hard look and then went up to the chest to collect his pick and shovel.

Charlie looked down at his hands for a few moments then he stood up. 'This is as good a time as any ter sort fings out,' he told his crew.

'Leave it out, son,' Sid warned him. 'It ain't werf the aggro.'

Charlie ignored him and walked up slowly to where Brody was standing. 'I got a complaint,' he said quietly.

Brody handed the last of the tools out to his men, ignoring him, but as he made to walk off the young man stepped directly in front of him.

'What's your beef?' Brody growled.

'I reckon that my crew are workin' at a disadvantage,' Charlie told him. 'I fink there should be a fairer share out o' the decent tools.'

'Oh yer do, do yer?' the foreman sneered. 'I'm in charge 'ere an' I'll decide who gets what.'

'Well, if yer don't sort it out I'll go an' see someone who can,' Charlie replied calmly.

Brody's face coloured up and he suddenly reached out to grab the younger man by the throat. Charlie was too quick for him and he slipped sideways, sending the huge foreman off balance. As he turned round Charlie was ready. He had grabbed a shovel and was holding it up like a club.

'Come near me an' I'll split yer crust open,' he growled.

For a few moments Brody looked as though he would

spring forward, but then his shoulders sagged and he pointed his finger at Charlie. 'I'll sort you out later,' he snarled. 'C'mon, lads, let's get ter work.'

'What about these dodgy tools?' Charlie persisted.

'Yer'll 'ave ter wait till termorrer,' the foreman growled as he led his men away.

'Yer done it all wrong, son,' Sid told him. 'Yer fronted 'im an' 'e's lost face wiv 'is crew. If I know Brody 'e won't let it end there. Take my advice an' watch yer back.'

Charlie delved down into the chest and grabbed a pickaxe and a shovel. 'C'mon, let's take these over ter the office. We can't work wiv these,' he said disgustedly.

Sid shook his head. 'Let's manage fer terday,' he replied. 'We'll give Brody a chance ter get 'em changed first.'

Charlie shrugged his shoulders. 'All right, but we're not workin' wiv this load o' rubbish after terday,' he said firmly.

'Fair enough. C'mon, lads, there's a bonus ter be earned,' Sid said, imitating the foreman.

The novice crew began the back-breaking job of digging a six-foot-deep trench with their ancient tools, and before the morning was out Charlie's hands were raw and bleeding again.

Some way along the wasteground Brody's team were making good progress, and as Brody dug his shovel deep into the damp clay his face was a dark mask.

'That flash monkey needs sortin' out,' one of the crew said to him.

'Don't worry,' Brody told him. 'I'll fix 'im fer sure termorrer.'

Carmody's novice trench-digging team were learning fast under the guidance of Sid Green the ganger. During their morning tea break he took time to explain to them the reason why the trench runs were marked out in such a fashion. Scratching in the dust with a stick he drew a rough plan of how the sewage pipes were to be laid out from the building that was going up behind them, linking up into one main pipe run which stretched down to the main sewers under Jamaica Road. Carmody's site manager had stipulated a length of trench which had to be cut out of the clay soil each day, and by that Friday evening the two gangs were expected to have reached the main pipe run and earned their bonus. The men could now see some purpose to the punishing work, but as they sat on the edge of the trench drinking their tea out of stained mugs even their ganger was despondent.

'We got about as much chance o' gettin' that bonus as gettin' Brody ter smile,' he told them. 'We're way be'ind already.'

'Talkin' o' Brody, d'yer fink 'e'll get these tools changed?' the fair-haired labourer asked, looking at Charlie.

The young man ran his boot over the diagram scratched out in the soil and looked up at him. 'Like I said, if 'e doesn't, I'm gonna go over the office,' he replied in a determined voice.

Sid gave Charlie an anxious glance and threw his tea leaves on the ground. 'Right, lads, let's see if we can make a bit o' progress,' he sighed.

The men jumped down into the trench and set to work once more. The hot dry weather had made the clay easier to cut up and handle and they all worked with a will, hardly stopping to catch their breath. Charlie laboured away with his pickaxe, trying to ignore the pain from his bandaged hands, while the other men shovelled out the large freed-up clods.

'Sod it!' one of them cursed as the wooden handle of his shovel split.

''Ere, use this pickaxe. I'm goin' over the office,' Charlie growled.

'Leave it, I'll go an' see Brody,' Sid told him, stabbing his shovel into the clay bed.

'What's the use?' Charlie retorted angrily. ''E'll only tell yer ter wait.'

Sid Green faced him closely, looking up at him with a determined expression on his stubbled face. 'I'm the ganger, it's my job ter get fings sorted out,' he replied sharply.

Charlie picked up the broken shovel. 'All right, you can do the askin', but I'm comin' wiv yer,' he said firmly.

Sid could see by the look in the young man's eyes that it was no use arguing and he nodded. 'Let's go an' see 'im then,' he said.

The two men walked purposefully across the waste-ground to where Brody's team were working. They could see that the first length of trench had been dug and the gang were tackling the second stretch. Brody was stripped to the waist, his broad shoulders and powerful biceps glistening with sweat as he heaved a large clod of clay up out of the deep hole. 'What d'you two want?' he called out.

'We got a problem,' Sid told him. 'We need anuvver shovel. This one's busted.'

'I've already told yer yer'll 'ave ter wait till termorrer,' he said, wiping the sweat from his brow with the back of his hand.

'What're we s'posed ter do wiv this?' Sid asked him angrily.

'I could tell yer,' one of the men called out.

'I'm talkin' ter the butcher, not the block,' the ganger told him.

Brody pushed his workman aside and climbed up out of the trench. 'Now listen. I'm tellin' yer once an' fer all that yer'll 'ave ter wait till termorrer,' he said with emphasis. 'It's a case o' makin' do. We all 'ave ter make do at times.'

Charlie could stand it no longer. 'You make do,' he snarled. 'I'm goin' over the office about this.'

Brody moved forward to grab him but Sid stepped in front of him. 'Look, we don't want no trouble, but yer gotta sort this out terday,' he said quietly. 'We're runnin' be'ind time as it is. What say yer come over the office wiv us?'

Brody was eyeing Charlie while Sid was talking, and after a moment or two he turned to the older man. 'All right, fer you, but not 'im,' he growled. 'Anuvver fing. Keep 'im away from me in future.'

Sid nodded and took Charlie by the arm. 'C'mon, son. We made our point,' he said calmly.

The sun had sunk low in the sky as Sid and his gang climbed out of the trench, very weary but happy with their progress. 'Well, lads, we made a bit o' ground up this afternoon now we've got some decent tools ter work wiv,' Sid said grinning.

Charlie pressed his thumb into the palm of his hand and winced. It felt raw and there was a dried bloodstain on the filthy strip of bandage. ''Ow far be'ind Brody's lot are we, Sid?' he asked.

The dapper little man spat out the dust from his mouth. 'I reckon we're not much more than 'alf a day adrift,' he told them. 'All bein' well we should make up the difference termorrer, if we put our backs into it.'

'My back's creased already,' one of the crew groaned.

'Yeah, mine too,' Charlie grunted as he arched himself painfully.

'A couple o' weeks an' yer'll all be top-grade diggers,' Sid said grinning.

Charlie looked over at the ganger and could not help but admire him. He was the oldest and lightest by at least a stone, but he worked as hard, if not harder than any of them, and now, when the rest of them were fit to drop, he looked as sprightly as when he had first jumped down into the trench that morning.

Sid led the way back to the tent where they found Brody and his gang already changing, and they placed their tools in the chest looking very pleased with themselves, to the cha-grin of Brody and his men. The two crews sat facing each other while they slipped out of their waterproofs and took off their clay-covered boots, both ignoring each other.

'I'll expert yer bright an' breezy termorrer, lads,' Sid said as he left. 'Remember there's a bonus ter be earned.'

As Charlie left, Brody got up and followed him out of the tent. 'I ain't fergot you,' he said darkly.

The young man turned and gave him a derisory glance. 'Are you worried we might just get a share o' that bonus, Brody?' he asked him with narrowed eyes.

'Yer too flash fer my likin', Bradley,' the foreman growled.

'That's your problem,' Charlie said as he walked on.

'We'll see whose problem it is,' Brody called out.

'Any time,' the young man called back.

Chapter Ten

When Linda got home from work on Tuesday evening her mother led her into the scullery and told her the news. 'Yer dad's gotta go in 'ospital,' she said. 'The specialist told 'im they need ter do some tests. They're takin' 'im in on Friday.'

''Ow is 'e, Mum?' Linda asked anxiously.

''E's in the parlour 'avin' a snooze,' Dora said. 'You can wake 'im up, I'll be servin' up tea in a few minutes.'

Linda went in and saw that her father was rousing himself. He looked pale and drawn but he managed a smile. ''Ello, luv. 'Ave yer just got in?' he asked.

The young woman sat on the edge of his chair and put her arm round his shoulder. 'Mum told me yer gotta go in, Dad. 'Ow yer feelin'?'

'It's not too bad,' he replied, suddenly wincing. 'I get a shootin' pain every now an' then. They'll sort it out, I'm sure.'

Linda kissed him on the forehead. 'Course they will,' she said encouragingly.

John eased himself in the chair and looked at his daughter. 'Yer mum tells me yer got a young man,' he said.

101

'Yeah, it's Charlie Bradley,' Linda replied. ''E's callin' round ternight.'

'So yer mum said.'

''E'll be round after tea. D'yer mind?'

'Course not,' John said, patting her hand. 'We know the Bradleys. Charlie seems a nice lad.'

''E is nice, Dad,' Linda told him with a big smile. ''E's got this job on a buildin' site down at Dock'ead an' I'm dyin' ter see 'ow 'e's gettin' on.'

John winced again as the pain caught him. 'Are you an' Charlie goin' steady then?' he asked.

'I fink so,' Linda told him.

'So 'e's comin' round ter break the ice,' John said smiling. 'Don't worry, we won't give 'im a bad time.'

'I know that. Charlie's not one o' those flash fellers,' she said quietly.

Dora came into the room and started to lay the table for tea and then James walked in, his heavily bandaged finger supported in a sling. 'So Charlie Bradley's comin' callin',' he said. 'I s'pose I'll 'ave ter straighten 'im out.'

'Yer'll do no such fing,' Dora told him sharply. 'Charlie's a nice lad. I know 'is mum, an' I knew 'is dad too. 'E was a very 'ard-workin' man. So you keep yer mouth shut, James.'

''E's only windin' yer up, Mum,' Linda cut in.

James smiled as he sat down in the armchair facing his father. 'Yeah, I was only jokin'. Charlie's a decent bloke. Me an' Frankie's 'ad a few drinks wiv 'im,' he said matter of factly.

'Listen ter the ole man talkin',' Linda said quickly. 'It's a wonder the guv'nor at the Bee'ive allows yer ter go in there. Yer not eighteen yet.'

'Yeah, but 'e finks I'm eighteen,' James replied smiling. 'I ain't gonna put 'im right, am I?'

John Weston glanced across at his son and had to admit that he looked older than seventeen. He had filled out, and was shaving regularly now as well.

Linda and her mother went out into the scullery to serve up the meal while the rest of the family gathered in the parlour. Pamela looked at her father with concern and Tommy also gave him a worried glance, but Ben sat in the corner on an upright chair reading the *Wizard*, and when the plates of hot food were brought in he was first at the table.

Charlie Bradley had a tired, pained expression on his face as he sat with his hands soaking in a bowl of hot salt water. His mother was standing over him, hands on hips as she made her point.

'I can't understand yer, really I can't,' she went on. 'You could 'ave gone back in the office, but no. Yer must be mad ter suffer like that when there's no need to. I've seen yer farvver come 'ome wiv 'ands like that in the winter after 'e'd bin 'andlin' those tiles an' slates all day. There's no need fer yer ter suffer like that.'

'Look, Ma, I told yer 'ow I feel about workin' in an office,' he said sighing. 'It's not fer me. Anyway this is only a temporary job, till I find somefing better.'

'If yer not careful those 'ands are gonna go septic, then yer'll know it,' May Bradley told him sharply.

'They'll be all right. They feel better already,' he lied.

May left the room sighing irritably and came back with bandages, lint and a jar of vaseline. Charlie dried his sore hands on a clean towel and watched as his mother applied the vaseline to strips of lint which she spread over the large raw patches on his palms.

'Yer won't be able ter work wiv these,' she told him firmly as she tore the wrapping off a roll of wide bandage.

Charlie sat forward in his chair studying his mother's thin, serious face as she bandaged his hands. It was understandable that she should want the best for him, he realised, but he was a grown man and had to make his own choices now. He had to pick his own friends too and not allow her to dictate to him the way she had before he went into the army. No doubt she would have something to say when he got around to telling her that he had a girlfriend; he might as well tell her now, get it over and done with.

'That's it,' May said as she knotted the bandage. 'It'll keep the dirt out.'

'I'm goin' over ter see someone after tea, Ma,' he told her casually.

'Oh?'

'Yeah, Linda Weston. We're walkin' out tergevver.'

''Ave yer just decided ter tell me?' May said offhandedly.

'We've only just got tergevver,' Charlie replied. 'Linda's a nice gel.'

'I know the family.'

'I'm meetin' 'em ternight,' he told her.

'I just 'ope yer not rushin' into anyfing,' May said quickly. 'After all yer've only bin 'ome two weeks.'

'We're just walkin' out tergevver, that's all,' he replied.

'I 'ope yer gonna bring 'er 'ome ter see me,' she told him. 'I don't like ter be kept in the dark.'

'No one's keepin' yer in the dark, Ma. I was gonna bring

'er ter see yer pretty soon,' Charlie said quickly, his temper rising.

'Just as long as yer don't go makin' a fool o' yerself,' May told him sharply. 'Too many young men get their girlfriends inter trouble and then they're burdened down fer the rest o' their lives. I want somefing better fer you.'

Charlie bit back on an angry reply. It was the way she was, she couldn't help it. She had been widowed for five years and now that his sister had left the nest she was focusing all her attention on him. He would have to make it clear he could not allow her to rule his life, but he would also have to treat her with kid gloves. She had been easily upset and prone to periods of depression before he went into the army, and things didn't appear to have changed much since he got out.

The night was warm and sultry, with a myriad stars dotting the deep purple sky. Across the River Thames the City lights were still shining, and eastwards loomed the dark sombre shapes of the factories and tanneries. Linda stood close to Charlie on the roof, feeling his arm around her as she rested her head against his shoulder.

'It was nice talkin' ter yer mum an' dad,' he said.

'Frankie an' James went out purposely,' Linda told him. 'They thought yer'd feel a bit uncomfortable wiv everyone there.'

'I know the boys anyway,' Charlie replied, smiling at her.

'I was really shocked when I opened the door an' saw those 'ands all bandaged up,' she said.

'Yeah, I feel stupid like this,' he laughed.

'What about termorrer?' Linda asked him. 'Yer won't be able ter go ter work, surely.'

'I've got to,' he told her. 'I've sorted an ole pair o' gloves out an' cut the fingers out of 'em. They'll do ter go over the bandages.'

Linda looked down at the dressings for a moment then her eyes met his. 'I'm worried about those 'ands, Charlie,' she said quietly.

'They'll be fine,' he said, smiling at her reassuringly. 'Even wiv sore 'ands it's better than goin' back ter that shippin' office. I couldn't stand that, Linda. Anyway it's only fer a while, till I sort fings out.'

She nodded slowly, her face still registering her concern. 'I 'ope yer can,' she replied.

Charlie stared up into the evening sky. 'I know what I'm doin',' he said firmly. 'I've got plans. I'm gonna make money, be somebody one day. There's no way I'm gonna work at a desk fer the rest o' me life, writin' entries in dusty ledgers an' bowin' an' scrapin' ter some jumped-up little office manager. I tell yer somefing, Lin. I 'ave nightmares about that shippin' office. I'm an old man an' I shuffle inter the manager's office ter collect me gold watch. Everyone's there, an' they all clap me as I put it inter me waistcoat pocket. Then I shuffle out an' go back ter the pile o' ledgers, but now the pile's grown right up ter the ceilin'. I wake up dreadin' the new day, till I realise that it's only bin a dream.'

Linda touched his arm. 'I'm sure yer'll get what yer want out o' life one day, Charlie,' she said softly.

'I don't want the 'ole moon, just a bit of it,' he replied as he turned to face her.

'I'd like a small bit of it too,' she said smiling at him.

They walked further into the shadows and Charlie slipped

his arm around her waist. 'There's enough ter go round,' he replied.

Linda sighed as she felt his arm tighten around her. 'Me dad wanted ter know if we were goin' steady,' she told him. 'We are, ain't we, Charlie?'

His lips brushed against her ear. 'If yer want us to,' he said quietly.

'It's somefing I've always wanted,' she replied, turning to him and lifting her head, hoping he would kiss her.

Charlie glanced over towards the stairway as they heard low voices. 'We're not alone,' he said in mock fear, his eyes widening.

'I don't care. Kiss me, Charlie.'

He lowered his head and their lips met in a gentle kiss. Linda put her arms around his neck and closed her eyes, feeling his body pressing against hers as she savoured his lips. It seemed unreal, she thought. Only a very short time ago she could only dream about him and now she was in his arms and he was kissing her passionately.

They could hear the low voices talking urgently as they moved apart and Linda looked up at him. 'That sounds like Kate Selby,' she remarked.

'No, Peter, no. I mean it,' the woman's voice said.

Linda put her hand up to her mouth to hide a grin and Charlie gave her a comical look. 'I'd better cough or somefing,' he said grinning. 'They don't know we're 'ere.'

Linda shook her head and smiled wickedly.

'But yer promised,' the man's voice said.

'I never did.'

'Yer could 'ave fooled me.'

'You fellers are all the same. That's all yer fink of.'

'No, it ain't.'

'I'm goin' 'ome.'

'Aw, Kate, don't go yet.'

'Yes, I am. Yer've upset me.'

'Don't go.'

Sounds of hurrying footsteps on the wooden stairs were followed by heavier ones and then it was quiet.

'That's Kate Selby,' Linda grinned. 'She's bin leadin' 'im on, that's fer sure.'

Charlie's arms went around her again and their lips met in a long, lingering kiss. When they parted Linda sighed deeply. 'I'd better be goin' now, Charlie,' she said. 'It must be gettin' late.'

They stepped out of the shadows into the light of the moon and walked to the end stairway. The small street was deserted as Charlie led Linda to her door. 'Until termorrer,' he said smiling.

The young woman reached up and brushed his lips with a soft kiss. 'Until termorrer, Charlie,' she whispered.

On Wednesday morning the sun rose in another clear blue sky, and as Charlie walked to work every muscle in his body still ached from the previous day's digging. He was feeling apprehensive. He knew that he would be able to work through the stiffness, but would his hands last out?

Brody and his men were coming out of the tent when Charlie arrived and the hulking foreman gave him a blinding look. Charlie ignored him and walked in to see Sid lacing up his boots. 'Mornin', Sid. Mornin', lads,' he said cheerfully.

'Bloody 'ell, mate, are you gonna be able ter work like that?' Sid asked him when he saw his bandaged hands.

'I got some gloves ter put over these,' the young man replied, pulling them out of his pocket. 'I'll manage. We gotta earn that bonus.'

The whistle sounded and when they came out of the tent they could see Brody and his men already clambering into their trench.

'They ain't wastin' no time,' the fair-haired crewman remarked.

'C'mon, lads,' Sid said encouragingly as he led the way across the wasteground. 'Let's get stuck into it.'

As they jumped down into the hole one of the men handed Charlie his pickaxe. ''Ere, mate, you 'ave that,' he said. 'It'll be better than usin' the shovel.'

Charlie thanked him and quickly set to work. The sun was not yet overhead and the crew put their backs into it, working hard to break up the base clay. They began to make good progress and when the tea-break whistle sounded they all climbed out of the trench bathed in sweat but pleased at what they had achieved. Sid was optimistic that they would make up the lost ground that day and he was first back into the hole when the tea break was over.

Charlie was in a lot of pain with his hands but he clenched his teeth and carried on. Every muscle ached unrelentingly and sweat ran into his eyes as he laboured with the pickaxe. The midday break was a brief merciful interlude from the agony, and when he had finished his sandwiches he sprawled out beside the trench on the warm earth along with the rest of the gang and tried to ease his protesting muscles. He knew he had to steel himself and not give in. Today they were in sight of their target and running almost neck and neck with Brody's gang.

As the sun rose high in the sky the team worked steadily, pacing themselves for the long afternoon, and Charlie wondered if he was going to last out. His stomach muscles seemed to be cramping up with the strain of lifting the heavy clay clods on the shovel and his hands throbbed nonstop. There was no time to waste today though, he told himself, and he gritted his teeth as he wielded his pickaxe once more, feeling utterly exhausted.

Sid had taken a short breather and he wiped his sweating face with a red-spotted handkerchief. 'We're doin' well, lads,' he said encouragingly.

Charlie stopped digging for a moment to arch his aching back and suddenly the gang felt a deep rumble under their feet and then men were shouting. Someone came running over. 'There's bin a cave-in!' he screamed out.

Everyone clambered out of the trench and saw dust rising up ahead of them. 'It's where Brody's workin',' Sid said, setting off at a trot.

When the gang reached the spot they stood transfixed. A large deep hole had appeared in the earth and down below men were fighting to free themselves from the loose soil. One of them had been buried up to his armpits and as he struggled to claw himself out he suddenly froze in horror. Right beside him, sticking out of the earth with its nose pointing to the sky, was an unexploded bomb.

'Gawd Almighty! Don't move, son!' the site foreman called out to him. 'That's right, keep dead still.'

Sid looked down into the large crater and realised what had happened. The bomb had burrowed down into the soft earth and lain there undiscovered ever since the Blitz. It would have left a tunnel which weakened the ground around it, and with all the activity above it and the hot weather drying out the clay subsoil, the surface had suddenly sunk.

The site foreman scrambled down into the hole followed by Charlie and the ganger. The rest of Sid's team made to follow but the foreman stopped them. 'Not too many! You men stay where you are!' he shouted urgently.

The three men reached the shocked labourer and they gently scooped the earth away from him with their hands, keeping their eyes all the while on the metal cone beside them.

'That's it, lads, now pull 'im out carefully,' the foreman told them.

Four more of Brody's gang had managed to struggle free but of the ganger himself there was no sign. ''E was standin' right next ter me,' one man said, gasping for breath.

Sid noticed a slight movement of earth. 'There! Over there!' he shouted.

Everyone started digging frantically with their bare hands and tense, endless seconds of desperate effort passed before they finally uncovered a boot. Spurred on, they soon managed to move enough of the earth to pull Brody free. He was barely conscious and white with shock. Charlie slipped his hands under the distressed man's shoulders and Sid and the site foreman each took a leg. Slowly they eased him up the side of the crater where willing hands were waiting. Once he was on level ground they turned him on to his back and someone wiped the earth from his face. Charlie leaned back on his haunches and Sid knelt on all fours gasping for breath.

'That was a close one,' the foreman said panting. 'A few minutes more an' 'e'd 'ave bin a goner.'

Brody opened his eyes and looked up at Charlie, then very slowly he lifted his forearm. 'I owe yer one, Bradley,' he gasped.

The young man grasped the ganger's hand. 'I fink you owe somebody,' he replied grinning. 'There's an unexploded bomb in that crater. Yer could quite easily 'ave caught it wiv yer pick.'

The area around the crater was quickly evacuated and Brody was taken off to hospital with suspected broken ribs. Charlie had lost his bandages during the frantic digging and after he had cleaned the soil from his raw hands the foreman put a temporary dressing on them. Now, as he sat with Sid in the site office drinking tea from an old cracked mug, he was in considerable pain.

'The area's bin roped off an' the bomb disposal squad are on their way,' the foreman told them as he came back into the office. 'We've gotta clear the site. You'd better get up Guy's wiv those mitts, Bradley.'

Chapter Eleven

The news of the unexploded bomb at Dockhead was being discussed on the doorsteps in Eagle Street and the two hawks stood with horrified looks on their pale thin faces as they spoke with Freda Colton from number 4.

'If that bomb 'ad gone up it would'a took 'alf o' Dock'ead wiv it,' Doris said. 'It makes yer fink.'

''Ow many more unexploded bombs are layin' under the ground, that's what worries me,' Phyllis said.

'There was enough dropped in the Blitz, that's fer sure,' Freda Colton added, her face set sternly.

Doris slipped her hands inside her pinafore and nodded over towards the Buildings. 'That Bradley boy was workin' on the site when it was found, by all accounts,' she told her friends. 'Mrs Akerman told me. She lives under May Bradley. She said the boy come in wiv 'is 'ands all bandaged up. It must 'ave burnt 'im.'

'Nah, it wouldn't do that,' Phyllis informed her. 'The bloody fing would be stone cold, the time it's bin layin' there.'

Doris looked peeved. 'Yer don't know about such fings,' she persisted. 'It's the chemicals they use on 'em. You take

113

them incendiaries. They was made o' phosphorus. That's why they flared so much.'

'Good Gawd,' Freda said, her hand on her chin. 'It fair scares yer.'

Dick Conners came along the turning humming happily to himself, until he saw the women gathered. 'Mornin', ladies,' he said, giving them a cheerful smile.

Freda Colton smiled back but the two hawks all but ignored him.

'Did you 'ear about that bomb in Dock'ead?' he asked them.

'Yeah, we was just talkin' about it,' Freda told him.

Dick shook his head slowly. 'Gawd knows 'ow many more there are,' he went on. 'There was enough dropped.'

'That's what I was sayin',' Freda replied.

The two hawks did not relish the street's drunk joining in their discussion and they turned their backs on him to continue. Dick Conners was well aware of their hostility and a brief, wicked smile appeared on his face. 'There's anuvver 'ole on the bombsite down there,' he said, nodding towards the space at the end of the turning. 'The council said it's rats, but I'm not so sure. Rats don't make 'oles that big. Yer could get a cart'orse down it.'

Phyllis and her friend Doris both gave him a questioning look.

'They could be sewer rats, I s'pose,' Freda said. 'They're enormous, some o' them.'

'I wouldn't fink so, luv,' Dick told her. 'I'm sure it's one o' those unexploded bombs. Anyway I've told old Ginny ter keep away from the winders while the men are takin' a look.'

'What men?' Doris asked him quickly.

'Why, the council men,' he told her. 'Someone in the pub said they was comin' down ter take anuvver look at it. Trouble is they go pokin' about wiv them sticks an' they're liable ter set it off. Still if it 'appened we wouldn't know much about it, would we?'

Phyllis looked shocked. 'Surely they wouldn't go pokin' about wiv sticks?' she queried.

'Don't you be so sure,' Dick replied. 'You take that turn-out over the water last year. They thought that was rats.'

'What 'appened?' Freda asked.

'Well, the fumigation men were sent for when someone found this bloody great 'ole on a bombsite. Stepney it was. Anyway, they started pokin' about an' whoosh.'

'What d'yer mean, "whoosh"?' Doris said gruffly.

'What I say, whoosh. Crash bang wallop.'

'Is it any good tryin' ter get any sense out of 'im?' Doris remarked, turning to her friend.

'Yer mean it was a bomb?' Freda asked.

'Too bloody true,' Dick replied. 'Up it went an' took them fumigation men wiv it. Never found a trace of 'em they never. Tell a lie, they did find a boot about six months later. Up on a roof it was. It 'ad a foot in it.'

'Oh my good Gawd!' Freda gasped, looking at the two hawks.

'It was lucky it didn't take more people wiv it, but it was factory land, yer see,' Dick explained. 'Now that one in Dock'ead would 'ave flattened the place if that 'ad gone off. Same as that 'ole down there. If there's a bomb down that 'ole yer can say goodbye ter this street, that's a stone cold certainty.'

'You mind what yer sayin', yer frightenin' these women,' Doris said sharply.

'Ain't you scared then? 'Cos as sure as Gawd made little apples I am,' Dick told her.

'When's them men comin' down about that 'ole?' Freda asked him, looking distinctly scared.

'I dunno. But if I get the word I'll come an' knock on yer doors,' Dick assured them. 'After all there's no sense in takin' chances, is there?'

The three women watched him walk away, and as soon as he was out of earshot Phyllis turned to the others. 'What's the good o' takin' any notice o' that drunken ole goat,' she said dismissively.

Freda was pinching her chin thoughtfully. 'I ain't noticed no big 'ole on that bombsite an' I pass there every day,' she said.

They all glanced fearfully along the street, and then went on to other business.

'Did I tell yer about that Mrs Bolter . . .' Doris began.

Charlie Bradley walked into the Beehive at Thursday lunchtime and saw the Carter brothers sitting at the usual table in the far corner, with two other men he did not recognise. When they saw him Nick Carter got up and walked over to the counter.

'What you bin doin', Chas?' he asked, putting his hand in his trouser pocket.

Charlie held up his heavily bandaged hands. 'It's a long story,' he said grinning.

Nick took out a pound note and laid it down on the counter. 'Give the lad a drink, will yer, Bert, an' 'ave one yerself,' he said, before turning to Charlie. 'Bring it over there, I wanna 'ave a chat,' he said amiably.

As soon as Charlie walked over to the far table Nick introduced the two strangers. 'This is Con Ashley, an' this is Billy Nelson,' he said. 'Lads, I want yer ter meet an ole pal of ours, Charlie Bradley.'

The two men nodded briefly and Charlie immediately guessed their role. Both displayed the marks of the ring. The man introduced as Con had a flat nose and puffed ears and the other, Billy, had some scarring over both eyes.

Tony 'Boy-boy' Carter stared at Charlie's hands. 'What's the trouble?' he asked.

'I bin doin' ditch diggin' an' they've rubbed raw,' he told him with a sheepish grin.

The younger Carter brother shook his head slowly. 'Is that why yer turned us down, Chas, so yer could go an' get yer 'ands all mashed up? Yer gotta be a clown.'

Charlie ignored the jibe, but seeing the amused smiles on the two heavies' faces he said, 'I'm not used ter the work. We never did much diggin' in the Kate Carney.' He smiled at the older brother.

'So 'ow long yer gonna be off work then?' Nick asked him.

'A couple o' weeks,' he replied.

'Look, I'm not tryin' ter twist yer arm, Chas, but yer made a mistake not chuckin' yer lot in wiv us, an' that's the result,' Nick said, nodding towards Charlie's hands. 'Now what about reconsiderin'?'

Charlie sipped his drink, aware that everyone's eyes were on him. He put the glass down and stroked his chin thoughtfully.

'Look, Chas, we got an arch full o' the stuff I was tellin' yer about,' Nick Carter went on. 'It don't need any puntin'. It sells itself. We can't produce enough.'

'I appreciate the consideration, Nick, but I would 'ave thought yer'd got it all set up by now,' Charlie said, briefly casting his eyes at the younger brother for some response.

'Yeah, what yer gotta understand is, me an' Tony 'ave bin puttin' ourselves about on the manor, but we've got too much organisin' ter do now an' we can't spare the time,' Nick explained. 'We got contracts lined up an' orders waitin', an' that's where you come in. We want someone we can rely on. Someone who'll take the orders an' deliver the stuff. Like I say, it don't want no puntin', they're cryin' out fer it. They can't get enough. Look, I tell yer what. Don't make a decision right now. 'Ave a drink on it an' then come round the arch ternight. We'll be there till about nine, nine-thirty, but don't leave it till the last minute. We got a lot ter show yer. What d'yer say?'

Charlie was about to concede but suddenly he pulled a face. 'I can't ternight. I got a date,' he said quickly.

Nick glanced at his younger brother and raised his eyes in exasperation. 'The boy's got a date,' he said with mock surprise, turning to Charlie. 'Who is she, one o' the local birds? Do I know 'er?'

'It's Linda Weston,' Charlie told them.

'Very nice too,' Nick said smiling. 'She's a nice sort. A bit quiet fer you though, I would 'ave thought.'

'We're goin' steady,' Charlie told him, his eyes widening just enough to show that he would not have anything said about her.

'That's no problem. Bring 'er round,' Nick Carter said, spreading his hands in front of him. 'We'll give 'er a complimentary bottle o' perfume.'

Charlie drained his glass, then looked from one to the other. 'OK. I'll do that,' he said smiling.

Nick seemed pleased but Tony Carter's face remained impassive. The two heavyweights looked blank too and Charlie guessed that the arrangement being discussed was going over their heads. They were employed as muscle, after all, and by the looks of them they would be more than competent in their field.

Charlie left the pub and strolled down to Dockhead. There were two days' wages to collect, and he was hoping he would get the chance to say farewell to Sid and the rest of the crew.

Dick Conners sat by himself in the public bar of the Beehive feeling a little put out by Bert Warner's continuing ban. After all he was a regular customer, not someone who used the pub as a convenience, like those sanctimonious priests. Never mind, Bert would come round in time.

''Ello, Dick, 'ow yer goin'?'

The drunk looked up to see Wally Gainsford standing there. 'Not so bad, Wally,' he replied. 'I was just finkin' as a matter o' fact.'

'That can be painful,' Wally said chuckling, his large belly wobbling over his tight leather belt. 'Fancy a drink?'

Dick had just bought a pint and he shook his head. Wally ambled over to the counter and brushed his hand through his rapidly receding fair hair. 'Gis a pint o' bitter, Bert,' he said cheerfully.

''Ow's fings, Wally?' the landlord asked as he pulled on the bar pump.

'Mustn't grumble,' the big man replied. 'Maggie's all

right, the kids are all OK, an' I'm still earnin' a crust.'

'I thought they was talkin' o' shuttin' that gasworks down,' Bert queried.

'Yeah, there was a lot o' talk, but that's all it was,' Wally told him. 'It'll be a few more years yet before they do anyfing about it. Well, at least I 'ope so. There's not many jobs goin' fer stokers the way fings are. It's all goin' over to electric.'

'You could always join the navy,' Bert joked. 'They're always in need o' qualified stokers.'

'Yeah, if the gasworks shut down I might do that,' Wally laughed. ''Ere Bert, what's the matter wiv ole Dick over there? 'E looks all mean an' 'orrible. You ain't bin upsettin' the poor sod, 'ave yer?'

'Nah, 'e's often like that, is ole Dick. On 'is own too much, if you ask me.'

'Who'd 'ave 'im?' Wally remarked, pushing a half-crown across the counter and picking up his frothing pint.

Bert leaned on the counter and looked over at Dick. 'I 'ad ter bar 'im from the saloon,' he said.

'What was that for?'

'Sedition, blasphemy, you name it.'

'Oh yeah?'

'I 'ad a group o' priests in 'ere the ovver day,' Bert told him. 'They was from St Mary's. On a seminar, I believe they called it. Anyway, they ain't bin in 'ere five minutes when Dick comes over an' starts rantin' off.'

'What for?'

'Well, one o' the priests was goin' on about the drop in church numbers, an' Dopey Dick 'appened to 'ear 'im,' Bert explained. ''E came over an' started goin' on about what's the good o' people goin' ter church if all the priests are out on the piss. I didn't know where ter put me face, but mind you they suffered 'im pretty well. One of 'em told 'im that churchmen needed sustenance too, an' Dick said 'e knew that 'cos they drunk enough o' that communion wine. Anyway I told 'im 'e was barred an' 'e started goin' on about me barrin' the priests too. 'E said that they started it by talkin' out their arses. Can you believe it? Gladys 'ad ter go in the ovver bar she was so shocked.'

'So yer banned 'im from the saloon. I wonder yer didn't bar 'im altergevver,' Wally remarked.

'Well, yer know 'ow it is. The poor sod's on 'is own an' this is the only place 'e's got. I couldn't do it, Wally.'

'Never mind, yer'll get yer reward upstairs,' Wally laughed.

''Ere, that reminds me, did you 'ear about the Allertons?'

'No, who's they?' Wally asked.

'They're a family who live in the Gale Street,' Bert told him. 'Now Mick Allerton was an atheist. 'E used ter come in 'ere an' lay the law down about there's no 'eaven an' 'ell, an' 'e used ter slag off the Salvation Army people too when they came in 'ere wiv the *War Cry*. Anyway Mick Allerton 'ad a stroke an' died a couple o' weeks ago. All the family were standin' round the coffin payin' their last respects when suddenly Mick sits up an' rubs 'is eyes.'

'Bloody blimey,' Wally said.

'Yeah, that's right. 'E sat right up in the coffin. 'E told the mourners that St Peter was at the gates when 'e arrived an' 'e sent 'im back.'

'Yer 'avin' me on, ain't yer?' Wally said, giving Bert Warner an incredulous look.

'Nah, straight up,' Bert replied. 'Anyway what 'appened

121

was, accordin' ter Mick, St Peter told 'im 'e wasn't welcome up there, an' Mick tried ter tell 'im about the good fings 'e'd done in 'is life. 'E told 'im about the five shillin's 'e'd put in the blind box an' 'e mentioned the five bob 'e gave ter the Salvation Army one Christmas. Anyway St Peter tells 'im to 'ang on while 'e 'as a word wiv God. Ten minutes later St Peter comes back an' beckons Mick over. "I've 'ad a word wiv the Lord," 'e says. "What did 'E say?" Mick asks 'im. So St Peter pulls out this money an' ses, "'Ere's yer ten bob back, now piss orf." '

Wally's raucous laughter filled the bar and Dick Conners looked over. 'What's that all about?' he asked.

'We were just talkin' about ole Mick Allerton,' Wally told him.

'Mick Allerton, who's 'e?'

Wally walked over to where Dick was sitting. 'Mick Allerton was an anarchist,' he began.

Chapter Twelve

Linda slipped her arm through Charlie's as they crossed Tower Bridge Road into Abbey Street, and when they were walking along the row of terraced houses she looked at him curiously. 'Won't yer tell me where we're goin'?' she asked him.

Charlie smiled mysteriously. 'Yer'll see,' was all he said.

At the bottom of the wide street they turned right before the railway bridge and carried on past a series of arches. Charlie stopped at an arch with a blue-painted wooden front and tapped on the wicket gate. It reminded Linda of the wine vaults, but when the door was opened to let them in an entirely different odour drifted out.

'It's perfume,' she said.

The smell was almost overpowering inside. When their eyes became accustomed to the dim light Linda caught her breath. Charlie too was impressed by what he saw. Sitting round a large wooden bench were at least a dozen women all filling tiny bottles with rubber-topped droppers and placing them on trays. Another woman carried a filled tray over to a second bench where more women were sitting.

Nick Carter smiled at the surprised look on the visitors' faces.

''Ello, Linda,' he said.

'Linda, you remember Nick Carter,' Charlie told her.

Boy-boy Carter ambled over and looked at the young woman. 'An' Tony Carter,' he said.

Linda smiled. 'Yeah, of course I do.'

'Well, what d'yer fink of it?' Nick asked Charlie.

'Everyone looks very busy,' he replied. 'What time do they work till?'

'Nine-thirty,' Nick told him. 'They're married women wiv kids fer the best part an' this is a chance fer 'em to earn some pin-money. It's clean work an' they get plenty o' breaks. We pay good wages too an' they get free samples as well. That's the good fing about it. Anuvver is, this stuff we use as a base ain't knocked off. We got a regular, legit supplier. All the bottles are bought on the straight market too, an' we print our own labels. All right so we're stampin' all over the patent laws an' connin' the public inter believin' that this gear's the real McCoy, but let me show yer somefing.'

Charlie and Linda followed him into a small office at one side of the arch. Nick picked up two tiny bottles which looked identical and gave them to Linda. 'Open that one,' he said, pointing to the bottle in her left hand. 'Smell it.'

Linda did as she was bid and then Nick pointed to the other bottle. 'Now that one.'

Once again the young woman put the bottle to her nose. 'They're both the same,' she said, looking from one to the other.

Nick smiled and pointed to the bottle in her left hand. 'That one is Elegance, pure French perfume,' he told her.

'Yer talkin' about five pounds or more fer a bottle that size. Now that ovver one we make up ourselves, an' we market it as Elegance at firty-bob. Only an expert could tell the difference, an' wivout bein' rude ter you women, luv, there's not many experts amongst our customers,' he said grinning.

Charlie shook his head slowly. 'Nick, I gotta 'and it to yer,' he told him.

Nick beckoned for them to sit down then he sat on the corner of his desk facing them. 'Now look,' he began. 'The young lady'll appreciate this, even if you don't. A bargain is a bargain in any language. People love ter get a good deal an' they don't usually ask questions. Am I right, luv?'

Linda nodded. 'I fink every woman's 'eard of Elegance but I don't know of anyone who's ever bin able to afford it,' she told him.

'Exactly,' Nick said triumphantly. He looked at her intently. 'Would you worry at all if I mixed them two bottles up an' gave yer one of 'em?' he asked.

Linda shook her head. 'If I could buy one of those fer firty-five shillin's I'd be very pleased.'

'There we are, Chas. Now what d'yer say? D'yer wanna go back ter that poxy trench you was diggin' an' do yerself anuvver mischief fer a fiver a week, or d'yer wanna come in wiv us an' earn that in a couple of hours?'

Charlie stared at Nick Carter, watching the grin hovering on his thin lips. 'Yer talked me into it,' he said smiling.

Nick got up and picked up the two small bottles from the desk. 'There we are, my luv, put them in yer 'andbag,' he told Linda. 'Compliments of Carter Associates.'

'Cor, fanks very much,' she said, her eyes opened wide.

Nick smiled benevolently. 'What are yer like wiv figures?' he asked her.

Linda shrugged her shoulders. 'I'm quite good at sums,' she said shyly.

'What about writin' letters an' answerin' the phone?' he went on.

'I can't type,' she told him.

'We ain't got a typewriter 'ere,' he said, his smile growing.

'Yeah, I can write letters an' answer the phone,' Linda replied.

'Well then, I can offer yer a job 'elpin' me get fings straight in the office,' he told her, 'as long as Charlie 'as no objections ter you workin' alongside o' me. Seven pounds a week an' complimentary perfume, what d'yer say?'

Linda looked shocked and she glanced from one to the other.

'Fine by me,' Charlie said grinning.

Nick was amused by the young woman's expression. 'Look, yer don't 'ave ter make yer mind up right away, but if yer decide it's yes I'll be wantin' yer ter start in two weeks time. OK?'

Linda nodded, still taken aback. Nick opened the office door and beckoned someone.

A middle-aged woman wearing a floral turban popped her head round the door. 'Yes, Mr Carter?'

'Bess, will you show the young lady round an' let 'er see the procedures,' he said, then turned to Linda. 'Yer'd like ter see the set-up, wouldn't yer, luv?' he asked her.

Linda nodded and followed Bess out to the bottling area, and Nick sat down facing Charlie. 'Now listen carefully, Chas,' he began. 'We've got our fingers in a lot o' pies at the moment but there's no need fer you ter worry yerself over them. Your concern is ter build up the trade in the Dock'ead area an' down as far as the tunnel. That was my area so, as yer can imagine, I've combed it thoroughly. The punters are there waitin'. They buy in bulk at fifty bob an' knock it out at fifty-five. Yer'll 'ave a list wiv contact places, like the pubs an' workin' men's clubs, as well as factory addresses. The facto-ries are yer best bet as it 'appens. I've built up some good contacts wiv the women workers. Your job is ter keep 'em supplied, see if they wanna up the orders an' then collect the money. Occasionally there'll be ovver commodities comin' on the market, but that'll be later. In any case the outlets are already sussed. OK?'

Charlie nodded, trying to take it all in. 'It sounds good,' he said enthusiastically.

Nick Carter opened a large ledger. 'Now, let's talk money,' he said.

There were serious looks on the faces of the young men who were sitting together in the Rising Sun, a little pub in the New Kent Road.

'Apparently they've got a good fing goin',' Tommy Kerrigan told them. 'My source tells me they're earnin' a fortune.'

The other five men did not make a comment. They did what they were expected to do: listen and wait for him to finish before they began asking questions. Feeling encour-aged, Tommy went on. 'What they do on their own manor doesn't concern us, but there 'as ter be a stop point short of our manor. We don't want the law runnin' bandy round 'ere an' pickin' up on our little schemes,' he reminded them with a dark look. 'Now what I intend ter do is call a meetin' wiv the Carters as soon as possible. If we can negotiate a deal ter buy the gear in bulk at a rock-bottom price an' do the puntin' ourselves we should earn well. We got enough punters ter push all we can get.'

The five men remained silent as they watched the tall lean figure sitting forward in his chair. Forty-two-year-old Tommy Kerrigan had a commanding presence. His eyes were deep-set and dark and his thinning dark hair was pushed back from his forehead to hide the bald patch. He was lighter than the others by at least two stone, but his knowledge of the manor, his contacts, and the very fact that he was the eldest of the four Kerrigan brothers meant that he held sway. Tommy was very powerful physically, despite his build, and he feared no one. He worked in the docks along with his three brothers and had gained much kudos when he and his team, as he liked to call them, put an end to a protection racket in what they considered to be their area, a patch that stretched from East Lane, Walworth, westwards to the Elephant and Castle and northwards to the Tower Bridge Road.

'Well? Any questions?' Tommy said, looking around him.

'Don't yer fink it's askin' a lot ter try an' do a deal wiv the Carters, considerin' we 'ammered 'em off the manor?' Bernie Kerrigan asked.

'Well, all we really did was tell 'em we wanted 'em outers, after all,' Tommy said with a faint smile. 'The 'ammerin' would 'ave come later, if they didn't comply. Which they did. Right, any more?'

'If they do give us a blank what do we do, swaller?' Joe Kerrigan asked.

Tommy turned to his youngest brother. 'Not exactly,' he replied in a quiet voice. 'We put pressure on. There's ways an' means.'

The Kerrigans' cousin Arthur Slade was the next to speak. He was the same age as Tommy but much more solidly built, with deep blue eyes and a mop of unruly flaxen hair. 'What about a trade?' he asked. 'We got our regular buyers amongst the lorry drivers who service the docks an' wharves. We could put a bit o' business their way.'

'Now that sounds likely,' Tommy said, nodding his head slowly. 'Anyfing else?'

'We could always muscle in,' Sam Colby said quietly. 'We're strong enough now ter spread a bit.'

Tommy had known Sam since they ran the streets together in Walworth and he knew that his boyhood friend would relish the chance. Sam had detested Boy-boy Carter ever since a confrontation in the Rising Sun when Carter had insulted his wife. It was only the intervention of the rest of the team that had prevented Sam from seriously hurting him. 'No, that's out fer the time bein', Sam,' he told him. 'Maybe circumstances'll change in the future, but fer now it's a no-go. Any more questions?'

Everyone sat silent and Tommy reached into his coat pocket and pulled out a bundle of notes. 'Right then. I've got some settlin' up ter do,' he told them, peeling a couple of notes off the bundle. 'Joe, can yer get a round? An' buy the bar one. They look a miserable lot ternight.'

Ginny Coombes sat at her front door in the cool of the evening with a shawl draped over her frail shoulders, watching while Dick Conners poured her out a stout from a pint bottle. 'Mind now, yer silly oaf. Look, yer spillin' it all,' she growled at him.

Dick grinned. 'It's only the froth. That's 'ow it should be,' he told her.

Ginny took the filled glass with a loud tut-tut. 'I dunno, I might as well do it meself,' she went on.

'There's no pleasin' you lately, is there, gel?' Dick said feigning a hurt look.

Ginny ignored him and took a long draught from the glass. 'Where d'yer buy this?' she asked sharply.

'Up the bleedin' pub. Where else d'yer fink I bought it, the oil shop?' he growled.

'Yer could'a done, by the taste of it,' she moaned. ''Ere, you taste it.'

Dick put the glass to his lips. 'Seems all right ter me,' he told her. 'I'd soon tell if it was off.'

'I ain't sayin' it's off,' Ginny went on. 'All I'm sayin' is, it don't taste right. It's got a sort of iron taste.'

'So it should, yer silly ole mare,' Dick said grinning. 'That's what does yer good. It's the iron.'

Ginny seemed mollified. 'P'raps it's me tongue,' she told him. 'It gets coated at times an' I 'ave a job ter taste fings prop'ly.'

'I dunno 'ow, yer silly ole bitch,' Dick mumbled. 'Yer tongue's never still long enough ter get furred up.'

'What you say?' she asked loudly.

'I said it could be furred up.'

'Yeah, like our kettle.'

'Yeah, that's right.'

Dick shifted his position against the door jamb. 'Shall I ask Albert if 'e wants a drink?'

Ginny leaned her head round. 'Oi, Albert. Dick said d'yer fancy a drink?' she called out.

'Yeah, I'd like a nice brown ale,' he called back.

'Wouldn't yer like a stout? We got stout,' Dick told him.

'Can't drink the stuff. It's too irony fer me,' Albert called back.

'Brown ale, yer say?' Dick called out.

'Yus please,' the old man shouted.

'It amazes me 'ow 'e can 'ear when 'e wants to,' Ginny remarked.

Dick was about to make his way to the end of the street to buy another pint of stout and a bottle of brown ale when he saw the two hawks leave their house. His face broke into a smile and he turned to Ginny, having already told her about his joke. ''Ere they come,' he hissed. 'Now don't ferget what I told yer, Ginny gel.'

'Evenin', Mrs Coombes,' the two said as they drew level, not giving Dick a glance.

'Evenin', Doris. Evenin', Phyllis,' Ginny replied in a syrupy voice. 'It's got bigger since they left.'

'What's that, Mrs Coombes?' Doris asked.

'Why, that bloody great 'ole, that's what,' Ginny told them. 'The men said it wasn't rats. They started pokin' about wiv a bloody great stick an' then they scarpered. Just as though they were taken short. I never seen workmen run like that before.'

Doris and Phyllis looked at each other in horror.

'They could'a found somefing, I s'pose,' Ginny went on, 'but they never tell yer anyfing these days, an' it's no good askin' 'em, is it, Dick?'

'Nah. I run after 'em an' asked 'em what it was they found

but they said it was nuffink,' Dick informed them casually.

Ginny leaned towards the two women. 'I fink 'e knows,' she said quietly. 'I fink 'e knows an' 'e ain't tellin' me. Mind yer, 'e does fink o' me. I s'pose if it was somefing bad 'e wouldn't say anyway. 'E is thoughtful is Dick. D'yer know 'e's even bin on ter me an' Albert ter move away from that bombsite. 'E's worried 'cos o' the damp. It is a windy corner in the cold weavver, I 'ave ter say. Anyway, don't let me keep you two gels. Oh an' mind 'ow yer go past that bombsite. Those pavin' stones don't seem too firm underfoot over there. It could be that 'ole doin' it, I s'pose.'

'I don't fink we'll bovver ter go far ternight,' Doris said, her eyes full of fear.

'No, my corn's started playin' me up,' Phyllis added quickly.

Dick and Ginny watched the two hurry back down the turning and then the street's drunk turned to his landlady. 'Ginny, you ought ter be on the stage,' he said chuckling.

'An' you ought ter be locked up, yer pissy-arsed cowson,' Ginny growled. 'Frightenin' old ladies.'

Chapter Thirteen

The Friday evening meal at number 6 was similar to normal, with Dora and the girls, Tommy and Ben sitting around the table together. Frankie and James were working overtime on the building site and their tea was being kept hot in the oven. Dora had gone to the hospital with John that morning, however, and during the meal Linda occasionally glanced across the table at her mother and saw the worried expression on her face. Dora had told her earlier as she was serving up that it was the first time they had been parted since getting married. Linda imagined how she must be feeling. She herself was very concerned about her father, as they all were. At the beginning he had seemed to be responding to the treatment his panel doctor had prescribed, but after a particularly bad day he had got progressively worse until he was in constant pain and not eating at all.

Lucy Perry had called in before tea that evening to offer her help if needed and had stayed for a while chatting. Listening in on the talk, though, Linda felt that she was a Job's comforter. Mrs Perry suggested that it could be a diseased kidney and John might have to have it removed, adding by way of reassurance that it wasn't as bad as it sounded since many people lost a kidney and survived just as well on one.

Linda knew that her mother was dwelling on what Mrs Perry had said and she noticed how her eyes filled up with tears when Pamela remarked cheerfully that their father would most likely be home in a couple of days. Tommy and Ben were unusually quiet around the table and they thoughtfully gathered up the empty plates without bidding after the meal was over. Tommy wanted to wash up and Ben offered to dry but Dora put on a brave face and refused them with a big smile. 'Me an' Linda'll do it, boys, 'cos we need ter be quick,' she told them. 'We're gonna pop over ter the 'ospital ternight wiv some o' yer dad's fings.'

Linda had not yet mentioned the job offer Nick Carter had come up with, and she prudently waited for the right moment as they set to work.

'It's gonna be a worry fer Frankie, what wiv 'im goin' in the army next week,' Dora said as she put the first of the washed plates on the draining board.

'It could be all sorted out by next Thursday, Mum,' Linda told her encouragingly.

'I do 'ope so, but these fings take time,' Dora replied. 'I'm gonna miss the money, too. Frankie's always bin good wiv what 'e earns. There's always a bit extra when 'e does overtime.'

'Never mind, Mum, Pamela starts work in September,' Linda reminded her.

'Yeah, but I wanted 'er ter go straight in an office,' Dora said. 'I know it don't pay as good as factory work ter start wiv but she'll benefit later. I was 'opin' I could manage wivout takin' most o' the money the poor little cow earns, but now yer dad's gonna be on sick pay fer a while it's different.'

Linda tried another plate and set it down on the scullery table. 'I can give yer extra, Mum,' she said tentatively.

'I don't want any more from you than yer give me now,' Dora said quickly. 'I couldn't take every penny off yer. No, I'll manage. Once we know more about what's gonna 'appen, I'll 'ave anuvver word wiv yer farvver. 'E's never let me go out ter work before. 'E reckons I've got enough ter do in 'ere, but ovver people 'ave ter manage. Look at Mrs Gainsford. She's got five all under ten an' she goes out office cleanin' every mornin'. The kids manage. They look after each ovver. At least you lot are off me 'ands. No, 'e'll 'ave ter change 'is mind an' let me 'elp wiv the money.'

Linda picked up another washed plate. 'I've got the chance of a job that pays fifty shillin's more than I get at the wine vaults,' she said.

'Doin' what?' Dora asked quickly.

'Workin' in an office.'

'An office? But you ain't got no experience, Lin.'

'But I've bin offered it, Mum,' she told her.

'Where?'

'Workin' fer the Carter bruvvers.'

'The Carters?' Dora said in surprise. 'An' they'd pay yer an extra fifty shillin's a week? That's seven pounds all told. What do they expect yer ter do fer that sort o' money?'

'Answer the phone an' keep their books tidy,' Linda explained. 'There's no typin' ter do an' I can manage the figures. That was one fing I was good at in school.'

Dora looked unimpressed. 'I don't like the idea of it, Lin,' she said. 'Those Carter boys 'ave got a bad name round 'ere. I don't want you gettin' mixed up wiv that lot.'

Linda put down the tea towel and sat down at the table. 'Look, Mum, it's just a job in an office. The Carters 'ave got this arch down at Abbey Street an' they've got women workin' part time fer 'em. They're doin' really good an' it's all above board.'

'What exactly are they doin'?' Dora asked as she sat down facing her.

'It's perfume. Real French perfume. They're doin' their own brand,' Linda told her, knowing that this wasn't strictly true.

'Perfume? 'Ow many people round 'ere can afford French perfume?' Dora said quickly. 'That stuff costs the earth.'

'Ah, but they sell it a lot cheaper,' Linda explained. 'It's goin' like 'ot cakes. They're earnin' a bomb.'

'I dunno, Lin, it sounds fishy ter me.'

Linda leaned across the table and took her mother's hand in hers. 'That job at the wine vaults 'as become a waste o' time lately,' she said quietly. 'We very rarely get the opportunity to earn our bonus, an' if fings continue ter go the way they are I can see some of us gettin' laid off. This is a chance fer me, Mum. I'm gonna grab it. Charlie took me along ter the arch an' I've seen it fer meself. Charlie's gonna work for 'em too.'

'I 'ope that lad's not bin twistin' yer arm,' Dora said quickly.

'No, Mum, Charlie doesn't know I'm gonna take it yet. Honest.'

Dora shrugged her shoulders. 'I wouldn't try an' stop yer, luv, if yer mind's made up,' she replied. 'After all yer not a child, but I'm askin' yer ter be careful. I don't trust them Carters.'

'I will, Mum, I promise,' Linda said, getting up and reaching for the kettle. 'This job could be a godsend to us.'

Bert Warner had had his doubts about the Carters, but, as he explained to Gladys, 'They come in the saloon bar an' sit over in the corner out the way, an' they don't interfere wiv the ovver customers. Besides, they spend well. I fink they just want a nice little waterin' 'ole, as the sayin' goes. They know very well that if they start cuttin' up rough they'll get barred. As a matter o' fact they've got a little business goin', so I bin told. P'raps that'll 'elp ter quieten 'em down a bit.'

Gladys did not look too happy and Bert tried to reassure her. 'When I was 'avin' a drink wiv ole Denny Somers from the Risin' Sun the ovver night, 'e put me wise to a few fings,' he went on. 'The Kerrigans use 'is pub a lot an' they never cause any trouble whatsoever. Denny said they bring a lot o' business in, an' when I told 'im about the Carters usin' my pub 'e said that provided they keep to themselves I shouldn't worry.'

'Well, as long as they do,' Gladys told him.

It was Friday evening, and Bert had just served Nick Carter with a round of drinks when Tommy Kerrigan walked into the saloon bar accompanied by a hefty-looking character with a ring-scarred face. The landlord knew Tommy Kerrigan by sight and he immediately looked over to gauge the Carter brothers' reaction. They had spotted the newcomers and did not seem put out in any way, but when Kerrigan and his friend carried their drinks over to the far table Bert watched out of the corner of his eye, half expecting all hell to break loose at any second.

Nick Carter nodded to Tommy Kerrigan and Sam Colby

but Tony 'Boy-boy' Carter's face was a set mask. Sam Colby eyed the younger brother across the table with distaste; then, while Tommy was speaking, he watched Nick's face for his reaction.

'I've asked fer this meet because I feel it's in our best interests ter pool our resources,' Tommy began.

Nick studied his half-empty glass for a few moments, then he looked up at Kerrigan. 'I was a bit surprised when yer phoned me, Tommy,' he said quietly. 'You was the last person I expected ter be callin' me, especially after yer made it clear we weren't welcome in your boozer any more.'

Tommy smiled briefly. 'It was fer the best, Nick,' he told him quietly. 'You an' your team were squeezin' us. You were off yer manor.'

'Yeah, we took the point, Tommy, but now we're on our own manor, an' I 'ope it's not the case that you an' your team are considerin' tryin' ter squeeze us.'

Tommy Kerrigan smiled. 'It's just a meet. Old enemies buryin' the 'atchet over a few drinks,' he replied calmly.

'Why don't we cut out the bollocks an' get down ter business?' Tony said sharply.

Nick lifted his hand up, his eyes flicking briefly to his brother. 'You were sayin' about poolin' resources. Would yer like to explain?' he asked.

'We understand you boys 'ave got a good fing goin',' Tommy resumed. 'What's more, we both know that you need good outlets.'

'We've got 'em,' Tony said quickly, his narrowed eyes going from Kerrigan to Colby.

'Just a minute, Tony,' his brother said with irritation. 'Let's 'ear the man out.'

'All right, so yer've got outlets, but we both know yer need ter spread,' Tommy went on. 'Punters tend ter swamp an area an' then it dries up. It's 'appened to us in the past. My proposition is fer you ter sell your commodity to us in bulk, at an agreed price, an' we'll do the marketin' on our patch. We could 'andle all you could supply us wiv. Progressively, o' course.'

'You fink so?'

'I know so. We got two good street markets on our manor.'

Nick stared down at his clasped hands for a few moments. 'What's ter stop us buildin' up our own business in the markets?' he asked quietly. 'We've got a team set up ter do just that.'

'Not on our patch, yer won't,' Sam Colby cut in.

'An' if we choose to ignore the warnin'?' Tony Carter said, looking directly at him.

'Then we close yer business down, simple as that,' Colby replied.

'I don't fink there's anyfing more ter be said then,' Tony told him sharply.

Nick gave Colby a brief hard look. 'I'll ignore that threat, fer the time bein',' he said calmly, then he turned to Tommy Kerrigan. 'You expect us ter go along wiv this idea o' yours. What 'ave yer got ter trade, except threats?'

Kerrigan glanced at his partner before he met Nick's steely gaze. 'We've got a group o' lorry drivers we do business wiv at the wharves. They buy all we can wrangle out. They'd be very good punters, an' they've got their contacts spread out all over the country. If we can agree a deal then we'll steer 'em your way. They'll bring yer their own business as well.'

Nick looked thoughtful for a while, then finally he nodded. 'OK. I'll think about it,' he replied. 'I'll need ter put yer proposition ter the rest an' I'll get back ter yer by Monday latest.'

The two visitors stood up to leave and Tommy Kerrigan reached into his pocket and took out a small card. 'Use that number,' he said, flicking it on to the table. 'I'll be waitin'.'

Eve Jeffreys had worked at the baker's shop on the corner of Eagle Street for over six years. She was a slightly-built woman in her late fifties, with a trim figure and neatly styled grey hair. Her pale blue eyes looked kind and she seemed never to have a bad word to say about anybody. Eve knew just about everyone in the street and she was renowned for her tact and diplomacy. She worked part time behind the counter, serving the batches of freshly baked bread and rolls, and when the last bake was finished and the shelves were cleared she went home to her neat and tidy house in Catford.

Eve had been widowed since before the war and she lived alone, her aged mother having passed away some two years ago. She had come to terms with her single life and had varied interests. She went to the Women's Guild on Tuesday evenings and would often visit the theatre with a good friend of her own age who was also widowed. Eve was a sociable sort who could never find it in her heart to pass by anyone she knew, not even the two hawks.

Doris Harriman and Phyllis Chaplin could find nothing nasty to say about the cheerful woman who worked in the bakery, much as they tried, and they reluctantly came to the conclusion that Eve was a nice person. They were also gratified by the complimentary remarks she directed at them and they usually found it possible to raise a smile whenever she approached them, which she often did on leaving the bakery.

At two o'clock on Friday afternoon Eve left the shop and saw the two women chatting outside Doris's house, so she crossed the street and gave them a cheery greeting. 'Your hair looks nice, Doris,' she said in her refined way. 'What have you been doing to it?'

'I just put it in curlers same as usual,' the hawk replied.

Eve knew that Phyllis would be a little put out if she did not receive a compliment as well so she thought quickly. 'Do you know, Phyllis, I was only saying to Mrs Sandwell this morning after you left the shop, doesn't Mrs Chaplin remind you of Bette Davis, the way she wears her hair and the way she's got of looking at you? She had to agree. I think you're the spitting image.'

'Get away,' Phyllis said, smiling self-consciously.

Doris did not pass any comment and Eve felt that perhaps she had leaned a little too far in one direction so she quickly went on to other things. 'By the way, I was going to ask you two ladies for some advice,' she told them sweetly. 'My friend Bella wants to buy me a blouse for my birthday and she said she'd leave the colour to me. What colour do you think would suit me? I'd wear it with this coat.'

'I should fink a lemon,' Doris said.

'Nah, yer need a pale pink wiv that oatmeal coat,' Phyllis said.

'What about a plain white?' Eve suggested.

'I s'pose yer could do. White goes wiv anyfing,' Doris replied.

141

'Do you think a white would do, Phyllis?'

Both women nodded and Eve gave them a big smile. 'I knew I could rely on you for some sensible advice,' she said. 'Some people have no colour sense.'

Doris happened to glance along the turning and she saw Dick Conners coming out of Ginny's house. ''Ere 'e comes,' she growled.

'Dear o' Lor, I 'ope 'e don't start chattin',' Phyllis remarked.

'Poor Mr Conners,' Eve said. 'Such a nice man when he's sober.'

'Which he ain't very often,' Doris piped in.

'He's really nice and polite when he comes in the shop for his bread,' Eve told them. 'I think the poor man's lonely.'

''E gives this street a bad name,' Phyllis said quickly.

''E needs a good woman ter keep 'im in order,' Doris remarked.

'Yer right there,' her friend said. 'I wish 'e would find someone. P'raps we'd 'ave some peace an' quiet then.'

'Is he as bad as all that?' Eve asked, looking suitably shocked.

'Worse,' Doris growled as Dick drew near. ''E comes out o' that pub at weekends practically legless. 'E urinates up the wall, 'e stands there singin' at the top of 'is voice, an' what's more 'e sits in the kerb an' falls asleep. I mean ter say, it's not very nice fer respectable people to 'ave ter put up wiv it, is it?'

Dick passed by without stopping, but he gave Eve a big smile and a wink. The women watched his progress and Doris shook her head in disgust as the drunk stood contemplating the Beehive's public-bar door, swaying from side to side. Suddenly he lurched forward and disappeared inside.

'I can see that you ladies have got a lot to put up with,' Eve said sympathetically.

'You don't know the 'alf of it, luv,' Phyllis told her.

'P'raps you should try and fix the poor man up with a nice woman,' Eve suggested. 'At least you'd get some peace.'

Phyllis and Doris were both prepared to let Eve Jeffreys know just how bad their trials and tribulations were, but she felt it was time to make her exit. 'Well, I'd love to stay chatting for a while. It's always so interesting talking to you, but I've got an appointment at the optician's this afternoon,' she told them.

The hawks watched Eve Jeffreys walk out of the turning and then Doris suddenly narrowed her eyes and stroked her chin. 'A good woman might make a difference ter that drunken whoreson,' she remarked.

'I'm sure she would,' Phyllis replied, then seeing the look on her friend's face her eyes narrowed too. 'Are you finkin' what I fink you're finkin'?' she asked her.

'She's bin widdered fer some time, an' that ole git's on 'is own,' Doris said grinning evilly.

'I fink me an' you should 'ave a chat,' Phyllis replied.

Chapter Fourteen

The hot dry weather was showing no sign of abating and every day the water carts were out swilling down the dusty streets and flushing the evil-smelling drains. Children played out in their bare feet, chasing behind the carts and holding old eye-glass lenses in the sun to scorch patterns on bits of paper, and they all began to get some country colour in their urban faces. The toffee-apple men and the ice-cream sellers called round twice a day and at weekends they never seemed to be out of the backstreets. A rag-and-bone man turned up now and then too, his laden cart pulled by a sorry-looking pony, and he exchanged goldfish in jam jars for old clothes and other rubbish.

Maggie Gainsford found a jam jar with a goldfish swimming round in it when she walked into her scullery on Saturday morning, having just got back from the market, and she sat down for a moment and wondered. She had hardly anything to give the rag man. Most of her family's everyday clothes were the worse for wear, it was true, and she would have loved to be in a position to give them all to him, but instead she had to make do and mend. Thus she was a little puzzled by the goldfish.

'Brenda?'

'Yeah?'

'What's this doin' 'ere?'

'I dunno. Nuffink ter do wiv me,' the eldest Gainsford child said positively.

'Ron?'

'Yeah?'

'Whose is this?'

'It ain't mine,' the eight-year-old said.

'Cassie?'

'Yeah?'

'I wanna know who this belongs to.'

'It's not mine,' replied Cassie, who was just seven.

'Bob, come 'ere.'

There was no reply from the six-year-old, but Michael the baby of the family put his head round the door. 'Bob's gone fishin' fer tiddlers at the canal wiv the Robinsons, but they wouldn't let me go wiv 'em,' he said in a sorrowful voice.

'I should fink not. Bob shouldn't be goin' neivver,' Maggie told him. 'I warned 'im about that canal. Children get drowned in there.'

Michael's head disappeared behind the door but Maggie called him back. 'Michael, do you know who brought this goldfish in?' she asked him.

The little lad's face took on an angelic look as he shook his head slowly and Maggie realised what was going on. Michael and Bob always played together outside the house and she knew from experience that Bob was the daring one whose exploits were loyally kept secret by his younger brother. Maggie felt that it was not a good thing to browbeat the youngster into telling on his older brother, so she decided to use a bit of guile.

'Michael, did Bob say we gotta feed this fish or will 'e do it when 'e gets in?' she asked him.

There was no answer and the harassed mother of five gave up, sighing deeply as she prepared herself for another long sweat over the copper. First though, the ash pan had to be cleaned out and the ashes raked. She went to the corner to get her old coat which she used for kneeling on and could not find it. She searched everywhere but it was nowhere to be seen. Finally she gave up looking, reminding herself to hide the goldfish before Bob got home – if it was his he would miss it. Her knees were sore by the time she had finished clearing out the copper, and as she sat at the scullery table with a cup of tea she remembered the other old coat of hers that was hanging up under the stairs. She would have to kneel on that when she whitened her front doorstep.

An hour later Maggie put the finishing touches to the step and got up painfully. That tatty cushion's useless to kneel on, she fumed. Wait till Bob gets home and I'll give him what for. Two coats for one measly goldfish. It was outrageous.

Linda went to the market on Saturday morning while her mother cleaned the house. They were going to the hospital that afternoon and there was much to be done. Pamela helped by hanging out the washing in the backyard and Tommy kept out of the way, taking Ben to the pie shop for their usual plate of pie, mash and parsley liquor before going on to the afternoon picture show at the Trocette.

Along the street Ginny Coombes sat outside in the sun

and Lucy Perry put a final polish on her parlour windows. Across the way, in Sunlight Buildings, the elderly Mrs Brown struggled down the flights of stairs from her top-floor flat and toddled along to the Beehive for her usual lunchtime Guinness, stopping en route to chat with Doris and Phyllis; while in the end block May Bradley was receiving a very rare visit from her daughter Sara and her grandson Peter.

'I can't understand him, Mum. The army must have turned his brain,' the younger woman was going on. 'Fancy going to work on a building site, and digging trenches at that.'

'I got on to 'im about goin' back in the office ter work but 'e got really shirty,' May told her. 'I'm sure it's the army done it to 'im. 'E was so sensible before 'e went in.'

'Cedric said that lots of young men get their heads turned by the army,' Sara replied. 'He's had shop assistants go back to work for him after they've finished their national service and they've been really bolshy. He doesn't put up with it, mind. He tells them either to knuckle down or leave. He's very firm, is Cedric. Always has been. No, darling, don't pull on the tablecloth like that or you'll upset the flowers.'

The two-year-old toddled over to his grandmother and leaned against her leg. 'I want a drink,' he said.

'Say please to grandma, sweetness,' Sara said smiling.

'No. I want a drink.'

'All right, precious, Mummy'll get you one.'

Once he had quenched his thirst the child decided to attack the tablecloth once more, unnoticed by his mother who was extolling Cedric's qualities. 'Do you know, he never loses his temper. I've never known a man to keep so cool,' Sara was going on. 'One day this nasty woman came in the

148

shop and actually asked what he had on offer in the way of black-market food. Well, Cedric was shocked and he told her in no uncertain terms to get out before he called the police.'

'Did she?' May asked.

'Oh yes. One look from Cedric was enough, but later that afternoon the woman's husband came into the shop and started abusing him,' Sara told her. 'He said that his wife had been insulted and he wanted an apology, would you believe?'

'And did Cedric apologise?'

'Of course not. He merely walked into the back storeroom and waited until the man left. It was all right, there was an assistant in the shop at the time. He's very cool is Cedric. Mind you, he did tell me later that he would have thrown the man out bodily, as big as he was, except for his back. You know he has to be careful since that strain he had. No, don't pull on that tablecloth, there's a dear, you'll pull the vase over and it's Grandma's best vase.'

May Bradley had one eye on her daughter and one eye on the china vase which was now moving perilously near to the edge of the table. 'Does he still get trouble with his back?' she asked.

'Not so much as he did once,' Sara replied. 'When he was eighteen it was very bad. It played him up quite a lot. As a matter of fact, Cedric always regrets the fact that his back kept him out of the services. He would have liked to go in the navy, but there you are. No, my little jumping bean, leave it alone. No, don't hang on it. Oh dear!'

May had made a grab for the vase but she was too late. It slipped from the table and shattered on the floor. The child stood crying loudly, a single, drawn-out note, hardly pausing to draw breath. May Bradley could cheerfully have strangled him but she swallowed hard and patted his head instead, which elicited another wave of wailing.

'Don't get upset, peanut, it was only an accident,' Sara told him. 'Grandma has another one.'

May wished she had. The vase had been more than fifty years old and quite valuable, so she had been led to believe. Seeing it lying in pieces on the floor with water spreading out all over the mat made her angry enough to choke.

'I've got to leave soon,' Sara informed her. 'Cedric's taking me to a grocers' dinner this evening and I've got to take my little sweet pea to his mother. She's keeping him there tonight.'

May wondered if Cedric's mother had ornaments about the place and what her reaction would be if the little bastard broke one.

'Is Charlie likely to be coming in soon, Mum?' Sara asked.

'I don't know, really I don't. 'E just seems ter use this place like a lodgin'-'ouse,' May told her with a sigh.

'He really will have to pull himself together,' the younger woman said. 'Would you like me to get Cedric to have a word with him? Cedric can be pretty firm when need be. Someone should say something to Charlie, for his own sake.'

May shook her head. Cedric would be asking for trouble the way Charlie was at the moment, she thought. 'No, I'll just see 'ow fings turn out,' she told her.

The young child had settled down to a steady sob, punctuated with wet sniffs, and May Bradley could hardly wait to see the back of him. 'Yer'd better be goin',' she said. 'I'll tell Charlie yer called an' was sorry yer never got the chance ter see 'im.'

Sara left the Buildings holding on to the protesting infant who was crying to be carried. It was one lie after another, she thought with a sigh. It was necessary, though, if her mother was not to worry. Yes, Cedric was going to the grocers' ball, but not with her. She would have liked to go, but there was no one she could leave the child with. Cedric's mother had minded him once, and that was only for a few hours when Cedric took her to see a film, but when they got home the exasperated woman was holding her hand to her head, a bottle of smelling salts at her elbow.

The child was bawling again and Sara shook him roughly by the arm. 'If you don't shut that row I'm going to smack your leg hard, you little brat,' she snarled at him.

With the shopping done, and the front-door sentinel duty over for the time being, the two scheming women from Eagle Street sat in Doris's parlour enjoying a cup of tea.

'The less we 'ave ter do wiv Dopey Dick the better, in the way o' speakin' to 'im, I mean, but we must get 'im ter fink that Eve fancies 'im,' Doris said.

'I fink we should 'ave a quiet word in Ginny Coombes' ear,' Phyllis suggested.

'Good idea,' Doris said, pouring the last of her tea into the saucer. 'She was sittin' outside 'er front door a little while ago. We could walk up there an' speak to 'er.'

Ginny saw them coming and groaned aloud. 'Stop in there, Dick, the ugly sisters are on their way,' she called up the passage.

''Ello, luv. Nice day again,' Doris said by way of greeting.

'Yeah, it is,' Ginny replied, eyeing the two up and down.

151

'Where's yer lodger, up the pub?' Phyllis asked her.

'Nah, 'e's gettin' ready ter go,' she told them, curious about their sudden interest.

'Did you know 'e's got an admirer?' Doris said.

'An admirer? An' who would that be?'

'Eve Jeffreys who serves in the baker's.'

'An' 'ow d'yer know that?'

'She told us,' Doris said smugly. 'We was speakin' to 'er yesterday an' she was sayin' what a nice man 'e was.'

'It makes a change fer someone to 'ave a good word fer 'im,' Ginny replied sarcastically.

'Eve's bin on 'er own fer a lot o' years now an' she's very smart,' Doris remarked. 'By the way she was talkin' I fink she's lookin' fer a nice man.'

'Yeah, an' she was tellin' us that every time Dick goes in fer the bread 'e 'as a chat wiv 'er an' 'e's very polite,' Phyllis added.

'She don't see 'im after 'e's bin on the turps,' Ginny growled.

Doris folded her arms and tried to look very knowledge-able. 'You know what I fink?' she said. 'I fink someone like Eve Jeffreys would be the makin' o' that feller. A man needs a good woman ter keep 'im in order, an' that's all Dick lacks. I know 'e's very lucky to 'ave you an' Albert, but yer know what I mean.'

Ginny wasn't too sure that she did, and the sudden enthusiasm of the two hawks made her suspicious. Normally they wouldn't even give Dick the time of day and now it seemed they were acting as matchmakers. Perhaps she was being too hard on them both, she thought. Maybe there was a spark of decency in them.

'Does the bakery woman know Dick likes a drink?' she asked them.

'I expect so,' Doris replied.

'What I mean is, does she know 'e gets blue blind, paralytic drunk as a matter o' course?' Ginny asked.

'No, she only works part time, in the mornin's, so she wouldn't see 'im when 'e's sloshed,' Phyllis explained.

Ginny looked them both up and down again. 'I'll 'ave a quiet word wiv 'im,' she told them.

Feeling that they had gone as far as they could for the time being, Doris and Phyllis bade Ginny good day and walked on, their eyes straying nervously to the bombsite as they gave it a wide berth.

Once they were out of sight Ginny shouted down the passage. 'It's all right, they've gone.'

Dick sauntered along to the front door and stood in the bright sunlight. 'I fink I'll go fer a pint,' he told his landlady.

'Before yer go yer wouldn't mind slippin' over the baker's, would yer?' she asked him. 'I need a fresh loaf.'

'I got yer one this mornin',' Dick told her.

'Yeah, but I need anuvver one.'

'If yer say so,' he replied, scratching his head.

'It's good bread over there. Always nice an' crusty,' Ginny remarked. 'They're very obligin' too. She's very nice is that Eve what's-'er-name. The one who works part time.'

''Ow would you know? Yer never go in the shop,' Dick said grinning at her.

'Maggie Gainsford told me,' Ginny replied. 'Anyway, that Eve likes you, an' she's a widow too, so I've bin told.'

'Who told yer that?' Dick asked.

'Never you mind. I'm just puttin' yer wise, that's all,' the old lady growled. 'Anyway, yer better go an' get me that loaf before they sell out.'

Dick Conners ambled across the turning to the baker's shop smiling to himself. There appeared to be some match-making going on and he would have to be very careful not to get sucked in too deeply. He was happy the way he was and he did not intend to let any woman come on the scene and try to change him. He was too long in the tooth now.

'No bread left?' he queried on seeing the empty shelves.

'I'm sorry, dear, but we've just sold out,' Eve told him.

Dick scratched his chin. 'Oh well, in that case Ginny'll 'ave ter make do,' he said. 'I got 'er one this mornin' anyway,' he said.

'Yes, I remember,' Eve said smiling.

'Well, I'm off fer a pint,' Dick told her.

'I'm off home now,' she replied.

'I'm gonna get drunk,' Dick announced.

Eve smiled benignly. 'Really?'

'Yep. I'm gonna get blind drunk, then I'm gonna go 'ome an' fall inter bed an' sleep it off,' Dick told her. 'When I wake up I'm gonna 'ave a wash an' brush-up, then I'm going' out again an' gettin' even worse drunk. I might even sleep in the gutter ternight, or in a shop doorway, if I'm very drunk. I shall most likely upset somebody in the pub. I usually do.'

Eve slipped her coat on and walked round the counter with a sad look on her face. The man was ill, she thought. Doris and Phyllis were right to be concerned about him, he was crying out for help. A typical case. A piece of flotsam adrift on the sea of life, just like that character in the play she had seen only last week. Meredith Jones had seemed to be beyond help, but he had been saved – recovered from the maelstrom, snatched back from the black depths at the very last moment. Dick Conners was just like Meredith Jones and he too could be saved.

'Dick?'

'Yeah?'

'Tell me something,' she said quietly. 'Would you like your life to be different? Would you like to get up one morning and know that you weren't going to touch a drink all day?'

The drunk stroked his chin for a few moments. 'That mornin' I'd 'ave a shave as usual, then while I 'ad the razor 'andy I'd cut me froat,' he told her.

Eve Jeffreys shook her head sadly and she watched him walk out of the shop. Yes, he was just like Meredith Jones.

Chapter Fifteen

The warm summer sky had dissolved into a glorious sunset, and the old man stood leaning on the balustrade watching the gold and the red fading slowly into purple night. He felt at peace as he listened to his flock cooing contentedly in the loft, their evening flight done. Monty had strutted about the roof while the rest of the birds whirled and dived overhead, and he had fluttered up on to the stonework beside him for a while as if to keep him company. Now he was cooing along with the rest, and Bill Simpson lit his pipe. The youngsters would be gathering soon and he would leave them to it, he thought. Jack Marchant would be calling for his usual chat and there was the regular Saturday night play to listen to before he went off to bed. Life was simple now, uncomplicated and easy, with a lifetime of memories to dwell on: memories of his travels to the far corners of the earth, of his friends long gone, and of the love of his life whom he often saw in his dreams and who would be waiting for him out there, up beyond the changing sky.

They came up on the roof, the young people of the street, and gathered together laughing and joking. Jenny Jordan was with them and her round flat face was wreathed in a smile as she stood talking to Kate Selby. 'I've got a date ternight. 'Is name's Brendan an' 'e's meetin' me 'ere soon,' she told her. ''E's really nice.'

'It's a bit late ternight fer a date, ain't it?' Kate queried.

'Brendan 'ad ter go somewhere an' 'e's 'opin' 'e'll be back in time,' Jenny replied.

'Where d'yer meet 'im?' Kate asked, a ghost of a grin on her face as she looked disbelievingly at the short chubby girl with her fluffy brown hair.

''E started work in our office two weeks ago,' Jenny told her. 'Brendan's an accountant. 'E's very clever wiv figures.'

Kate Selby was aware that the others were listening and she went on with her cross-examining. 'What's 'e like, I mean ter look at?'

''E's good-lookin' in a manly sort o' way,' Jenny replied with a shrug of her shoulders. 'I s'pose yer'd call 'im attractive.'

'Good fer you,' Kate said with a growing smile. 'Is it serious?'

Jenny nodded, suddenly aware that they were all looking at her, and she flushed angrily. 'What about you an' Peter Ridley? Are you an' 'im still tergevver?' she asked, trying to divert their attention.

'Yeah, just about,' Kate told her.

A young man walked out on to the roof and stood looking around for a few moments.

'Cor, who's that?' one of the young women said to her friend.

''E's tasty,' another remarked.

The young man was tall and fair-haired and his handsome

158

face broke into a broad grin as he spotted Jenny and walked over to her.

'I wonder what 'e sees in 'er?' Kate said uncharitably to the group as Brendan walked off towards the stairway with Jenny, his arm around her.

Charlie Bradley clasped Linda's hand in his bandaged one as they left the Buildings and walked over to the Beehive. 'I'm glad that's over,' he said smiling.

'D'yer fink she likes me?' Linda asked him.

'Course she does,' Charlie told her. 'Yer not exactly a stranger, are yer?'

'She seemed very quiet,' Linda remarked.

'That's just 'er way,' Charlie said reassuringly. 'She's 'ad a bad day terday. Me sister came visitin'. She can be a bit overbearin' at times.'

They walked into the public bar and Charlie smiled as he noticed the serious look on Linda's face. 'Relax,' he whispered.

They ordered their drinks and found a corner, and Linda looked around at the familiar faces. She saw the Perrys, and Wally Gainsford talking to Dick Conners, who was nodding his head vigorously. There were other faces, neighbours and acquaintances, and a few she had not seen before.

''Ere's ter you an' me, kid,' Charlie said, adopting an American accent as he lifted his glass of beer.

Linda sipped her drink and then looked up at him. 'I've decided ter take the job,' she told him.

'I was 'opin' yer would,' he replied. 'You should do very well there.'

'I 'ope so,' she said. 'It's gonna be different.'

159

'Nick's OK. There's nuffink ter worry about there,' Charlie said encouragingly.

'I was always frightened of 'im, an' 'is bruvver, when I was small,' Linda confessed.

Charlie took another sip from his glass. 'As I said, Nick's fine, but I can't take ter that bruvver of 'is,' he told her. 'Boy-boy's always bin trouble, ever since we were kids ter-gevver. 'E got turned down fer the army, an' no one seems ter know why. 'E never talks about it.'

'I remember Nick bein' in uniform,' Linda replied.

'Yeah, 'e went in towards the end o' the war. 'E was in the Rifle Brigade,' Charlie told her.

''E's not married?'

'Nah. Nick's goin' wiv one o' the women who works at the arch. She's the supervisor there, as a matter o' fact, an' she's a married woman too. Gilda 'er name is. Yer'll be meetin' 'er soon.'

'What about Boy-boy?' Linda asked.

Charlie shook his head slowly. 'There's a trail o' destruction be'ind 'im,' he replied. ''E's bad news to any gel. I 'eard 'e's payin' someone maintenance.'

'What about you, Charlie? Are yer lookin' forward ter workin' fer the Carters?' Linda asked him.

The young man glanced down briefly at his bandaged hands, and when he looked up there was a hard glint in his eyes. 'I've realised that there's no future in sweatin' fer a livin',' he said with passion. 'I've got plans.'

'Do they include me?' Linda said quietly.

Charlie's eyes became soft as he met her gaze. 'That's the reason I wanna get somewhere, be someone,' he told her seriously. 'My farvver worked 'ard till the day 'e dropped, an' look at your dad. Where's all that 'ard work got 'im?'

Linda could sense the fire burning inside him and she reached out and touched his hand. 'Just don't let yer ambitions spoil it fer us, Charlie,' she said softly.

The young man stared at her, feeling a sudden need to hold her, caress her and feel her young vibrant body next to his. 'Listen, Linda,' he said in a husky voice. 'You're more important ter me than any ambition I've got, an' I want yer ter know that whatever I do, it's wiv you in mind. I tell yer that 'cos the simple trufe is, I'm fallin' in love wiv yer.'

'I already 'ave,' she replied quietly. 'It seems like I've loved you fer as long as I can remember.'

Charlie waited until she had finished her drink then his eyes met hers. 'Shall we go?' he said.

They left the pub and crossed the street, without speaking, both knowing instinctively where they were making for, and when they reached the top of the stairway and stepped out into the shadows on the roof he took her in his arms. They kissed long and passionately and she could feel his urgency. She let him kiss her neck and felt shivers of pleasure coursing up and down her spine, and she did not resist when his hand wandered on to her breast and then strayed down her side to the top of her upper thigh. Her breath was coming faster now as he slipped his hand between her legs and moved upwards under her flared cotton dress. The bandage felt clumsy but he pressed his open palm on to her mound of hair, his fingertips gently searching for her most intimate spot. She gave a deep sigh of pleasure and then suddenly she stopped him, pulling on his arm. 'No, Charlie, no,' she moaned.

161

He was breathing deeply as he fought to regain his composure. 'Yer drivin' me mad,' he said in a voice he hardly recognised. 'I can't stop finkin' about yer. I need yer, Linda.'

'I feel the same way, Charlie,' she sighed, 'but I can't, I just can't.'

'If yer loved me as much as I love you, yer would,' he told her.

'If yer loved me that much yer'd wait,' she replied quickly. 'It's too soon. We've only bin goin' wiv each ovver fer a few days.'

'It doesn't matter if we love each ovver,' Charlie said sulkily.

'It does ter me,' she told him firmly.

They moved apart, both leaning against the stairway wall, and for a few moments they were silent. Charlie spoke first, his voice little more than a whisper. 'I do love yer, Linda. There's no doubt in my mind.'

'I love you too, very much, but yer must be patient, Charlie,' she replied, moving towards him.

They kissed tenderly and he slipped his arm around her waist as they walked out of the shadows to the stone balustrade.

Tony 'Boy-boy' Carter banged his fist down on the table, his pointed chin jutting out menacingly and his pale eyes wide with anger. 'What gives 'em the right ter come round 'ere demandin' we cut 'em in,' he snarled. 'Put it the ovver way round. What joy would we get if we went on their manor readin' the riot act? They'd feel obliged ter sort us out, an' that's what we should be doin', not suckin' up to 'em. I fink Nick's lost 'is bottle.'

Billy Nelson nodded. 'I couldn't believe I was 'earin' it,' he replied. 'We can match that bundle o' shit any time. If it was down ter me I'd sort 'em out once an' fer all.'

Boy-boy looked at the big ex-pugilist and nodded. 'We'd only need ter fix Tommy Kerrigan. The rest would bottle out straight away,' he growled.

'We'll need ter make a good argument when we get round the table termorrer,' Billy said, draining his glass. 'We know Don Jacobs an' George Morrison'll side wiv Nick but we might 'ave a chance o' pullin' Con Ashley in wiv us. It'll certainly put the cat amongst the pigeons.'

Boy-boy Carter picked up the empty glasses, a smile hovering on his lips. 'Even if we can't rope Con Ashley in, it's not all lost,' he said. 'Tommy Kerrigan ain't made of asbestos. 'E can burn same as anyone else.'

Dick Conners left the Beehive late on Saturday night feeling a little cross with his neighbours. Wally Gainsford had been asking him a lot of questions about that silly woman in the baker's shop. How did he feel about her? Would he like to get something going with her? Had he ever thought of getting married? It was obvious Wally had been listening to his wife Maggie, who had been talking to Ginny, who had heard a whisper from someone in the street about the woman. What did they take him for? If he was in any way interested in the silly cow he would have put his hat in the ring long ago. As it was, he was happy to be fancy free with only himself to please, and they wanted to marry him off to the first person who showed some interest in him. Maybe the woman really was interested in him and had said something to the ugly sisters. She was always talking to them, and they would jump at the chance to interfere in someone's life as much as they possibly could. The ugly cows did not bother to hide their disgust whenever they saw him pass by the worse for drink. He had actually heard them say that his drunken behaviour gave the street a bad name. Did they think it was a problem that could be solved by their meddling? It was obvious that they were the ones who had put the idea in Ginny's head. He knew that Ginny Coombes was genuinely concerned for him, and through a natural desire to see him get married to some respectable woman she had clearly been drawn into their stupid game. It was too obvious for words, sending him over the baker's for an extra bloody loaf.

Well, if they wanted to play their silly games let them, he told himself. He would soon have Eve Jeffreys moaning to the ugly sisters that she wouldn't marry Dick Conners if he were the last person on earth.

''Ello, Dick, you look surprisin'ly sober,' Ginny remarked as he walked in.

'Yeah, I got side-tracked by Wally Gainsford an' 'e can chew the 'ind legs orf a donkey,' Dick growled. 'I 'ad ter drag meself away from 'im every time I wanted a refill.'

'What was 'e talkin' about then?' Ginny asked him.

'What everybody's talkin' about. Me an' that Eve woman, that's what,' Dick told her. 'The bloody questions 'e was askin' me! I ain't got no desire ter get married, Ginny.'

'You could do a lot worse than Eve Jeffreys,' she told him.

'I'm not disputin' that,' he replied. 'If I was intendin' ter get married I'd most likely pick someone like 'er, but I'm not, so there!'

'All right, all right, don't get shirty,' Ginny said frowning. 'People are only showin' interest 'cos they've got some regard for yer.'

'Or they want me out o' their 'air,' he growled.

'What yer talkin' about?' Ginny asked quickly.

'Why, them two ole biddies o' course,' Dick replied. 'I know their game.'

Ginny shifted her position in her chair and looked him squarely in the eye. 'Now listen 'ere, luv,' she began. 'No one wants ter see yer married off more than I do, but fer the right reasons. Me an' Albert won't last fer ever, an' who the bloody 'ell's gonna take you on when we've gorn? Who else is gonna put up wiv yer fallin' in an' out o' the 'ouse pissed out o' yer brain?'

Dick walked over and put his arm round his landlady's shoulders. 'Nobody would, 'cept you an' Albert, luv, but that's me point. That's what I'm tryin' ter tell yer. I can't change an' no woman can make me. I am what I am, a good-fer-nuffink piss artist. I wouldn't put meself on any woman. I couldn't expect any woman ter put up wiv it.'

'You could change. You could change yerself, if yer've the mind to,' Ginny told him firmly.

'Yeah, but that's just it. I don't want to,' Dick said quietly. 'Drink shuts all the bad fings out. I can live wiv meself when I'm drunk. I can't when I'm sober.'

'All right, Dick, I'm not gonna argue wiv yer any more,' she told him. 'An' I ain't gonna send yer over the bloody baker's shop fer no more extra bread. Just ignore the woman an' she'll get the message.'

'Ter be honest, I fink she's the victim, same as me. I just wish people would mind their own business.'

'Just ferget it, Dick, or yer'll work yerself up into a state,' Ginny said sighing. 'Now reach down in the corner. There's a couple o' bottles o' stout there. Yer might find a light ale if yer lucky.'

Kate Selby came down from the roof and took Peter Ridley's arm as they walked quickly to the end house in Eagle Street. 'We can't be too long, in case me mum an' dad come 'ome early,' she told him.

Peter nodded, his face flushed with expectation as she slid the key into the lock. 'We'll be as quick as we can,' he said urgently.

'Anyone would fink we're talkin' about doin' the washin' up,' Kate giggled.

'I love yer, Kate,' the young man gasped as he grabbed at her in the passage.

'Not 'ere, yer dopey fing. Upstairs.'

'I do love yer, Kate.'

'All right, let me get me coat off.'

'Yer've got a lovely figure.'

'Did yer remember ter get anyfing?'

'Yeah, course I did.'

'All right, don't rush, I'm not goin' anywhere.'

'Yer got a smashin' pair o' legs.'

'Shush! Oh it's all right, I thought I 'eard the front door go.'

'Yer've really got a lovely figure.'

'Don't do that, it tickles.'

'Oh darlin'.'

'Peter, what's wrong?'

'I don't fink I'm gonna be able ter manage it.'

'Yes, yer can. Just take it easy.'

'Was that the front door?'

Kate sat up on the bed and adjusted her cotton dress. 'C'mon, let's go out fer a walk.'

'I'm sorry, Kate. I'm too nervous 'ere,' Peter told her. 'I'm expectin' that front door ter go any minute.'

'P'raps it's fer the best,' she replied.

'Kate?'

'Yeah?'

'Let's go back up on the roof. It'll be quiet by now.'

'If yer like.'

They climbed the stairs and slipped into the deep shadows.

'I love yer, Kate.'

'I love you too.'

'Oh, Kate.'

'Oh, Peter.'

'Kate.'

'What now?'

'We can't.'

'Why not?'

'I've left them fings on the chair by yer bed.'

Chapter Sixteen

Charlie Bradley walked through the Monday morning market with a feeling of excitement. It was to be his first day working for the Carters and he self-consciously pulled on his open shirt collar as he crossed the thoroughfare into Abbey Street. Nick Carter had told him the sky was the limit and he wanted to prove to him that he was capable of doing the job.

He reached the railway arch and took a deep breath before tapping on the wicket gate. It creaked open, and as he ducked into the dimly lit interior he saw the day staff hard at work and was immediately assailed by the exotic aroma of perfume.

Nick closed the gate and slid the bolt. ''Ow's the fryin' pans?' he asked.

Charlie showed him the small squares of plaster on his palms. 'A couple more days should do it,' he said cheerfully.

Nick led the way to the office. 'Take a seat, Charlie,' he said, seating himself behind a small desk. 'As yer chuckin' yer lot in wiv us it's only right yer should know the full score.'

'Would I want to?' Charlie said smiling.

'We've 'ad a visit from the Kerrigans,' Nick told him

quietly. 'They know about the business an' they want a split.'

Charlie looked shocked. 'That's out of order,' he replied. 'Did yer tell 'em where ter go?'

Nick smiled. 'I could 'ave done, an' that's what Tony wanted me ter do, but it's not that simple,' he said. 'We need ter push it out in their area, on their manor, an' that's the problem. Tommy Kerrigan spelled it out. 'E insists on controllin' 'is patch, naturally. They buy bulk from us at a basement price an' do the sellin' on their manor. We were told that if we said no they'd shut us down.'

'Would they be able to?' Charlie asked him.

'It wouldn't take much ter set this place alight, would it?' Nick replied. 'Then there's the punters who'd sell the stuff on 'is turf. Kerrigan's got the muscle be'ind 'im ter scare 'em off if they tried ter push it wivout 'is say-so.'

'D'yer fink they were bluffin'?' Charlie asked.

'I was tempted ter call Tommy's bluff, but there's the women ter consider. I couldn't guarantee their safety if someone lobbed a petrol bomb in the arch.'

'So where's that leave you?'

'We're goin' along wiv their suggestion, but I've managed ter negotiate a better price than they first put on the table,' Nick said, affording himself a smile. 'The Kerrigans are gonna work their own manor an' we warn our punters ter keep well clear.'

'Was Tony upset?' Charlie asked.

'Yer could say that,' Nick replied. ''Im an' Billy Nelson wanted us ter call their bluff. The rest backed me. Anyway, I fink it'll work out. Once Kerrigan gets ter see the earnin' potential 'e'll want the supply ter continue. I know they could copy our setup easily enough, but wivout the base oils they're cattled, an' there's only enough brought 'ere fer a day's blendin'. The rest is under lock an' key. It's our insurance.'

Charlie leaned back in his chair and looked at him. 'Tell me, 'ow did the Kerrigans get on ter this?' he asked.

Nick looked down at his clasped hands for a moment or two. 'It could 'ave bin one o' the women chattin', though they've bin warned that it could be dangerous ter let on about this setup. We told 'em the reasons why an' they understood, so I don't fink it was one o' them.'

'Yer mean ter say yer might 'ave a grass on yer payroll?' Charlie remarked.

Nick nodded. 'I've got my suspicions but I'm leavin' it at that fer the time bein'. I'll find out though, an' when I do . . .'

Charlie saw a dangerous look flare up in Nick Carter's eyes and it said everything. 'Right then, what d'yer want me ter do?' he said smiling.

Nick reached into his desk drawer and took out a sheet of foolscap. 'There's the list of names an' addresses,' he told him. 'They spread from round the corner ter the tunnel. Yer just make contact an' take the orders. They pay one over one. In ovver words, if yer don't pick up the cash fer the last order they don't get the next one. It's all down on the list what yer s'posed ter collect. Any bad payers are your responsibility. It'll be up ter you ter put the frighteners in, but if it gets nasty we'll supply the muscle ter do the persuadin'. OK?'

Charlie nodded then he clicked his fingers. 'I almost fergot. The gelfriend, Linda. She's put a week's notice in. She'll be ready ter start next Monday.'

'That's fine,' Nick told him. 'I need ter get out on the

streets but I'm tied up 'ere wiv all this paperwork. Linda seems a smart kid. Once she's learned the ropes I'll be able ter leave 'er to it. Right then, I'll introduce yer ter Gilda. She's got yer orders made up already. Yer'll carry 'em in a canvas bag. One ovver fing. If the Ole Bill pulls yer up an' they wanna take a gander in yer bag, don't worry. Just refer 'em to us. You're a bona fide representative, an' anyway we're payin' enough ter keep 'em sweet. Good luck, Charlie.'

The young man stood up and clasped Nick's outstretched hand. 'Fanks fer the chance,' he said. 'Yer won't regret it.'

Linda walked to work on Monday morning with mixed feelings. She was looking forward to her new job but was sorry to leave the girls she had befriended over the past two years. They were a good bunch, she thought: Doll, Kate Madigan, Fat Mary and Irene Cutler the forelady. They would have to continue chasing bonuses, struggling to make ends meet on the low wages they earned for the most part. She was fortunate. There was a chance for her to better herself and she could not afford to let it pass.

They all looked sad when she told them she was leaving at the end of the week and Fat Mary shed a few tears. 'Yer'll 'ave ter be all 'oity-toity in an office,' she said.

'Not in the office I'm gonna be workin' in,' Linda assured her.

Irene was in good fettle that morning and she cheered the women up with her little anecdotes. 'I remember this gel who got a job in an office,' she told them, her eyes twinkling. 'It was an 'olesale chemist firm. The young gel was a real scatterbrain. Couldn't get anyfing right. 'Ow they come to employ 'er, I'll never know. Anyway, she 'ad ter take orders over the phone an' she kept gettin' 'em mixed up. One day the guv'nor called 'er in an' told 'er she'd 'ave ter go. The gel started bawlin' an' pleadin' fer anuvver chance but the guv'nor was adamant. She'd lost the firm two good customers. What she'd done was send two cartons o' sanitary towels ter the Old Westonians Rugby Club an' a gross o' French letters ter St Mary's Covent.'

'So the poor cow got the sack,' Doll said.

Irene shook her head. 'The sales manager 'ad taken a fancy to 'er an' 'e pleaded on 'er be'alf,' she went on. 'The guv'nor said that if 'e could win the customers back 'e'd give 'er anuvver chance. Now this sales manager was the best, an' yer know what 'e done?' The women all shook their heads. 'Well, 'e got on ter the rugby club first an' got 'em ter take the sanitary towels at a discount, then 'e got on ter the convent an' they did the same.'

''Ow comes?' Doll asked.

'Well, whenever the rugby players cut their 'eads open they used the towels as bandages,' Irene told her. 'They swore by 'em after a while, by all accounts.'

Fat Mary was scratching her head and looking puzzled. 'What about the french letters?' she asked.

'The sales manager suggested the nuns could keep 'em fer Christmas decorations. Anyway that Christmas the Cardinal visited the convent an' 'e complimented the Muvver Superior on the lovely balloons. The nuns 'ad blown the jolly bags up an' painted 'em all different colours, yer see.'

'I don't believe that,' Fat Mary said.

'It's true, as sure as I'm standin' 'ere,' the forelady told her, shifting her position on the hard stool. 'Nuns can be very out of it, especially those ones who've bin shut up fer a lot o' years.

I 'eard once that there was a farmer in Italy who 'ad this donkey an' it 'ad a great big dingle. It was so big it slowed the animal up, so one day the farmer sent fer a vet who lopped it off. The vet took the ole John Thomas away wiv 'im an' as 'e was passin' this great big wall 'e chucked it over. Unbeknowns' to 'im it was a convent an' the nuns went mad when they saw it lyin' there. One of 'em shouted out "'Oly Mary, somefing terrible's 'appened ter Farvver Francisco."'

The bawdy banter went on, helping to make the day pass quickly, and Linda was grateful. She was anxious to get home and find out what the kidney specialist had said to her mother that afternoon.

Eve Jeffreys had a soul-searching weekend. Her life was well-ordered and quite disciplined, but she had come to realise how very empty it was. She had good friends, and there was the library; the Women's Guild was a boon too, but there seemed to be no purpose, nothing to strive for. Eve had come to the conclusion that she was just going through the motions, and she needed the excitement that might be found in attempting the near impossible, tackling the sheer cliff face, moving the immovable. She could have gone on waxing lyrical for evermore, but she was determined to recognise the challenge when it appeared, and it had, there in Bermondsey at her place of work, and it was called Dick Conners.

On Monday morning Eve Jeffreys went to work with new vigour and purpose, and she felt more alive than she had for a long time.

'Good morning, Mr Conners,' she said breezily when Dick came in for a split-tin loaf.

'G'mornin', luv,' he said grudgingly.

'Did you have a good weekend?' Eve asked him.

'Yeah, what I can remember of it,' Dick told her.

'I want to show you something,' Eve said quickly. 'Just let me serve these two ladies first.'

Lucy Perry and Freda Colton picked up their crusty loaves and left the shop reluctantly, wondering just what it was Eve had to show the drunk.

'Ginny's waitin' fer me ter take this loaf back,' Dick told the inspired shop assistant. 'She's waitin' ter do some toast fer Albert. 'E ain't too good this mornin'.'

'Oh, I am sorry. Anyway this won't take a minute,' Eve said, reaching under the counter.

Dick took the proffered pamphlet and glanced it over, narrowing his red-rimmed eyes. 'What's it say? I ain't got me glasses wiv me,' he told her.

'It's a revue they're putting together at the Palace Theatre. *Old Soldiers Never Die*,' she read out to him. 'I thought you might like to see it, you being an old soldier. I've been given two complimentary tickets and I'd be happy for you to join me.'

'Well, that's very nice of yer, luv, but I dunno,' Dick told her hesitantly. 'Trouble is I usually go fer a drink in the evenin's.'

'That's no problem,' Eve replied smartly. 'They've got a nice bar in the theatre and you can get a drink in the interval.'

'Yeah, but the pubs'll be shut by the time I get back,' he said, grinning triumphantly.

'No, they won't. Not if we go to the first performance. It's twice nightly, you see.'

Dick growled under his breath, then he rallied as another excuse came to mind. 'I would go, believe me I would, but me ole wound's bin playin' me up lately,' he told her. 'I got speared in the leg while I was in the Khyber. I can't go traipsin' round the West End.'

'You won't have to,' Eve said brightly. 'We can get a number one bus almost to the door. There'll be no walking to do.'

Dick was getting desperate but, much as he wanted to tell the woman to leave him alone, he couldn't. He did not have the heart to wipe that happy smile from her face with a cutting remark. Better to ease his way out of it, he thought. 'That's good ter know,' he said, 'but the trouble is I get fidgety in those seats. I go ter the pictures over the Trocette now an' then but I can never sit frew the 'ole show. I get too stiff an' 'ave ter come out.'

'Dear oh dear, you are making excuses, Dick,' she remarked with an indulgent smile. 'Those seats at the Palace are some of the best you could possibly imagine. Why, it's like sitting in your own armchair. And just think of it. The revue has been put together by ex-servicemen. You'll enjoy it, and besides, think of the memories the show will revive.'

'I dunno,' Dick said falteringly. 'I still 'ave nightmares about some o' the fings what 'appened ter me when I was a servin' soldier.'

'There must have been many good moments too, and that's what this show's been put together for, to revive the good memories,' Eve told him.

'When is it?' he asked her.

'The tickets are for this Friday,' she replied.

'That's a shame,' Dick said smiling. 'I 'ave ter push Mrs

Coombes up ter Spa Road in 'er wheelchair every Friday so she can get 'er weekly barf.'

Eve was not going to be put off at this late stage. This was a real challenge, and nothing was too difficult to surmount if the will to win was there, she reminded herself. 'Look, Dick, I should be finished here by two o'clock,' she told him. 'I'll come along and have a chat with Mrs Coombes. Perhaps I can arrange for someone else to push her to the baths on Friday evening.'

The drunk winced noticeably. Ginny Coombes always took her weekly bath in the scullery, in the old tin bath that he filled with hot water from the copper, and she wouldn't have it any other way. 'It's all right. I can get Mrs Gainsford ter push 'er round ter Spa Road,' Dick said, sighing in defeat.

'Very good,' Eve said smiling broadly. 'You'll need to be ready by six o'clock. If you're ready on the dot we may have time for a quick drink at the pub next door. I usually enjoy a nice port and lemon before I go to a show. And just think of it: you may even meet a few of your old comrades in arms.'

Dick left the shop feeling utterly routed. There was no way he could have got out of it without insulting the woman. Maybe it won't be too bad, he thought on reflection. He used to enjoy a revue at one time. Ginny would be surprised, though, after all the things he had said to her. At least he would be able to get a drink and be back in time to get to the Beehive before it closed.

'What you lookin' so miserable about?' Ginny asked him as he put the bread down on the table.

'I'm goin' to a revue,' he said flatly.

'Oh yeah? Who wiv?'

'Eve Jeffreys,' he told her.

Ginny nearly fell out of her chair with surprise. 'Why, you crafty old sod,' she said smiling. 'After all yer said about the woman.'

'I wasn't 'avin' a go at 'er in particular,' the drunk replied meekly. 'I was just sayin' about people interferin' in me life, that's all.'

'What revue is it?'

'It's the one at the Palace.'

'I just bin readin' about it in the *Daily Mirror*,' she told him. 'It's fer ex-soldiers. There's a picture in the paper showin' the ole boys wearin' their medals. Yer'll be able ter wear yours. You ain't wore 'em since VJ night.'

Dick's face brightened. 'Yeah, that's right. I fink I'll sort 'em out. They could most likely do wiv a bit o' spit an' polish.'

Chapter Seventeen

Dora Weston's eyes were swollen from crying but she put on a brave face as she gathered her children around her on Monday evening. 'Yer dad's gotta 'ave a kidney removed,' she told them quietly.

Pamela immediately burst into tears and Tommy lowered his head sadly. Ben looked up into his mother's white face. 'Dad won't die, will 'e, Mum?' he asked fearfully.

Dora put her arm round the lad's shoulders and smiled at him. 'Course 'e won't, but 'e's gonna be off work fer a long time. Yer dad's strong an' 'e'll be 'ome in a couple o' weeks. In the meantime we've all gotta 'elp each ovver.'

Linda was comforting her younger sister. 'Now come on, stop cryin' or yer'll upset everybody else. Dad's gonna be fine.'

Dora sat down in the armchair and stared down at her clasped hands. 'The specialist said that the right kidney was diseased but the ovver one was fine,' she told them. 'Yer dad's cheerful enough an' 'e sends 'is love. After the operation we can all go in an' see 'im.'

'When are they doin' it?' Linda asked.

'This Thursday.'

'The day Frankie goes in the army,' she pointed out.

'Yeah, I know,' Dora sighed. 'It can't be 'elped. P'raps we'll be able ter phone the camp an' let 'im know that 'is dad's all right.'

Ben went to the front door and sat on the step with his chin cupped in his hands, noticed by the two hawks as they stood chatting a few doors away.

'She must 'ave told 'em,' Doris said quietly.

'Yeah, it seems like it,' Phyllis replied.

'I was shocked when she told me,' Doris went on. 'I was just dustin' me mats when she come past. I felt obliged to ask 'er 'ow 'e was.'

'I wasn't surprised when yer told me,' Phyllis said. 'I was expectin' it. Look at that Mrs Gatley. She 'ad pains fer months an' they told 'er ter drink loads o' barley water. She ended up 'avin' it out.'

'Yeah, that's right,' Doris replied. 'Mind you though, she was up an' about in no time at all.'

'John Weston seems a strong sort o' bloke. 'E'll soon get over it, I should fink,' Phyllis remarked.

'Look at that poor little sod sittin' there,' her friend said, nodding towards Ben. ''E looks really upset.'

'I've a good mind ter go an' speak to 'im,' Phyllis told her, 'but yer don't know if yer doin' right, do yer?'

'P'raps it's better we leave 'im alone,' Doris said.

The two women stood looking sympathetically at the sad little boy; Doris with her hand held up to her chin and Phyllis with arms folded and her head resting against the brickwork. They remained there for a while, quite still, staring along the turning, and then Doris finally decided that a cup of tea might be in order. 'I dunno, if it's not one fing it's anuvver,' she said sighing. 'C'mon, let's put the kettle on.'

Ginny Coombes was trying to communicate with Albert but was having little success as usual. 'I said Dick's goin' to a revue,' she shouted.

'View? What view?'

'I said revue, yer silly ole sod.'

Albert winced. 'Yer'll do me eardrums in one day, shoutin' in me ears like that,' he grumbled.

'I gotta shout wiv you. Yer can't 'ear me ovverwise.'

'What's this about a revue? I ain't interested in no revues.'

'I ain't talkin' about you. It's Dick. 'E's goin' wiv Eve Jeffreys.'

'Where to?' Albert asked.

'A revue.'

'I know that, but where?'

'The Palace.'

'Alice? Alice who?'

'I said "Palace",' Ginny shouted. 'Look at me lips.'

'The Palace. I got yer now. That's a nice place. What's 'e goin' there for?'

'I give up,' Ginny groaned.

Albert settled himself in the armchair and picked up the *Radio Times*, then as an afterthought he said, ''Ere, what's Dick doin' wiv 'is medals? 'E's got 'em laid out on the scullery table.'

'Yer should 'ave asked him,' Ginny shouted.

'I did, an' 'e told me 'e's gonna meet the King.'

'P'raps 'e is.'

'What?'

181

'I said 'e might be.'

Albert grinned, showing a lone tooth. 'What's 'e goin' to, a garden party? I can just see it now. "What's that medal for, Dick?" the King'll ask, an' 'e'll say, "That's fer long service an' good conduct at the Bee'ive, yer Majesty." Then when it comes ter goin'-'ome time they won't be able ter find 'im. 'E'll be under the table pissed as an 'andcart.'

'Shut yer silly row up an' read yer paper,' Ginny growled.

'Any Brasso in the cupboard, luv?' Dick asked as he popped his head round the door.

'I fink I'm out of it,' she told him.

'Never mind, I'll get some termorrer at Cheap Jack's,' he said.

'Can yer pop out fer a paper, they should be up by now,' Ginny reminded him.

Dick strolled along the turning whistling his regimental march, imagining himself on parade with his full row of medals glistening on his chest. 'Company, halt!' he called aloud as he reached the Westons' house and saw Ben sitting on the doorstep with his chin on his knees. 'Why the long face?' he asked.

'Me dad's gotta 'ave an operation,' Ben told him, looking up at the tall gaunt figure.

Dick frowned. 'Is that so? What sort of operation?'

''E's gotta 'ave 'is kidney out,' Ben informed him.

The street's drunk was saddened by the news. He had often passed the time of day with John Weston and enjoyed an occasional drink with him in the past. He bent down and propped himself against the brickwork at the child's elbow. 'Is yer dad in 'ospital now?' he asked him.

Ben nodded. ''E's 'avin' the operation soon,' he said.

'I am sorry,' Dick said quietly, studying the lad's face. 'Anyway, there's nuffink ter worry about. I 'ad my kidney out years ago, an' look at me.'

'Did yer?' Ben asked him.

'Cross me 'eart,' the drunk said.

'Me dad won't die, will 'e?'

'Course not. Take my word fer it,' Dick said smiling. 'When the Lord made us 'E said to 'imself, I'd better give 'em all two kidneys, just in case. 'E was very clever, yer see. I wouldn't 'ave thought o' that, would you?'

Ben shook his head. 'We've only got one 'eart though.'

'Yeah, but that's different,' Dick replied with a chuckle. 'When we're 'appy we feel it 'ere in the 'eart, an' when we're sad it's the same. Just imagine what it'd be like if we all 'ad two 'earts. We'd be 'appy an' sad at the same time an' we wouldn't know whevver ter laugh or cry.'

The young boy looked at the drunk. 'We've got two eyes though,' he said.

'Yeah, an' we got two arms an' two legs as well,' Dick said beaming. 'I fink God made a good job of us, don't you?'

Ben's face broke into a grin. 'Yeah, I reckon so.'

'Right then, I'd better be off,' Dick said, struggling to his feet.

'I gotta go in fer tea,' Ben told him.

'Now don't you worry, son. Everyfing's gonna work out just fine,' Dick said with a cheerful smile.

The sun was dropping down over the chimney pots as he crossed the Tower Bridge Road to the newsagent's. The evening was still warm and people were hurrying to and fro. Trams rattled along the steel tracks and buses lumbered past laden with tired workers. Dick thought about Eve Jeffreys and wondered why she should have been so insistent that morning. Why should she bother with the likes of him? She knew of his reputation. He was a habitual drunkard who would only bring her grief. Was she embarked on a personal temperance crusade, or did she really have some feeling for him? Whatever the reason, he had been targeted and he would have to play it very cagily.

Tommy Kerrigan looked very pleased with himself as he faced his associates round the table in the Rising Sun saloon bar. 'They're deliverin' the first batch termorrer,' he told them. 'Sam, I want you to organise the market traders. Get Manny an' Lennie Brookes ter do the business there, an' make sure you impress on 'em that this is an ongoin' fing. I don't want 'em pricin' 'emselves out o' business. Arfur, you'd better work the Borough end. Mind who yer rope in, an' the same applies there. The Carters 'ave put a ceilin' on the retail price. It's firty-five bob, so make sure no one goes above that. It allows a good margin fer profit anyway.'

Sam Colby's face was dark with anger as he looked at the leader. 'When are we gonna sort Boy-boy Carter out?' he asked, his jaw muscles working.

'Look, I know yer feeling's fer that nonsense case, Sam, but we gotta be patient,' Tommy told him. 'I'm meetin' wiv our contact in a few days' time an' by then 'e reckons 'e'll 'ave the full s.p. We can't make a move till then or we'll bugger it all up. Don't worry, I'll let you take care o' Boy-boy, once we can move safely. Fer the moment we collect the stuff an' build up the business.'

Colby was not satisfied with the answer he had got and Tommy Kerrigan knew it. 'Sam, me an' you need ter talk.

Give us a few minutes, will yer, lads?' he asked them.

Bernie and Joe Kerrigan and their cousin Arthur Slade got up from the table and went over to the counter, and as soon as they left Sam leaned forward in his chair. 'Tommy, 'e's takin' the piss,' he growled.

'What's the score?' Tommy asked him.

'Boy-boy's knockin' Gwen's sister off. I got it out of 'er last night. Gwen knows I can't abide the geezer, not after the way 'e slagged 'er off in the pub that night, so she didn't wanna tell me, up till now.'

'What's changed?' Tommy asked.

Hatred burned in Sam Colby's eyes as he gritted his teeth. ''E's started knockin' 'er about,' he replied. 'Gwen went round there ter see 'er the ovver evenin' an' she was gutted. When Mandy opened the door my missus nearly passed out. The gel's got a black eye an' scuff marks down one cheek, an' a cut on 'er fore'ead. Gwen said 'er boat race looked like someone 'ad bin usin' it as a football.'

'I understand yer reasons a bit better now, Sam, but like I said, I want yer ter bear wiv me fer a few more days,' Tommy urged him. 'I've got good reasons fer askin'.'

'A few more days then,' Sam said sighing heavily.

Tommy Kerrigan leaned back in his chair and folded his arms. 'Tell me, Sam, yer not finkin' o' toppin' 'im, are yer?'

The henchman smiled and shook his head. 'We'll do this very professionally, don't worry. Carter won't see our faces an' 'e won't know who's be'ind it. We'll put it to 'im that Mandy's ole man got to 'ear of 'er infidelity an' it's retribution day.'

Tommy Kerrigan nodded slowly. 'That's the way it's gotta be, Sam,' he told him quietly. 'We can't afford open war wiv

185

the Carters just yet, there's too much at stake. Once we get our 'ands on the ingredients, we're in business an' they become expendable. Until then we play their silly games.'

Sam nodded. 'I take it there's no chance of our contact playin' us along fer Carter's sake?'

Tommy shook his head emphatically. 'None whatsoever. 'E's got good reason fer wantin' the Carters stepped on. Take it from me.'

Sam Colby had known Tommy since they were kids on the street and was aware that he played his cards very close to his chest. He was obliged too: they were in a dangerous game and one slip could very well be their last.

Gilda Jacques was nineteen when she married Alan Bristow and was widowed before she was twenty. Alan had been her childhood sweetheart and they married before he went to France, where he died on a beach at Dunkirk. Gilda joined the ATS in 1941, and after the war she met Perry Walters, a successful businessman who had made his fortune during the Thirties in the clothing trade and had done quite well with government contracts during hostilities. Gilda married him in 1945, and their life together totalled less than eighteen months. Bad business dealings in a changing market cost Perry dearly, and when he discovered that he had been cheated by one of his associates he purchased a service revolver and shot the man in the head. The gun was traced, and for premeditated murder Perry Walters paid the ultimate penalty. He was hanged in Wandsworth Prison in January 1947.

Gilda was widowed for the second time and was still only twenty-six. She struggled on alone, feeling that there was little to live for, and she finally tried to end it all with an overdose of sleeping tablets. She was destined not to die, however, for a friend of her late husband Perry found her just in time. She spent a lengthy time in a psychiatric hospital and was discharged in 1949, but this time she was not alone. Martin Lowndes, the man who had saved her life, was on hand and he courted her with old-world charm. Gilda had grown very fond of Martin, and although she was not in love she married him, disregarding the fact that he was almost twenty years older than her. They set up home in Bermondsey Square, in a two-storey Victorian house, and Martin concentrated his energies on his fancy leather goods business. He was forced to travel around the country quite a lot, and while he was on one of his lengthy trips his very lonely and vibrant young wife fell for the charms of Nick Carter.

Gilda had only known one true love and he had been snatched from her by the cannon shell of a Stuka dive bomber. Her second husband, Perry Walters, had been self-centred and a mediocre lover, while Martin was devoted to her but unable to satisfy her basic needs. He went in fear of losing his pretty young wife and believed that if he gave her the freedom and independence she needed with no questions asked she would stay with him. Gilda understood what he was doing and swore to him that she would never leave him, which made Martin Lowndes a happy man.

Nick Carter was introduced to her at a party and they were immediately aware of the animal attraction between them. Within two weeks they had become lovers. Gilda made it clear from the very beginning that they could be nothing more than that, which suited the suave Nick Carter admirably. He had plans of his own and did not want any family commitments. Now, with his new venture getting under way, he had installed Gilda as an overseer. She organised the women competently and saw to it that the orders were ready on time, enjoying the responsibility. Like her lover she did not care to be deskbound, and it was on her insistence that he sought a young woman to look after the office.

In the cellar of Gilda's house in Bermondsey Square, and unknown to her devoted husband, two drums of exotic base oils were secretly stored. Each morning before leaving for work she went down and drew off one day's measure of the mixtures. She understood very well the reasons for the secrecy, but had she known what lay ahead she would have had nothing whatsoever to do with the whole business.

Chapter Eighteen

Frankie Weston clicked his small suitcase shut and grabbed it up from the bed, taking one quick look around his bedroom before he hurried down the stairs.

Dora looked up as he walked into the parlour and smiled at him. She could see the undisguised excitement on his clean-shaven face and the look of concern for her in his large dark eyes.

''Ave yer got time fer a quick cuppa before yer leave?' she asked him.

Frankie shook his head. 'I'd better get goin', Ma. I don't wanna be late fer the train.'

Dora got up and put her arms around him, wanting to hold on to him and not let him go. He was a man now, full-grown and stocky like his father, but she still considered him to be her little boy. 'Yer won't ferget ter write, will yer, Frankie?' she said, holding back her tears.

'No, course I won't. Try ter get word ter me about Dad,' he replied.

Dora stepped back a pace, still holding him by the shoulders. 'Take care, son, an' don't go lettin' anyfing 'appen ter yer.'

'Course I won't,' he said grinning. 'Anyway I'll be 'ome again in six weeks. Take care, Mum, an' don't worry, Dad's gonna be fine.'

Dora watched him walk along the passage and once the front door had closed behind him she let the tears fall. He had asked her not to stand at the door waving to him as it would embarrass him if the neighbours were about and she understood. He was a proud lad, was Frankie, and never a minute's trouble. It was his first time away from home and he saw it as an adventure. As he had said, it was only Winchester, not the other side of the world.

Dora made herself a cup of tea and sat deep in thought in the quiet room. It had been an emotional time at the hospital the previous evening. John had been in pain but he had put on a brave face when Frankie walked down the ward towards him. Pride had shone in his eyes, she could see, and concern for his son was there too. They had always been a close family and they had managed to stay together during the war, John being downgraded at his army medical through defective eyesight. He had been thirty-five at the time and willing to go but Dora had given thanks that it was not to be. She knew many families who had waved their husbands and fathers off, never to see them again. She had been lucky – they all had – and now they had to be strong and hope and pray that her husband, their father, made a speedy recovery.

The knock startled Dora and she opened the door to see Maggie Gainsford standing there.

'I just seen Frankie marchin' off,' she said quietly. 'I thought yer might need a bit o' company.'

'C'mon in, luv,' Dora told her. 'It's anuvver scorcher terday. Fancy a cuppa?'

Maggie nodded as she sat herself down in the armchair. 'I bet yer'll miss that lad,' she said. ''E's a nice boy.'

Dora sighed sadly as she lifted the cosy from the teapot. ''E couldn't wait ter go,' she said smiling bravely. 'I just worry 'e's gonna be all right.'

'Fortunately mine are all still kids, but I can understand 'ow yer must be feelin',' Maggie replied.

Dora filled a cup and added milk. 'Two sugars?'

'Yes, please. I'm s'posed ter cut down on it,' Maggie told her, 'but I can't stand tea wivout sugar.'

Dora looked up at the clock on the mantelshelf. 'John'll be goin' down about now,' she remarked, nervousness working away at her stomach.

''E'll be all right,' Maggie said encouragingly. 'I bet yer'll miss 'is money though.'

'Yeah, it'll be a squeeze, 'specially now John's on the panel,' Dora told her. 'Never mind though, we'll manage. Pam starts work in September an' Tommy next year. We're gonna need their money 'cos James goes in the army as well next year.'

They sipped their tea, Dora's eyes occasionally straying towards the clock. 'Did yer know our Lin an' Charlie Bradley 'ave got tergevver?' she asked after a while.

'Yeah, I've seen 'em tergevver,' Maggie replied. ''E's a nice lad, is Charlie. She could do a lot worse.'

Dora nodded. 'John likes 'im, an' so do I. She's a strange woman though, 'is muvver.'

'Yeah, I know,' Maggie agreed. 'Yer can never seem ter get talkin' to 'er. She's a bundle o' nerves.'

'Linda's startin' a new job on Monday.'

'Oh yeah? Where at?'

'She was offered a job workin' fer the Carter boys,' Dora told her. 'They've rented an arch in Abbey Street by all accounts.'

Maggie pulled a face. 'They're a dodgy pair. What they doin'?'

'Perfume. They're makin' it in the arch. It's s'posed ter be genuine French perfume,' Dora explained.

Maggie shook her head slowly. 'French perfume, all the way from Bermon'sey. It's just like them. Yer wanna make sure your Lin gets 'er wages every week.'

Dora smiled. 'She's got 'er 'ead screwed on all right. Anyway she's gettin' two pounds more a week than at the wine vaults.'

'Good luck to 'er,' Maggie said.

Dora put her empty cup down on the table. ''Ere, I was talkin' ter Lucy Perry at the market yesterday. She said that Eve at the baker's shop 'as got 'er eyes on Dick Conners.'

'Yeah, that's right,' Maggie replied. 'Mind you though, 'e won't take kindly to 'er makin' up to 'im. Ole Dick likes 'is independence. 'E'll see it as an 'indrance.'

'Especially if she expects 'im ter stop drinkin',' Dora remarked.

'She's got about as much chance o' that as I 'ave o' gettin' the pools up, an' I don't do 'em,' Maggie laughed. She put her cup down on the table and sighed. 'Well, I'd better be gettin' back,' she said. 'I've got a load of ironin' ter do.'

Dora looked up at the clock again. 'Yeah, me too. Anyway fanks fer lookin' in luv, I appreciate it.'

Boy-boy Carter pushed the empty teacup away from him and picked up the morning paper, his pale eyes glancing at the young woman as she came into the kitchen. 'What did she 'ave ter say when she saw yer face then?' he asked her.

Mandy wrapped the towelling dressing-robe tightly round her and pulled on the tie band. 'She wouldn't 'ave it that I'd 'ad too much ter drink an' fell on me face,' she said offhandedly.

Boy-boy sniffed and opened the paper. 'Yer shouldn't wind me up, yer know that, don't yer?' he growled.

'I wanted ter get back at yer. Yer've bin ignorin' me,' Mandy said quietly.

'Just don't ever try that on again, that's all,' he told her with venom. 'Yer my gel an' that's the way it's stayin'. If I ever catch you flirtin' in front o' me again I'll change the shape o' yer face permanent.'

'I'm sorry, Tony, I mean it,' she said, coming behind him and kneading his neck with her fingers.

Tony folded the newspaper and then reached up and pulled her down on to his lap. 'Yer should'a remembered I 'ad fings on me mind,' he said, nuzzling her throat. 'We're busy settin' up the business an' I was preoccupied. Anyway I was good last night, wasn't I?'

'The best,' she sighed.

'I look after yer, don't I? I buy yer fings. Why d'yer get doubts?'

'I dunno,' Mandy replied, looking down at the blue-chequered tablecloth. 'I just can't bear ter fink of you 'avin' somebody else.'

'There's nobody else,' he whispered in her ear. 'You're my gel an' that's the way it's gonna stay, so don't go windin' me up any more. I don't like gettin' rough, but sometimes you ask fer it.'

Mandy stood up and slowly undid the knot in her dressing-robe. 'Yer do like my figure, don't yer, Tony? It does do fings ter yer, doesn't it?'

The young man watched as she slipped the robe from her shoulders and let it fall to the floor. She was wearing just tiny black knickers and she posed provocatively. 'Yer not busy just now, are yer, Tony?' she purred.

He stood up and went to her, forcing her backwards against the heavy Welsh dresser. He cupped her full breasts in his hands, his body pushing against hers, and she groaned and pulled his head down, her open mouth pressing on his. 'Love me, Tony. Love me now,' she moaned.

He slid her knickers down over her thighs as she arched her body backwards against the corner of the dresser and entered her quickly. She moved on him, her rotating thrusting hips driving him wild, her tongue moving against his as her passion grew. He could feel her long fingernails pressing into his neck and her teeth gripping his lip and he groaned loudly as he fought to satisfy her craving. She was like a wildcat, hardly able to restrain herself as she thrust in time with him, faster and faster, until he felt his strength draining, then suddenly she gave out a low cry and shuddered violently. Tony gasped for air, his chest rising and falling rapidly as she clung to him, and he let his exhausted body sag.

The morning sun shone into the smartly furnished front room as, later, Tony lounged back in the luxurious divan and watched her moving about in front of him. She wore a short bathrobe, her blonde hair tied up on top of her head with a black ribbon, and she smiled wickedly at him as she straightened the cushions and tidied up the newspapers. The marks on her cheek had faded and the small cut on her forehead had closed, but the discolouring around her left eye was still prominent and he sighed sadly. He knew he loved her but she had a way of bringing out the worst in him, the animal instinct within him that knew no bounds, and he was aware that at such times he could quite easily kill her.

'Gwen'll be callin' later,' she said, giving him a reassuring smile. 'Don't worry, darlin', I'll be singin' yer praises.'

Tony scowled. 'She's a troublemaker, Mandy,' he told her gruffly. 'She carries everyfing back ter that maniac Sam Colby.'

'She's me sister, Tony, I can't ignore 'er,' Mandy said in a hurt voice.

'Yer know the Kerrigans are after rowin' 'emselves in on our business,' he growled.

'Gwen never talks about Sam's business,' she replied.

'Well, I'm tellin' yer. Just watch what yer say to 'er.'

Mandy came over and knelt down in front of him. 'Is there anyfing yer'd like me ter do?' she said in a husky voice.

He pushed her aside and stood up quickly. 'You're insatiable,' he muttered. 'Later. I've gotta get ter work.'

Linda Weston felt as though the morning would never pass. There were no big orders outstanding and the little work available was being done at a leisurely pace. It made the hours drag by, and when Irene Cutler signalled that it was time for lunch the young woman breathed a sigh of relief. Often the girls went to one of the many cafes in the area or took their sandwiches and flasks of tea to a nearby public garden now it was summer, but today Linda felt sick inside and she decided to take a stroll in the warm sunshine. Her father would be having his operation about now and she wanted to be alone with her thoughts.

As she walked out of the vaults and turned towards London Bridge she saw Charlie crossing the road towards her. He was wearing a single-breasted grey summer suit and black patent shoes and his blue shirt was open at the neck. There was a canvas bag under his arm and he sported a big smile. 'I was wonderin' if yer'd care fer some company,' he told her. 'I've bin waitin' over the road till yer come out.'

'I've bin missin' yer, Charlie,' she said as he slipped his arm around her waist. 'I've seen 'ardly anyfing of yer since the weekend.'

'I've bin so busy,' he told her. 'I thought yer might need a bit o' support terday.'

'That's very nice of yer,' she replied. 'I'm so worried.'

Charlie gave her a squeeze as they walked on. 'Everyfing's gonna turn out just fine, you'll see,' he said with a big smile.

'I do 'ope so,' she sighed. 'Mum was cryin' this mornin', what wiv Frankie goin' away as well.'

They walked up the steep hill to London Bridge and turned towards the City. Down below, the river was running fast and a tug boat chugged under the centre span, fighting against the tide. On the south side they saw the small freighters berthed at the wharves and on the City side the stout walls of the Tower of London. The expanse of water between London Bridge and Tower Bridge, known as the Pool of London, was shimmering in the sunlight, and up on the bridge a light salty breeze carried the faint tang of sour mud.

'See over there, look, where the little gate is on the waterline? That's Traitor's Gate,' Charlie told her.

Linda smiled. 'Yeah, I know. Me dad showed me when I was little.'

Charlie was quiet for a while as they stood looking down on the eddying tide, then he turned his head and looked sideways at her. 'I've bin missin' yer, Lin,' he said quietly. 'As a matter o' fact, I dreamed about yer last night.'

'Yer did?'

'Yeah, we were up on the roof an' all the lads were millin' around yer. You 'ad this lovely dress on, all sort o' billowy an' I was tryin' ter get yer ter notice me, but yer wouldn't look at me. Then suddenly everyone 'ad gone. There was just you an' me an' we could 'ear this loud roarin' noise. You were very scared an' I put me arm round yer. We just sat there up on the roof in the shadows, an' we were kids again. After a while the noise stopped an' we went over ter that stairway post where I'd carved out the love'eart. Anyway I 'ad this big knife an' I finished it. I carved your initial next ter mine.'

'That proves yer must 'ave bin finkin' of me when yer closed yer eyes last night,' Linda said smiling.

'I fink of yer all the time I'm not wiv yer, an' last fing every night,' Charlie replied quietly. 'Next time we go up on that roof I'm gonna carve yer initial just like I did in the dream.'

Linda slipped her hand in his. 'Don't do it yet, Charlie,' she said in a soft voice. 'Wait till you're truly mine, really an' truly mine.'

'But I am yours,' he told her.

She looked out at the water and beyond, through the span of Tower Bridge to where the water met the sky. 'Wait till we've made love, Charlie. Wait till then, 'cos then I'll feel that you're really an' truly mine.'

He nodded, a warm smile on his lips, then he picked up

his bag and slid his other arm round her waist as they walked off the bridge, down to the bustling wharves and narrow cobbled lanes. They kissed tenderly in a secluded spot and he could feel her love, sense the passion she was holding in check, and he knew that very soon he would do her bidding and take his knife to the rooftop post.

They walked along to the vaults and he left her there. Linda stood in the doorway, watching him until he was out of sight, then she went inside, into the cool cavern to face the long afternoon.

Chapter Nineteen

Dora spent the morning ironing, and when the ironing was finished she looked for other things to do. She cleared the copper pan out and scrubbed the scullery table until her fingers were sore. She tidied the parlour and dusted the whole house through. Time seemed to be standing still and she tried to find something else to do that might make the empty moments pass more quickly. She had thought of going to the market but there was nothing she needed, and there were sure to be people she knew there all asking the same questions.

When she had exhausted all means of making the hands of the clock move faster, Dora made herself a cup of tea and sat down with the leather-bound photograph album that Linda had bought for her and John last Christmas. She had crammed it full of old snaps that she had dug out of drawers, cupboards and other nooks and crannies. She pored over one particular family snap taken at Margate the first August bank holiday after the war. Frankie would have been fourteen then and still at school. He looked very young, she thought. James had that cheeky smile and Linda had her arms around Pamela, Tommy and baby Ben, who were all pulling faces. John was standing next to her, looking handsome in his grey flannels and open-necked shirt. Those had been happy days with her brood around her. Now, though, they were beginning to fly the nest: Frankie had left and James would follow him next year; Linda was courting and would no doubt be getting married in a couple of years.

Dora leaned her head back in the chair and closed her eyes. There was time to relax, she told herself. Time to let her jangled nerves settle down. The steady loud tick of the chimer on the mantelshelf filled her mind, like a pendulum eternally returning, and under its hypnotic influence Dora drifted off to sleep.

The white walls hurt her eyes and she blinked. He was standing over her, a huge figure with spiky ginger hair and eyes that seemed to shine out of a flat red face. He was shaking his head sadly and she fought against him. She could smell ether and hear the clicking of tongues. Panic seized her and she shook her head. 'No. No, it can't be true. 'E mustn't die. I won't let 'im die,' she shouted.

'You should have been here, Mrs Weston. He was calling for you.'

'I wanted to but I couldn't,' she screamed.

'That's a poor excuse. Isn't it a poor excuse?'

Heads nodded and tongues clicked, and then the man with the spiky hair gave her a notepad and pencil. 'You must write it all down. Write it down before you leave.'

'She must write it all down. All down,' the voices chorused.

Dora struggled against the hands which were holding her down and she tried to scream but nothing came out. Then she saw John. He looked sad as he passed by and he shook his head at her disapprovingly.

'John!' she called out, and then she heard the quiet, soothing voice of reassurance. 'Mum. Mum, wake up. Yer've bin dreamin'.'

Dora opened her eyes and saw James kneeling down beside her chair. He was holding her by the arms. 'What are you doing' 'ome? What time is it?' she said in a panicky voice. 'I gotta run down the road an' phone up the 'ospital.'

James smiled at her. 'There's no need,' he said quietly. 'We finished the job terday so we all got away early. I've already phoned Guy's. Dad's OK. They said 'e's come out o' the anaesthetic an' 'e's sleepin' quite comfortably.'

She stared at James for a few moments until his words finally registered, then she threw her arms around him. 'We must let Frankie know,' she gulped between tears. 'I wonder if Linda's bin able ter phone up.'

'I'll take a stroll up there an' tell 'er,' James volunteered.

'Would yer mind, luv?'

'Course not. I'll go right away,' he told her, needing to get away from all the unleashed emotion.

Ginny Coombes was fussing around Dick Conners. 'Well, where did yer put the bloody fing?' she asked him in exasperation.

''Ow the bloody 'ell do I know?' he replied. 'I was pissed at the time.'

'Tell me somefing I don't know,' she scolded. 'Yer always bloody pissed.'

'I dunno what yer makin' such a song an' dance about,' he growled. 'I got ovver shirts.'

'I ain't sendin' you out lookin' like a poppy show,' Ginny told him.

'Sendin' me out? Sendin' me out? Yer sound like my ole muvver.'

'I'm responsible for yer while yer under my roof, an' don't you ferget it, Mr Grumpy. That shirt yer so conveniently lost just 'appens ter be yer best one, yer one an' only best one. The ovvers 'ave got the collars and cuffs all frayed. I ain't sendin' you out in any o' them so yer better start lookin'. Understand?'

Dick went up to his room and continued the search there, while downstairs in the parlour a very irritated landlady looked around the room, puffing loudly. 'I can't understand that feller, really I can't,' she grumbled to Albert who sat watching her antics. 'I wouldn't mind but 'e's only got the one.'

'One what?' Albert asked.

'Don't you start. I ain't got time fer a deaf an' dumb lesson,' she growled.

'What yer lookin' for?' Albert asked.

'Dick's best shirt,' she screamed in his ear.

Albert jumped a foot. 'Yer'll end up doin' my ears in one day, woman,' he shouted back at her.

Dick came back into the room. 'Well, I've looked everywhere an' I can't find it,' he said in a subdued voice.

Ginny stroked her chin. 'That's a lovely shirt. I said so when yer got it, didn't I, Albert? Oh never mind. I said, never mind.'

Dick hid a grin. 'I'm sure I gave it ter yer fer washin' an' you put it in the copper an' then 'ung it out on the line,' he told her. 'Yeah, I'm sure yer did. I remember yer tellin' me not ter go gettin' smudges on it when I walked past it.'

'In that case it'd be folded up 'ere in this room ready fer

ironin',' Ginny replied. 'Eivver 'ere or in the scullery an' it's definitely not out there. I've 'ad the bloody room inside out.'

'Look, it won't 'urt me goin' in one o' me workin' shirts,' Dick told her. 'As long as it's clean an' pressed.'

Ginny puffed loudly. 'I can see it now,' she growled. 'There'll be someone big inspectin' the ole soldiers an' they'll come up ter you. It could be the Duke o' York or the King 'imself. "This is Dick Conners of Bermon'sey, yer Majesty," they'll say. The King'll look at yer nice suit I pressed for yer an' yer shiny row o' medals, then 'e'll spot yer frayed shirt. 'E'll fink yer tryin' to insult 'im. "Is that ole bastard takin' the piss?" 'e'll say. Then the flunkies'll whisk you off somewhere till the inspection's over. What a disgrace. They'll all blame me. "It's that Mrs Coombes who's ter blame. She's never got a shirt ready fer the poor ole bastard." '

Dick was laughing aloud at Ginny's carryings-on and she herself had to smile.

'What you two laughin' at?' Albert asked.

Ginny shook her head and Dick sat down to catch his breath.

'That's right, ignore me,' Albert moaned. 'I'm gonna make a cup o' tea.'

Dick watched him climb out of his chair and suddenly a big grin spread across his face again. 'Ginny.'

She followed his eyes and then, as she spotted the shirt, her face knotted up. 'Albert, yer bin sittin' on the shirt, yer great big lummox.'

'Shirt? What shirt?'

'God give me strength,' Ginny gasped. 'Dick, do us a favour, will yer? Take 'alf a crown out o' my purse an' fetch

203

me a stout from the off-licence, before I 'ave a nervous breakdown.'

Charlie Bradley whistled to himself as he walked along the quiet street. He had arranged to meet one of the punters at the Swan public house at nine sharp and Nick Carter had been suspicious. He had been monitoring Charlie's meeting places and he knew the Swan to be a haunt of some teara-ways from Dockhead known as the Malandane mob. He had already warned the punters not to do any business in that particular establishment. There was a risk of that mob seeing the money and goods change hands and they might well jump both the punter and his supplier. Charlie had met the contact previously and he did not think there was any need to worry, but Nick Carter had not been convinced.

Charlie walked into the public bar and ordered a pint of bitter. It seemed quiet enough, with a few old men sitting around over their drinks and one or two couples chatting together. He took his pint and found a table by the door, placing the bag at his feet. It was ten minutes to nine and the young man sat back and sipped his beer. Things had been going well and already his commission was building up nicely. He thought of Linda and wondered how her father was. Talking with her that lunchtime had instilled a strange sense of excitement in him. He wanted her badly, and now he was sure that she needed him just as much. She had made it apparent by the way she let him know that they would soon become lovers. It was a sweet gesture, wanting him to seal their love by carving her initial on the post. It was childish, maybe, but romantic nevertheless.

At nine sharp the punter walked into the bar and nodded

as he went to get a drink. Charlie watched him and thought that the man seemed nervous. He was glancing around and twitching his shoulders as he waited to be served. Finally he came over and sat down facing Charlie across the table. He was a short, slightly built man in his forties, with a pale face and shifty eyes. Charlie had already delivered an order to him and collected the money outstanding at a cafe in Dock-head and the transaction had taken place without a hitch. This time he had to collect over fifty pounds and give him a fresh supply.

'Yer got the necessary?' Charlie asked.

The man tapped his coat pocket. 'Yer got the stuff?'

Charlie smiled and reached down to his bag.

'Not 'ere,' the man said quickly. 'It's a bit risky. Outside in the gents.'

Charlie shook his head. 'It's quiet enough 'ere. Let's see the cash.'

The man became fidgety. 'All right, I need a leak first though. I won't be long.'

Charlie watched him leave the bar, warning bells ringing in his head. This could be a setup, he thought.

The punter came back a few minutes later and sat down again. He looked around the bar and then fished into his coat pocket and took out an envelope. 'There's fifty-two pounds there,' he said.

Charlie quickly counted the money and then put it safely away in his pocket. He took out a small carton from the bag and handed it over. 'That's yer full order. Thirty bottles,' he told him.

The man put it under his coat and got up quickly, walking out of the bar without another word, and Charlie's heart sank when he saw the frightened look on his face. He knew instinctively that he was going to be jumped as soon as he left the pub and he cursed himself for not taking heed when Nick Carter had warned him. He realised he had much to learn.

Charlie finished his pint and left the pub holding his breath. It seemed quiet enough as he glanced quickly left and right. He clasped the bag tightly and set off home. He had only gone a few yards when he was suddenly surrounded. Four well-built young men had come out of a doorway and stood leering at him. 'I fink we'll take a look in that bag,' one said.

'Piss off,' Charlie said with bravado.

'I don't fink so,' the young man said. 'Give us yer bag, pal.'

Charlie tried to push past them and a hard blow whacked into the side of his head. He staggered back and then they all jumped him. The bag was torn from his grasp and a boot thumped into his midriff. Suddenly he heard heavy footsteps. He was dazed from the punch to his head but he could see three of the men running away. The man who had first accosted him was being held by Nick's minders, Con Ashley and Don Jacobs.

'You all right, son?' Con asked.

'Yeah, fanks,' Charlie managed to reply.

'We've bin watchin' out fer yer. Nick was worried,' Don Jacobs told him with a wide grin, his flat boxer's face flushed with exertion. 'There's yer bag. Yer better be gettin' off 'ome. We've got a little bit o' business ter take care of.'

The man they were holding looked terrified. 'Let me go,' he panted.

'All in good time, pal,' Con told him. 'First though, yer

gotta be made to understand that our carriers 'ave right o' way on this manor. From now on they go un'indered.'

'It's understood,' the man gasped.

'It will be, very shortly,' Don said. 'But before that yer gonna need a lesson in obedience. Savvy?'

Con nodded to Charlie. 'Off yer go, son. This ain't gonna be very pretty.'

The man was dragged off and Charlie could not help but feel sorry for him. Both Con Ashley and Don Jacobs were ex-boxers, and they would no doubt make sure that their lesson stuck in the unfortunate man's mind.

Gilda came into the room and handed Nick Carter a drink before she slid down beside him on the large settee. 'Martin's gone to Glasgow. He phoned me earlier from the station,' she told him. 'He's due back next Tuesday.'

Nick smiled and pulled her to him. 'Remind me ter leave in good time,' he said smiling.

Gilda slipped her arms round his neck and kissed him hard on the mouth. 'I'll warn you, darling, in plenty of time,' she purred.

The phone rang and she reached over to the small marble-topped table beside her. 'It's for you,' she said, pulling a face.

Nick took the receiver from her and listened for a few moments, then his face relaxed. 'Well done, Don. Is Charlie all right? Good. See yer termorrer.'

Gilda waited till he put the receiver down then she snuggled up close. 'What was all that about?' she asked him.

'It's nuffink fer you ter worry yer pretty little 'ead over,' he said smiling.

'Patronising sod,' she said, nuzzling his ear. 'Tell me, Nick, were you serious about moving those drums?'

His face took on a worried look. 'I don't want you put at
any risk if fings get nasty, an' they could do,' he told her.

Gilda slipped her arm through his and nestled closer.
'Look darling. Those drums are as safe here as anywhere,
safer in fact. Leave them where they are. Come on, let's go to
bed.'

Chapter Twenty

Dora Weston was up early that Friday morning, but she barely had time to toast a couple of slices of bread under the gas-stove grill before James came hurrying down the stairs, still buttoning his shirt. He very rarely spoke more than two words first thing in the morning but today he was slightly more communicative. 'I expect we'll see a big improvement in Dad ternight,' he said, sipping his mug of hot sweet tea at the scullery table.

Dora nodded as she put the plate of buttered toast in front of him. 'It's obvious 'e's gonna be in a lot o' pain fer a few days but please Gawd 'e'll soon be on the mend,' she replied.

James finished his rushed breakfast and reached for his coat. 'I wonder 'ow Frankie's gettin' on,' he remarked.

'I bet 'e felt strange wakin' up in a different place,' Dora said, grabbing a teacloth as her son made for the door. 'Come 'ere, yer got grease all round yer mouth.'

James grinned as his mother tried to get the margarine off his face and he grabbed the cloth from her and did the job himself. 'See yer ternight, Ma,' he said as he hurried out of the house.

Linda came down to the scullery a few minutes later. She

had already eaten her breakfast and there was time to chat for a few minutes before leaving for work. 'Well, it's my last day at the wine vaults terday, Mum,' she remarked. 'I shan't be sorry ter go, though I'm gonna miss the gels.'

'As long as fings work out for yer,' Dora replied.

'Course they will. The new job can't be no worse than stickin' labels on bottles,' Linda told her.

'You mind yer time,' Dora said, getting up and refilling the kettle. 'I'd better rouse those kids or they'll be late.'

Once Linda had left the house, Dora poured a cupful of Quaker Oats into a heavy saucepan and stirred it thoughtfully for a few minutes while it came to the boil. She added a pinch of salt and turned the gas down before popping her head round the stairs. 'C'mon, you lot, or yer'll be late fer school,' she shouted.

'I'll be glad when September comes,' Pamela remarked as she stirred fresh milk into the stodgy mass of porridge on her plate.

'Yeah, I'll be glad when I leave school as well,' Tommy told her. 'I wanna work wiv James on the buildin'.'

'I wish I was old enough ter go ter work. School's borin',' Ben moaned, sprinkling a spoonful of sugar over his porridge.

'Yer'll soon wish yer was back at school, me lad,' Dora told him. 'Now come on, eat that breakfast up an' not so much talkin'.'

'My friend Carol's got a job at the clothes factory at Tower Bridge,' Pamela said. 'She earns good money. She's a machinist.'

'I've told yer before I don't want you workin' in a factory,' Dora said sharply. 'Yer'll do much better goin' in an office.

Some offices send their staff on typin' an' short'and courses.
Yer could end up bein' a secretary.'

Pamela did not seem too enthusiastic about this prospect
and she pulled a face as she shrugged her shoulders. Tommy
was busily stuffing food into his mouth but Ben had a few
more words to say. 'I'm gonna be a barrer boy when I leave
school,' he announced. 'My mate's bruvver's a barrer boy an'
'e earns a lot o' money.'

'Right, you lot, that's enough,' Dora told them firmly.
'Now c'mon or yer'll all be late.'

'Can we go in an' see Dad ternight?' Tommy asked.

'Me an' Linda's goin' in ternight an' there's only two
allowed round the bed,' Dora explained. 'You can see yer
dad in a few days' time, when 'e's feelin' a bit better.'

Breakfast over, the Weston children left for school, and Dora
allowed herself a few quiet minutes enjoying a cup of tea
before going off to the market. The neighbours and stallholders would all be asking about John and she would most likely
have to run the gauntlet. Doris and Phyllis would expect to be
the first to know and they were no doubt chatting together
outside at this very moment, she imagined.

The two viragos were indeed keen to get the news about
John Weston at first hand, and at that moment they were
standing outside Doris's front door.

'I'd go an' knock but she might fink we were just bein'
nosy,' Phyllis remarked.

'I shouldn't fink so,' Doris replied. 'After all, we are
neighbours.'

'I know what I'll do,' Doris said. 'I'll go an' ask 'er fer
change fer the gas,' reaching into her apron pocket for her
purse.

Five minutes later the two hawks walked out of the small backstreet into the busy morning market feeling prepared. Ten minutes later Dora set off to get her shopping, and she was not surprised that everyone she met already knew that her husband was making progress.

Dick Conners went to the baker's shop on Friday morning with Ginny's words ringing in his ears. 'Eivver try ter look 'appy, or tell the woman yer've decided not ter go,' she had said. 'Don't mess the poor cow about.'

'Hello, Dick. You look very spruce this morning,' Eve remarked with a big smile. 'Usual, is it?'

Dick nodded, feeling liverish and aware that he looked anything but spruce. 'I've polished up me medals all ready,' he said flatly, hoping that wearing them on his suit coat would put the woman off.

'How nice,' she said, still smiling at him. 'I'll be very proud to be escorted to the show by a veteran.'

'Will yer?' Dick replied.

'Why of course,' Eve told him enthusiastically. 'There'll be lots of veterans there.'

Dick picked up the hot crusty loaf from the counter. 'I'll see yer in the Bee'ive then,' he said with a long face.

Eve Jeffreys watched him leave, smiling to herself. He was trying to make her feel that he wasn't too keen on going to the show but she hadn't been fooled. Once he saw those smart old soldiers carrying themselves with pride he would soon start to think. He was one of them and would want to be every bit as upright and proud as they were.

Nick Carter sat at his office desk with his hands clasped on the leather top. 'I knew that particular pub spelt trouble,' he said. 'In future take notice, Charlie. We can't always guarantee a minder's gonna be on 'and ter nursemaid yer.'

Charlie nodded dutifully. 'I'm sorry, Nick,' he replied. 'I won't make the same mistake twice.'

Nick afforded himself a smile. 'As it 'appens Don Jacobs an' Con Ashley gave the geezer a good goin'-over,' he told him. ''E's got the message an' 'e'll pass it on, that's fer sure. Anyway it's all over an' done wiv. I'm more concerned now about that bruvver o' mine. 'E's got 'imself tied up wiv one o' the Kerrigans' women. Apparently the bird 'e's knockin' off is Sam Colby's sister-in-law. She's gone a bundle on 'im but Sam ain't too pleased – there was bad blood between 'im an' our Tony before this little episode. Tony 'ad too much ter drink one night an' insulted Colby's wife. I've warned 'im ter give this bird the elbow but 'e won't listen. I can see trouble brewin'. Tommy Kerrigan would love an excuse ter get 'is 'ands on this little setup but 'e needs the formula. That's our trump card.'

'S'posin' the Kerrigans came round 'ere mob-'anded an' walked out wiv those oils yer use. What then?' Charlie asked him.

Nick shook his head slowly. 'That won't 'appen,' he replied. 'We only bring enough in every day fer blendin'. We supply the Kerrigans wiv their cut-price order an' they're doin' very well on the deal. The only way they could better that would be if they produced it themselves. As it 'appens, nobody but me knows where the stuff's kept. That's the way it's gonna stay, at least till we know fer sure if someone's grassin' us up.'

George Morrison popped his head in the office, a serious

expression on his wide flat face. 'Sully's outside,' he said. ''E wants ter see yer.'

'Show 'im in, George,' Carter told him, then he turned to Charlie. 'We'll talk later.'

Detective Inspector Dan Sully came into the office and waited until Charlie had left before sitting himself down in the chair facing the desk. He was tall and overweight, and he sighed as he brushed his hand through his thinning fair hair. 'There was a message waiting for me when I got in this morning, Nick,' he said. 'Late last night one of our bobbies found Terry Malandane tied to a lamppost. He'd taken a bad beating. I've just had a word with the bloke but I couldn't get anything out of him. I suppose there's no chance of you being able to throw any light on it, is there?'

Nick Carter nodded. 'Malandane an' a few of 'is team tried ter jump one of our boys last night,' he replied. ''E 'ad ter be disciplined.'

'Look, I don't want a gang war on my patch,' the inspector told him sternly. 'Things are nice and quiet at the moment and that's the way I like it.'

'There's no fear o' that,' Nick replied. 'It could 'ave got a bit nasty, ter tell yer the trufe, but we've nipped it in the bud.'

'Just so long as I don't have to pull the rug from under you,' Sully said. 'You're getting a good living and I'm happy with the arrangement we've got. Apart from the perfume company whose stuff you're imitating, no one's getting hurt. Let's leave it at that. Don't spoil it for both of us by coming on too heavy.'

'You understand that if I don't get safe access fer my people all this is gonna fold like a deck o' cards,' Nick warned him. 'I'll only act when my lads are threatened. I've no ambitions outside my own manor, yer've got my word.'

'That'll do me,' Sully said, getting up. 'Oh by the way, what's the s.p. on the Kerrigans?'

'They're buyin' supplies direct from us an' pushin' 'em on their own manor,' Nick told him.

'Are they happy with that?' Sully asked.

'They've no choice,' Nick replied, smiling craftily as he reached into the drawer of his desk and took out a sealed envelope.

Sully slipped it into his coat pocket. 'Don't forget what I said,' were his parting words as he left the office.

Linda put the last of the bottles into a carton and arched her aching back. The day seemed to have flown by and now that the order had been finally completed there was time for Irene Cutler to make her little speech.

'We've all 'ad a whip round, Linda, an' we've got yer a little goin'-away present,' she said smiling as she took out a small parcel from her apron pocket.

Linda flushed up as she accepted the gift. 'Fanks very much. It's very nice of you all,' she replied.

'Go on, open it,' Fat Mary told her.

'Yeah, go on, we 'ope yer like it,' Doll added.

Linda tore the wrapping from the parcel and saw that it was a silver compact. 'Oh, it's really lovely,' she gasped.

'We got yer name inscribed on it,' Irene told her.

Kate Madigan dabbed at her eyes. 'We're all gonna miss yer, Lin,' she said in a croaky voice.

'I'm gonna miss you lot too,' Linda replied. 'I've 'ad some good laughs 'ere.'

Kate put her arms around her and hugged her tight. 'I'm

really gonna miss you, Lin,' she said tearfully.

Linda hugged each of her workmates in turn and then came to the forelady. 'Fanks fer everyfing,' she said quietly.

Irene made light of it with a wave of her hand. 'That's what foreladies are for. Now come on, all of yer, let's get off 'ome.'

Linda walked home in the warm summer evening with mixed feelings. She felt sad having to say goodbye to all her workmates, yet excited about the new job. It would mean that she could put some extra money into the home now it was needed, and she might be able to save a few shillings each week for some new clothes, the sort Kate Selby wore.

Ginny Coombes nudged Albert out of the way and reached up for the freshly ironed shirt that she had hung up on the parlour doorframe. 'There you are, an' don't get no smudges on it puttin' it on, d'you 'ear me?' she said sharply to the subdued-looking Dick Conners.

'Fanks, gel. Yer done that a treat,' he told her.

Albert was grinning as he stood watching Dick's reaction. 'Just mind yer don't get all paint an' powder on it,' he said chuckling.

'Eve Jeffreys don't wear paint an' powder, yer silly ole sod,' Ginny growled. 'She's a nice refined woman. Any man'd be proud ter be walkin' out wiv the likes of 'er.'

'I ain't walkin' out wiv 'er,' Dick was quick to point out. 'I'm just goin' ter this revue fing wiv 'er.'

'Well, it's as good as walkin' out wiv 'er. Anyway yer'll be able ter judge fer yerself what she's like after ternight.'

'Don't go gettin' pissed ternight, or that will do it,' Albert told him, the grin getting wider.

'Albert's right. Don't go showin' the woman up,' Ginny said. 'Just take it careful.'

'Bloody 'ell, Ginny, yer make me feel like some 'orrible ole git who don't know 'ow ter be'ave prop'ly,' Dick said quickly. 'I'll 'ave you know I used ter be pretty suave in the sergeants' mess, 'specially when we invited the officers an' their wives.'

'Yeah, well you ain't in no officers' mess now, me lad, so don't ferget yer manners, an' don't get in no arguments wiv anybody.'

'Who me? I'm the soul o' discretion,' he told her solemnly.

'Right, let's do that tie for yer,' Ginny grumbled, 'yer look like a bundle o' shit.'

When she was satisfied with her efforts the landlady helped him into his coat and gave it a last brush down. 'There we are. 'E looks quite smart, if I say so meself. Don't yer reckon so, Alb?'

'What yer say?'

'I said 'e looks quite smart.'

'I fink 'e looks quite smart, as it goes,' Albert said.

Dick gave them both a weak grin and made to leave but Ginny tugged at his arm. ''Ere, put that in yer pocket,' she said, handing him a pound note. 'The drinks might be dear in that place.'

The drunk gave his landlady a quick peck on the cheek. 'Fanks, luv. I'll give it yer back if I don't need it,' he said.

'It's all right – it ain't mine,' Ginny said grinning, 'it's Albert's bettin' money.'

''Ere, you ain't bin goin' down my winnin's, 'ave yer?' Albert asked as he saw the money change hands.

'Course not, yer silly old sod. That's out me 'ousekeepin',' Ginny replied, winking at Dick.

Dick Conners left the house and walked slowly along the turning. He could not remember the last time he had been out with a woman; certainly not since the war ended, he thought. Anyway it was supposed to be a good revue and he might meet someone he knew from his army days. Eve wasn't a bad-looker for her age and she had no objection to him having a drink. It might not be too bad after all, he concluded.

Chapter Twenty-One

Tommy Kerrigan leaned back in his chair and smiled at the men gathered around the table in the Rising Sun. 'Well, lads, it's bin a good first week,' he told them. 'We can 'andle all the stuff we can get. I'm gonna up the order fer next week.'

'Yer don't fink they'll put a ceilin' on it, do yer?' Bernie Kerrigan asked.

'I don't see any reason fer that,' Tommy replied. 'They agreed the price an' it's all cash in the bank fer them anyway.'

'It'll be cash in the bank fer us, once we get our 'ands on that oil they're usin',' Joe Kerrigan remarked.

'Yeah, well we gotta be patient,' he was told. 'Nick Carter's guardin' it wiv 'is life. Accordin' to our contact, none of 'is associates knows where it's bein' stored an' 'e's gotta tread very carefully.'

Sam Colby looked across the table at Tommy. 'What about Boy-boy? Wouldn't 'e know?'

'I shouldn't fink Nick Carter would take 'im into 'is confidence,' the gang leader replied. 'Boy-boy's a liability. 'E's prone ter gettin' boozed, an' we've seen 'im in action. Would you trust the geezer, even if 'e was family?'

Colby's jaw muscles tightened. 'Yer know my feelin's,' he growled.

Tommy Kerrigan took a sip from his glass and met Colby's gaze. 'Nick Carter's got a married woman in tow, so I've bin told,' he said. 'She's workin' at the arch. Apparently she brings in just enough o' the oil each day. She collects it from somewhere.'

'Yer don't fink she's storin' it at 'er place?' Colby asked him.

'It's a bit doubtful, but we can't discount it,' Tommy replied. 'Anyway, we'll just 'ave ter see what our man can come up wiv. In the meantime we'll play it nice an' cool.'

Sam Colby had other ideas but he held back from telling them his own view on how it should all be handled. Tommy Kerrigan was allowing their rivals to become too established, he thought. Their business was growing and with it their power. They would soon be in a position to exercise that power and market the perfume direct. Maybe Kerrigan and his brothers were content to tread the safe path but he was not. There had to be a confrontation sooner or later. Why wait until the Carters were in a commanding position?

The man who had just walked into the saloon bar was known to the Kerrigans and he waved a greeting as he spotted them. Colby gave him a quick wink and waited for an opportunity to talk privately to him. The chance came when Tommy Kerrigan drained his glass. 'I'll get these,' Sam offered.

As Sam put the empty glasses down on the counter the newcomer leant towards him. 'I've contacted Patrick an' 'e can sort it out,' he said quietly.

'When?'

'It'll take a couple o' weeks.'

'Can't 'e 'ave it ready sooner?'

'Yer gotta understand, Sam, the stuff ain't easy ter come by,' the man told him. 'Besides, it's gotta be assembled. There ain't no margin fer error, not wiv that stuff. It all takes time.'

'Right then, tell 'im ter get started soon as 'e can,' Colby said as he picked up the replenished glasses.

Dick Conners relaxed in the comfortable seat of the theatre and looked around. The plush red stage curtains were drawn and illuminated by soft light. The air was scented with various perfumes, and as he looked up at the ornate figuring Eve nudged him gently. 'Look, Dick, the orchestra are taking their places,' she whispered.

He nodded and glanced down at the programme he was holding but the print was too small for him to read without his glasses, and they were lying on the chair by his bed, the lenses having been shattered when he trod on them a few nights ago after a lengthy session at the Beehive.

'Would you care for a wine gum?'

Dick shook his head. The one drink he had had at the pub next door was still working on his system and he did not want to nullify it by sucking on sweets.

The conductor tapped his baton and suddenly the murmuring ceased. The lights dimmed and the music struck up, and without meaning to Dick Conners found that he was tapping his feet in time with the martial rhythm. When the overture finished and the orchestra leader had taken the applause, the show began with a rousing opening number. The sketches were based on life in the services and the individual artistes performed comical variations on the theme. Dick found himself chuckling at first and then as the show warmed up he was laughing aloud. Eve too was enjoying it and occasionally their eyes met in appreciation of what was going on.

After a very funny sketch in which the new recruit was trying to fit all his battle equipment together, the theatre lights came up.

'Let's get a drink,' Eve said.

They walked down into the bar and joined the throng at the counter. Dick could see that there were a lot of elderly men wearing campaign medals and he began to feel more and more relaxed. 'Lovely show,' he remarked to a veteran standing next to him.

'Jolly good,' the man answered in a cultured voice.

'Takes yer back, dunnit?'

'It does that.'

Eve had managed to catch the barman's eye and she ordered for them both. They found a seat and Dick took a long draught from his glass of bitter.

'That tastes like the nectar o' the gods,' he said gratefully.

'Are you enjoying the revue?' Eve asked.

'Yeah, I am,' he replied. 'It certainly takes me back.'

'You were in the army before the war, weren't you?'

'Yeah, before the second lot. I signed on in 1919. I was just twenty years old.'

'What made you do it?'

Dick studied his pint for a moment or two. 'Fings were bad at the time,' he told her. 'I was the youngest of a large family an' both me parents 'ad died. I was workin' in a tannery an' one day I got talkin' to an ole soldier who'd just started work there. The stories 'e told me about India an' ovver countries 'e'd bin to got me finkin'. I wanted ter see these places fer meself. Then one day the foreman at the tannery started ter give me some lip, so I got 'old of 'im an' chucked 'im in the tannin' pit. That was that. I went straight down ter the recruitin' office an' signed on the dotted line.'

'Did you ever regret it?' Eve asked him.

'Never,' he said firmly. 'Never once did I say ter meself, Dick, yer've made a mistake. Mind yer, it wasn't exactly a piece o' cake in some o' the places I served in, but like I say, the army gave me the chance ter see somefing o' the world an' it taught me what comradeship was all about.'

Eve nodded, her eyes searching his face. 'Would you mind me asking you a very personal question?' she said in a quiet voice.

'Fire away,' he replied.

'Why do you drink so much, Dick?'

He smiled disarmingly and looked down at his glass. 'I dunno really,' he said. 'Yes, I do. Course I do. I drink ter make me feel better. I've got a good friend in the bottle. Me best. When I'm drunk everyfing seems bearable. I can even tolerate meself.'

Eve's face looked sad. 'I can understand in a way,' she told him. 'When I lost my husband, life suddenly became meaningless. I struggled to face every day, and there were times when I thought about ending it all.'

'Yeah, me too,' he replied. 'I'd spent a lot of 'appy years in the army. There were good friends an' excitement, then suddenly it's all gone. Almost twenty years I done in the colours, then I was pensioned off wiv a disability. I'd lost a kidney, yer see. Anyway, wiv the war loomin' I felt there was

223

still fings fer me ter do, so I signed on as an air-raid warden.'

'Was there never a woman in your life, Dick?' she asked.

His face dropped. 'There was, but she was killed in the Blitz.'

'Oh, I'm sorry,' she said, looking down at her hands with a grave expression.

Dick nodded, twisting his mouth. 'That night in May when the last big air raid was at its worst I was wiv Sheila. That was 'er name. I 'eard the bomb fallin'; it was like someone shakin' a corrugated metal sheet. I grabbed 'er an' pulled 'er down on the floor. I remember shieldin' 'er wiv me body an' then the lights went out. When they finally dug me an' Sheila out from under the rubble I was still alive an' she was dead. That's why I drink, Eve. Ter kill the pain. Ter ferget that one night in May.'

'No one should be alone wiv those memories, Dick,' Eve said quietly. 'Do you still feel so alone? You've got Mr and Mrs Coombes, and . . . well, there's me too . . .'

'I'm beyond redemption, luv, an' I'm not the sort o' person you should be wastin' yer time wiv,' he told her with a cold smile.

The second half of the performance was about to begin and as they stood up to leave Eve slipped her arm through his. 'Let me be the judge of that,' she said in a quiet voice.

The balmy night brought little breeze and the velvet sky was full of stars as the two strolled down the Strand. They reached a little public house and Eve tugged on Dick's arm. 'We could have a drink here if you like,' she said smiling. 'We've got time before the last train.'

Dick Conners was suddenly filled with remorse. He had

wanted her to be shocked by his behaviour, embarrassed by him flaunting his medals and put off by his coolness towards her, but she had taken it all with a smile, returning his lack of grace with nothing but kind words. She was a good woman who had known heartache herself and she seemed to have a warm spirit. 'I'd be delighted to buy you a drink,' he told her with comical grandeur.

They sat in a corner of the lively pub and chatted over a pint of bitter and a port and lemon. Eve was telling him about her liking for the theatre and her interest in the Women's Guild when she suddenly became quiet. Dick noticed a change in her expression and he touched her hand gently. 'Is there anyfing wrong?' he asked quietly.

'I can be such a fool sometimes,' she answered in a sad voice.

'What d'yer mean?' he asked.

'Oh, it's nothing really. It's nothing for you to concern yourself with.'

'Looking at that sad face, I am concerned,' he replied quickly. 'Tell me. What's upset yer?'

Eve smiled wanly. 'I live a comfortable life,' she told him. 'I have my friends and my interests and I have no desire to take another man into my life, and I should be content, but no. I suddenly see myself as a crusader, a saver of souls, and to be perfectly honest I go about it like a bull in a china shop. I saw you as the ideal person to save. I can do it, I told myself. I could see it clearly too. With my help and support you'd become an upright, happy soul who had cast out John Barleycorn and I would be looking around for other poor mortals to save. God, how stupid I am!'

'Yer far from stupid, luv,' Dick said kindly. 'Yer've got a

feelin' fer people. Yer concern yerself, an' that can't be bad. Yer could 'ave steered me past this pub, an' preached ter me about the evils of strong drink like ole Frederick Charrin'ton did to all those people over the Mile End Road way back in the eighties, but yer didn't. Yer talked ter me an' brought me out o' meself. Whatever yer was finkin' of don't matter. It's what yer done that counts. Yer've enjoyed yerself an' so 'ave I, an' I didn't fink I would. The way I see it, we're both adults who lead our own lives the way we see fit. We can be advised an' encouraged ter change, Gawd knows I 'ave bin, but at the end o' the day we do what suits us. As fer me, I'll most likely go on doin' what I've bin doin' fer the past ten years. I've got too much of a taste fer it now. It's part o' me.'

She looked into his sorrowful eyes, knowing that there was nothing more she could say, nothing more that would reach him, and she squeezed his hand in hers. They left the pub and walked the short distance to Charing Cross Station where they boarded the last train to Catford. Dick got off at London Bridge and left her with a cheery wave and a smile. 'See yer termorrer, gel,' he told her. 'Don't be late fer work.'

Up on the roof the young folk gazed up at the pinpoints of light and made their own secret wishes. Jenny Jordan snuggled close to her young man and whispered into her ear as they hid in the shadows. Some distance away Kate Selby and Peter Ridley were feeling slightly less romantic.

'You weren't even careful,' she complained.

'What was I s'posed ter do?' he asked her.

'Yer could 'ave said no,' she suggested.

'You're the one who's s'posed ter say no.'

'I got strong feelin's an' I can't turn 'em on an' off like a tap,' she went on.

'That goes fer me too,' he sighed in exasperation.

'Anyway it's all right. I started terday.'

'Yer might 'ave told me before yer started leadin' off,' he growled.

'I wanted ter frighten yer.'

'Well, yer did.'

'Good, I'm glad.'

'I sometimes wonder if yer really love me.'

'Course I do,' she told him.

'Well, yer got a funny way o' showin' it.'

'Peter?'

'Yeah?'

'Cuddle me gently.'

'Oh, all right.'

Behind the stairway roof and the chimney pots Bill Simpson stood by his pigeon loft talking with Jack Marchant. 'I watched 'em from up 'ere, Jack,' the older man said. 'They was up an' down the street wiv their tape measures an' their clipboards.'

'It don't mean nuffink,' Jack replied. 'It could be somefing ter do wiv the drains, or the electrics. They 'ave ter take measurements.'

'Nah, it was in the local paper some time ago,' Bill told him. 'I remember it well. They was talkin' about pullin' the 'ole lot down an' buildin' a modern block o' flats 'ere. Right over Eagle Street.'

'Who was?'

'Why, the Borough Council.'

'They ain't got no bleedin' money fer new flats,' Jack said

dismissively. 'They can't even maintain the ones they 'ave got. Take that block in Tooley Street. Fallin' down round their ears, it is.'

'Those buildin's don't belong ter the council,' Bill told him. 'They're private just like these.'

'Nah, the council took 'em over. They bought the lease, so I bin told.'

'Who told yer, that scatty mare next door ter yer?'

'Nah. Someone else,' Jack replied.

'Anyway, I see the men wiv them tape measures an' I ses ter meself, aye, aye, what's goin' on 'ere,' Bill went on. 'I got worried. Not fer meself, yer understand. I was worried about what was gonna 'appen ter me birds. I mean ter say, yer can't take 'em in those new flats they put up these days.'

'Nah, it's a bloody shame,' Jack agreed. 'The same fing 'appened to ole Jumbo's mate, Phil Mascall.'

'What did?' Bill asked.

Jack took off his cap and proceeded to scratch his bald head. 'Well, Phil Mascall lived in one o' those old 'ouses in Dock'ead,' he began. 'Now Phil kept chickens an' rabbits in 'is backyard an' one day 'e won a pig in a raffle.'

'Yer takin' the piss, ain't yer?' Bill said quickly.

'Strike me dead if I'm tellin' a lie,' Jack replied with passion. 'Phil 'ad bin on a coach outin' ter the country an' they all went in this pub in Kent. All the locals was goin' in the raffle an' Phil went in just fer a laugh. Course the laugh was on 'im. 'E won the pig an' 'e 'ad ter bring it 'ome on 'is lap. It shit all over 'im, it did. Stunk the bloody coach out. The driver wasn't very pleased, as yer would imagine, nor was the rest o' the passengers, but anyway Phil gets it 'ome

228

an' builds a little pen for it in 'is backyard. It was quite a big backyard as it 'appens.'

'Yeah, it'd 'ave ter be,' Bill remarked yawning.

'Now ole Phil become really attached ter this porker,' Jack went on. ''Is ole woman wanted 'im ter do it in fer the Christmas table but 'e wouldn't 'ear of it. 'E treated it as one o' the family, an' finkin' about it the bloody fing looked like 'alf 'is family. Anyway, one day they all got notice down the street. The places 'ad bin condemned, yer see. Now Phil's ole woman's over the moon. She can't get out quick enough, but Phil finks ovverwise. 'E's more worried over 'is chickens an' rabbits, an' this pig what's grown really fat. Now when the council man calls ter look fings over Phil tells 'im 'e wants a place wiv a backyard, an' when the man asks why 'e takes 'im out an' shows 'im the pig an' the rest o' the menagerie. You can imagine this geezer's face. Livid 'e is. 'E tells Phil that if the pig's not out o' the place in twenty-four hours the council are gonna serve a summons on 'im.'

'So what 'appened?' Bill said impatiently as Jack took time out to light his pipe.

'Phil told 'im ter piss off,' Jack continued. 'Next fing there's the police an' the 'ealth inspector, an' Gawd knows who else all knockin' at Phil's front door. The newspaper reporters were there too, an' the photographers. There's always one comic in the bunch an' when one o' the reporters asked this bloke about the pig 'e told 'im it wasn't a pig at all, it was Phil's ole muvver-in-law who'd come ter stay fer a while. Well ter cut a long story short, Phil finally agrees ter give the pig up as long as a good 'ome's found fer it. Now while they're ummin' an' ahhin', Phil's ole woman slaughters the pig an' 'angs it up be'ind the carsey door. Anyway the council van turns up an' when they go ter collect the animal it ain't in the pen. Phil told 'em it must 'ave 'eard 'em comin' 'cos it suddenly snorted an' then jumped over the wall. Phil's ole woman told 'em that someone shouted over the wall to 'er that the pig 'ad bin seen leggin' it over Tower Bridge.'

'Didn't the men see the carcass 'angin' up on the carsey door?' Bill asked him.

'Nah, the door was swung back, yer see,' Jack told him. 'Anyway ter make a short story shorter, everyone in the street 'ad pork fer their Sunday dinner that week, all except Phil that was. The poor bastard was in mournin' fer that porker. Strange when yer come ter fink of it 'ow people get attached ter pets.'

'Yeah, yer right,' Bill replied as he leaned on the balustrade and looked out over the rooftops at the moonlit sky. 'When I go I want yer ter release all them birds.'

'But they'll come back,' Jack said.

'No, they won't. Not if yer shut the loft up. They'll know it's time ter find a new nestin' place.'

'What about Monty?' Jack asked. ''E won't fly off. I fink the bleeder's fergot 'ow ter fly.'

''E will, you mark my words,' Bill told him.

Chapter Twenty-Two

John Weston sat propped up with pillows on Saturday afternoon, his face pale and drawn, but he managed the occasional smile as he chatted with Dora and Linda. 'So 'ow are you an' Charlie gettin' on?' he asked.

'Ter be honest, I've not seen much of 'im this last week,' Linda told him, looking downcast. ''E 'as ter work awkward hours on this new job of 'is.'

'What about you? You won't 'ave ter do the same sort of hours, will yer?'

'I'm in the office, Dad. It'll be nine till five,' she said smiling.

'Our little office gel. Fancy that,' John said affectionately.

'It'll certainly be a nice change from the wine vaults, that's fer sure,' she told him as she gathered up her handbag. 'Look, Dad, I'm gonna give you an' Mum some time on yer own. I'll see yer termorrer.'

John smiled at her as she bent and kissed his forehead, then he reached out and clasped Dora's hand as the two of them watched Linda walk away down the ward. 'D'yer fink she's 'appy?' he asked.

'Yeah, but she's missin' Charlie,' Dora said.

'What about this new job she's startin'? It sounds a bit dodgy ter me,' he remarked.

'Yeah, it does ter me too,' Dora replied, 'but she's old enough ter make 'er own mind up, luv. We ain't got the right to interfere.'

'We're still 'er parents though,' John told her. 'I don't wanna see 'er get inter bad company.'

'Charlie's a good lad,' Dora said quickly.

'I know that. I'm talkin' about the Carters,' he replied.

'I don't fink yer need ter worry. Our Lin's a sensible gel. If fings wasn't right she'd soon leave,' Dora told him. 'She could always get anuvver job.'

John seemed satisfied and he gave her a smile. 'What about you? D'yer miss me?'

'Course I do,' she said coyly.

John's face was wreathed in a smile. 'Six kids we've 'ad tergevver an' I can still bring a blush ter yer face,' he chuckled.

Nick and Tony Carter had had a hard upbringing in Bermondsey. Their father had drunk himself into an early grave and their mother had struggled on alone, compelled to take in washing to make ends meet. The boys ran the streets and soon got into bad company – the local policeman's knock on the door was a common occurrence. A few clips round their ears and a good telling off were enough to keep the lads out of serious trouble, but when their mother died of pneumonia and the old and respected beat bobbie retired, the two boys ran riot. A well-meaning aunt and a few of the neighbours contrived to keep the family house clean and tidy and they cooked meals and did the washing and ironing, until Nick Carter was called up midway through the war and his younger brother was sentenced to one year in Borstal for looting bombed properties.

With the rent running into large arrears the landlord decided to repossess the family house, and when Tony Carter came out of Borstal he was compelled to find lodgings. The war over, Nick Carter returned to Bermondsey and soon became involved in the flourishing black market. Along with Tony he made a good living 'ducking and diving', as he described it, and soon he was able to rent a small terraced house for the two of them in Abbey Street. Nick Carter had big ambitions and he recruited a few hard characters who had fallen on bad times and were not too fussy about what they did for a living.

George Morrison was the first to join the Carters. He had been a talented amateur boxer but had had the misfortune to be spotted by a shady manager, who took him on as a professional and mismatched him until the young man was almost punch-drunk. Every up-and-coming heavyweight fought George and in boxing circles he eventually became a laughing stock.

Nick Carter had taken an interest in boxing, often going along to the local gym to watch the fighters train, and it was there that he first got to know George Morrison. He felt sorry for the likeable character who was now employed as a sparring partner and general dog's-body and he offered him a job helping in the yard he had rented in Abbey Street.

George Morrison proved to be a loyal servant and Nick knew he could be trusted to keep quiet about the devious goings-on there. Now, across the road in the arch he had become the overseer. He was responsible for supplies and deliveries and worked closely with Gilda, who had taken a liking to the quiet hulk of a man who said very little.

On Saturday afternoon Nick Carter worked alone at the arch. He had blended a new batch of perfume ready for an early start on Monday and had taken an inventory of phials, labels and the fancy packaging. He intended to change a tyre and do a service on the Commer van which was garaged in the yard across the street, but there was time first for a break, and as he brewed tea on a gas ring he was deep in thought. Someone had leaked information to the Kerrigans and he was puzzled as to who exactly might have been responsible. It might well have been one of the women innocently chatting to a neighbour who had passed it on, but he could not rule out the possibility that it was one of his associates.

As he sipped his tea Nick mulled over the problem. George Morrison could not even be considered, he told himself. He would bet his life on the man's loyalty. What of the others though? Con Ashley, Don Jacobs and Billy Nelson were all ex-fighters whom he had known since he was a kid on the streets, and had come recommended by George Morrison. Their hard looks and ability to handle themselves very well had been the main reason they were recruited. Other gangs jealously guarded their own areas but sometimes they had ambitions to spread out in to other areas. Only when they saw powerful opposition were they dissuaded. Nick Carter had realised early on that it was the law of the jungle, a dog-eat-dog world where only the fittest survived.

The loud ticking of the clock and the occasional rumble overhead as a train went by were the only distractions in the heavy silence as Nick Carter went through a list of suspects in his mind. Con Ashley and Don Jacobs were close friends who could be relied upon to deliver the perfume orders to their respective punters without fear of attack from local villains. They were well known locally and both had lots of contacts, which resulted in them earning very good commissions on top of their basic income. Both men were in their early forties, married with grown-up children, and neither had ever shown any desire to become businessmen in their own right. They went along with his decisions and rarely questioned them.

The other member of the team, Billy Nelson, was the youngest, and Tony's personal friend. Short and stocky, his rugged complexion, deep-set grey eyes and sandy hair made him a favourite with the ladies and he never lacked female company. Self-assured and fearless, he had been on hand to ease Tony out of many a scrape, and together they led a very charmed life with the women they came into contact with. According to Tony, he was currently involved in a torrid relationship with a married woman whose husband was serving a long sentence for armed robbery. Like the other members of the team, Billy Nelson went along with policy, although he would always back Tony all the way. He too was earning very well from the business and Nick thought it very unlikely that any of them would be in the pay of Kerrigan and his crowd.

As improbable as it seemed, Nick could not get rid of his gut feeling that information was being leaked back to his rivals from someone close, and he realised that the only way to satisfy himself was to adopt a process of elimination. To that end he pondered long into the afternoon.

Charlie called at the Weston home in the late afternoon and arranged with Linda to have a night out together after he had made a delivery in Dockhead. He had been very secretive and as she got ready Linda was feeling happy. She had missed him all week and was beginning to think he was losing interest in her, though she tried to convince herself that it was not the case. He had to work during the evenings and she knew how determined he was to make a success of his new job. They went along with his decor...

Linda brushed out her shoulder-length fair hair and then heated up her curling tongs over the gas. Her hair waved to her satisfaction, she applied a light powder base to her face and used a very pale shade of lipstick. Her best emerald-green cotton dress had been pressed ready and she had bought herself a pair of silk stockings at the market to go with her black patent shoes. Charlie would be calling for her very soon and she wanted to look her best. She smiled to herself as she dabbed a touch of Elegance behind her ears and on her cleavage, and then picking up her small patent-leather clutch bag she went downstairs to wait.

Dora was getting ready to visit John at the hospital and she smiled appreciatively as Linda twirled round in front of her. 'Yer look very nice,' she said. 'Come 'ere, let's fix that dress, there's a piece o' cotton 'angin' down.'

''Urry up, Mum, Charlie'll be 'ere any minute,' she said anxiously.

'Now calm down,' Dora told her quickly. 'The lad won't mind waitin' a second. Yer wouldn't wanna look anyfing but yer best, now would yer?'

Pamela came into the scullery and gave her sister a saucy whistle. 'You look nice,' she remarked.

Tommy had followed her into the room and he watched idly in the doorway as his mother knelt down to adjust the dress.

'It's the seam come loose,' Dora said.

'Oh no!' Linda gasped.

'Now, don't get all agitated, it won't take a minute. Tommy, go an' fetch me my sewin'-box. Down by the armchair.'

''Urry up, Tommy,' Linda called out in panic.

'Gis a chance,' the young lad yelled back.

A few minutes later the job was completed and Dora grunted as she got up from her knees. 'It 'ad ter be fixed or you'd 'ave caught yer 'eel in it,' she said.

Linda gave her mother a grateful smile. 'Am I OK?' she asked.

'Yer look really nice,' Dora told her.

She sat down straight-backed at the table and immediately there was a knock on the front door.

'That'll be Charlie,' Linda said, jumping up quickly and kissing her mother on the cheek. 'Give my love ter Dad.'

Charlie stood on the doorstep holding a brown paper parcel. He was wearing a grey single-breasted suit with a blue shirt open at the neck, his dark wavy hair brushed back from his forehead. He smiled approvingly as Linda stepped out and his smile widened as she slipped her arm through his.

'It won't take me a few minutes ter deliver this an' then the night's our own,' he told her cheerfully.

At number 9 Eagle Street Ginny Coombes was finishing off her portion of haddock and she glanced up at Dick Conners across the table. 'Wasn't that nice?' she asked him.

'Yeah, it was lovely, but I wasn't all that 'ungry,' he replied.

'I dunno what's wrong wiv yer,' Ginny said sharply. 'Yer bin mopin' about all day. Ain't yer feelin' well?'

'I ain't bin mopin' about,' Dick replied quickly. 'I went down the market fer a stroll this mornin', then I went up the Bee'ive fer a pint or two, then I come back fer a nap. I ain't exactly bin sittin' about all day.'

'Well, yer don't look yerself,' Ginny insisted as she laid her knife and fork down on her empty plate.

'What's the matter wiv yer fish?' Albert asked.

'I ain't 'ungry,' Dick told him with a sigh.

'Ain't you 'ungry?'

'No,' Dick shouted at him.

Albert got on with his meal and Ginny reached for the teapot. 'I was wonderin' if yer'd 'ad words last night,' she probed. 'Yer seemed very quiet when yer come in.'

'No, I never 'ad words,' Dick told her. 'As a matter o' fact, I 'ad a good night out an' we didn't 'ave words.'

'Yer never said if Eve 'ad anyfing ter say about last night,' Ginny went on. 'Yer saw 'er this mornin', didn't yer?'

'No, I never. She wasn't in this mornin'.'

'That's unusual fer 'er. She don't lose any time as a rule.'

'I was just wonderin' if she's all right,' Dick remarked.

'So that's why yer bin all moody,' Ginny said nodding her head. 'Yer like 'er, don't yer?'

'She's very nice as it 'appens,' Dick said quietly.

'Will you an' 'er be goin' out again?'

'We ain't made no plans.'

'But yer might?'

'I shouldn't fink so.'

'Why not?'

Dick puffed loudly. 'Look, Ginny, she just asked me if I wanted ter go to a show wiv 'er, that's all. She thought I might like it, as it was a service revue. She ain't got no designs on me, nor me on 'er.'

"Ow d'yer know about 'er?' Ginny pressed him. 'She likes yer, she said so.'

'We 'ad a long chat,' Dick told her. 'We both agreed we're a bit too long in the toof ter change our ways. I got my way o' carryin' on an' she's got 'ers.'

'We all 'ave ter make some changes when we get ourselves attached to anyone,' the landlady went on. 'Look at me. I was the belle o' the street at one time, not so's yer'd know it now. I could 'ave 'ad me pick o' the young men, an' look who I chose.'

Albert was carefully buttering another slice of bread, blithely unaware that he was being discussed.

'I bet 'e cut a dash when 'e was a young buck,' Dick remarked.

Ginny's eyes softened and she nodded her head slowly. 'As a matter o' fact, Albert wasn't the best-lookin' man in the street, but 'e was the kindest, most lovely feller a gel could wish for. D'yer know what? The first day 'e asked me out I 'ad 'alf a mind ter turn 'im down, but there was somefing about the way 'e asked me. I dunno what it was, but I just couldn't say no. That was more than forty-five years ago an' I ain't bin able ter say no to 'im since. Yer wouldn't fink so, just lookin' at 'im, would yer?'

Albert looked up and saw them both staring at him. 'Whassa matter wiv you two?' he asked. "Ave I got me dinner round me face or somefing?'

'Get on wiv yer grub, yer silly ole sod,' Ginny told him with a big grin.

Dick Conners leaned back in his chair. 'I fink I'll give the pub a miss ternight,' he said quietly.

'Gawd 'elp us,' Ginny exclaimed. 'Yer must really be feelin' ill.'

The two young people strolled hand in hand down Shaftesbury Avenue, through the West End theatre crowds and the milling visitors to the metropolis, and Linda sighed happily. The film had made her weep and she had felt Charlie's hand tightening over hers at the crucial moment when the lovers said their last goodbye. She knew that the story had touched him too and she was pleased. They had left the cinema in Leicester Square and strolled along to a little restaurant off Regent Street where they enjoyed a meal of grilled plaice served with new potatoes and peas. The sweet was hot apple pie with cream and they had lingered over strong coffee. Charlie asked her if she wanted a brandy with it but she had declined. It was the first time she had visited a West End restaurant and to start with she had been very nervous of doing something wrong. They were in a secluded position, however, and Charlie had encouraged her to relax, smiling at her in that special way of his.

Now, as they reached Charing Cross Road and turned towards Trafalgar Square, Linda thought how magical the night was. High above the bright lights and the bustling crowds, stars twinkled in a velvet sky, and the air was balmy, as it might be in some far-off tropical land. Charlie was close to her, happy and attentive, her father was making steady progress after his operation, and a new chapter was about to begin in her life. Yes, it was all just right.

'Yer know what I'd like ter do right this instant?' Charlie said suddenly.

'Tell me,' she smiled at him.

'I'd like ter take yer in my arms an' kiss yer breathless,' he said softly.

'Soon, Charlie,' she told him. 'Up on the roof, in our secret spot.'

'Let's get the fast train,' he said, rolling his eyes suggestively.

Chapter Twenty-Three

Nick Carter was on hand on Monday morning when Linda arrived at the arch. 'Look, I've got some business ter take care of,' he told her. 'I'll introduce yer ter Gilda. She runs fings 'ere. She'll get yer started, OK?'

As soon as Nick had left the office, Gilda smiled at Linda and waved her arm theatrically. 'This is your domain,' she declaimed. 'Don't let the fellers take liberties by lounging about the office. Just tell them to vamoose.'

Linda looked a little frightened and she smiled nervously at the striking redhead. 'I've never worked in an office before,' she told her.

Gilda smiled kindly. 'There's nothing to it. Just pick up the phone when it rings, open the mail every morning, and there's not much of that, and file papers in that ugly-looking cabinet over there. Make yourself a cup of tea when you feel like it and generally make yourself at home.'

Linda started to feel better. 'I know you must be kept busy, but can I come ter see yer if I get any problems?' she asked.

Gilda nodded. 'Of course you can. I used to have to combine this with the rest of the work and it was me who

243

coaxed Nick into taking someone on. He wasn't too keen at first. You understand how difficult it is bringing a stranger into this setup, but once he knew that young Charlie was coming in and you and he were together he grabbed the bull by the horns, so to speak.'

'I just 'ope I can do a good job,' Linda said.

'You'll be fine,' Gilda assured her. 'One thing though. Be careful when Boy-boy's about. Charlie's probably told you what he's like and you might already know anyway, but I wouldn't be doing the right thing if I didn't warn you. Between you and me, Tony Carter is a lecherous, no-good sod who tries it on with everybody. Give him half a chance and he'll have your knickers off. I detest the feller, and he knows it. He pestered me once and I told Nick. He sorted him out. It's never happened since. I'm sorry if I've frightened you but you need to know the score.'

Linda smiled. 'I'm not frightened of 'im,' she told her. 'We all grew up tergevver in the street an' 'e knows me an' Charlie are datin'. Charlie wouldn't stand fer any ole nonsense.'

'Good fer 'im,' Gilda replied. 'I like Charlie. He's a nice lad.'

The phone rang and Linda jumped, to Gilda's amusement. 'Go on then, love, answer it,' she told her.

Linda picked up the receiver and pulled a face at her. 'Hello, Carter Brothers here,' she said in her best voice. 'Oh, I see. Yes, I will. Goodbye.'

'Who was that?' Gilda asked, her green eyes widening.

'Tommy Kerrigan. 'E wants ter double the order fer this week,' she told her.

Gilda's face became more serious. 'We can cope with it,

but I don't know if Nick'll agree,' she said. 'Anyway it's up to him. He'll be back soon. I'd better be getting back out there. Just make yourself at home, Linda. Sort the office out to suit your own working and don't forget I'm on hand if you need any advice.'

'I'm really grateful, Gilda,' Linda told her.

The redhead paused in the doorway. 'By the way, did you know me and Nick are a number?'

Linda nodded smiling. 'Charlie did tell me.'

Dick Conners woke up early on Monday morning and rolled on to his back, painfully aware how his body was protesting. On Saturday evening he had fought the urge to go to the Beehive and that night he had found sleep almost impossible. On Sunday lunch time he had gone along and limited himself to two pints of bitter. He had felt ill in the pub, and after dragging himself home he sat alone in his room in agony. His stomach was seized by cramp and his chest pounded. He expected to die there in the darkness and his heart went out to Ginny and Albert Coombes. They had taken him in and cared for him when he most needed kindness and now he was going to die miserably without being able to thank them for their generosity and compassion.

The knotting in his stomach eased and Dick said a few silent words of prayer for his deliverance. He had felt upset and confused during the weekend but things were much clearer to him now. His mind was alert and lucid, and he put his hands behind his head and stared up at the cracks in the ceiling. He had been worried about Eve Jeffreys, fearing the worst. He had imagined her pinned under the wreckage of a train or lying in a hospital bed after a terrible accident on her way home. She had given up her free time to accompany him to a show, feeling that she could help him, and in return he had been less than grateful, in his thoughts at least. Ginny was right: Eve was a good woman. Her kindness had touched him and he had wanted to prove to himself that he could change for her sake, as a sort of private tribute to her. It had been madness and he realised only too clearly now that any change he wanted to make in his life would have to be gradual. Years of heavy drinking had altered his body, befuddled his mind and taken away his self-esteem. He could not expect to change overnight, not even for Eve.

Dick climbed from his bed and washed himself in cold water. He was feeling better when he went downstairs and he gave Ginny a smile.

'I 'eard yer last night,' she told him. 'I sent Albert in ter see what was wrong. I thought yer was dyin', the bloody noises yer was makin'. It frightened Albert too.'

'It must 'ave bin the cramp,' Dick told her sheepishly.

'Cramp? More like the bloody D.T.s, if you ask me,' she growled. 'Anyway yer better sit down. Albert, pour 'im a cup o' tea while I do the toast.'

'Ginny, I've bin a bloody fool,' he said meekly. 'I tried ter do wivout gettin' sloshed over the weekend. I stayed in Saturday night an' I only 'ad a couple on Sunday. Me insides must 'ave bin rebellin'.'

'Why the sudden change after all these years?' Ginny asked him.

'I've got ter dislike meself, that's why,' he told her. 'I've 'ad it driven 'ome ter me in no uncertain way.'

'That woman's bin gettin' on ter yer. I knew it. I could see

246

it in yer face when yer walked frew that door on Friday night. I said to Albert there was somefing wrong wiv yer. She should mind 'er own business. It ain't nuffink ter do wiv 'er or anybody else fer that matter what you do. If yer wanna get pissed every night it's up ter you, nobody else.'

Dick waited patiently till she had finished her tirade and then he looked into the old lady's grey eyes. 'Listen, Ginny. I really 'ad a good night out. Eve went in the pub wiv me an' never once did she say anyfing to upset me. In fact I was more than surprised the way she was. Like I told yer yesterday, we 'ad a good chat an' she agreed that we were both too old ter change our ways, an' she also let slip that she 'ad no plans ter take anuvver man on. She's got no designs on me, luv.'

'Well, that's all right then,' Ginny said quickly. 'Now when yer've 'ad yer toast yer better get over the shop fer me loaf before they all go.'

Boy-boy Carter started up the Commer van and revved the engine for a while to warm it up. 'I tell yer, Billy, if it was down ter me I'd 'ave given Kerrigan's mob the elbow straight away,' he growled. 'It seems every time they want somefing our Nick jumps. Fancy 'im agreein' ter supply that pile o' crap wiv our gear. Next fing we know our own manor'll be swamped by their punters. If it was down ter me I'd stop tradin' wiv 'em pronto.'

Billy looked serious as he lounged against the door of the vehicle. 'If yer did that it'd certainly force Kerrigan's 'and,' he remarked.

'Too bloody true,' Boy-boy growled. 'That's what's needed. I can't stand this softly-softly approach. Us an' the

Kerrigans are never gonna exist tergevver. One or the ovver of us 'as gotta bow out, an' I ain't intendin' it ter be us. If we let 'em get established wiv this perfume they'll be wantin' more an' more till the day comes when we can't supply. They'll be powerful enough by then ter take over this setup an' we'll end up wivout a pot ter piss in.'

Billy stepped away from the Commer as Carter crashed in the gear, and when the van was outside the yard he closed the gate and snapped the padlock back in place. Boy-boy drove the van across the street at speed and screeched to a halt outside the arch, and as Billy followed him over he jumped out of the cab and slammed the door with an angry expression on his baby face. 'I'm just a poxy delivery boy fer that load o' crap,' he said with venom.

He swaggered into the arch and saw George Morrison standing by a stack of cartons. 'Is that the lot?' he asked him.

'Yer gotta wait till Nick comes back,' George told him. 'Gilda said the order might be changed.'

The younger Carter gave him a quizzical look and walked over to where the women were seated round a long wooden bench. Gilda was chatting to one of the workers and she looked up as he came over. 'Tony, Tommy Kerrigan's phoned in. He wants the order doubled from today,' she told him.

Boy-boy's face took on a hard look. 'What did Nick say?'

'We're waiting for him to come back,' she replied. 'He shouldn't be long.'

Carter stormed away cursing, and the women exchanged surreptitious smiles.

'I can see a confrontation,' Gilda told them under her breath.

Linda was going through the sheets of paper that were strewn over the desk and she looked up as Boy-boy walked into the office.

'So yer decided ter join us,' he said.

Linda smiled. 'Yeah, why not?'

Boy-boy came over and sat on the edge of her desk. 'Seen much o' Charlie lately?' he asked, giving her a lecherous grin.

Linda had known him since they were kids on the street but had always kept her distance. She had always been frightened by his aggressive attitude and general manner, but things were different now. She was part of the setup here and would have to deal with him, like it or not. 'Yeah, we went out over the weekend,' she told him calmly.

'I don't s'pose 'e's got much time fer courtin' these days,' Boy-boy remarked.

Linda gathered up a pile of papers and shuffled them neatly together. 'We manage,' she replied with a smile.

He looked at her intently, searching for some sign of encouragement or weakness. 'If Charlie starts ter neglect yer you come an' see me,' he told her, grinning.

Linda met his gaze. 'If Charlie starts ter neglect me I'll be 'avin' words wiv 'im,' she said quickly.

'I bet yer a little fireball,' Carter said, his eyes moving over her as she got up and walked over to the filing cabinet.

'P'raps you should ask Charlie that question,' she told him cuttingly.

Boy-boy's smile left him and he got up from the desk and made for the door. 'Did Nick say 'ow long 'e'd be?' he asked her.

'Gilda said 'e should be back soon,' Linda replied.

As he walked out of the office Nick stepped into the arch. 'Ain't you delivered that lot yet?' he said.

'Yer better talk ter Gilda,' Boy-boy told him.

'Nick, Kerrigan wants the order doubled this week,' Gilda called over to him.

The gang leader stood thinking for a few moments then he nodded. 'Yeah, that's all right, if we can 'andle it,' he called back.

'No problem,' Gilda replied.

'Right then, Tony. Yer can start loadin' that lot an' I'll get George ter bring the rest out ter yer.'

Boy-boy gave him an icy look and stormed out of the arch. Nick smiled self-consciously and followed him out. ''Ave you got the needle?' he asked.

His younger brother rounded on him. 'Yer bet yer life I got the needle. Why did you agree to up the order? Why didn't yer tell 'em ter get stuffed?'

'I got my reasons,' Nick told him sharply. 'At the moment, if Kerrigan wanted ter treble the order I'd accommodate 'im, an' I'll tell yer why. I'm givin' 'im enough rope to 'ang 'imself. 'E didn't fink we could cope wiv the doublin' up, an' a refusal was all 'e'd need ter fink 'e could start screwin' us. We might not be able ter guarantee deliveries to our own punters an' they'd probably be 'ammered too.'

'Yer mean ter say Kerrigan's mob would move in on us?' Boy-boy queried. 'I don't fink 'e'd try it on our manor.'

Nick took his brother roughly by the arm. 'Now, you listen ter me,' he growled. 'You know that Charlie Bradley got jumped last week in Dock'ead by the Malandanes. What yer don't know is that one o' Kerrigan's mob set it up.'

''Ow did yer find out?' Boy-boy asked.

'I've just bin down the station ter see Sully. I'd phoned 'im last week ter see if 'e could find out whevver Terry Maland-ane 'ad bin approached by anybody ter do the business. The way I figured it, the Malandanes are just aggravaters, they ain't got a brain between 'em. They wouldn't know 'ow ter go about settin' anyone up. Anyway Sully leaned on Terry Malandane an' put the fear o' Christ into 'im. 'E told 'im 'e was gonna fit 'im up wiv somefing if 'e didn't come clean. Take it as gospel, Kerrigan was be'ind it.'

'So what do we do about it?' Boy-boy asked him angrily. 'Yer said just now yer givin' 'im enough rope to 'ang 'imself. What yer got in mind?'

Nick leaned against the back of the van and folded his arms. 'As I said, Kerrigan thought we couldn't supply the double order, an' the reason why 'e thought that is 'cos 'e was told.'

'What yer gettin' at?' Boy-boy asked, frowning.

'Kerrigan found out about this setup an' then 'e got ter know that we was runnin' low on supplies because there's a grass feedin' 'im the information,' Nick said quietly. 'Yer see, we wasn't runnin' low. I got Gilda an' George ter store most o' the filled cartons out o' sight. They purposely left only a few on the bench. It was just a feelin' I 'ad that whoever's grassin' us up would notice the shortage an' let Kerrigan know. I expected right from the start that Kerrigan would try an' put pressure on us ter supply more o' the perfume than we could manage. So I wasn't surprised when Gilda told me 'e'd bin on the phone.'

The younger Carter looked subdued. 'Who is it, Nick?' he asked, narrowing his eyes.

'I've spent a lot o' time puzzlin' it out an' I fink I've got a good idea,' he replied. 'I'm callin' a meetin' termorrer night at the Bee'ive. I want everyone there. An' listen, Tony, I want no argument from you, whatever I say or whatever I come up wiv. Just stay calm an' let me do what I gotta do. Will yer go along wiv that?'

Boy-boy nodded. 'Yer'll get no grief from me,' he said firmly.

George Morrison had the rest of the order ready and the van was soon loaded. Boy-boy locked the back doors and climbed in the cab, and as he started the engine Nick walked up to the door. 'Kerrigan might 'ave primed 'is ole woman up, so if she does ask 'ow the stock's goin' when yer make the delivery just say we're workin' flat out an' just about copin'. OK?'

When the van pulled away Nick went back into the arch and saw George and Billy Nelson talking together. 'The Bee'ive, eight o'clock, termorrer night. OK?'

The men nodded and he walked into the office. 'Well, 'ow's my new secretary copin'?' he joked.

Linda flushed slightly. 'There's bin two phone calls,' she told him. 'I've written the messages on the pad by the phone, an' there's the mail opened ready. I've filed away all the papers.'

'Well, that's a good start,' Nick replied. 'Yer'll find it'll be quiet fer a few days but we're settin' up a phone-in system, so yer'll be kept pretty busy takin' orders. By the way, I want yer ter buy some National Insurance stamps, an' keep the women's cards stamped up ter date. Gilda'll go over it wiv yer first. There's nuffink ter worry about.'

Linda had seen the cards in the filing cabinet and she took them out to check the amount of stamps needed, feeling happy that there was something she could get on with.

Nick Carter left the arch and strolled through the morning sunshine. That lunchtime he had arranged to meet with some lorry drivers from a local haulage firm, who had suggested distributing orders outside London. It could be a good deal, he thought, but the nagging feeling persisted that Tommy Kerrigan was scheming. True to his word he had put the drivers in touch and things were running smoothly at present, but it would only last while the location of the base oils used in the perfume remained a secret. If Kerrigan ever found out where the drums were being hidden he would certainly seize them by force, blackmail, or any other means he could devise. Nick Carter knew he had to expose whoever it was that was passing the information, and quickly.

The gang leader walked into the Crown public house at Dockhead still turning things over in his mind. Tomorrow night's meeting would sort it all out, he told himself, provided the bait was accepted. If his hunch was right then it would be poetic justice. A few years had passed, but he still remembered her words ringing in his ears. He had to face the possibility that his past had come back to haunt him.

Chapter Twenty-Four

Doris and her next-door neighbour Phyllis were looking very pleased with themselves on Monday morning as they stood in the street chatting together.

'Yer could 'ave knocked me down wiv a feavver when she said 'er an' Dopey Dick were goin' ter see a show,' Doris was going on. 'I couldn't believe it.'

'I was the same,' Phyllis replied. 'What really surprised me though was seein' 'im walkin' up the street on Friday evenin' wiv all those medals on.'

'It must 'ave bin one o' those ex-servicemen's shows they're puttin' on,' Doris remarked. 'I tell yer what, I bet ole Ginny 'ad a rare old time gettin' 'im ready. 'Is suit was all nice an' pressed an' 'e was wearin' a clean shirt too.'

'His boots too. They was all polished,' Phyllis reminded her. 'It just shows yer what 'e could be like if 'e 'ad a mind to.'

Doris folded her arms and scratched her elbow. 'I ain't seen 'im comin' out the pub pissed neivver, not since Friday.'

Lucy Perry and Maggie Gainsford came along the turning carrying shopping bags and chatting together.

'We was just talkin' about old Conners,' Doris told them as they drew level.

'Why, what's 'appened to 'im?' Maggie asked.

'Nuffink. Well, nuffink bad,' Phyllis told them with a smug smile. 'Dick's courtin'.'

'No,' Maggie replied with raised eyebrows, trying to look surprised.

'S'right,' Doris said. ''E's walkin' out wiv Eve Jeffreys from the baker's.'

'Good Gawd,' Lucy exclaimed. 'Who'd 'ave thought it.'

'I fink 'e's off the piss too,' Doris added.

'Well, if she's managed ter get 'im off the booze she deserves a medal,' Lucy remarked.

Maggie Gainsford had a soft spot for the street's drunk and she did not like to hear him run down indiscriminately. The man had always treated her with respect and he never passed by her children without a few kind words. What was more he had often knocked with a bagful of fruit when one of them was sickly. 'There's nuffink wrong wiv ole Dick that a good woman couldn't put right,' she said forcefully. ''E's just lonely, but I tell yer what, 'e'd make a good 'usband. The man's 'eart's in the right place.'

Doris and Phyllis did not want to disagree with their neighbour. They were feeling very charitable that morning and wanted everyone to know that they had played a part in Dick's good fortune. 'Yer quite right, Maggie. It's just what I was sayin' ter Doris,' Phyllis told her. 'As a matter o' fact, we was talkin' ter Ginny Coombes only last week an' we were the ones what told 'er that Eve in the shop 'ad 'er eye on Dick. Didn't we, luv?'

Doris nodded her head vigorously. 'No one wants ter see the feller settled down wiv a good woman more than we do. I fink she'll be the makin' of 'im.'

Maggie wanted to tell them both that they were a pair of two-faced, interfering old goats, but she managed to refrain. 'She's a nice woman, Eve,' she said nodding.

Lucy Perry nodded too. 'I've not seen much o' Dick this weekend,' she remarked. ''E normally stands outside my winder on the way 'ome from the pub an' sings a song or two.'

'I tell yer what, Eve wasn't in the shop on Saturday,' Phyllis told them. 'Me an' Doris was surprised. Wasn't we? I ses to 'er, aye, aye, they must 'ave 'ad a good time last night. Eve 'ardly ever loses any time.'

'She's in this mornin', though,' Doris said. 'We was gonna ask 'er 'ow they got on, but the shop was packed. It don't do fillin' people's mouths so we didn't say anyfing. I expect she'll tell us on 'er way 'ome. She normally stops fer a chat.'

Dick Conners was feeling much better after seeing Eve that morning and as he stepped out of his front door he had a happy expression on his face, until he spotted the gathering at the end of the turning. He walked towards them, hiding his displeasure. Maggie Gainsford was a good woman and Lucy Perry had never given him any reason to dislike her but the two hawks were a different kettle of fish, he told himself. The interfering old biddies would get their comeuppance one of these days.

'Mornin', ladies,' he said cheerfully.

'Mornin', Dick,' they chorused.

'Anuvver nice one,' Maggie said smiling.

Dick glanced at Doris and Phyllis, who were looking more sanctimonious than ever. 'If yer see Eve, will yer tell 'er I'm in the Bee'ive gettin' sloshed?' he asked them. 'Tell 'er there's a drink waitin' for 'er.'

Maggie and Lucy exchanged a quick glance and smiled at each other but Doris and her friend looked horrified as they watched Dick walk away, a wicked grin on his face.

'Did you ever,' Phyllis gasped.

'The man's beyond it,' Doris said, shaking her head.

Dick Conners chuckled to himself as he sat sipping his pint of bitter. He had been overjoyed that morning to find that Eve was safe and sound. She had given him a friendly smile and told him that she overslept on Saturday morning after their late night out. He told her how worried he had been to find that she hadn't arrived for work on Saturday, and mentioned in passing that he was going to be in the Beehive at lunchtime if she cared for a drink. He warned her that the hawks would no doubt be hovering, wanting to know everything that went on.

'Watch'er, Dick. 'Ow's it goin'?' Wally Gainsford said as he walked in with the midday edition of the *Star* under his arm.

'Not so bad, Wol,' Dick told him.

''Ow's yer love life? I've 'eard all about it,' Wally said grinning widely.

Dick Conners' face remained serious. 'Me an' Eve Jeffreys went out ter see a show tergevver 'cos she 'ad a spare ticket,' he sighed. 'That was it, Wol, nuffink more. So I wouldn't go listenin' ter the tittle-tattle. They'll all 'ave me married off in no time.'

Wally collected his pint from the counter and sat down beside the drunk. 'I'm on lates terday,' he said. 'I was just gonna try an' pick a few winners out. By the way, Dick, I wouldn't want yer ter fink our Maggie's bin gossipin'. She don't give it 'ouseroom.'

'I know that, Wol. Yer got a good 'un there,' Dick told him.

'Jus' so's yer know,' Wally said.

'As a matter o' fact I've asked Eve ter pop in fer a drink,' Dick remarked, picking up his glass. 'I dunno if she will or not.'

Wally nodded and put on his tin-rimmed glasses. 'I'm gonna do an 'alf a crown win double terday,' he said. 'I've 'ad a tip. If they come in, the money'll go on gettin' Maggie an' the kids away fer a week at Margate. Maggie likes Margate.'

Dick sipped his drink quietly while Wally Gainsford immersed himself in the runners and riders at Ascot. The two old biddies would no doubt pass his message on word for word, and hopefully Eve would see the joke. It would be nice to have another quiet chat with her that lunchtime. She had been a good listener and had been very honest with him, as he had with her. She understood the situation but he hoped they would remain friends.

Wally left the pub to put his bet on and ten minutes later Eve looked in the door and saw him sitting alone at the table. 'I've just been talkin to Doris and her friend Phyllis,' she told him with a smile. 'They were quick to point out that you would most likely be under the influence by now.'

Dick smiled back at her. 'What is it, a port an' lemon?'

'No, I think I'd like a nice shandy, if you don't mind, Dick,' she told him.

'Comin' right up,' he said, getting out of his chair.

Bert Warner gave him a knowing look as he passed over the shandy. 'I 'ope yer not gonna lead 'er astray, Dick,' he said with mock seriousness.

'I'm gonna drop some fag ash in 'er drink an' then 'ave me way wiv 'er,' he replied with a straight face.

Eve delved into her handbag and took out a small mirror which she held up to her face, moving her little finger along her bottom lip to smooth the pale lipstick she had on. She noticed the slight puffiness under her eyes and the lines around her mouth and sighed in resignation. Joe used to tell her she had a face that looked lived in but was still a very attractive woman, and she had been inclined to believe him. Joe had never been one to give out compliments profusely, in fact he had never had much to say for himself at the best of times. How she missed him though. Thirty-five years was a long time to be together, and he was the only man she had ever been with. Never once, until last Friday, had she been alone in another man's company, but she did not feel guilty. Joe would approve, she felt sure. Dick Conners was a nice man despite his heavy drinking, and he reminded her of Joe in a lot of ways.

'There we are,' Dick said, placing the glass down on the table in front of her.

Eve took a quick sip. 'You've cut yourself shaving,' she remarked.

'Yeah, me 'and was none too steady this mornin',' he told her. 'I ain't bin drinkin' much over the weekend. I was worried sick in case anyfing 'ad 'appened to yer.'

'You shouldn't have. I was all right,' she said smiling.

'Yeah, but I wasn't ter know, was I?' he replied. 'I was imaginin' all sorts o' fings.'

'So laying off the drink makes your hands shaky,' she said. 'I would have thought it was the other way about.'

'Maybe wiv most people, but wiv me I'm as steady as a rock once I've 'ad a few,' he told her with a grin.

Eve took another sip from her glass then put it down on

the table. 'Dick, I hope you don't think I'm being pushy,' she said tentatively, 'but I may be able to get a couple of tickets for a very good play that's coming to the West End soon. Would you like to come? Say no if you'd sooner not. I'll understand.'

The drunk stroked his chin thoughtfully for a few moments. 'Eve, I like yer company, an' I'd like ter see a West End play,' he said quietly, 'but ter be honest I don't fink it's a good idea. We talked about us on Friday night. We're both set in our ways an' fings could get complicated. I mean yer a smart, attractive woman, an' if I was lookin' fer female company I'd be over the moon ter be walkin' out wiv you.'

Eve smiled. 'It's all right, you don't have to explain, Dick. I understand. You're probably right. Things could get complicated.'

They finished their drinks in silence and then Eve picked up her handbag. 'Well, I'd better be going,' she told him. 'I've got a woman friend calling tonight. I've enjoyed the drink.'

Dick sighed sadly as he watched her leave. Maybe he was being a fool in not nurturing the friendship, he thought, but what could he offer her? He couldn't raise himself to her level, only bring her down to his. No, things were better left as they were.

He got up and walked over to the counter. 'Fill it up, Bert,' he said.

Charlie had enjoyed a lie-in that morning and when he finally walked into the front room, May Bradley gave him a searching look. 'Don't you 'ave ter clock in on that job of yours?' she asked him.

Charlie grinned. 'I fix me own times, Ma,' he replied, picking up the teapot. 'I do a lot o' the business in pubs an' dockers' clubs an' the like. It's a lot of evenin' work.'

'I don't like the sound of it,' she told him sharply. 'It's not a real job. 'Ow long's it gonna last?'

Charlie felt irritated as he poured the tea. 'Course it's a real job,' he answered. 'I'm earnin' a sight more pushin' perfume than I would be pen-pushin'. Besides, it's varied. I can meet people, fix me own times an' please meself what I do, plus the fact that I don't 'ave ter bow an' scrape ter some tuppenny-'a'penny office manager. "Yes sir, no sir, three bags full sir".'

May was not satisfied and she shook her head slowly as she watched him tip cornflakes into a cereal bowl. 'What's gonna 'appen if that perfume company find out yer usin' their trademark?' she asked him. 'They'll take yer ter court.'

'That's the Carters' problem. I let them worry about that,' he told her. 'I'm only a salesman.'

'Yer in it wiv 'em an' you'll be roped in as well,' May told him. 'Yer farvver must be turnin' over in 'is grave.'

Charlie swamped the cornflakes with milk and then sprinkled sugar over them. 'Look, don't worry, Ma,' he said, sighing with exasperation. 'I'm only in it until I can get a few bob be'ind me. Then I'm gonna start up meself.'

'Doin' what?' his mother asked quickly.

'I bin finkin' o' goin' inter the 'olesale business,' he replied. 'I'll rent an arch an' peddle the stuff meself till I get established.'

'That sounds as chancy as the perfume,' May said dismissively. 'I dunno what's got inter you since yer come out the army.'

'I'm finkin' more clearly, that's what,' he told her quickly. 'I've got plans.'

'I've 'eard that said before,' she replied. 'I can see you endin' up wivout a penny ter yer name an' an 'ouseful o' kids runnin' round yer ankles. Yer'll be sorry then. Yer'll wish yer'd taken my advice an' gone back in the office.'

Charlie pushed the bowl away from him and leaned back in his chair. 'Look, Ma, I ain't got any plans ter get married too soon,' he told her quickly. 'Anyway, me an' Linda's not even engaged yet, an' she's gotta put every penny in at 'ome while 'er farvver's off sick.'

'Yeah, but what 'appens if yer get the gel pregnant?' May said cuttingly.

'She's not a slut, Ma. We're not 'avin' it off,' he said angrily.

'I didn't say she was but these fings do 'appen,' May retorted. 'No one knows what's in the cards.'

Charlie sighed in resignation. He could see that his mother was getting upset and knew that she would use her tears to try to force her will upon him, the way she always had, even when his father was alive. 'Listen, Mum,' he said quietly. 'I understand 'ow worried you are, but in a year or two yer'll see that I was right an' yer'll be pleased for me. Besides, I'll be able ter make life easier fer yer. Yer'll 'ave the fings yer've never bin able to afford before. I'll pay fer yer to 'ave a nice 'oliday somewhere.'

'You're gonna do a lot,' she replied sarcastically. 'Yer'll need all yer money ter get married. Fings won't be no better fer me, it'll still be the same as it always 'as bin, 'and ter mouth.'

'Yer shouldn't spend so much time sittin' 'ere durin' the

day worrin' about fings,' Charlie told her quietly.

'I wish I didn't 'ave to,' May replied. 'I wish I was well enough ter go back ter work but yer know I can't. Me nerves won't stand it. Doctor Swain said I need more time. 'E understands 'ow I am.'

Charlie sighed wearily. She had been like this for six months or more, he realised, and the doctor seemed to be content to pander to her instead of encouraging her to pick up the pieces of her life. 'Why don't you go an' stay wiv Sara an' Cedric fer a few days?' he suggested. 'The change'll do yer good.'

'You just don't understand, do yer?' she rounded on him. 'My nerves ain't up ter lookin' after young Peter, an' that's all I'd be doin' if I went there. Besides, Cedric don't 'ave much ter say fer 'imself ovver than work. Nah, I'd much sooner stay where I am.'

Charlie felt it was useless to carry on, unless he wanted to end up as depressed as she was. 'Well, I'd better be off,' he said. 'By the way, don't wait up fer me, I've got me key.'

Chapter Twenty-Five

Nick Carter let himself into the terraced house in Abbey Street and immediately knew that Mrs Samuels had been in. The place reeked of fly spray and everything was neat and tidy. The passage had been swept and the parlour dusted and polished. There was a pile of ironing folded neatly on the scullery table, and his freshly pressed grey summer suit was hanging up over the door. He found a new loaf in the bread bin and an unopened pint of milk and the butter dish standing in the stone sink with a wet cloth over them. There was some cheese in the larder and a bowl of fruit on the dresser.

Nick smiled to himself as he slipped off his shirt and shoes. It was a hot day and Mrs Samuels had no doubt agonised over what to do about the food, he thought. She was a treasure. Nearing seventy and still very sprightly, she came in every day to clean and tidy up, making sure as well that there was enough to eat in the house. Often the bread would go stale and the milk curdle when he was staying with Gilda and Tony was with his lady friend, but Mrs Samuels persevered, happy to do so for the generous wages she earned.

Nick made himself a cup of tea and cut two thick slices of bread. The butter was almost liquid but the cheese was fresh, and when he had made the sandwich he took it into the parlour with his mug of tea and sat back in the armchair. Gilda's husband was home from his trip and would not be going off again until Thursday, which meant he would have to get Mrs Samuels to stock up on food. He would have to remind her about that fly spray too. The place stank of it and his eyes were beginning to itch.

The clock had stopped and Nick switched on the wireless to get the correct time. His housekeeper was very efficient but she steadfastly refused to touch the chimer after the time she attempted to adjust it and one of the hands fell off.

Nick was deep in thought as he sipped his tea, waiting for his younger brother to arrive. The meeting tonight would have to be handled very carefully and Tony needed to be put in the picture and told exactly what his role would be, he realised. There was no margin for error. It was a bad business. In the aftermath questions would be asked and answers demanded, and he would have to be prepared. The whole sordid truth would have to come out eventually.

Linda had spent the afternoon bringing the women workers' insurance cards up to date with help from Gilda and time had flown. The clock said quarter to five and the two women sat sipping tea.

'All you need to do now is make sure the cards are stamped every week,' Gilda told her.

'I've still gotta get ter grips wiv the filin' system,' Linda said.

'I shouldn't worry too much,' Gilda replied smiling. 'Nick

seems to use that filing cabinet as a dustbin. Any system you start up must be an improvement. Anyway, you are settling in OK?'

'Yeah, I like it,' Linda told her. 'It's very different from the wine vaults.'

'Tony Carter's not been making a nuisance of himself, I hope?' Gilda asked.

'No, I've not seen much of 'im, ter be honest,' Linda replied.

'I won't be seeing much of Nick for a couple of days, outside of work that is,' Gilda said grimacing. 'My husband's home. Terrible, isn't it? I bet you think I'm a real scarlet woman.'

Linda laughed aloud. 'Course I don't.'

'We are what we are, I'm afraid,' Gilda sighed. 'I love Nick, but I love my husband too, in a different sort of way. I wouldn't do anything to hurt him, and I'd never leave him. He needs me, but not in the way Nick does. Fortunately Nick understands and accepts things the way they are.'

'Does your 'usband suspect anyfing?' Linda asked her.

Gilda ran her finger round the rim of her cup. 'I'm sure he does,' she said quietly, 'but he never talks about it. We lead separate lives. He travels a lot and I never ask him about what he gets up to, and he never quizzes me about what I've been doing. It's an arrangement that wouldn't work for most couples, but it does for us. You need to know Martin to understand. He's my third husband actually. As a matter of fact I married my first husband when I was nineteen. He was killed at Dunkirk six months later.'

'I'm very sorry,' Linda said quietly.

'Alan was my first love and I'll never forget him as long as I live,' Gilda told her, still fingering her cup. 'There were thousands of women just like me. Young women who got married and were widowed shortly afterwards. My biggest regret is that I never had his child. I dearly wanted to get pregnant but there was so little time.'

Linda felt an effortless closeness to the woman. She had never met anyone so open and honest before. 'I 'ope I 'ave children,' she told her.

'With Charlie?'

'Yeah.'

'Are you sleeping with him yet?'

Linda flushed slightly. 'No, not yet.'

'Well, you just be careful when you do get round to it,' Gilda warned her. 'There's plenty of time for kids. Enjoy each other. Learn to please him and make sure he pleases you too. That's the secret. Your children will be conceived in love then. They'll be wanted and loved and I'm sure the two of you will be very happy. Well, that's enough of my preaching for one day. Come on, let's get off home.'

The Carter team had gathered together in the saloon bar of the Beehive and Bert Warner remarked on the fact to Gladys. 'It looks like they're 'avin' a bloody board meetin',' he quipped.

'As long as they've not brought any choppers wiv 'em,' Gladys remarked smiling.

Tony Carter ordered the drinks and carried them over to the far table where the team were sitting, all looking a little apprehensive. Charlie Bradley glanced from one to another and could see from the expressions on their faces that they were wondering what the hastily called meeting was all about.

'Right then, lads, let's get started,' Nick told them. 'Ter begin wiv, I want yer all ter know that we've got a problem. The base oils we're usin' are runnin' very low. I fink we can only count on two more days, at the rate we're goin'.'

'We can get a fresh supply, can't we?' Con Ashley asked.

Nick shrugged his shoulders. 'When I first picked up the drums I was told there'd be more where they came from. As a matter o' fact a dozen drums in all were smuggled inter the country. Four were bought straight away by a team from Glasgow an' we took two fer starters wiv an option ter buy four more.'

'What's the problem then?' Billy Nelson asked. 'Surely we can just go an' pick 'em up?'

'That would be the natural assumption, sure, but the customs 'ave bin sniffin' around an' they've 'ad ter be moved,' Nick told them.

'Are yer sayin' that yer don't know the new location?' Don Jacobs cut in.

'Oh yeah, I got a phone number all right, an' the name o' the contact,' Nick replied, looking very serious. 'I wrote it down in the office diary. The trouble is, it's gone missin'.'

'Yer jokin', ain't yer?' Con Ashley said sharply.

'I wish I was,' Nick told him, matching his angry stare. 'It went missin' last week. It was always on the desk, by the phone. I've turned the office upside down an' I've bin frew the arch inch by inch. It's nowhere ter be seen.'

'Yer mean ter say someone's deliberately nicked it?' Billy Nelson queried. 'I can't believe that.'

'The only ovver explanation is it's bin mislaid,' Nick

replied. 'But where? The book never leaves the office. It's got me beat.'

'Are yer dead sure it ain't in the office?' Don Jacobs asked.

Nick nodded. 'Definitely.'

'It wouldn't be in the van fer some reason, would it?' George Morrison asked him.

The gang leader wanted to hug him. It was the response he had been hoping for. 'That's the only place I've not looked, ter tell yer the trufe,' he replied, stroking his chin and looking thoughtful. 'I'll take a dekko first fing in the mornin'. If it's not there I dunno where else it could be.'

'What about termorrer's orders?' Charlie asked him.

'They're already packed ter go,' Nick replied.

Billy Nelson looked angry as he eyed his boss. 'So the trufe o' the matter is, one poxy book goes missin' an' we end up goin' out o' business,' he growled.

'That's about the strength of it, I'm afraid,' Nick told him. 'Anyway it's not come ter that yet. It might be in the van, or there's a chance it might miraculously turn up, if whoever's nicked it 'as a change of 'eart.'

'None of us 'ere would wanna take it, surely?' Con remarked, looking round the table.

'What about the women?' Billy asked. 'Could one o' them 'ave took it out the office?'

'They never go in there, they've got no reason to,' Nick replied. 'Anyway I've always kept it locked when I go out, 'cos o' the money stored in there.'

'Well, let's 'ope it's in the van then, fer all our sakes,' Don Jacobs said, picking up his pint.

Nick Carter waited till he saw the chance then he gave Tony the signal with a brief wink. 'Look, I've gotta meet

Gilda in a few minutes,' he told the group. ''Ere, Tony, get everyone a drink.'

Boy-boy took the pound note. 'Yer better not keep 'er waitin' or she'll 'ave yer guts fer garters,' he joked.

Nick left the pub and hurried along the quiet Tower Bridge Road knowing that he had played his part well. The rest was up to Tony.

The Beehive was reasonably quiet that Tuesday evening and the landlord found time to stand at the counter talking to an elderly customer while he polished the glasses. He was feeling quite pleased that Boy-boy Carter had taken him into his confidence a minute or so before when he came over to place the order.

'I won't be a second, Sid,' he told the customer, popping his head into the public bar. He came back and gestured over at the far table. 'Tony, yer wanted in the public bar,' he called out.

'Who is it, Bert?' he asked.

'It's a lady,' Bert replied.

Boy-boy's eyes widened and he grinned at the rest as he got up. 'I won't be five minutes,' he told them.

A pale moon was rising in a clear sky as the group left the Beehive and went their various ways. One of the men walked quickly along Tower Bridge Road and turned right into Abbey Street, glancing behind him to make sure no one was following. He walked along purposefully, his mind on the job in hand. He stopped at the yard and felt into his pocket for the key to the padlock. Checking that the street was deserted, he opened the gates and stepped inside. He climbed into the Commer van and a few moments later he gave a grunt of satisfaction as his hand closed over the thin book that was wedged down the back of the passenger seat. He quickly jumped out of the cab and closed the door quietly. Suddenly a beam of light blinded him and he shouted in fright as he shielded his eyes.

'I see yer've found what yer came for, Billy.'

'I . . . I was jus' passin' so I thought I'd take a look,' he said quickly.

Nick lowered the torch slightly. 'Don't try ter lie yer way out of it, Billy,' he said slowly. 'We both know why yer here, don't we? It's OK. I might 'ave bin tempted ter do the same meself, if I was in your shoes.'

Billy Nelson's face screwed up with hate. 'Yer mean if I'd killed your sister, 'cos that's what yer done, as good as stickin' a knife in 'er yerself. Sendin' 'er ter that backstreet butcher to 'ave your baby cut out of 'er,' he sneered bitterly. 'Yer know somefing? The saddest fing is, she could 'ave kept it. 'Er 'usband who she was so terrified of died in action a few weeks later, you dirty bastard.'

Hidden by the darkness, Nick Carter's face had gone white. 'So yer decided ter sell yer soul ter Kerrigan,' he said icily. 'That way yer'd not only bring me an' Tony down but everyone else involved wiv us. Why didn't yer come an' face me? I'm the one who caused yer the grief. Why, Billy?'

'Don't fink fer a second I bottled out,' he snarled. 'If it 'ad bin left ter me I'd 'ave cut yer froat first opportunity. It's a promise I made ter me muvver on 'er death bed that keeps you alive, that stops me from doin' yer. She'd promised Josie never ter say who the farvver was – what d'yer fink that done to 'er, Carter? She watched 'er daughter die, 'cos o' you, an' there was nuffink she could do. When she lay there at the end, ramblin', it was your bloody name she kept repeatin', the thought o' you an' what yer done that was torturin' 'er, but she made me promise not to kill yer.'

'I guessed yer'd found out, some way or ovver,' Nick said slowly. 'As soon as I knew someone was leakin' ter Kerrigan I 'ad you in the frame. I never knew you was Josie Kelly's bruvver, till yer went to yer muvver's funeral. Me an' Tony watched it. Someone who knew 'er well told me then that she'd bin married twice an' 'er first 'usband's name was Nelson.'

'So now yer know it all,' Billy growled.

'Yeah, that's right,' Nick told him. 'I also know that I've gotta live wiv it. Just as you've gotta live wiv what you've bin doin'. Yer muvver told me once that my past would come back to haunt me one day. P'raps it always 'as.'

Billy threw the book he was holding on to the floor. 'I'll be wiv Tommy Kerrigan from now on,' he said bitterly as he shouldered past. 'Yer days are numbered, Carter. I'll see yer crawlin' in the gutter before I'm frew.'

Chapter Twenty-Six

Linda leaned on the balustrade and stared out at the City lights. 'The week seems to 'ave flown by,' she sighed.

Charlie slipped his arm around her waist and pulled her closer to him. 'Yeah, what a week,' he replied. 'Everyone was shocked ter find out what Billy Nelson 'ad bin doin'.'

'Gilda said terday that fings are gonna get rough,' Linda told him. 'What exactly did she mean, Charlie? I asked 'er but she wouldn't say no more.'

'When Nick got us all tergevver ter tell us about Billy Nelson, 'e 'ad ter face a lot o' criticism,' Charlie explained. 'Don Jacobs an' Con Ashley felt 'e was bein' too soft wiv the Kerrigans an' Boy-boy backed 'em up. The result was, Nick's gonna cut their order back ter the original amount an' up the price. It's bin forced on 'im. 'E was outvoted.'

'What about you, Charlie? Did you side in wiv the rest?' Linda asked him.

He shook his head slowly. 'I said I felt we should back Nick's judgement an' I got slagged off,' he told her. 'Me an' Boy-boy got arguin' an' it got a bit unpleasant, ter say the least.'

'Well, I'm proud of yer,' Linda said smiling.

'What for?' he asked.

'Fer bein' honest. I expect it would 'ave bin easier ter side in wiv the rest,' she replied. 'That's my Charlie.'

The young man smiled briefly, then his face grew serious again. 'Maybe you should consider gettin' anuvver job, Linda,' he told her. 'I'd never fergive meself if you got 'urt. Don't ferget it was me who took yer ter the arch in the first place.'

'Yeah, but it was Nick who offered me the job, an' me who made the decision ter take it,' she countered. 'It was nuffink ter do wiv you.'

'That's as it may be but I'd still feel better if yer got anuvver job,' he pressed.

'No way. I like what I'm doin' an' I'm gonna stay where I am, so let's ferget it,' she said firmly.

'Let's walk round the ovver side,' Charlie suggested.

Linda took his hand and as they walked past the pigeon loft they saw Bill Simpson and Jack Marchant sitting together on a low wooden bench. Both men were puffing away on their pipes and Linda smiled at them as they passed by.

'You two are keepin' late hours,' Charlie joked.

'We're waitin' fer the shower,' Jack told them.

'I don't fink there's any chance of it rainin' ternight,' Linda remarked.

'The silly ole sod's talkin' about a star shower,' Bill told them, turning to Jack. 'Why don't yer say what yer mean?'

'A star shower?' Linda queried.

'Yeah, there's one due ternight, accordin' ter the paper,' Bill replied. 'It's a shower o' meteors.'

'They're like shootin' stars,' Jack started to explain.

'That's what they are, shootin' stars,' Bill told them. 'It's s'posed ter be lucky ter see 'em. Yer gotta watch carefully. It's over in a second or two.'

Jack reached down and picked up a quart bottle of brown ale and two glasses. ''Ere, 'old on ter these, Bill,' he told him.

The older man took the glasses and held them out for his friend to fill. 'It's a nice clear night ternight, so we might be lucky,' he said. 'The papers said it'd be around ten o'clock.'

Jack took out a silver pocketwatch from his waistcoat pocket. 'It's almost that now,' he remarked.

Linda looked over at the loft. ''Ow's the pigeons?' she asked.

'They're all well. They've 'ad their evenin' flight, an' their corn,' Bill told her.

''E's a bit concerned about Monty, ain't yer mate?' Jack remarked.

'Monty?' Charlie said smiling. 'Who's Monty?'

'It's one o' the pigeons,' Bill told him. ''E's a cock. 'E landed on the roof one day exhausted an' 'e's bin 'ere ever since.'

'We named 'im Monty 'cos o' the way 'e struts about. Yer know, like the Field Marshal,' Jack added.

'Oh I see,' Charlie replied.

'Yeah, 'e struts about, but 'e won't fly wiv the rest,' Bill went on. 'There's nuffink wrong wiv 'im, as far as I can see. 'E just waits around up 'ere on the roof. Sometimes 'e flutters up on the wall an' looks up at 'em as they come swoopin' over an' then I finks ter meself 'e's gonna fly off any minute, but 'e never does. Strange one that.'

''Ow long 'ave yer kept pigeons, Mr Simpson?' Linda asked.

'Must be more than twenty years now,' the old man replied.

'Well, we're gonna walk round the roof an' watch out fer that shower,' Charlie told them.

'Watch carefully or yer'll miss it,' Jack warned them.

The two young people smiled at each other as they walked on to the far corner where deep shadows hid them from view. There in the darkness Charlie took Linda in his arms and kissed her open mouth. She pressed her body to his, wanting to tease him, urge him to be more daring, but he moved away.

'Look, Lin, I don't want yer ter take this the wrong way, but yer told me that yer dad was comin' out of 'ospital termorrer so I want yer ter take this,' he said, handing her an envelope.

'What is it?' she asked, frowning.

'It's some money.'

'I can't take this,' she said, looking inside. 'It's forty pounds. I couldn't possibly.'

'Linda, it's not fer you, it's fer yer folks,' Charlie said quietly. 'It'll take yer mum an' dad an' the kids on a week's 'oliday ter Margate or somewhere. It's nice at Margate.'

Linda's eyes filled with tears. 'Charlie, it's a lovely thought, but I couldn't possibly accept it,' she said quickly. 'Yer mum could do wiv extra money, yer said so yerself, an' there's fings you need as well. No, I couldn't take it.'

'Look, I've sorted me mum out, truly,' he replied. 'I've earned well this last couple o' weeks. I can afford it. Take it. Yer dad'll need buildin' up after the op.'

'I dunno what ter say,' she murmured.

'There's nuffink to say,' he told her. 'Just put it in yer bag.'

Linda grabbed him and kissed him on the mouth. 'I love you, Charlie,' she whispered.

'I love you too,' he said, his arms crushing her to him.

'I want yer ter love me soon. I can't wait much longer,' she gasped as she felt his passion growing.

'I want you too, more than I can tell yer,' he whispered, nuzzling her ear.

She arched her neck, her eyes open to the heavens as his lips sought her throat. 'Look, there it is!' she exclaimed.

Charlie looked up and saw it too, a bright, moving path of light, like stardust sprinkled through the night by some giant hand, its glitter falling in a long curving trail to disappear suddenly near the horizon.

'Did yer see it?' she asked him excitedly.

'Yeah, I saw it,' he told her. 'Bill said it was s'posed ter be lucky.'

'We will be lucky, you an' me, Charlie,' she whispered, shivering despite the heat of the night.

'C'mon, let's walk yer ter yer door,' he said.

'Will yer dream about me ternight?' she asked him.

'All night long,' he replied.

Sam Colby looked hard at the slightly built man facing him across the table in the late-night Elephant and Castle cafe. 'I don't need excuses, Maurice, I need you ter tell me when yer man can deliver,' he growled.

'I understand yer impatience, Sam, but I can't rush 'im,' Maurice told him. 'Patrick's a moody sort o' bloke. 'E'll deliver, make no mistake, but in 'is own time.'

'Well, you tell that moody mick that if I don't get it soon I'm comin' lookin' fer 'im, an' you tell 'im Sam Colby's feelin' all mean an' 'orrible at the moment.'

'I'll do me best, Sam, an' that's a promise,' Maurice said, feeling uncomfortable under the maniacal stare.

Sam Colby got up and buttoned up his coat. 'I'm countin' on yer, Maurice,' he growled.

Maurice watched him leave and breathed a sigh of relief. He had been to see the Irishman only that day and found to his dismay that he had not even started the job of work. He would have to be warned, he thought. Sam Colby was one of the worst. His violent temper was legendary. If Patrick didn't get moving soon he could quite well go around for the rest of his life missing an ear.

Nick Carter lounged back in the cushions and sipped his Scotch, watching Gilda over the rim of the glass as she walked to the drinks cabinet. 'D'yer fink I should 'ave fronted 'em?' he asked her.

'No, I think you did right,' she replied, turning to face him. 'At least they know now you're willing to listen. You tried it your way and gained time. They've pushed the decision on you, and they'll have to live with the consequences.'

'Kerrigan's mob won't take this lyin' down, that's fer sure,' he said sighing.

'What do you see them doing?' Gilda asked him, pouring gin into a tall glass.

'I fink they'll put the squeeze on the punters first, wherever they can,' he replied. 'They'll pay a few o' their contacts ter cause aggro an' make fings as difficult as possible. Of course they'll be after the oil, that's obviously their prime target, an' that's what me an' you 'ave gotta talk about, Gilda.'

'Look, Nick, the subject's closed,' she said sharply. 'It stays here. I know you're worried on my account and I love you for it, but believe me it's as safe here as anywhere.'

'But s'posin' they realise you've got it 'ere, an' they come after yer. What can you do?'

'That front door is really solid and I always keep the bolts on when I'm here alone,' she replied. 'What's more I always look out of the upstairs window to see who's there before I answer a knock. Then there's the phone. If I'm worried at all I can soon phone the police.'

'I'm still not convinced,' Nick told her. 'You don't know the Kerrigans like I do. They're as carney as a cartload o' monkeys.'

'Darling, please don't worry,' she said, coming over and sliding down beside him with a mischievous smile. 'Would you like me to entertain you?'

Nick nodded, his eyes fixed on hers, fascinated by her allure, the strangeness in her. 'I'd like that,' he whispered in her ear.

Gilda took a sip from her glass and then got up without a word, went over to the walnut record cabinet and lifted the lid. She selected a record and put it on the turntable. The exotic sound of Rimsky-Korsakov's 'Song of India' shimmered out of the silence; the soft, hoarse tone of the oboe like a lonely voice from another world. Gilda turned off the light and left just one table lamp burning, and in the pink subdued glow she pulled the slides from above her ears and let her long red hair flow down over her shoulders. Her head was arched back as she swayed in time with the music, like a snake, her lithe body coiling from side to side, her hips twisting sensuously as she slowly undid the buttons of her cotton dress.

281

Nick sat gripping his glass, the drink forgotten as he watched, enthralled by her movements, held by the music and the exotic promise she exuded. She was sliding the dress over her wide shoulders and down her shapely body and with a little wriggle it dropped to the floor. She stood before him, wearing just a black bra and panties, her feet unmoving on the carpet while her body indolently swayed. As the music became more dreamy she reached behind her back and loosened her bra. The flimsy garment fell from her voluptuous breasts, her nipples standing out like ripe cherries. They moved as she swayed, and she glided her hands down across her belly to her panties, her thumbs sliding under the band. Slowly, in time with the languid music, she lowered them, over the round of her hips and down her thick, shapely thighs.

Nick's eyes explored her naked, undulating body, her wide hips exciting him as she sashayed slowly from side to side. She grinned as she gracefully thrust her sex at him, and as the music died he stood up. She came to him, her arms outstretched, and with a quick movement he swept her up in his arms and carried her over to the divan. There in the dim light he stripped quickly and lowered himself over her. She held him, stroked him until he gasped with pleasure, and then wrapped her legs around his waist and moved on to his manhood with an upward thrust of her hips. She sought him, urging him still faster till the vital moment of exploding passion. She groaned with delight as their bodies locked in love and he arched over her, his tensed arms shaking with exertion.

'Was I good?' she asked breathlessly.

Nick swallowed hard. 'You were wonderful,' he gasped. 'What a woman.'

'I've been missing you, the past few days, darling,' she sighed.

'I've missed you too,' he said, his lips brushing her forehead.

'You'll never stop loving me, will you, Nick?'

'Never, not ever, not as long as there's breath in me body,' he whispered in her ear.

Outside, high above in the night sky, the shooting star fell to the horizon and was gone.

Chapter Twenty-Seven

On Saturday morning Eagle Street came alive early. Children played in the warm sunshine, feeling happy now that the schools had closed the previous day for the six-week summer holiday. The toffee-apple man called on his rusty bicycle, the rag-and-bone man pushed his barrow into the turning and sat on the handles rolling a cigarette, and two olive-skinned women with their dark hair covered by headscarves came into the street carrying baskets of heather. One of them walked down the row of terraced houses and the other went into the Buildings.

Doris pulled a face after she and Phyllis had both bought a spray of the purple bloom. 'I never like refusin' them Gipsies,' she told her friend. 'They're s'posed ter curse yer if yer refuse 'em. It's a bit of a bloody nuisance really.'

'Well, she called this lucky 'eavver. I 'ope it brings me a bit o' luck, I could do wiv some,' Phyllis remarked.

'Yeah, me too,' Doris replied.

The two stood in the sunshine watching one of Maggie Gainsford's children digging dirt out of the gutter with a thin stick of wood.

'I shouldn't do that,' Doris called out to the child. 'Yer'll catch a fever.'

Cassie was only seven but she already knew enough not to argue with the hawks. Her big eyes grew even larger at the reprimand and she hurried away.

'I s'pose we've gotta put up wiv it fer six weeks now,' Phyllis said sighing.

'Yeah, I was just finkin' the same,' Doris replied. 'It's too long, six weeks. The kids get bored after a week or two, an' Gawd knows what their muvvers must feel like wiv 'em round their ankles every day.'

Dora came hurrying out of her house looking agitated. 'I gotta get the shoppin' done, John's comin' out this mornin',' she told them as she passed.

'I'm very pleased to 'ear it. 'Ow is 'e, luv?' Doris asked her.

'Well, he's still very sore but 'e looks fine,' she replied. 'Gotta 'urry. See yer later.'

'She's 'ad a lot ter put up wiv,' Phyllis remarked. 'What wiv 'er ole man an' the boy goin' in the army.'

'Mind you, 'er Linda's a good kid,' Doris said. 'She 'elps out a lot. I saw 'er out 'ere first fing this mornin' doin' the step. She cleaned the winders too. She does work 'ard.'

Kate Selby came along the street holding on to her mother's arm, and they were soon within firing range.

'Don't they look alike, them two,' Doris said nodding towards them.

'She's a stuck-up cow, that Liz Selby,' Phyllis growled. 'She don't 'ave a lot ter say to anybody.'

'Mornin', Liz, mornin', luv,' Doris said as they drew level.

'Mornin', ladies,' Liz said smiling. 'Done all yer shoppin'?'

'Not yet,' Phyllis replied, forcing a smile and giving them a little wave as they walked on. 'Nosy mare,' she declared when they were out of earshot.

Doris nodded. 'I can see that Kate gettin' 'erself inter trouble,' she remarked. 'She's always 'angin' round the blokes.'

'I make yer right,' her friend replied. 'She's all done up like a little tart.'

'Oh well, I'm gonna put the kettle on then I must get down the market,' Doris announced.

As he left the house that morning to get his landlady's fresh bread, Dick Conners was pleased to see that he did not have to run the gauntlet, and he whistled cheerfully to himself as he entered the corner shop.

'Morning, Dick,' Eve said, giving him a big smile.

'Mornin', Eve. Anuvver lovely day,' he answered.

She finished serving a customer and turned to him. 'Usual?'

He nodded. 'Ginny's not too good this mornin',' he remarked. ''Er back's playin' 'er up.'

'Sorry to hear it,' Eve told him. 'Give her my best. Tell her to take it easy.'

Dick picked up the wrapped loaf. 'Well, I s'pose I'd better be gettin' back,' he said, not moving.

'Mrs Weston was in early this morning,' Eve told him. 'Her John's coming out of hospital today.'

'I'm pleased to 'ear it,' Dick replied.

More customers came into the shop and he stood back. 'Well, I'd better be goin',' he said, giving her a smile.

'Take care, Dick. See you on Monday?'

He nodded and waved a goodbye as he left the shop.

★   ★   ★

At eleven o'clock, as Dora and Linda left the house for the hospital with a suitcase containing John's clothes, Mrs Iris Brown left her second-floor flat to go to the Beehive for a stout. She had not been feeling very well and had forced herself out of bed early that morning. Iris was eighty years of age and still very independent. The stairs were increasingly a problem for her but she was determined not to become totally housebound. Mrs Garrity next door got her shopping and the morning papers, but Iris insisted on going to the pub for a drink. It was not the same sitting by the hearth with a bottle of stout, she felt.

The old lady painfully managed to reach the lower landing where she stopped to catch her breath. Her heart was pounding and she clung to the banisters till she felt able to continue the journey. Finally she stepped out of the block into the bright sunlight and sighed sadly to herself. Children came running by and people were out chatting on their doorsteps but no one seemed to acknowledge her or wave to her as she passed by on the other side of the street.

Had Iris looked back she would have seen the sad glances and the shaking of heads as her neighbours saw the bowed figure in the shabby coat and hat shuffle by. They noticed that her shoes were down-at-heel and her thick lisle stockings were hanging down over her ankles, and they could see the marks of snuff around her nose. They had long since refrained from chatting with her because she never quite seemed to comprehend what they were saying and reacted so aggressively. Instead they shook their heads and left her to herself.

''Ello, gel. The usual?' Gladys Warner asked her.

Iris nodded as she placed her handbag on the counter and fiddled with the clasp. 'Bloody fing's stuck,' she grumbled.

Gladys finished pouring the stout into the glass and placed it in front of the old lady. 'Come 'ere, luv, let me 'elp yer,' she offered.

'It's all right, I can manage it,' Iris said irritably.

Gladys stood back and watched for a few seconds. 'Let me do it,' she said again.

Iris pushed the tatty handbag towards her with a puff and looked around the bar. They were all strangers, she thought. None of the old faces were there. Where were Mrs Franklin and Mrs Parson? What had happened to that nice lady who always shelled her peas into her apron while she chatted away ten to the dozen? They were all gone. They must have been in earlier.

'There we are, luv,' Gladys said.

Iris delved into her handbag and then looked puzzled. 'I 'ad it wiv me. I put it in 'ere, I know I did,' she mumbled.

'What yer lookin' for, luv?' the landlady asked her.

'Why, me purse,' the old lady said sharply. 'I 'ad it 'ere, I know I did. There's me week's rent in it an' Alf's club money. 'E'll be upset if I don't pay it in for 'im.'

Dick Conners was sitting nearby and he had been watching with a sad expression on his face. He got up and came over. ''Ere we are, gel. This just dropped out o' yer bag,' he told her, handing her a ten-shilling note.

She took it without a word and handed it over the counter. Gladys looked at Dick and shook her head sadly then she rang up the price and handed the old lady her change. 'Now put that away safely,' she told her.

Iris sat down on the bench seat near the door and took a

sip from the glass. That woman behind the counter was new, she told herself. Jack Sweeney always used to serve behind the public bar. It's all different, all changed. The beer didn't taste the same either. They must be watering it down. What day was it? Sunday? No, it couldn't be Sunday. Too many kids out on the street. On Sundays they'd all be at church or Sunday school. No, it must be a weekday. Funny how the days get mixed up lately.

Iris finished her drink and sat for a while staring over at the counter. She would normally have had a second bottle of stout but today she did not feel she could manage it. Besides it didn't taste very nice. One time she would have been able to drink the place dry, and dance the night away. Where were they all? Perhaps they would be in later. That was it, she was too early. They were all doing their shopping. Better to go back home and take a short nap.

As the old lady struggled up and made to leave Dick Conners and Gladys exchanged pitying glances and Dick jumped up to open the door for her. She crossed the street and walked slowly to her block, feeling the sadness weighing on her. She was alone and nobody cared. Alf had gone. They'd all gone. What was there left for her to live for? Just pain and misery. They didn't care. None of them did.

Iris climbed the first flight of creaking stairs and by the time she reached the first landing she felt exhausted. It was wrong for an old lady to have to live up on the second floor, she told herself as she fought for her breath. When she had recovered enough she started off again, and this time she had to stop halfway up the flight of stairs. Finally she reached her landing, white-faced and shaking with the effort. She pulled on the doorstring and let herself into the dark, dingy flat, easing herself into the armchair with a deep sigh. She would take a short nap and then tidy the place up in case anyone called. Alf might pop round, or Mrs Wickstead. No, she wouldn't be calling. She was very ill. Never mind. Not to worry.

A taxi pulled up at number 6 Eagle Street and Dora climbed out, followed by Linda who helped her father out. Dora paid the driver and took John's arm. 'Welcome 'ome, luv,' she said smiling at him.

John Weston felt embarrassed at being the centre of attention and he was glad when the front door closed and he was able to sit down in his favourite armchair.

'You talk ter Dad an' I'll put the kettle on,' Linda told her mother.

Pamela and Tommy came bounding into the room. ''Ello, Dad,' they shouted together.

Dora had a pillow ready. 'Let me put this be'ind yer back,' she said. 'It'll make yer feel more comfortable.'

'Where's young Ben?' John asked her.

'I expect 'e's at the pie shop,' Dora told him. 'I gave 'im the money ter go. Oh, by the way, we 'eard from Frankie. 'E seems cheerful enough accordin' ter the letter.'

Linda came in with a pot of tea and John sighed contentedly. 'It's nice ter be 'ome,' he said smiling at them.

Dora looked stern. 'Now yer gotta take it easy, John. Drink that tea, then you can 'ave a nap.'

Iris woke up with a start and looked up at the clock. 'The bloody fing must be goin' wrong,' she said aloud, fixing her eyes on the empty chair facing her. 'The 'ands ain't moved.

It's like me, I'm goin' wrong. I should fink it's about time I stopped tickin', fer all the good I am. Wouldn't that give 'em a shock. They'd be sorry, all of 'em. Come ter fink of it, I'd be dead an' buried before they noticed I was gone. I could die up 'ere an' nobody would find me fer months. I might as well chuck meself under a bus. At least then they'd know.'

The old lady shuffled out into the filthy scullery and made herself a cup of tea. For a long while she sat contemplating things, then suddenly a smile wreathed her ancient lined face. She got up and slipped on her coat. 'Better leave me 'andbag,' she said aloud as she walked out of her flat without bothering to shut the front door. The journey to the roof did not seem to tire her as much as her first trip that day had, and when she had recovered her breath Iris picked up a stool that she found by the stairway and carried it to the balustrade.

Maggie Gainsford had warned her brood to stay in the street and when she went out to the front door to check on them she saw a group of children pointing to the roof of Sunlight Buildings. 'Oh my good Gawd!' she gasped.

High above her Iris Brown stood with arms outstretched like a priest giving a public blessing. Just then Lucy Perry came to her door.

'Look! Up there!' Maggie shouted to her. 'It's ole Mrs Brown. She's gonna jump.'

People were gathering, their eyes fixed on the figure above them.

'Get the kids indoors,' someone shouted.

'Stay where you are, Iris,' another shouted up to her.

Wally Gainsford came running out and dashed over to the

292

Buildings. Other people were going into the blocks and more people were beginning to gather at the end of the turning as they spotted the old lady.

'It's Mrs Brown. She must 'ave gone off 'er 'ead,' a stallholder said as he stood watching.

Wally reached the roof and found people standing by the stairway.

'Don't go near 'er!' a man shouted at him. 'She's threatened ter jump if anyone goes near 'er.'

Suddenly Bill Simpson walked out on to the roof carrying a bag of corn. 'Iris, I'm gonna go an' feed my pigeons,' he shouted to her. 'I won't try an' stop yer jumpin'.'

The old lady looked round at him and reverted her gaze to the street below. Bill walked slowly along the roof behind her, keeping a safe distance, then a few feet past her he stopped. 'I 'ave ter feed 'em every day or they suffer,' he told her.

'Don't you come near me,' she said loudly.

'Like I say, I'm only interested in feedin' me pigeons, not you, luv,' he told her. 'As far as I'm concerned you can do what yer like.'

'I'm goin' to, make no mistake,' she called back.

'I shouldn't be in too much of an 'urry though,' Bill said, walking towards the balustrade at an angle so as not to alarm her. 'Look down there. It's fillin' up nicely. Anuvver couple o' minutes there'll be 'undreds watchin'. That's what yer want, ain't it? 'Undreds ter watch yer jump. Mind you though, yer gonna make a nice splash. It's not the way I'd choose. Much too messy fer me. They'll 'ave ter scrape yer orf the pavement. Nah, I'd prefer ter put me 'ead in the gas oven, or take a dose o' carbolic. Any way's better than that.'

'Leave me alone, yer silly ole sod,' Iris called out.

'That's right, 'ave a nag. Everyone else does,' Bill said, leaning his elbow on the wall and resting his chin in his hand. 'I bet I can give you a few years. Eighty-four this month I was. I bet you're nowhere near eighty. I should be the one up there, not you. Compared ter me yer a young woman.'

'Why don't yer shut yer noise, yer silly ole git,' Iris growled. 'Just do me a favour an' go an' feed them poxy pigeons.'

Bill studied her, wondering how best to approach her. She was standing on a stool and her knees were level with the top of the wall. She would only have to lean forward. The only way to stop her would be to creep up behind her and grab her from the back. But if she turned suddenly and spotted someone approaching she would probably jump. No, the only way was to keep her talking, he figured.

''Ere, by the way. Did you 'ear the Buildin's are comin' down?' he went on. 'That's what the men were 'ere for. We're all gonna be re'oused in nice warm flats on the ground floor. Us old ones' that is.'

'It won't concern me,' Iris told him. 'I'll be well out of it.'

Two policemen had reached the roof and they realised that the old man was doing a good job in distracting her. They stood with the rest waiting for the right moment to grab the old lady.

'It should concern you,' Bill growled. 'We've earned our place. Not like them people down there. What do they know about us old 'uns? They ain't lived yet. All they want is ter see you jump orf this roof an' splatter yerself on the pavement. Charmin', ain't it?'

'Go an' feed yer pigeons an' leave me alone,' Iris pleaded.

'That's just what I'm gonna do,' Bill told her. 'I s'pose I better say goodbye ter yer then, 'cos yer won't be 'ere when I get back, will yer?'

'I shouldn't fink so,' she said.

'Well cheerio, Iris. Sorry yer goin' out this way, but still everyone ter their likin',' he said quietly. 'Personally I fink it's a bad way ter go. A coward's way when yer come ter fink of it. Anyway, before yer go will yer do me a favour?'

'What's that?' she asked.

'Can yer give us yer key?' he said. 'Yer left yer front door open. Yer wouldn't want everybody goin' frew yer fings, now would yer?'

'I ain't got me key, now piss orf.'

'Oh yes, you 'ave. I've known yer long enough ter know where yer keep yer key,' the old man persisted. 'You always keep it in yer apron pocket. Yer told me once you always keep it in yer apron so yer don't shut yerself out.'

Iris swayed slightly as she started to unbutton her shabby old coat and Bill's heart nearly missed a beat. He had been inching along the wall very carefully and now he was only three feet away from her. 'Don't worry, I'll give the key ter Mrs Garrity. She'll know what ter do wiv it,' he told her.

The old lady turned and fished into her apron pocket and as she was bent slightly away from the balustrade Bill made a grab for her. His hand closed over her open coat and he tugged with all his might. Iris swayed backwards towards the edge, pulling him with her but the policemen pounced, dragging them away from the sheer drop just in time.

Bill disentangled himself and sat down on the roof, his

face white and his breath coming in short gasps.

'Are you all right, old chap?' one of the policemen asked him.

'Yeah, 'ow's the ole lady?' he replied.

'She's all right. There's a doctor waiting to take a look at her,' the constable told him. 'She needs some hospital care.'

'She needs company more than anyfing,' Bill said shaking his head sadly. 'That's the trouble wiv old age. Loneliness. It's a killer.'

John Weston woke up and yawned, then he rubbed his hand over his face and looked across at Dora. ''Ow long 'ave I bin asleep?' he asked her.

'About two hours,' she told him. 'Ben came in an' took a look at yer. 'E's gone back out ter play.'

'Yer should 'ave woke me up,' he told her.

'Why? Yer've not missed anyfing,' she said smiling. 'Well, not much, anyway.'

Chapter Twenty-Eight

Ginny Coombes did not usually travel very far from her home these days. She found it difficult to walk any distance with her bad legs and her suspect back, but she sometimes took a stroll through the market on the arm of Lucy Perry, or occasionally with Maggie Gainsford. Other than those trips, which tired her out considerably, Ginny stayed at home. She did make the most of the warm and sunny days however, sitting at her front door in a wicker chair with a cushion at her back. The children did not worry the old lady. They held her in awe for the most part and discreetly kept their distance. She chuckled as she watched them at play, nodded amicably to passers-by, and, fortified by a stout that Dick Conners fetched her from the pub, she enjoyed the occasional chat with some of the neighbours.

'They're all springin' up, ain't they?' she remarked to Maggie.

'Yeah, they are,' her neighbour replied. 'Young Ron's gonna be like 'is dad. Bob favours me in colourin' but Gawd knows where I got Michael from. Wally reckons 'e takes after the milkman. I told 'im chance'd be a fine fing.'

297

Ginny chuckled. ''Ave you 'eard 'ow Mrs Brown's gettin' on?' she asked.

'Yeah, she's a lot better, accordin' ter Mrs Garrity,' Maggie told her. 'She went in ter see 'er yesterday. She was tellin' me she looks very perky.'

'I see there was a nice bit about ole Bill Simpson in the paper,' Ginny remarked.

'Yeah, I read it,' Maggie said, one eye on her youngest child Michael who had decided to run off with his older brother's marbles. 'Oi, Michael, bring them back!' she called out to him. 'I dunno, they drive yer up the wall at times. It's the first week o' the 'olidays an' I'm a bundle o' nerves already.'

'Yer should get Wally ter put yer on the stout. It's good fer the nerves,' Ginny told her.

'Wally only knows one way ter get me stout,' Maggie said grinning.

Ginny eased her position in the chair and glanced up at the old tenement block. 'I wonder what's gonna 'appen ter that place,' she said. 'There's bin a lot o' talk lately, an' I've seen some men 'ere the ovver day doin' a lot o' measurin'.'

'There's bin bits an' pieces in the papers about this street,' Maggie told her. 'They reckon the 'ole lot'll go before long. They're plannin' ter put a big block o' flats 'ere.'

'Well, I 'ope I ain't still around ter see it,' Ginny said with passion. 'I don't fink they should do away wiv these old 'ouses. They should do 'em up instead. I wouldn't wanna live in a flat wiv people over me.'

'I don't s'pose it'll be fer ages yet,' Maggie said reassuringly. 'They take years an' years ter make up their minds.'

The warm sun and the stout she had just finished helped

to lull Ginny off to sleep, and Maggie went inside to prepare the evening meal. Further along the turning preparations were going ahead for the holiday.

'I've done yer best shirt an' pressed yer suit,' Dora said, pinching her bottom lip thoughtfully. 'I'd better make sure the kids 'ave got enough socks an' vests. I wonder if Maggie's got a suitcase she can lend me? I'll 'ave ter remember to ask 'er.'

John Weston sat polishing his shoes. 'I didn't like the idea of acceptin' that money off Charlie,' he remarked. 'I know it was very good o' the lad, but I feel obliged.'

'I felt the same,' Dora replied, 'but we couldn't refuse wivout seemin' ungrateful. Anyway once yer get back ter work an' Pamela starts work we'll be able ter make it up to 'im.'

John nodded. 'I s'pose yer right,' he said. 'It'll seem strange our Pam workin'.'

'I don't fink she was too 'appy about waitin' till September, but I didn't want 'er goin' straight inter work,' Dora told him. 'I said to 'er she might as well wait till then. Anyway she couldn't really start now an' expect ter get a week off right away ter come ter Margate wiv us. She saw the sense in what I was sayin'.'

'It'll make a nice break fer all of us,' John remarked. 'The boardin' 'ouse seems very nice, judgin' by the letter they sent back.'

'I 'ope Linda an' James are gonna be all right while we're away,' Dora said, looking worried.

'Course they will,' John told her. 'They're both adults, Dora. The trouble wiv us is we still see 'em as kids. There's Frankie in the army an' Tommy startin' work next year. They're all growin' up fast.'

'Yeah, it makes yer feel old, dunnit?' she sighed. 'Well, I'd better get on. There's so much ter do yet an' we've all gotta be up early in the mornin'.'

The landlord of the Rising Sun looked worried as he passed the drinks to Tommy Kerrigan. He had heard enough of the conversation between the brothers to gather that the Carters were meeting them that evening and he sensed the tension. His predecessor had told him of the rivalry between the Kerrigans and the Carters during the change-over and about how the Carters had been ousted from the pub. Trade was good and there had been no trouble of any sort since he took over. Now it could all blow up, he fretted.

On the stroke of nine Nick Carter walked into the saloon bar accompanied by Don Jacobs and Con Ashley. They nodded curtly to the Kerrigans who were seated at their usual table and ordered their drinks.

Tommy Kerrigan walked over to them. 'This one's on me,' he said, placing a pound note down on the counter.

Nick picked up his pint and held it up. 'Cheers,' he said. 'Where do we talk?'

Tommy pointed to a vacant table at the other end of the bar. 'Let's sit over there,' he said, nodding to Sam Colby.

Once they were comfortable Nick pushed his glass to one side and leaned forward on the table, clasping his hands. 'We need ter resolve our differences,' he began. 'Our supply's runnin' short an' there's no way we can get more, not fer the present anyway.'

'Assumin' that's right, where does that leave us?' Tommy asked him.

'In the same boat as us,' Nick replied shortly. 'So we've

gotta make the best use of what's left.'

'An' what exactly does that mean?' Sam Colby asked.

'It means that you get yer original order on a weekly basis till the blendin' oils run out, or till we can get a fresh supply,' Nick told him. 'Also the price'll 'ave ter be upped. It's a case o' supply an' demand.'

'Upped ter what?' Tommy enquired.

'Twenty-five bob per bottle.'

'That's not acceptable.'

'Nor is supplyin' you wiv treble the original amount fer peanuts when the well's runnin' dry,' Nick said sharply.

'Well then, it looks like we're at stalemate,' Tommy said in an icy tone.

Sam Colby's face darkened. 'I fer one don't believe the well is runnin' dry,' he growled. 'The way I see it is, you let us open the market on our manor an' get it established, an' now you intend ter take it over yerself.'

'That's crap an' you know it,' Nick told him. 'You run yer own manor efficiently, so I'm led ter believe, which means our punters wouldn't exactly be made welcome, now would they?'

'Punters are punters all the world over,' Tommy Kerrigan replied sharply. 'If we can't supply 'em they'll come ter you. We couldn't shut the door completely on the trade.'

'So the ideal fing is fer you to accept our new terms,' Nick replied. 'Which means that you get exactly 'alf of our weekly output but at a sensible price. That way we both survive.'

Tommy Kerrigan studied his glass of Scotch for a few moments then he looked up at Nick Carter. 'I gotta 'and it ter yer, Nick,' he said quietly but with malice in his voice. 'That was a shrewd move yer made unmaskin' Billy Nelson.

'E fell fer it, where 'e should've bin a bit more suspicious an' a bit more patient. Mind you, I can understand. 'Is judgement was clouded by 'is feelin's towards yer. As it 'appens though, Billy did come up wiv a few good pointers. 'E tells me that yer've got somefing goin' wiv a married woman who works for yer an' apparently she brings in the blendin' oils every mornin' – just enough fer the day, 'e ses. 'E reckons you're storin' the finished article. Buildin' up a reserve if yer like. Which leads me ter fink that there's no shortage o' the oils. I read somefing inter that. In fact I'm inclined ter see it the way Sam does.'

Nick smiled mirthlessly. 'I'm afraid Billy Nelson's got it wrong,' he replied. ''E's never bin able ter keep 'is eyes off the woman an' 'e's done 'is fair share o' chattin' 'em up at the arch. 'E's bin listenin' ter too much idle gossip. Take it from me, there's no trufe in it, an' yer can believe it or not. Personally I don't care eivver way. Like I said, Tommy, yer've got a choice ter make: eivver you accept my terms, or yer don't get anuvver bottle. That's my last word.'

Sam Colby leaned forward over the table. 'Yer gonna live ter regret it, Carter,' he snarled.

Tommy Kerrigan gave him a warning glance, then he met Nick Carter's hard gaze. 'Yer'll know by Monday, eivver way,' he said abruptly.

As soon as they were alone Sam Colby rounded on his boss. 'I warned yer, didn't I?' he flared. 'They've bin playin' fer time. We've gotta get our 'ands on the oils an' quick.'

'Talk sense, Sam,' Kerrigan told him. 'Let's assume that Carter's woman is storin' the oils at 'er place an' we pay 'er a visit. What then? Can you blend the stuff? Do you know 'ow ter turn out the identical article, 'cos I don't.'

Colby's eyes narrowed. 'Yer led us ter believe that was yer plan: ter get the oils an' 'old the Carters up ter ransom.'

'Yeah, well I've changed me mind,' Kerrigan told him quietly. 'We're earnin' well out o' the stuff we get each week. Why should we 'ave all the aggro attached ter producin' it?'

'So yer gonna go along wiv the new deal?'

'No, I'm callin' their bluff.'

'What d'yer mean?'

Tommy Kerrigan leaned back in his chair. 'I'm gonna tell Nick Carter that we'll accept the original order, but at the original price, not the new price,' he explained. 'All right, it's a compromise, but the ovver way means that people are gonna get 'urt.'

'*They*'ll get 'urt, yer mean,' Colby hissed, his eyes wide with anger.

'Sam, I know yer got this fing about Boy-boy, but that's yer own personal business, not ours,' Kerrigan reminded him. 'We've got a good setup at the docks an' this perfume business is a money-spinner. Why chuck it all away?'

'Tell me somefing, Tommy. What if Carter calls yer bluff?' Colby asked him.

'I don't fink 'e will,' Kerrigan replied. ''E came to us wiv a business proposition. 'E knows that ter get a bit yer gotta give a bit. I got the feelin' 'e'll play along. After a while we can up the order as before an' by then 'e'll be feelin' confident that we've got no designs on takin' 'im over. I've given this a lot o' thought, Sam. I reckon if we play it cool we'll soon be able ter get as much as we can push.'

'S'posing' yer wrong? S'posing' yer fall flat on yer face? What then?' Colby asked him.

'I stand down an' you take over. That's what yer've always wanted, Sam.'

Colby smiled craftily. 'Yer've misjudged me, Tommy,' he replied. 'I'm 'appy the way fings are wiv us, but not wiv the Carter business. I want us ter get tough wiv 'em. We should take the bastards over. If we do it my way we pay Carter's bird a visit, impound the oils an' use that as the lever. Once we know where ter get fresh supplies an' we've bin shown 'ow ter produce the finished article, we'll release just enough ter let Carter's mob tick over on their own manor, an' we'll 'ave the lion's share.'

'Surely you're fergettin' one important point,' Kerrigan said quietly. 'Assumin' we muscle 'em out, what's ter stop Carter gettin' 'is own supply an' settin' up somewhere else?'

'Look, Tommy, they know they'd be wastin' their time,' Colby went on. 'They know we wouldn't let 'em market the stuff anywhere local. We can muster enough support from the lads in the docks ter prevent that 'appenin'.'

Tommy Kerrigan nodded. 'All right, we'll talk it over wiv the rest,' he said quietly. 'You can 'ave your say.'

Sam Colby looked satisfied as he stood up. 'I'll get us a drink,' he said, suddenly noticing the man standing at the counter. He casually walked over and stood beside him.

''Ave yer got anyfing fer me, Maurice?' he asked in a low voice.

'Patrick told me ter tell yer it's all ready an' waitin',' Maurice replied.

'Right, you set up the meet, Maurice, an' be careful,' Colby growled. 'I don't fancy puttin' meself in the frame, if yer get me drift.'

'I understand, Sam,' he replied. 'I'll call round your gaff termorrer evenin'. OK?'

Bernie Kerrigan had walked over to where his older brother was sitting. 'What's Sam doin' givin' that ponce 'ouse-room?' he asked.

''E worries me at times,' Tommy told him.

'Are we gonna to be put in the picture about the meetin' then?' Bernie asked when Tommy was not forthcoming.

'I need time ter weigh fings up, Bern. We'll talk termorrer,' he told him.

Bernie nodded. 'Please yerself, bruv,' he said, 'but don't let Sam Colby lean on yer. That man worries me too.'

Chapter Twenty-Nine

Linda got up early that July Saturday morning and saw another clear blue sky outside the window. The hot weather was holding out and she hurried downstairs to find her mother standing over the gas stove watching the kettle with an anxious look on her face.

'A watched kettle never boils,' Dora said sighing.

Linda smiled at her. 'There's plenty o' time, Mum, don't get all agitated,' she told her. 'I'll take the teas up, you get yerself ready.'

'I 'ope the weavver stays nice,' Dora said. 'The 'oliday'll do yer dad the world o' good.'

'Are the cases packed?' Linda asked her.

'Yeah, there's just the soap, flannels an' toofbrushes ter put in,' she replied.

James came down and sat at the scullery table with his customary grunt, to the amusement of his older sister.

'You're givin' that overtime a canin',' she remarked.

'Yer gotta get it while yer can,' James replied, shaking cornflakes into a cereal bowl.

'What time d'yer finish, twelve?' Linda asked him.

James nodded and both women knew that there was little

more they would get out of him that morning. Five minutes later he grabbed his coat and gave his mother a peck on the cheek. "Ave a nice 'oliday, Mum,' he said.

Dora smiled at Linda as the front door closed behind him. 'Well, that was an interestin' conversation,' she said.

By nine o'clock the children were ready and waiting. John sat reading the morning paper unconcerned by the activity around him as Dora and Linda fussed over the last-minute preparations. 'Now yer know what ter do,' Dora went on. 'There's the food money in the cup on the dresser an' the rent's under the clock. Don't ferget ter make sure James 'as a change o' clothin' an' remember ter give Maggie Gainsford the rent ter pay. Oh by the way, don't ferget ter tell the milkman ter cut it down ter two pints a day this week. The milk money's in the cup as well. Shut the door when yer go out an' keep the place tidy. Leave the ironin', there's nuffink important. Yer could do a wash though.'

'Mum, stop fussin',' Linda told her calmly. 'I've got it all under control. Just ferget everyfing an' enjoy yerselves.'

'C'mon, John, put yer coat on, Charlie'll be 'ere soon wiv the taxi,' Dora told him.

'There's time yet, Mum. Charlie said 'e'll be 'ere about 'alf nine,' Linda reminded her.

'Yeah, but we don't wanna keep it waitin', do we?' Dora replied.

Charlie had walked to the cab rank in the Old Kent Road and found a taxi waiting. He directed the driver into Eagle Street and jumped out smiling as he saw Linda standing at her front door. "Ere, give that ter yer dad ter pay fer the cab,' he said quickly, slipping two one-pound notes into her hand. "E'll take it from you.'

The two of them watched as John, Dora and the children climbed into the taxi. 'Now don't ferget what I've told yer,' Dora called out as the cab pulled away.

Linda grabbed Charlie's hand. 'Come in fer a few minutes an' I'll get yer a cuppa. I'm bein' mum this week,' she told him, grinning.

Sam Colby climbed the wooden stairs to the top floor of the dingy tenement block in Waterloo Road and tapped on the door.

'Who is it?'

'It's Colby.'

'Just a minute.'

The sound of bolts being drawn was followed by a scraping noise and then the door creaked open. 'You're early,' the dark-haired man said in a broad Irish accent as he stood back to allow Sam Colby in.

'Maurice told me it's ready,' Colby said curtly.

'Sure it is,' Patrick replied. 'Take a seat an' I'll fetch it.'

Colby remained standing while Patrick slid the bolts back in place. He looked around the sparsely furnished room with a sense of distaste and spotted the empty whisky bottle lying on its side in the hearth. Maurice had told him that the Irishman was a heavy drinker and he hoped that the man had at least been halfway sober when he assembled the item he had called for.

'There we are,' Patrick said as he came out of a back room and laid a small metal box on the table.

Colby saw that there were two cables wrapped around the box, one red, one black, and he looked curiously at the Irishman. 'Are yer sure this'll work?' he asked him.

Patrick smiled and nodded his head. 'It'll work, believe me,' he replied, picking up the box. 'Now all you have to remember is where these leads go. There's the diagram I've drawn. It's very simple.'

Colby took the sheet of paper and studied it for a few moments. 'That looks straightforward enough,' he remarked, slipping his hand into his coat pocket and taking out an envelope.

The Irishman took it and put it down on the table. 'Pleased to have done business with you,' he said smiling broadly.

'Don't yer wanna count it?' Colby asked him.

'I trust you,' he replied.

Sam Colby took out a folded brown paper shopping bag, opened it up and slipped the device inside. Patrick smiled as Colby walked to the door. 'At least you won't look conspicuous carrying a shopping bag,' he told him.

'I wasn't intendin' ter put the fing under me arm,' Colby replied.

The Irishman slipped the bolts, then turned to him before he opened the door. 'I must warn you that this little transaction would be frowned upon by my masters, so secrecy is all important,' he remarked.

'Don't worry, I'm not about ter make it public,' Colby said sarcastically.

Dick Conners folded the evening newspaper and slipped it down the side of the armchair. 'I dunno if I'll be goin' out ternight, Ginny,' he told her.

'What's the matter, are you boracic?' she asked.

'Nah, I just don't feel like it,' he replied.

Ginny looked at him closely. 'I can't make you out lately,' she said. 'Yer've bin mopin' about the place ever since that Friday night out.'

'That's got nuffink ter do wiv it,' he retorted.

'Well, yer could 'ave fooled me,' Ginny told him.

'I don't feel 'undred per cent, gel. I must 'ave somefing workin' round me,' he said, rubbing his hands together.

'You ain't feelin' cold, are yer?' she asked. 'It could be a summer chill.'

'Nah, I dunno what it is.'

'It's 'er. I can tell.'

'What yer talkin' about?'

'You know what I'm talkin' about.'

'No, I don't.'

'Eve Jeffreys.'

'Don't be silly.'

'Never mind about don't be silly,' Ginny said sharply. 'Ever since that night out wiv 'er yer've bin moochin' about the place like a lovesick calf. Even Albert's noticed it. Yer've bin tryin' ter lay off yer beer an' it's bin a shock ter yer system. It stands ter reason.'

'Well, what d'yer want me ter do about it?' he asked her.

'Eivver ask 'er out or go out an' get pissed, one or the ovver. Don't sit round me wiv the 'ump.'

'Well, I couldn't very well ask the woman out now, could I? The bloody shop's shut,' Dick growled.

'Well, go an' get pissed ternight an' ask 'er out on Monday,' Ginny growled back at him.

'Yer don't understand,' he said sighing.

'Oh yes I do,' Ginny told him. 'I ain't exactly senile yet. Yer like the woman but yer scared of 'er. Yer scared o' changin' an' yer 'idin' be'ind yer weakness fer the booze.'

'What are yer talkin' about, woman?' Dick replied irritably.

'You know what I'm talkin' about,' she went on. 'Yer know as well as I do that yer gotta pull yerself tergevver before yer can ask the woman out an' yer lookin' fer an excuse ter go an' get sloshed. That way yer don't 'ave ter face 'er. Yer can sit 'ere instead, wallowin' in yer own self-pity, tellin' yerself yer not good enough for 'er.'

'I dunno what I'm doin', Ginny,' he sighed. 'I'm scared o' goin' in the pub in case I get pissed an' I'm scared o' fightin' the demons inside me when I'm sober.'

'I've known a few piss artists in my time,' Ginny said quietly. 'Mostly I've seen 'em drink 'emselves into an early grave. I knew one feller who beat it, though. Gawd knows what 'e went frew in the process, but I do know 'e didn't do it on 'is own. 'E 'ad the 'elp of a good woman. What I'm tryin' ter say is, if you're really keen on Eve Jeffreys ask 'er out, an' then lay yer cards on the table. Yer've got nuffink ter lose.'

Dick nodded his head slowly. 'I'm goin' fer a walk, Ginny,' he told her. 'I've got a lot o' finkin' ter do.'

Linda slipped her arm through Charlie's as they left the little riverside pub and strolled down the cobbled lane. They could smell the sour river mud and hear the swish of the ebbing tide against the stanchions of the wharves, and high above in the sky a pale moon hung behind a wisp of cloud. Linda sighed and leaned her body against his as they walked out into the main thoroughfare. 'It's a lovely night,' she said quietly.

Charlie smiled, appraising her with his dark eyes, and she melted.

'Let's go back ter my place,' she whispered.

'What about James?' he asked.

''E's gone to a party,' she told him. 'James usually manages ter find a party on Saturday nights. 'E won't be 'ome till late, if at all.'

They walked on in silence, both nervous and expectant, and as they passed a tall warehouse Charlie took her by the arm and pulled her into a dark doorway. Their bodies touched and their lips met in a soft passionate kiss. Linda shivered with pleasure as she felt his hands running down her back and she pressed tightly to him. 'I want yer badly, Charlie,' she gasped.

'I want you too,' he sighed.

They moved out of the shadows, and walked through the quiet street into Tower Bridge Road, eager to get back. Lights were blaring out from the Beehive, and the sounds of the piano playing and singing voices carrying along the road, and as they turned into Eagle Street they saw Dick Conners saunter out of the public bar, pause, and then go back inside again. Linda took out her key and let them into the house, closing the door quickly and turning to him in the dark passage. His lips closed over hers and she put her arms around his neck. 'I'm scared, Charlie,' she whispered.

'Of me? Of makin' love?' he asked.

'I want it ter be good. I want you ter like me,' she said.

'I love yer, darlin',' he told her softly, his lips brushing her neck.

She took his hand and led him up to her bedroom. 'I'm shakin' for yer,' she sighed.

313

Charlie kissed her gently in the darkness, fighting to keep control of his bursting feelings as he unbuttoned her dress. Linda felt it slip down her body and then she was in his arms and he was caressing her small firm breasts. He was having trouble undoing her brassiere and she reached behind her back to help him. As she stood there by the bed, he lowered his mouth, closing his lips over her hard pointing nipples, and she moaned with pleasure and thrust herself forward. Charlie quickly slipped out of his trousers and shirt, then he moved his hands down over her hips and slid her panties down her thighs. Her breathing was faster now as she felt his fingers exploring her body and she gasped as her hand closed over his stiff member. She moved backwards, down on to the bed, feeling his weight above her as he lowered himself on her hot body. 'Be careful darlin', I'm a virgin,' she whispered.

Charlie pressed into her slowly and he felt her hands suddenly grip his shoulders and her body tense, then she gasped and pulled him to her, her hips thrusting forward. He entered her fully and she cried out as she felt him inside her, her first and only man. She was loving him now, her breath coming in gasps and her open mouth pressing against his, her tongue teasing him as she moved with him. He moaned with pleasure as suddenly he reached his peak and Linda shuddered as she felt the deep explosion of his passion. He sank down spent on top of her, and for a time they lay together still locked in love. In the stillness she could feel the beating of his heart.

'I'm yours now, Charlie,' she said. 'Yours for ever.'

'I'm yours too. For ever and ever,' he sighed.

Sounds of singing and footsteps in the street below drifted

up into the quiet dark bedroom as the lovers quickly dressed. They could hear laughter, then a solitary voice singing, 'On Mother Kelly's Doorstep'.

'That sounds like old Dick Conners,' Charlie said.

Linda pulled the curtains to one side and looked down into the street. Charlie came up behind her and clasped his hands around her waist. 'Just look at the poor ole sod,' he said. ''E can 'ardly stand up.'

Linda drew the curtains together. 'Kiss me, Charlie. Kiss me breathless.'

Ginny Coombes cut thick slices of bread and coated them liberally with margarine, then she laid slices of cheese on them and sliced an onion onto it. 'Pour the tea, Albert,' she shouted at him as she closed the sandwiches and halved them with a sharp carving knife.

'I wonder if 'e'll come in pissed ternight,' Albert said as he stirred sugar into the tea.

'It's a stone-cold certainty,' Ginny replied.

Chapter Thirty

Mandy Davis sat at her dressing-table on Sunday night combing out her long blonde hair. The hour was late but she felt wide awake. Her body still tingled from the long, passionate session that evening and she smiled to herself as her eyes strayed towards the bedroom door. He had loved her fully but she was eager for more. She pulled her dressing-robe tightly round her ample figure and then leaned forward to study her face. The discolouring around her eye was almost gone and the cut on her forehead had healed. Tony Carter was a good lover but very dangerous when angered, and she realised that she would have to be careful not to rile him in future.

The tap on the front door startled her and her heart missed a beat. She hurried along the passage. 'Who is it?' she called out.

'It's me. Gwen.'

'Whatever's wrong?' Mandy asked as she let her sister into the flat.

'Mandy, are you alone?' Gwen asked her.

The blonde nodded towards the bedroom door and saw the anxious look in her sister's eyes. 'It's all right,' she said quietly.

'Mandy, I'm worried,' Gwen told her. 'Somefing's goin' on. I'm scared.'

'C'mon in an' sit down, luv. What is it?'

Gwen shook her head as she slumped down on the divan. 'We went out ter the pub as usual ternight but I thought Sam seemed preoccupied,' she began. ''E wasn't 'imself. Anyway when we got back 'e started on the rum. Yer know 'ow moody 'e gets when 'e drinks rum. I asked 'im ter come ter bed but 'e said 'e 'ad somefing ter do, somefing that should 'ave bin done long ago. Mandy, if yer'd seen that look in 'is eye. It frightened the life out o' me. I was in bed about ten minutes then I 'eard 'im go out. I couldn't sleep so I got up. I thought of you. I know that you an' Tony Carter are seein' each ovver an' I thought yer might know somefing, somefing that Tony told yer. Where would Sam be goin' this time o' night?'

'I dunno, Gwen. Tony never talks about what 'e gets up to,' Mandy told her. 'All I know is, there's no love lost between the Carters and the Kerrigans.'

'I know that much,' Gwen replied. 'This is somefing else though. I can feel it. I wish Sam'd confide in me, but 'e never does.'

'I wish I could 'elp yer, Gwen. Can I get yer a drink, or a coffee?' Mandy asked.

'No, I'd better be gettin' back,' she replied. 'I don't want Sam ter know I've bin over 'ere.'

'Will you be all right?'

'Yeah, course I will.'

As soon as her sister had left Mandy went to the bedroom. 'Did yer get the drift?' she asked.

Billy Nelson nodded. 'Yeah, I did. I wonder where 'e's off to?'

★ ★ ★

Sam Colby walked back to his house through the empty street feeling satisfied at a job well done. It had gone without a hitch and he smiled to himself. Very soon now he could make his move. Tommy Kerrigan was too family-minded. His thoughts and actions were not those of a man totally in charge. He should have been able to see that events over the past couple of years had left power vacuums. Areas of south-east London were ready for the taking, and one powerful group with enough muscle and know-how could make the whole south-east area their own. Once he had spelt it out he felt sure that Tommy Kerrigan and his brothers would fall into line behind him, and so would the Kennedys and Danny Kellerman's mob.

Colby reached his house and let himself in. The clock said two-thirty and he went quietly into the bedroom, where Gwen appeared to be sleeping peacefully. He undressed and slipped into bed beside her. He could feel the warmth of her body and hear her steady breathing and he smiled to himself. She was a good woman who deserved the best. Soon she would be able to have all she wanted. People would treat her with respect and point her out as the number one's wife. He would be the undisputed leader and command due respect too. He would put his mark on south-east London and rule it ruthlessly. That was the mistake of people like Tommy Kerrigan and Nick Carter. They didn't think big. They could see no further than their own manors. It was all there for the taking, and the process had already begun.

Boy-boy Carter had made his excuse to Mandy that morning, but as he shuffled and dealt the cards he wished he had never agreed to join the card school at Peckham. Moishie had convinced him that his bookmaker friends were not exactly professional gamblers where poker was concerned and were good for the taking, but it was not working out that way and already he was fifty pounds down. The cards were not running for him and he cursed his luck as he ran his fingers through his greasy hair. The hour was late and the Scotch was beginning to work on him.

'I'll take one,' Moishie Firman said.

'I'll ride wi' these,' Stan Longman told him.

'One fer me,' Mal Wallace said.

The bidding began and the kitty grew. Boy-boy Carter threw in his weak cards with disgust. 'That's me cleaned out,' he growled.

Sara Wallace brought in a tray of sandwiches and gave Carter another meaningful wink as she set them down on the sideboard. 'Is this game likely ter be goin' on fer much longer?' she asked her husband.

'Yeah, it's just warmin' up,' he told her.

'Well, I'm off ter bed,' she replied. 'Night, fellers.'

'I'm off too,' Boy-boy told them. 'I got a busy day termorrer.'

Sara Wallace was waiting by the front door and she moved close to him as he went to leave. 'It was nice meetin' yer, Tony,' she said, giving him a seductive smile.

'Me too,' he said, eyeing her up and down and then looking furtively along the dark passageway.

'It's all right, they're too concerned wiv the game ter worry about us,' she told him. 'Would yer like ter kiss me goodnight?'

Boy-boy took her in his arms and kissed her roughly and

she responded by reaching between his legs.

Mal Wallace threw his hand in and got up quietly. She was at it again, he realised. She thought she was being clever; thought he hadn't noticed the come-on looks she had been giving that slimy young git all night long.

The passage light being switched on startled them and Boy-boy pulled his hand away quickly from under Sara's dress.

'You dirty little whore!' Mal Wallace shouted as he rushed forward and gave her a backhander which sent her reeling.

Carter tried to fend the heavily built bookmaker off but he was hopelessly outweighed. A fist caught him full in the face and then a knee came up in his groin. He doubled up in excruciating pain, only to be dealt another heavy blow on the side of his head. Lights flashed before his eyes and he was being slowly choked by a massive pair of hands. His head pounded and there was a rushing sound in his ears. He felt himself slipping and then a sensation of falling. Something exploded in his head and then came blackness.

Sara Wallace sat sobbing in a chair, holding a cloth up to her face as the men argued.

'I'm truly sorry, Mal,' Moishie told him. 'I feel I'm ter blame.'

'I'm gonna cut that lecherous little bastard's froat,' Mal snarled.

'Leave 'im. I'll get 'im out of 'ere,' Moishie pleaded with him. ''E's not werf it.'

'Pour yerself a stiff drink, Mal,' Stan Longman told him. 'Yer'll feel better.'

The irate bookmaker looked over at his distraught wife. ''Ow could yer do it ter me?' he shouted at her. 'Don't I always treat yer well? 'Ow many women'd like to 'ave 'alf the fings you've got. Yer nuffink but a scrubber.'

Moishie took him by the arm. 'You stay in 'ere, mate, I'll sort Carter out,' he said firmly.

Mal Wallace did not reply and Moishie nodded to Stan Longman. 'Give us an' 'and wiv Carter will yer, Stan?'

The two men went outside the house and saw Boy-boy huddled in a heap at the bottom of the stone steps where Mal had thrown him. He was bleeding from a head wound and he started to come round a little as they picked him up.

'Grab an arm, Stan,' Moishie told him. 'Let's get 'im off the street.'

'What we gonna do wiv 'im?' Stan asked.

'If we leave 'im 'ere the ole bill are gonna pick 'im up,' Moishie said. 'Let's dump 'im on that bombsite. Once 'e recovers enough 'e'll find 'is own way 'ome.'

Nick Carter woke up early on Monday morning and went down to the scullery to make a cup of tea. He remembered that Tony had still been out when he went to bed and assumed he was with Mandy Davis. He was playing a dangerous game with her, he thought. She was too close to the Kerrigans and he had told him so, but Tony had merely laughed it off. He was an out-and-out womaniser and one day he was going to pay the price, he felt.

Nick sat sipping his tea, turning things over in his mind. Tommy Kerrigan was due to phone in that morning and he guessed that the man would be looking for a compromise. He had given Kerrigan room to manoeuvre and he felt confident that things could be worked out to suit everyone.

By the time he had washed and shaved and had his

breakfast it was nearing nine o'clock and still there was no sign of Tony. It was unusual for him to be so late, Nick thought. Assuming that things went as expected with Kerrigan there would be the usual delivery to be made, and Tony normally had the van ready outside the arch for loading by nine thirty.

As he slipped on his coat Nick heard the front door open and he saw his younger brother stagger into the passage. 'What the bloody 'ell's 'appened ter you?' he asked, shocked by Tony's appearance.

'I dunno. I got turned over, up at Peckham,' Boy-boy groaned.

'What d'yer mean, turned over?' Nick asked sharply.

'I was at a card school an' there was a bit of an argument.'

'By the state o' you it looks like it was a war.'

Boy-boy slumped down into a chair. His nose was bloody and his lips were bruised and swollen. His fair hair was matted with blood and his face was ashen. 'I need ter rest up, Nick,' he groaned.

Nick poured him a cup of strong tea and brought it over to him. "Ere, drink this. Then yer better get up the 'ospital,' he remarked. 'That looks a nasty cut on yer barnet.'

Boy-boy nodded and sipped his tea gratefully. 'What about the delivery?' he asked.

'It's down ter Kerrigan,' Nick told him. 'If fings work out OK we'll be supplyin' 'im as usual. Don't worry about that though. I'll make the delivery meself. You'd better get yerself sorted out.'

Work was well under way in the arch. The women were chatting together as they labelled and packed the small bottles of Elegance in the fancy boxes and Gilda was talking to George Morrison as Nick walked in.

'I'll be in the office, Gilda,' he said. 'I'm expectin' a call.'

Linda was busy opening the mail when he walked in. 'Good mornin', Nick,' she said smiling brightly.

'Mornin', Linda. Any phone calls?' he asked.

'There's bin a call from Tommy Kerrigan,' she replied. ''E didn't leave a message. 'E said 'e'll ring back later.'

Nick picked up the opened mail and scanned through it. 'Lin, will yer do me a favour?' he asked. 'Can yer go an' ask Gilda ter pop in? I need ter see 'er fer five minutes. You can go an' 'ave a chat wiv the gels. OK?'

As Linda left the office the phone rang and he picked it up quickly. Gilda came in and waited until he put the receiver down. 'You look all pleased with yourself,' she said smiling as he got up from the desk.

Nick took her in his arms and kissed her on the lips. 'The day's started well,' he told her with a smile. 'Tommy Kerrigan's agreed ter go back ter the original order but 'e wanted the price adjusted.'

'And?'

'I told 'im we could accommodate 'im.'

'After you argued, of course.'

'Of course,' he said grinning.

'I'll ask George to start getting the order out to the van,' she told him.

Nick took her by the hands and moved backwards, sitting down on the corner of the desk and pulling her to him so that she was standing between his legs. 'Tony's not gonna be makin' the delivery terday,' he told her. ''E came in this mornin' lookin' like 'e'd bin put frew a mincer. Apparently 'e got involved in a scrap over a card game last night. I told 'im ter rest up.'

'Are you sure it was a card game and not a woman?' Gilda queried.

'That's what 'e said,' Nick replied, shrugging his shoulders. 'Anyway, is Martin off on 'is travels this week?' he asked, placing his hands on her waist.

'He left early this morning. He'll be back on Thursday,' she said, smiling seductively as she moved closer.

'Can I see yer ternight?' he asked.

'I'd be very upset if you didn't,' she replied.

Nick stood up and took her into his arms. 'I loved that show yer put on fer me,' he whispered.

'There could be a repeat performance, if you play your cards right,' she told him.

At ten o'clock exactly that fine sunny morning Nick Carter left the arch and crossed the road to the yard, unlocked the gate and threw it open. His mind was on Gilda and the promise of an exciting evening to come as he opened the door of the Commer van and climbed into the cab. He was unaware that a sweating, breathless figure was running along Abbey Street towards him, his face grey and his wide staring eyes full of fear and dread.

Nick made himself comfortable behind the steering wheel and leaned forward to switch on the ignition just as the running man reached the gate.

Chapter Thirty-One

Gwen Colby had twisted and turned all night, feigning sleep when her husband came back in the early hours. Now, on a bright sunny Monday morning, she knew that she must face him, have it out with him. For too long she had been kept in the dark. Sam ran with hard men and she felt that he was perhaps the hardest of the lot. True, he had gone along with Tommy Kerrigan and his brothers, even though she knew that he often disagreed with them, but Sam had always been a leader, a very strong character who would never be subservient to anybody for long. He had spent much of his adult life in the docks. The hard tough life suited him and he had become a ganger while still quite a young man. She knew that Sam feared no one. Whatever he was up to was of his own making. He had said last night that what he was about to do was something he should have done a long time ago. She could only suppose that it involved the Carters, and in particular Tony Carter. Sam had detested the man ever since he insulted her in the Rising Sun. Carter was lucky that time, but since then the rivalry between the two groups had intensified to such a degree, from what she could gather, that there was now every likelihood of violence breaking out between them.

Sam walked into the kitchen with a bathrobe wrapped round him and he looked relaxed. He gave her a brief smile and sat down at the table.

'Sam, where did yer go last night?' she asked him as he reached for the teapot.

'Look there's nuffink fer you ter trouble yerself wiv,' he replied. 'It wasn't anuvver woman I was goin' ter see, that's fer sure.'

'I know that,' Gwen replied quickly, 'but I was worried. Yer've looked troubled lately an' I could see there was somefing on yer mind while we was at the pub last night.'

'It's business, that's all,' he answered.

'So it's business. Does that exclude me altogether?' she asked.

'Yer wouldn't be interested,' he told her.

'Try me.'

'Let it rest, Gwen.'

'No, I won't.'

Sam looked at her in surprise. She had never worried too much about what he did or where he went before. He leaned forward across the table. 'Now listen, luv,' he began. 'I've never messed around since we've bin married an' I've always looked after yer. Yer've only 'ad to ask me fer anyfing an' it's yours. Why all this sudden interest in what I'm doin'? Yer know I'm in wiv the Kerrigans an' we do a lot o' duckin' an' divin'. It sometimes means that we 'ave ter take care o' fings. We can't pick the hours ter suit us all the time.'

'Was that what yer was doin' last night, or should I say early this mornin', takin' care o' fings?' she asked him.

'Yeah, I was, as a matter o' fact,' he replied, a ghost of a smile playing on his lips.

'Sam, yer not lettin' the Kerrigans coax you inter doin' their dirty work, are yer?' she pressed.

Sam Colby's face took on a hard look and his eyes flared. 'Now you listen ter me, woman,' he growled angrily. 'I don't let nobody walk all over me, an' I don't let the Kerrigans use me as a messenger boy. As a matter o' fact, I've bin leanin' on them quite a bit lately, an' fer good reason. Tommy Kerrigan's gone soft. 'Is bottle's gone. If I let 'im go down 'e'll drag 'is bruvvers, Arfur an' me down wiv 'im. So the trufe o' the matter is, I'm gonna ease 'im out, ter put it kindly. What I've done, an' what I'm gonna do, is of me own makin' an' they'll be obliged ter live wiv it or take a walk. Yer'll see it all come off pretty soon.'

'Sam, I've never queried what yer do, nor 'ave I ever moaned about it,' Gwen told him, frightened by the maniacal look in his large dark eyes, 'but I don't want you settin' yerself up at the top. Yer'll be the target fer any young up-an'-comin' mob who fancy their chances. I want you ter get out while we still 'ave a life tergevver, 'cos I tell yer straight, we won't once yer take over from Tommy Kerrigan.'

'It's too late now. The die's cast,' he said, breaking into a cold chuckle. 'The Carters are finished.'

'Sam, what 'ave yer done?' she cried out.

'When Boy-boy Carter goes ter get that van out this mornin', 'e's gonna get a nasty surprise,' he told her, stirring his tea with a satisfied smirk on his large flat face.

'You're mad!' Gwen screamed at him, getting up from her chair and standing over him. 'All this 'as got ter yer, turned yer brain!'

'Shut it!' he shouted back at her. 'I know what I'm doin'. Don't you start puttin' your oar in. Just leave it.'

'I won't,' she replied, her voice breaking. 'I can't sit back an' let you ruin it for us, not after all these years tergevver. I want you ter get out while yer still can.'

'I told yer once, it's too late,' he growled. 'Anyway I can't sit 'ere arguin' wiv yer. I gotta get ter work.'

Gwen Colby watched him storm out of the room and then she lowered her head and cried. He had planned something terrible and she felt powerless to do anything about it. She sat down heavily, staring into the empty grate, and after a few minutes she heard Sam leave the house. Somehow she must warn Carter, she told herself. Mandy would most likely know how to locate him. She would have to move fast.

Billy Nelson was sitting at the breakfast table with Mandy when the loud knocking sounded on the front door, and taking his cue from her he went quickly into the bedroom.

'Mandy, can yer get 'old o' Tony Carter quick?' Gwen said breathlessly as she hurried into the flat.

'No, I can't,' her sister replied. 'Whatever for?'

'Sam's planned somefing terrible. 'E told me this mornin',' Gwen gasped. 'It's somefing ter do wiv Boy-boy. Sam's fixed 'is van.'

'What are yer talkin' about?' Mandy said frowning.

'Mandy, listen ter me, fer God sake,' Gwen cried out. 'Sam's done somefing ter Carter's van. Yer've gotta warn 'im. We got no time ter lose. Whatever it is it's gonna 'appen this mornin'.'

'All right, calm yerself. Just sit down an' get yer breath,' Mandy told her, hurrying to the bedroom.

Gwen Colby looked up in surprise as Billy Nelson walked out from the bedroom behind her sister. 'Billy's bin stayin' wiv me,' Mandy said calmly. 'I've told 'im what yer just told me.'

'Are yer sure?' Billy asked her. 'Could it 'ave bin just talk?'

'I know my 'usband well enough ter know it wasn't just talk,' Gwen told him sharply. 'Someone's gotta warn Tony Carter before it's too late.'

Billy Nelson looked down at the distressed figure for a moment or two then he turned to Mandy. 'I'd better see if there's anyfing I can do,' he said quickly.

A few minutes later Billy hurried out of the backstreet into the New Kent Road and broke into a trot along the main thoroughfare. It was nearing ten o'clock and he had a terrible feeling that he was going to be too late to warn Boy-boy. At the Bricklayer's Arms he dodged between trams and buses and broke into a full run along the Tower Bridge Road. His breath was coming in gasps and a band seemed to be tightening around his chest as he reached Abbey Street. Ahead he could see the railway arch over the road and the line of arches on both sides. As he drew near he saw that the yard gate was open and he speeded up, gritting his teeth with the effort. He skidded to a halt as he reached the entrance and saw Nick Carter sitting behind the wheel. 'Nick! No!' he shouted.

The deafening explosion blew the van apart. The radiator grill smashed into Billy and threw him out on to the pavement. Nick Carter's mangled body came to rest in the back of the wrecked vehicle, and for a moment or two there was deathly silence. Further along the turning, front doors opened, and people started running out from the nearby arches. George Morrison and Charlie Bradley reached the yard and knelt down over the badly injured Billy Nelson. He was groaning, his head and face bleeding badly. One arm was bent at an oblique angle and one leg was folded under him. George nodded gravely at Charlie who stood up and went into the shattered yard. He saw what was left of Nick Carter's body and was immediately sick.

When he staggered back on to the street, Charlie's face was ashen and he was trembling violently. He could see two women bending over Billy trying to stem the bleeding with towels and he looked at George with devastation in his eyes. 'Nick's in there,' he gasped. ''E's dead.'

George looked at him disbelievingly. 'Kerrigan wouldn't 'ave done this, would 'e?'

Charlie looked over to the arch instinctively and stared at Gilda being restrained by Con Ashley and one of the women. It was a few moments before he realised through his shock that she was screaming hysterically and he hurried across the street. 'Get 'er inside,' he said, nodding his head at Con.

Boy-boy Carter came running along the turning, roused by the explosion, and he glanced in horror at the unconscious figure on the pavement, then hurried into the yard. He came out white and shaking and knelt down over his old friend. 'Who did it, Billy?' he screamed out at him.

''E can't 'ear yer,' the woman tending him said.

'Billy, who done it?!' he cried out again.

The badly injured young man's eyes flickered open and he tried to speak. The words stuck in his throat and Boy-boy put his ear close to his mouth.

A police car screeched to a halt outside the yard and then

an ambulance with its bell ringing came racing along under the railway arch.

'It must 'ave bin gas,' one onlooker said.

'More like a bloody bomb,' another remarked.

Con Ashley and the woman worker managed to get Gilda into the office and sat her down in a chair. Linda knelt down in front of her and took her hands in hers, not knowing what to say.

'Nick!' Gilda called out, her eyes going up to Charlie. 'Nick's dead,' she said desolately.

''E couldn't 'ave felt anyfing,' Charlie told her in a soft voice.

Con Ashley went out to speak to the shocked women who were standing around talking in low voices and Linda looked up at Charlie. 'Stay wiv 'er while I make 'er a cup o' strong tea,' she told him.

Alice Baker sat with her arm round Gilda's shoulders, patting her back gently. 'There, there,' she said softly.

Charlie stood beside them, not knowing what to do, and Gilda suddenly looked up at him, fighting to compose herself. 'You'd better send the women home for the day,' she gulped.

George Morrison looked in the office and beckoned to Charlie. 'They've just took Billy Nelson away in the ambulance,' he said as Charlie stepped outside.

'Where's Boy-boy?' Charlie asked him, getting no response. 'George, listen ter me. Where's Boy-boy?'

George seemed dazed as he shrugged his shoulders. 'I dunno. 'E just took off,' he mumbled.

Charlie walked over to the women. 'Gilda wants yer all ter go 'ome fer the rest o' the day,' he told them. 'We'll let yer know more when yer come in termorrer.'

'Was Nick badly 'urt?' one of the women asked.

'I'm very sorry ter tell yer Nick was killed in the explosion,' Charlie said in a low voice.

Some of them became tearful. 'Was it a bomb?' one girl asked him.

'Nah, it was prob'ly a gas explosion,' another told her.

Charlie watched the women leave, then he turned to George Morrison. 'I fink we'd better leave Gilda wiv Linda,' he said. 'P'raps we should go back over the yard. The police are gonna be askin' questions.'

George nodded, still obviously shocked. 'I can't believe it's 'appened,' he said in little more than a whisper.

The two men walked across the street which was now full of curious bystanders. Another police car had arrived and uniformed officers milled around the entrance to the yard. A police sergeant stood writing in a notebook and he looked up as Charlie and George came over. 'I understand that this yard is rented to the Carter brothers,' he said.

'Yeah, that's right,' Charlie told him. 'That's Nick Carter's body in there.'

'One of our men went in the ambulance with the injured man,' the sergeant went on. 'He was identified by one of the women who was tending him as Billy Nelson, an employee of the Carter firm. Is that right?'

'Ex-employee,' Charlie corrected him.

The police officer looked up quickly. 'You say ex-employee?'

'Yeah, 'e left last week.'

'That's strange. I wonder what he was doing here this morning then?'

'I really don't know,' Charlie told him.

The sergeant put his notebook back in his breast pocket. 'This yard will have to be roped off till the forensic people get here,' he said. 'We'll be wanting to talk to you later. Will you be over there?' he asked, nodding towards the arch.

'Yeah, someone'll be there,' Charlie replied.

When they had got back to the arch George turned and shook his head slowly. 'Boy-boy's gotta be found,' he said. 'The police are gonna need ter talk to 'im.'

Linda came out of the office, her face smudged with tears. 'Alice said she'll stay wiv Gilda fer a while,' she told them. 'Whatever 'appened over the yard, Charlie? Was it a bomb?'

'It 'ad ter be,' George cut in.

'The police wanna talk ter somebody 'ere,' Charlie told her. 'I'll need ter warn Tony. I'd better see if 'e's at 'ome.'

Gilda came out of the office. Her face was very pale and her eyes red-rimmed, but she walked upright and unaided. Alice stood beside her looking concerned and Gilda squeezed her arm in a friendly gesture. 'I'm all right, Alice. Really,' she told her. 'You go home now. And thanks.'

She looked across at Charlie. 'Tell me exactly what happened,' she said calmly. 'Was it deliberate?'

'We can't be sure yet, but it looks that way,' he told her.

Her face suddenly became set hard. 'Where's Tony?' she asked.

'I was just goin' ter find out,' Charlie replied. 'The police'll be 'ere askin' questions any minute.'

'Find him, Charlie.'

Just at that moment the door opened and Boy-boy Carter walked in.

'Where were you this morning?' Gilda asked him icily.

Boy-boy's shoulders slumped and he lowered his head in anguish. 'It should 'ave bin me, not Nick,' he croaked. 'I wish ter God it 'ad bin me.'

Everyone looked at his battered face in silence, except Gilda. 'Nick was killed because of you,' she said, her voice level. 'That's something I'll never forget.'

Boy-boy looked at her, his eyes filling with tears. 'I've gotta live wiv it too, fer the rest o' me life,' he told her, his voice breaking.

The door suddenly opened and Detective Inspector Dan Sully stepped into the arch. He glanced around at everyone present before his eyes fixed on Boy-boy. 'We need ter talk,' he said.

Chapter Thirty-Two

Dan Sully sat facing the ashen-faced Tony Carter, studying him closely while the sound of a train rumbled overhead. 'This is a terrible thing,' he said as the noise faded. 'I wish I could delay this, but I can't. I need leads, answers, anything that will help me find out who was responsible, and fast. Who did it, Tony?'

The younger man shook his head. 'I dunno,' he replied. 'Yer know from yer dealin's wiv Nick that us an' the Kerrigans 'ave bin at each ovver's froats lately, but I can't bring meself ter believe that Tommy Kerrigan would sanction puttin' a bomb in our van. That's not the way 'e does fings.'

'We don't know for sure it was a bomb,' Sully reminded him.

'Come off it, I've just seen what's left o' Nick in that tangled mess,' he replied sharply. 'It 'ad ter be a bomb.'

'Until we get the official forensic report we can't be sure about anything,' Sully told him. 'In the meantime I need something from you. Have you and Nick been threatened by anyone lately? Have you got yourselves involved in anything political?'

'That's a stupid question,' Boy-boy replied angrily.

337

'I have to ask,' Sully said quietly. 'Planting a bomb is not generally the method used by a rival gang in my experience, certainly not in this country anyway, but going on the assumption that it was a bomb which killed your brother, I have to look at all possibilities.'

'I dunno who did it, Dan,' the young man replied, his eyes narrowing, 'but I tell yer one fing. I only 'ope you find 'im before I do.'

'That's one thing you can't do, take the law into your own hands,' Sully said firmly. 'We'll find whoever did it, make no mistake about that.'

Boy-boy dropped his head into his hands. 'I just can't believe this,' he groaned. 'Nick, dead!'

Dan Sully sat quietly, waiting until Boy-boy had regained some of his composure. 'This lad Billy Nelson who was injured in the blast,' he went on. 'I know he's one of your men, but the police sergeant's got him down in his report as an ex-employee. Could you put the record straight?'

'There was a difference of opinion, nuffink bad,' Boy-boy told him. 'So Billy decided 'e wanted out. That was it.'

'What was he doing at the yard then?' the policeman queried.

'I honestly don't know. P'raps 'e wanted ter see Nick about somefing,' Boy-boy suggested.

Sully nodded, then he leaned forward in his chair. 'Tony, you realise you'll have to finish with this perfume business right away,' he warned him.

The young man nodded. 'Yeah, I realise that,' he replied.

'Because of the seriousness of the crime, Scotland Yard have been called in and the Special Branch are involved as well,' Sully continued. 'The trouble is, a lot of the IRA activists who were interned at the outbreak of the war are back on the streets now and the Yard are worried that this could be the start of a new terrorist campaign. They'll certainly be calling here to find out if there's any possible link. They'll want to know what you're trading in, and who your customers are. Those boys don't leave any stones unturned. If they see those labels and the packaging they'll pass it over to the fraud squad and you'll be done for criminal deception, transgressing the patents act, or whatever . . .'

Boy-boy lowered his head and ran his fingers over his forehead. 'Look I understand what yer sayin' but I can't fink straight at the moment,' he said. 'I'll talk ter Gilda an' the lads. We'll sort somefing out.'

'Well, you'd better, and quick,' Sully warned him. 'I kept the station off your backs, but I can't anymore, not now.'

'Don't worry, I'll sort it out,' Boy-boy replied.

Sully got up from his chair. 'Are you quite sure you don't know who did this?' he asked, his eyes narrowing as he stood over him.

'I'm sure,' the distraught young man told him.

'If you learn anything bring it to me personally,' Sully said as he walked to the door. 'We'll get whoever it was before very long, and they'll swing for it, make no mistake.'

As soon as the policeman left, Gilda came into the office with Linda and Charlie. 'I've sent George home,' she said. 'He's taking it bad.'

'Sully said Scotland Yard 'ave bin called in an' 'e's warned us ter get rid o' the labels an' packagin' before they pay us a visit,' Boy-boy told them. ''E said they'll be lookin' frew everyfing ter find out who might 'ave bin responsible.'

Gilda sat down heavily, her shoulders rounded and her face pale and drawn. 'Burn it all, Charlie,' she said quietly.

'What about the bottles?' Charlie asked.

'Don't worry about the bottles. They could be used for half a dozen different brands,' she replied. 'As far as the police are concerned we're just in the cheap scent business.'

Boy-boy stood up. 'I've gotta pay a call,' he said, a distant look in his eyes.

'Tony, if yer got a clue about who did this take it ter the police,' Charlie told him quietly.

Boy-boy rounded on him. 'An' what then? They go an' take a statement an' the bastard just denies it. It's 'is word against mine. The ole bill won't be likely ter find any pointers in what's left in that yard.'

Gilda looked up slowly and fixed Boy-boy with her sad eyes. 'You know who did it, Tony, don't you?'

'Yeah, I know,' he growled. 'Billy Nelson managed ter tell me before they took 'im away in the ambulance.'

'Tell me,' she said.

'I'll tell yer, when I've finished wiv 'im.'

'Tell me! I've a right to know!' she shouted at him.

'Don't take the law inter yer own 'ands, Tony. Go ter the police wiv what yer know,' Charlie pleaded.

'No!' he shouted. 'I'm gonna make sure of it meself. Nick was my bruvver. I loved 'im.'

'I loved him too,' Gilda gulped, her eyes filling with tears.

Linda put her arm round her shoulders and did her best to comfort her as she broke down and sobbed loudly.

'Who was it, Tony?' Charlie pressed him. 'Tell us. We've all got a right ter know.'

Tony Carter spat out the words: 'Sam Colby.'

Come on, let's go ter the police right away,' Charlie urged him.

Boy-boy pushed past him and hurried out of the office and Charlie went after him.

'Let him go,' Gilda called out.

Boy-boy turned swiftly as he reached the main door. 'If yer try an' stop me I'll put this frew yer,' he snarled, pulling a flick knife from his pocket and clicking the blade out.

Charlie stood back and watched him leave, then he slowly walked back to the office. 'There was no stoppin' 'im,' he sighed. 'I'd better get started destroyin' the labels an' the rest o' the stuff.'

'Let me get a cab an' take yer 'ome, Gilda,' Linda said.

'Later,' she replied frowning. 'I can't just sit around doing nothing. There's so much to be done here.'

Charlie looked down at the distressed woman and gave Linda a despairing glance. 'What should we do?' he asked her quietly.

'If you get us a cab I'll take Gilda 'ome,' she told him. 'I'll stay wiv 'er fer a while.'

Charlie hurried from the arch and was back within a few minutes. 'The taxi's waitin' outside,' he said.

Linda took the protesting woman's arm and helped her out to the car, and as soon as they had gone Charlie set to work.

The Carters' yard stood adjacent to a bombed-out factory on one side and a large transport yard on the other, so the blast had not caused any damage to the houses in Abbey Street. The noise of the explosion had brought all of the residents out on to the street, however, and as was to be expected the news travelled like the wind. In the nearby Tower Bridge Road market the stallholders were told all about it several times that morning and they passed it on. Backstreets were buzzing and Eagle Street was no exception.

'Did you 'ear the news?' Doris Harriman said to Phyllis when she answered the knock. 'A bomb's gone off in Abbey Street!'

'Oh my good Gawd! Was anyone 'urt?'

'Mrs Williams from the Buildin's told me a few minutes ago,' Doris went on. 'She don't normally stop ter talk but she came up ter me as I was shakin' me mats. She said one o' the costers told 'er the bomb went off in a yard near the arches. Apparently there was a bloke lyin' on the pavement outside badly 'urt an' they took 'im away in an ambulance.'

'Was there anyone in the yard?' Phyllis asked.

'I dunno, but the police were all over the place by all accounts.'

The two stood at Phyllis's front door shaking their heads and looking horrified and as neighbours came along the turning the news spread.

'Yeah, I've just 'eard about it,' Lucy Perry replied when the hawks accosted her. 'Someone said there was people in the yard at the time.'

Even Ginny Coombes made her way along the street to talk to the little group that was gathering. 'I went cold when Maggie Gainsford told me,' she said.

'I reckon it must be the IRA started up again,' Doris informed them all. 'I remember those bombs they used ter put in the postboxes.'

'Yeah, so do I,' Phyllis replied.

'I shouldn't fink it was them,' Ginny remarked. 'There's a

lot of Irish people live round 'ere an' there's never bin any friction between us an' them. Besides, it's ordinary people live in Abbey Street, not yer nobs an' politicians.'

'It could 'ave bin a gas explosion,' Lucy offered.

'Nah, they said it was a bomb right enough,' Doris replied.

Gladys Warner had been for the morning paper and she had more to relate. 'I just bin talkin' ter Sammy Israel on the fish stall an' 'e reckons Billy Nelson was outside the yard an' 'e got badly 'urt.'

'Billy Nelson?' Doris queried.

'Yeah, 'im who goes wiv the Carter boys,' Gladys told her. 'Billy Nelson an' Boy-boy Carter are always tergevver.'

The congregation outside Doris Harriman's house grew, observed by Jack Marchant as he stood on the roof of Sunlight Buildings. ''Ere, Bill, come over 'ere a minute,' he called out to his friend who had just released the pigeons for their morning flight. 'Look down there. Some-fing's up.'

'I wonder who they're gassin' about terday,' Bill said grinning.

'Look, someone else 'as just come up to 'em,' Jack remarked. 'It looks like a right ole muvvers' meetin'.'

Bill Simpson leaned on the balustrade for a while, looking down at the gathering below, then losing interest he turned his attention to Monty who was strutting along the roof. 'I wonder if that lazy little git will ever take off,' he said out loud.

'It don't look like it,' Jack replied, filling his pipe.

Bill raised his arms quickly as the flight of pigeons swooped down and then went off on another circuit of the

Buildings. ''Ave you 'eard 'ow ole Mrs Brown's gettin' on?' he asked.

'Yeah, she's doin' quite well by all accounts,' Jack told him as he held a match to the bowl and puffed away.

Footsteps sounded on the stairs and Alice Toomey came out on to the roof carrying a wicker basket full of freshly washed bedding-sheets. ''Ave you 'eard about the bomb in Abbey Street?' she asked them, putting the basket down at her feet.

'So that's what they're all natterin' about,' Bill remarked.

'The IRA 'ave let a bomb off in a yard in Abbey Street, right by the arches,' she went on. 'They say they was after the railway.'

Jack Marchant had steered clear of talking to Alice Toomey after Bill's story about her and Jumbo Bennett but his curiosity got the better of him. 'When did this 'appen?' he asked her.

'This mornin',' she said. 'As a matter o' fact I 'eard a bang when I was doin' me washin' out in the scullery. I fought it was a lorry backfirin' an' I took no notice, but when I went down the market fer me taters an' greens everyone was talkin' about it. Apparently there's bin people killed. It worries the life out o' yer, dunnit?'

''Ow do they know it's the IRA?' Bill asked her. 'It could 'ave been a gas explosion.'

'No, it was a bomb right enough,' Alice said forcefully as she bent down to pick up the washing basket. 'They know the difference.'

Bill did not feel like getting into a long discussion with the woman and he nodded acquiescently.

'I can see you've bin busy,' Jack remarked, feeling suddenly daring.

'Yeah, I do love the feel o' clean sheets on me bed,' Alice told him smiling.

'Are you gonna 'ang that lot up now?' Bill asked her.

'Yeah, why?'

'I should wait till the pigeons come back ter the loft if I was you, in case they shit all over it.'

Alice pulled a face at the old man and turned her attention to Jack Marchant. 'I ain't seen you about, Jack,' she remarked. ''Ow yer keepin'?'

'I ain't so bad, gel,' he replied. 'Me back gives me gyp at times an' me ole corns play me up now an' then but I mustn't grumble.'

'You look quite chirpy ter me,' she said smiling at him.

Warning bells began to ring in Jack's head. 'Yeah, I mustn't grumble,' he told her, looking down distractedly at the women gathered together in the street below.

Alice began pegging her washing out and Jack sidled over to the loft.

'Yer wanna be careful of 'er,' Bill warned him. 'I told yer about 'er an' old Jumbo, didn't I?'

'Yeah, I was just finkin' o' that,' Jack replied. 'I wouldn't like 'er gettin' 'er 'ooks inter me. The woman's a bloody sex mechanic.'

Dick Conners had been to the baker's shop early that morning and he had smiled sheepishly at Eve as she wrapped up the loaf. 'I blotted me copybook over the weekend,' he told her. 'I'm afraid I got sloshed.'

She smiled back at him. 'Oh dear, never mind. You seem to have recovered.'

Dick had felt a little put out by her apparent indifference

and he pondered over it as he strolled down to the Beehive at lunchtime. Ginny had brought the news of the bomb back to him while he was shaving and now everyone in the pub was talking about it. He decided he had heard enough for one day and found a table in the far corner, where he sat brooding over Eve's reaction that morning. He had made his choice though and reverted to his usual drinking habits, he told himself. Why should he worry what she thought?

The drunk took a long draught of his drink and shut his ears to the excited chatter around him. As much as he tried to deny it, the truth of the matter was he did concern himself with what Eve Jeffreys thought of him. She had been in his mind a lot over the weekend and he had wanted to see her that morning, if only very briefly. Why should he suddenly feel this way about a woman at his time of life? But then Eve was no ordinary woman. She was attractive and smartly dressed, and a very warm and kind person. She made him feel of some worth, and what was more she had got him thinking.

Dick took another gulp from his glass. Maybe his landlady was right when she went on about him hiding behind his weakness, he reflected. She was a shrewd one was Ginny, and she had sussed that he was frightened of wooing the woman because of the changes to his life he would have to make. He had thought about this quite a bit over the weekend and every time he asked himself the question the answer was always the same. It was Eve or the booze, as simple as that. There could be no in between.

Dick finished his pint and rubbed his chin thoughtfully for a few moments as he stared down at his empty glass, then he got up and left the pub with a determined look in his eye, much to Bert Warner's surprise.

As he walked into the baker's shop Eve was dusting down the empty shelves with a soft brush. 'Hello, Dick, did you forget something?' she asked.

'Eve, I just wanted ter say that I fink you're a very nice lady an' I didn't get sloshed at the weekend, so if yer still wanted me ter go to a show wiv yer in the future I'd be only to 'appy to accompany yer,' he blurted out.

Eve Jeffreys' eyes widened in surprise and her charming smile made Dick's heart leap. 'Yes, I'd like that very much,' she told him.

'Well, that's that then,' Dick said, turning on his heel and walking out of the shop feeling elated.

As he strolled back to the Beehive he was determined to make the next pint his last. Until the evening, at any rate.

Smoke rose up in the air from the backyard behind the arch in Abbey Street as Charlie set about burning the whole supply of labels and packaging. It all seemed so unreal to him. Just a couple of hours ago Nick Carter was alive and now he was gone. As he watched the flames rising up from the oil drum, Charlie sighed sadly. Life could be a bitch at times, he thought. One day the future looked rosy and the next day it was all going up in smoke. One second of lunacy had taken the life of someone who had proved to be a good friend, and caused much misery to everyone concerned. Gilda was distraught, and Boy-boy had dashed off like a madman, hellbent on revenge. Where was it all leading to?

Chapter Thirty-Three

The customers standing at the counter in the Shepherd and Flock public house in north-west London were enjoying a joke, but the men gathered together in a small room above were all serious-faced as they waited for the commander to arrive. Sean McNally looked along the table at Brendan Quaid. 'It seems I was proved right after all,' he remarked.

'You were right, Sean. We all knew it, but there were problems at the time,' Quaid replied.

'And I suppose we have no problems now,' Sean went on sarcastically. 'We should have acted when I first suggested it but you all voted me down.'

Declan Kennedy held up his hands. 'It's no good arguing amongst ourselves,' he said quickly. 'Let's just quieten down and wait till Fitzpatrick arrives.'

Ten minutes later a tall, lean man, wearing rimless spectacles and a trilby cocked over one eye, walked into the room and threw the evening paper down on the table. 'They're trawling deep waters, gentlemen,' he announced.

The men remained silent while Walter Fitzpatrick took his seat, all eyes fixed on him, and it was Sean McNally who spoke first. 'This is a setback for us,' he remarked. 'The last thing we needed was a maverick getting involved with private quarrels, especially while we're in the process of establishing a network over here.'

Heads nodded and Fitzpatrick took off his hat and dropped it on to the table. 'One of our men in south London has confirmed that it was Patrick Foley who supplied the bomb and he's waiting for instructions,' he informed them. 'We'll have to act quickly. The British government is waiting for our reaction and since we're not going to claim responsibility we'll need to provide them with a suitable alternative, considering our trademark was on the bomb. Our sleepers in the area are generally well established and respected and I don't want to comprise their position by getting them to act for us so I feel that we should deal with the problem from this end. Sean?'

Sean McNally stood up. 'I should be able to have everything settled by tomorrow morning, if I leave now,' he told the gathering.

Boy-boy Carter walked through the quiet New Kent Road with an evil-looking flick knife rolled up in an old cap and stuffed down in his coat pocket. That morning he had run from the arch like a demon from hell, bursting to find Sam Colby and stick him like a pig on the spot, but as he prowled the streets the red mist before his eyes had eventually cleared and he had gone home to think things through. Now, as the evening shadows lengthened, his mind was focused on his sworn task and he felt in control of the situation. Hatred for the man who had robbed him of his brother burned hungrily inside him like a black flame and he knew that he would never rest, never shut his eyes until Nick had been avenged.

The daytime hours had dragged past agonisingly at the house he and Nick had lived in since the war. He had gone from room to room, picking up pieces of clothing, touching things that Nick had handled, staring up at framed photographs of them together, as he tried to come to terms with his grief. He had had to tell Mrs Samuels of his brother's death and she had taken it very badly. Now the waiting was over, and as he neared his destination he knew exactly what he had to do.

In her second-floor flat in a backstreet off the New Kent Road Mandy Davis moved around adjusting the cushions, gathering up the newspapers and fussing over the appearance of the room while she waited for Billy's knock. He would be arriving soon and she wanted everything to look nice. She had worried about him when he hurried out that morning but she knew that Billy could look after himself and the whole thing was probably a storm in a teacup. Gwen was inclined to panic. Anyway he would soon be with her and she could ask him all about it then.

The clock struck eight and Mandy looked around the room once more before going to her bedroom and putting on some of the perfume Billy had bought her. She realised that she was playing a very dangerous game entertaining Billy Nelson but she trusted the handsome ex-boxer to take care of her from now on. Tony had not contacted her for some time anyway and she suspected that he was seeing someone else.

She smiled to herself as she heard footsteps on the stairs and a gentle tap on the door. He was a little early, she thought as she slipped the catch and pulled the door open.

''Ello, Mandy,' Boy-boy said, walking past her into the room.

She turned quickly and followed him. 'I wasn't expectin' yer, Tony,' she said, looking anxious.

Boy-boy sat down heavily in the armchair. 'My bruvver Nick was killed this mornin',' he said, looking up at her.

'Oh no!' she gasped. ''Ow did it 'appen?'

'Don't you ever read the papers or listen ter the wireless?' he asked sharply. 'Nick was blown up at our yard. That bastard Sam Colby planted a bomb in our van. Billy Nelson tried ter warn 'im but 'e was too late. 'E got the blast right in the face.'

'Oh no!' Mandy murmured, collapsing on to the divan. 'Billy? Is 'e . . .'

''E was alive when they took 'im in the ambulance, just about,' Boy-boy replied.

Mandy dropped her head in her hands, unable to contain her feelings, terrified as she was that Tony would realise the truth about them. 'Billy Nelson's your best friend. 'Aven't you bin in ter see 'ow 'e is?' she asked, avoiding his eyes.

''E's no friend o' mine, not anymore,' Boy-boy growled. ''E was in the pay o' the Kerrigans an' that bastard bruvver-in-law o' yours.'

'But 'e tried ter warn yer bruvver,' Mandy sobbed.

'That changes nuffing,' he told her quickly, his eyes narrowing as he studied her.

'Billy was really concerned fer Nick this mornin',' she said tearfully, lifting her eyes to meet his. 'An' now 'e's got 'urt tryin' ter save 'im.'

'Billy was 'ere?'

'No, no   me sister Gwen told me.'

''Ow did Billy find out about the bomb in the van?' Boy-boy asked her quickly.

'Gwen prised it out o' Sam.'

'Then yer sister just 'appened ter know where ter find Billy.'

'Yes.'

'Yer lyin' ter me, Mandy. Billy was 'ere last night, wasn't 'e?' Boy-boy pressed her, getting up and going over to her.

'No, 'e wasn't. I swear.'

He leaned down and pulled her up to him. 'You're a lyin' little toe-rag,' he snarled, his face inches from hers. 'It all fits tergevver nicely. You 'ardly knew Nick, so yer not sheddin' any tears over 'im. It's Billy you're cryin' about. You always fancied 'im, didn't yer? I could see it in yer face whenever 'e was around us. An' then when I walked frew that door ternight – I could see the disappointed look on yer face when yer saw it was me. You was expectin' 'im, wasn't yer? You've even put on perfume for 'im, an' I can tell it's not the one I gave yer. Yer smell like a Lisle Street whore wiv that crap yer've doused yerself in. That's where yer should be, up Soho, floggin' it.'

Mandy looked into his wild, staring eyes. 'You're not a patch on Billy!' she screamed. ''E's more considerate, more feelin', an' yeah, 'e's better in bed.'

Boy-boy suddenly leaned back and hit her hard on the side of her face with the back of his hand, and as she fell to the floor he kicked her viciously in the ribs. Mandy cried out in pain and cowered beneath him, curled up in a ball as she waited for the next blow. Boy-boy stared down at her, but as he pulled back to kick her again he suddenly realised that if he went much further she would be in no condition to help him trap Colby. He bent down and dragged her to her feet before pushing her down roughly into the divan. 'Now listen ter me, you little slag,' he growled. 'The reason I came 'ere ternight was ter get Sam Colby's address from yer, an' ter find out if 'e's likely ter be at the pub ternight. Fings 'ave changed now, though. Yer gonna get 'im 'ere, d'yer understand? Yer gonna write a message ter yer sister on a scrap o' paper that ses I came in 'ere pissed an' beat yer up bad. Yer gonna tell 'er yer got busted ribs an' yer can't move very far. That should do it. Yer gonna tell 'er I passed out in the bedroom an' yer terrified I might start on yer again when I wake up. That'll certainly get Colby round 'ere. Then when yer've written the message yer gonna knock next door an' ask ole Muvver 'Ubbard ter take it ter yer sister straight away. I'll be just inside the door listenin' an' if yer try an' pull a fast one an' warn 'er I'll slit yer froat an' take the consequences, I swear.'

'I won't do it,' Mandy told him.

'Oh yes yer will,' he scowled.

'Yer can do what yer like ter me, I won't do it.'

Boy-boy slowly unfastened his belt and wrapped one end round his hand, leaving the buckle end hanging loose. With a quick movement he brought the belt round in a swinging arc and the buckle skimmed her scalp. 'The next one's gonna change yer face,' he snarled.

'I don't care,' she cried. 'Yer can't make me do nuffink.'

At the look of hatred in her eyes all his self-control left him and he brought the belt down hard around her shoulders. She screamed in agony and he suddenly realised that the neighbours would hear her cries. He grabbed her up and hit her hard on the jaw with his clenched fist and she fell to the floor in a heap. He stood over her for a while fuming, furious that it was not working out the way he had planned, and he looked around the room, trying to think clearly. Suddenly he saw her handbag lying on the sideboard and he grabbed it up and searched through it for Sam Colby's address, but without success. As he searched through the flat he grew more and more frustrated, and finally, when he had exhausted all possibilities, he slumped down in the armchair and stared down at Mandy's prone figure. She was lying perfectly still and he bent down and turned her on to her back, putting his ear close to her chest. He could hear her heart beating but she was still unconscious and he stood up, cursing his luck. There was one last chance to lure Colby to the flat, he decided. Failing that he would have to take the more dangerous option and go looking for him.

Tommy Kerrigan sat in the Rising Sun along with his brothers Joe and Bernie and their cousin Arthur Slade; all looked grim-faced as they waited for Sam Colby to arrive. They had heard about the explosion that morning and had read the account in the evening paper, which reported one person killed when a bomb was detonated at a yard in Abbey Street, the victim being one Nicholas Carter, a local businessman who rented the yard. The report went on to say that no one had claimed responsibility and that the one other person injured in the blast was in a serious condition at Guy's Hospital.

'Colby's talked enough about what 'e's gonna do ter Boy-boy Carter, but I can't believe this is down to 'im,' Joe said.

'Well, I don't fink it's the IRA neivver,' Tommy replied.

'The Carters could 'ave bin takin' liberties wiv some ovver mob,' Arthur Slade remarked.

'Plantin' a bomb under a van ain't the way fings are done around 'ere,' Tommy told them.

Sam Colby came into the bar and walked straight to the counter to get a drink, with just a brief nod to the Kerrigans.

'Are yer gonna front 'im?' Joe asked.

Tommy did not answer, and when Colby joined them he looked him straight in the eye. 'Did yer read about the bomb in Abbey Street?' he asked him.

Colby smiled mirthlessly. 'Yeah, shame ain't it?' he replied, sipping his beer.

'This alters everyfing,' Kerrigan said, his eyes still fixed on Colby.

'Why should it?' Colby asked him.

'Well, fer a start, Scotland Yard's involved. They'll close the Carters' perfume caper down fer sure, if they find out it's a brand name that's bein' copied.'

'I should fink Boy-boy's already sorted that out,' Bernie cut in.

Sam Colby looked around at the group. 'The time's arrived fer us ter make our move,' he told them. 'The Carters are finished now. Boy-boy's a nutter. We pull in the rest o' the mobs under us an' we can spread our net. We'll take control from 'ere down as far as Deptford. All the dock area an' the street markets'll be controlled by us. The prospects are endless.'

'And who's gonna be the big man in overall control?' Tommy Kerrigan spat out. 'Who's gonna be the little Caesar, the Al Capone? Not me.'

'Now listen ter me. The rest o' the local mobs are gonna

fall inter line, I've got assurances,' Colby went on. 'You eivver fall inter line too or concentrate all yer efforts on scratchin' a livin' on the quayside. There's no sittin' on the fence.'

'Well, I must say I always suspected that you 'ad ambitions, Sam, but this is madness,' Tommy said, his eyes narrowing. 'Tell me straight up. Was you responsible fer that bomb terday?'

Before he had a chance to reply the landlord called out. 'Sam, yer wanted on the phone.'

'We're waitin' fer an answer, Sam,' Kerrigan said, his voice rock hard.

Colby merely grinned lopsidedly as he walked over to the counter.

'Come frew,' the landlord told him, lifting the bar flap.

Colby walked into the small back room and picked up the receiver.

'Mr Colby? Mr Sam Colby? I'm Mr Collis who lives next door ter yer wife's sister Mandy. We 'eard a lot o' noises comin' from 'er flat an' my wife knocked ter see if everyfing was all right. I'm afraid Mandy's bin beaten up pretty badly. I've called the ambulance but she wants ter see you. She told us yer might be at the pub and you'd know what ter do. She said ter tell yer it was the same one as last time.'

'What else did she say?' Colby asked quickly.

The phone suddenly went dead and as he stood holding the receiver the landlord put his head round the door. 'Is anyfing wrong?' he asked.

Colby ignored him and hurried over to the Kerrigans. 'I've just 'ad a phone call ter say Gwen's sister's bin beaten up,' he told them. 'It could be a setup but I'll 'ave ter take that chance. I can't leave the gel, she's asked fer me. I'll 'ave ter go.'

'Well, yer better get movin' then, 'adn't yer?' Tommy Kerrigan told him, an icy tone in his voice.

Colby had expected at least one of them to volunteer to go with him as a backup, but as he looked from one to another he saw only hostility. He gritted his teeth in anger as he turned on his heel and stormed out of the pub.

As soon as he had left Tommy Kerrigan started the ball rolling. 'Bernie, Joe, we need ter meet wiv the ovver teams as soon as possible,' he declared. 'Arfur, contact Robey an' Dorkin. Bring them in as well. We'll make it the Samson's Arms termorrer night. Eight sharp.'

''E didn't 'ave to own up, did 'e?' Joe said disgustedly. 'Yer could see it in 'is eyes.'

Sam Colby hurried into his house near the pub and emerged a few seconds later with a length of lead piping tucked into his belt and a cutthroat razor in his coat pocket. He strode through the quiet backstreet and turned into New Kent Road. A short distance up ahead was the street where his sister-in-law lived, and as he hurried into the quiet turning he saw a hunched figure wearing a cap pulled down over his ears, beckoning to him. As he reached him the man straightened up and Colby gasped as he saw the face. At the very instant his hand closed over the lead piping, a long-bladed knife was plunged into his chest up to the hilt.

Chapter Thirty-Four

Charlie walked out of Sunlight Buildings early on Tuesday morning and crossed the street to knock for Linda. She looked pale and heavy-eyed as she stood back to let him in.

''Ave you 'ad yer breakfast?' she asked him.

The young man nodded as he walked into the parlour. 'Yeah, an' a long ear'ole bashin' from me muvver as well,' he told her. 'She's terrified I'm gonna be the next one ter get it.'

'Charlie, don't!' Linda said, looking horrified. 'I've 'ad no sleep all night worryin' about everyfing. Even James started quizzin' me before 'e went off ter work. 'E said that if Mum an' Dad 'ear about the killin' they'll come 'ome straight away.'

'P'raps they won't get ter know,' Charlie said hopefully. 'After all, it's not a local matter where they are.'

'Yeah, but they could 'ear it on the news broadcasts, an' it'll be in the national newspapers,' Linda replied.

Charlie watched her pour the tea. 'I know what. Why don't yer phone their lodgin's? 'Ave yer got the number?'

'Yeah, it's up 'ere on the mantelshelf.'

'We could go down the post office this mornin',' he suggested.

Linda handed him his tea. 'What we gonna do about the job, Charlie?' she asked.

'We'll just 'ave ter wait an' see,' he replied. 'I dunno about Tony. The way 'e stormed out o' the arch yesterday anyfing could 'ave 'appened.'

'What about Gilda? D'yer fink she'll come in?' Linda asked.

'She's a very strong woman,' Charlie said. 'I fink she will.'

A short while later they walked out into the market and made their way to the post office next to the Bricklayer's Arms. Linda made the call and after a couple of minutes she came out of the booth smiling. 'They'd just read about it in the mornin' papers,' she told him. 'I 'ad a good chat wiv Mum an' she's all right now. They were worried sick an' thought they'd better come 'ome terday.'

'Well, that's one fing sorted out,' Charlie said as he took her arm. 'Let's get down the arch.'

The morning was cooler than of late with light fluffy clouds drifting high in a bright blue sky. Trams and buses rumbled along the busy Tower Bridge Road as they always had and people passed to and fro beside the stalls, where the market traders were busy and shoppers stood chatting together about the prices and their children. They were the same sights and sounds that had greeted Linda every morning on her way to the wine vaults, but today everything seemed unreal to her. She gripped Charlie's arm and tried to control her nervousness as they turned into Abbey Street, knowing that they would have to pass the shattered yard.

'They've taken everyfing away, even the gates,' Charlie remarked as they reached the entrance.

When Linda looked down and saw the dried bloodstains

on the pavement she shuddered and averted her eyes. 'I wonder 'ow Gilda is?' she said quickly, trying to get the image of the blood out of her mind.

They crossed the street and knocked on the door of the arch, hardly expecting a response, but the bolts were immediately drawn back and Gilda stood before them with a sheaf of papers clasped in her hand.

'The police are calling very soon,' she announced. 'They want us all here.'

Charlie looked at her closely: she appeared to be quite calm, though pale and drawn. 'Are yer feelin' OK?' he asked her.

She gave him a wan smile. 'I took a couple of sleeping tablets last night,' she replied.

They went into the office and Gilda sat down at the desk. 'I've got the books ready,' she said. 'They show our trading figures and orders. The police will definitely want to see these. We must stick to our story: the perfume we produced was a cheap imitation scent that we supplied to local traders. We'll say that the business has folded and at the moment we're looking at the possibility of going into the leather trade. It's something I know a bit about and I can answer any awkward questions if the need arises. Charlie, have you destroyed all the labels and packaging?'

'Every bit,' he told her.

'That's good,' she said nodding.

''Ave yer seen Tony this mornin'?' Charlie asked her.

She shook her head. 'I couldn't see anything in the morning papers but I'm convinced Tony's killed Sam Colby,' she said quietly. 'If he has it'll certainly be in the midday edition.'

'The police'll wanna talk to 'im,' Linda remarked.

361

'We'll have to cover for him,' Gilda told her. 'We'll say he's taking it very badly and we'll get him to call in the station as soon as we see him.'

'What about the women?' Charlie asked.

Gilda sighed sadly. 'I had to lay them off with a week's pay, and a promise that we'll take them back on later, if at all possible,' she replied. 'There was nothing else I could do.'

'No, of course not,' Charlie said supportively.

'I've asked them to come back this afternoon for their money,' she added. 'I'll need you to help me get it ready, Linda.'

'Yeah, sure,' the young woman told her.

Gilda stared down at her clasped hands for a few moments. 'Con Ashley and Don Jacobs came in early and I explained everything to them,' she continued. 'They understood the position. As a matter of fact they left a few minutes before you got here. I haven't seen anything of George Morrison, though. He was close to Nick and he was very cut up yesterday.'

Linda was watching Gilda intently while she spoke and was amazed at her calm, businesslike manner. Her voice was level and unemotional and there was an air of steely control about her. It was as though she had closed the door on a large part of herself, shutting it off from her mind, and was determined to carry on as if nothing had happened to her.

'I'm just hoping Tony will turn up before the police get here,' Gilda went on. 'He's walking a tightrope if he did kill Sam Colby last night. Even if no one saw anything, it could still get really serious if Billy Nelson rallies enough to make a statement. As a matter of fact Don Jacobs told me he tried to get in to see him but he wasn't able to. He found out from one of the hospital porters that the police have got a round-the-clock guard at his bedside.'

'Is there anyfing more we can do now?' Charlie asked her.

'No, Charlie. There's nothing you can do right now,' she replied. 'There's nothing any of us can do.'

'Shall I put the kettle on?' Linda suggested

'That's a good idea,' Gilda said, forcing a smile.

Patrick Foley smiled to himself as he took his mug of coffee into the front room early that morning and sat down by the empty hearth. He hadn't lost his touch, evidently. The device had worked and one more grievance had been settled. It was a pity someone had to die, but that was no fault of his. He was a craftsman, like the carpenter who builds the scaffold or the gunsmith who tools the rifle or revolver. There had always been means available to deal out retribution, from the arrow and club to the gun and explosive, and he was willing to argue that his way was the most efficient.

The Irishman sipped his coffee, aware that, since the IRA would not claim responsibility for the bomb, the police would know that it was a private assassination. This would widen the scope of their investigations, making their work much more difficult. All he had to do was take care. There was nothing that could lead the law to his door. Maurice would lie low for fear of being charged as an accessory before the fact and the only other player was the man who had ordered the device. All the same, maybe he should take the opportunity of going back home for a week or so until things cooled down.

The knock on the door jerked him out of his reverie. 'Who is it?' he called out.

'It's Sean McNally. We have a job for you.'

Patrick's eyes widened with surprise. He had been in place for just six months now and had not expected to become operational for some time yet. The command must be moving fast. He threw back the bolts and opened the door. 'Sean, it's good to see you after all this time,' he said smiling. 'Come on in.'

The stocky man in a dark suit walked into the shabby flat and looked around with distaste. 'I'm afraid that you've upset the commander, Pat me boyo,' he said quietly.

'No, Sean. Not me.'

'Oh yes,' the visitor replied. 'You were put here as a sleeper, obliged to wait patiently for our alarm call. You didn't.'

'I don't understand,' Patrick said quickly, suddenly frightened.

'I think you do,' the stocky man said, sliding his hand into his coat pocket.

'No, Sean! No!'

The revolver came up slowly to Patrick's head and the last thing he focused his eyes on in this world was the silencer screwed to the barrel of the gun. There was a dull phutt! and a red hole appeared in the middle of Foley's forehead.

Dan Sully sat in his office at Dockhead Police Station at Tuesday lunchtime talking to Divisional Inspector Harold Sandford and he was on his guard.

'Well, we can rule out an IRA campaign now,' Sandford was saying. 'The blast had all their markings and frankly speaking we half expected a call from them, but the execution in Waterloo this morning changes everything.

Sully nodded. 'The victim was Irish and there was bomb-making equipment found in his flat. The Abbey Street blast had obviously embarrassed them and they've responded in their own unmistakable way.'

'Someone was responsible for planting the bomb though, Dan,' Sandford went on. 'There's a killer walking the streets who's gone to drastic lengths to settle a dispute. To my way of thinking that makes him very dangerous.'

'It's very puzzling,' Sully remarked. 'Nick Carter was a local small-time villain. No convictions, but he was known to the police. He and his brother were suspected of being involved in the black-market business, but nothing more serious.'

'Let's assume that the Carters had turned someone over, or leaned on someone. Do you know of any mob who would be likely to retaliate by putting a bomb in their yard?'

Dan Sully shook his head. 'The usual outcome in this area would be a punch-up in one of the pubs, or on the street,' he answered.

'Exactly,' Sandford replied, stroking his chin thoughtfully. 'This man found stabbed to death off the New Kent Road late last night – a Mr Samuel Colby – you read the report the Borough police sent on. What did you make of it, Dan?'

'Dock worker. Known to associate with the Kerrigan brothers, also dock workers and small-time villains. No convictions,' Sully rattled off.

'Coming so soon after the Carter killing, do you feel there could be some link?' Sandford pressed him.

'It's a bit off the Carters' manor,' Sully said, mindful of what Boy-boy had told him about the altercation with the Kerrigans. 'Besides, there were no clues forthcoming from the victim's wife. They're usually quick to point fingers.'

'But not if it's likely to open a can of worms,' Sandford reminded him.

'Granted. Mobs usually take their own measures,' Sully replied.

Harold Sandford shifted his position in his chair and took off his thick-rimmed glasses, running a hand over his wide flat face before he put them back on. 'Well, you know we'll be leaving this to you local chaps now that the IRA connection has been ruled out,' he said. 'But first I'd like to visit the Carters' establishment. Call it professional curiosity.'

Dan Sully was relieved that the investigation was reverting to local level, but he was not quite out of the woods yet. He knew Harold Sandford well and was aware of the man's ability to sniff out any devious goings-on. He was notorious for it. 'I phoned the arch first thing,' he told him. 'I said we'd be calling today.'

'You know something, Dan. I've got a gut feeling about this bomb blast,' Sandford said as he stood up. 'I think the answer lies with that poor chap in Guy's.'

'Billy Nelson,' Sully replied. 'He was a Carter man until last week according to the report. He left after a disagreement. What was he doing there at the yard yesterday morning?'

'He's not been able to make his contribution to the investigation, so far,' Sandford said. 'Let's hope he'll recover enough to make a statement.'

The Abbey Street explosion had been discussed to exhaustion, and the killing in New Kent Road was far enough away to merit only a brief mention by the two hawks as they sat sipping tea in Doris's parlour. The main topic of conversation was Dick Conners and the two women were angry.

'I really thought 'e'd turned over a new leaf,' Phyllis remarked disdainfully. 'I was shocked when I saw the performance on Sunday night.'

'So was I,' Doris replied. 'Blind drunk, 'e was. It's a bloody shame. She's such a nice woman too.'

'She's better off wivout 'im, that's fer sure,' Phyllis declared.

''E was in the pub yesterday an' terday,' Doris said. ''E'll never change.'

'It's funny, yer know, but I got the feelin' Eve Jeffreys is tryin' to avoid us,' Phyllis remarked. 'She always used ter stop fer a chat but she ain't bin near since last week.'

'P'raps she's too upset.'

'Yer might be right.'

'I fink I'll mention it when I get me bread termorrer,' Doris told her friend.

'I'll come over there wiv yer,' Phyllis replied, 'then we can go down the market tergevver.'

They sat sipping their tea in silence for a while, then Doris put her cup down and folded her arms. 'I wonder what sort of a week they're 'avin',' she said.

'Who?'

'The Westons.'

'I saw that Charlie Bradley goin' in there last Saturday night.'

'You know 'ow it is, luv; while the cat's away the mice'll play.'

With all angles thoroughly covered the two decided to call it a night.

'By the way,' Doris said as her friend was about to leave. 'Did you 'ear about Mrs Faraday? You know, 'er what lives over the bootmender's in Bermondsey Street.'

'I know 'er. Wiv the big earrin's.'

'That's the one. Well I 'eard . . .'

Half an hour later Phyllis left her friend's house with her head ringing, suitably shocked by the licentious carryings-on of the woman with the big earrings.

Chapter Thirty-Five

Gilda and Linda had set to work making up the women's money and cards, and everything had been ready when the first of them called at the arch. Gilda found it a sad duty having to lay them off, feeling that she was saying goodbye to friends. She promised to call them back again if at all possible, however, and it made her feel slightly better.

Linda had watched the women come and go, impressed by the way Gilda handled the situation. When Alice called in, Gilda had put her arms around the elderly woman and the two shed a few tears. Now it was quiet in the office and, as she cleared the desk and put the last of the papers away in the drawer, Linda felt close to tears herself.

Gilda took out an envelope from the safe and handed it to Linda. 'Thanks for what you've done, Lin, and your support,' she said. 'There's a week's pay in there. I'm sorry it's got to be this way.'

Linda smiled warmly. 'I'm gonna miss yer, Gilda,' she told her. 'I 'ope we can stay friends.'

'I'm sure we will,' the older woman said as she gave her a hug. 'You and Charlie must call on me soon.'

Linda looked around the office. 'Yer know, I was just

beginnin' ter feel at 'ome 'ere,' she remarked.

'Never mind,' Gilda said with a wan smile. 'At least you've got Charlie. Just hold on to him, he's a good lad. Now put the kettle on before I get all weepy again.'

Charlie had swept the backyard clean and was tidying up the work area when Dan Sully called, accompanied by the Divisional Inspector. The young man led them into the office and, after making the introductions, Sully turned to Gilda. 'I expected Tony Carter to be here,' he said.

'He's taken it very badly,' she replied. 'He's probably still at home. It's only at the other end of the street. I could send for him.'

Sully glanced briefly at his colleague. 'It's all right, we'll call on him later,' he told her.

'I know this is a sad business for you all, but you understand we do have to ask some questions,' Sandford said, looking from one to another.

'Yes, of course,' Gilda replied.

'What exactly are you trading in?' he enquired.

'Until yesterday we were bottling and marketing a cheap brand of scent,' she told him.

'And you no longer intend to carry on with it?' he queried.

'This was Nick Carter's business,' Gilda replied.

'What about his brother? Won't he take over?' Sandford pressed.

'As I just said, Tony's in no fit state to run the operation, not at present anyway.'

'I suppose you kept records of all transactions?'

'Yes, here they are. Every transaction is recorded in this ledger,' Gilda said, taking the book from the desk drawer.

Sandford took it and flipped quickly through the pages. 'I

see these are names of individuals and not companies,' he remarked.

'That was the way we traded,' Gilda explained. 'They were our punters. They bought from us in bulk and sold the scent in their own areas.'

'Has there ever been bad feeling between the company and any of the punters, as you call them?' Sandford asked.

'Not to my knowledge,' she replied calmly.

'Did you ever supply the scent to any of the local mobs, or gangs, to your knowledge?' the inspector asked.

Gilda paused before answering him. 'Not knowingly,' she said. 'One or more of the punters may have been involved with gangs or mobs, but we couldn't be expected to know. As I said, all our contacts were with individuals.'

Sandford turned to Charlie and Linda who were sitting to one side. 'What exactly do you do here?' he asked them.

Charlie spoke first. 'I 'elped get the orders ready an' delivered some of 'em.'

'I worked in the office,' Linda added.

Sandford nodded and then turned to Gilda once more. 'Would you mind if I had a look round?' he asked her.

'Of course not,' she said, getting up from the desk. 'I'll come with you.'

They walked out into the cool arch and Sandford strolled up to the long wooden bench. His eyes alighted on the stack of shallow cardboard boxes. 'What's this?' he asked her.

Gilda opened the top box. 'As you can see, they're the bottles we used for the scent,' she said.

'What about the packaging?'

'We burned it all yesterday.'

Sandford raised his bushy eyebrows. 'Why?'

'We rent the arch and before we leave we'd be expected to clear all our stuff out, so we burned what we could,' Gilda explained.

'It was rather a sudden decision, wasn't it?'

'Maybe it was,' she said, 'but you have to remember every one of us was in a state of shock yesterday. We were looking around for things to do to take our minds off the tragedy.'

'Yes, I understand,' Sandford replied. 'It was a tragedy. It was also a very unusual method of killing somebody. We tend to associate bombings with political groups, not warring villains.'

'Nick Carter was not a warring villain,' Gilda said sharply.

The inspector raised his eyebrows once more. 'I hope you won't take this as an insult, young lady, but I have to ask,' he said. 'Were you and Nick Carter more than just business associates?'

'I'm not insulted,' Gilda replied, forcing a brief smile. 'Yes, we were. We were lovers.'

'Thank you for your frankness,' Sandford said, returning her smile. 'I understand that this must be a terribly painful time for you, but you'll appreciate I have to ask these questions. My prime concern is the apprehension of whoever perpetrated this crime. The man's obviously dangerous and the sooner he's behind bars the better for all of us.'

Gilda nodded slowly. 'The whole thing is a mystery to me, to everyone. Nick never had an enemy, as far as I know. He was fair in his trading and he took on men to work for him who were down on their luck. He was very well thought of.'

Harold Sandford saw the tears beginning to form in the young woman's eyes and he coughed. 'Er, perhaps you could

372

tell me about this Billy Nelson who was injured in the explosion,' he said quietly. 'I understand he left the business only last week.'

'Yes, that's right,' Gilda replied, taking a deep breath.

'Can you tell me why?'

'Billy wasn't happy in the job.'

'A clash of personalities?'

'No, I don't think so.'

'He just wanted to move on?'

'Yes.'

'Why do you think he was at the yard that morning?'

'I haven't the faintest idea.'

'Could he have been trying to warn Nick Carter?'

'You mean he knew that the bomb was planted there?'

'Possibly.'

'But how could he have known?' Gilda queried.

'That's the mystery, if indeed he was trying to warn him,' Sandford replied, stroking his chin thoughtfully.

'It seems very unlikely,' Gilda remarked.

'I understand from the report that Tony Carter usually drove the van,' the inspector went on. 'Yesterday morning however his brother took his place. Would it be at all possible that Billy expected Tony Carter to be driving it that morning, and when he found out that Nick had taken his place he tried to warn him?'

'Are you suggesting that Billy Nelson wanted Tony to die in that explosion? That he planted the bomb himself?' Gilda asked quickly.

'It's another possibility.'

'It's preposterous. Billy and Tony were very good friends.'

Harold Sandford looked at her closely. 'He could have

fallen out with Tony, let's say over a woman friend for instance.'

'But he only left the business last Friday,' Gilda said dismissively.

'Yes, but the differences between them could have been simmering for some time,' the policeman pointed out.

'No, it's unthinkable,' she said shaking her head. 'Besides, Billy wasn't that sort. He got aggravated occasionally like the rest of us do, but whenever he did he was always apologetic very soon after. To be perfectly honest, inspector, I'd stake my life on Billy having nothing whatsoever to do with planting that bomb. In fact he wouldn't be capable of anything like that.'

The inspector looked around the arch, his eyes darting here and there. 'Where does that door lead to?' he asked.

'The backyard,' she told him.

'Do you mind if I take a look?'

Gilda led the way and leaned her weight on the locking bar. Sandford helped her push the heavy door back and they stepped out into the sunlit yard.

'This is where you burned all the labels and packaging, I see.'

'Yes.'

Sandford kicked the oil drum. 'There seem to be a lot of ashes here,' he remarked. 'You must have had quite a lot to burn.'

'Quite a lot.'

'Who made the decision to burn everything?'

'I did.'

'Shouldn't it have been Tony Carter?'

'Tony Carter wasn't all that interested in the day-to-day

running of the business,' Gilda told him. 'He was quite happy for me to take decisions.'

'But it was his decision to close the business down?'

'We both agreed it was the best thing to do. It was his decision though,' she explained.

'Forgive me, but I'm rather puzzled,' the policeman went on. 'If Tony Carter was quite happy to let you get on with the day-to-day administration, why wouldn't he let things tick over? He could have put you in complete control – even offered to sell the business to you.'

Gilda found her temper rising and she looked hard at the inspector. 'I can't speak for Tony Carter, you'll have to talk to him about that,' she said sharply. 'What I can say is, I have no desire to remain here now that Nick is dead. I'm sure that Tony feels the same way. The business was Nick's brain-child.'

Sandford appeared to be satisfied with her answer and he nodded. 'I think that's all the questions I have. I'm very grateful for your co-operation, Mrs Lowndes.'

They walked back to the office to find Dan Sully going through the ledger. Charlie and Linda were sitting together, both looking a little bemused, and they glanced at Gilda enquiringly. She gave them a secret wink and smiled at Sully. 'Is there anything else we can help you with, inspector?' she asked him.

'No, I think we've finished,' Sully replied, looking inquiringly at his colleague.

Sandford nodded. 'Yes, that'll be all for now. Thank you for your time,' he said.

The two policemen walked out of the yard into the bright sunlight.

'What conclusions have you drawn, Dan?' Sandford asked him as they walked along Abbey Street.

Dan Sully looked thoughtful. 'I've got a feeling that this vendetta stems from something outside the business, to be quite honest, Harold,' he told him. 'My opinion is that Nick Carter had got himself into some sort of trouble with the big boys. It could have been to do with gambling. I don't hold with the possibility of it being a local gang.'

'Well, it's your pigeon now, Dan,' Sandford replied. 'In my opinion Nick Carter was marketing a brand-name perfume, hence the sudden decision to burn the evidence. Gilda Lowndes and Tony Carter made a joint decision to cease trading, so the woman told me. They would, wouldn't they, knowing that our investigations would be certain to uncover the fraud. I should rope in a few of the punters and lean on them a little, if I were you.'

Sully nodded dutifully, hoping that the divisional inspector was not going to come up with any more bright ideas, but he was disappointed.

'I should liaise with the Borough station over this Sam Colby killing, Dan,' he suggested. 'I've a feeling it might prove profitable. By the way, are you still mounting a twenty-four-hour guard over Billy Nelson?'

'Yes.'

'Good man. Insist that it stays, at least until the poor chap dies, or until the doctors say there's no chance of him rallying.'

'Will do,' Dan told him.

'Come on, Sully, I'm going to let you buy me a pint,' Sandford said smiling smugly. 'Then we'll pay Tony Carter a visit.'

★ ★ ★

Gilda had relayed the gist of the inspector's questions to Charlie and Linda, and they were sitting thinking things over as they sipped their tea.

'In my opinion the man's as crafty as a cartload of monkeys,' Gilda remarked. 'He was trying to trap me, make me say the wrong thing, I could feel it.'

'Well, they can fink what they like. At least they couldn't find anyfing 'ere that'd incriminate us,' Charlie said.

'It didn't look good, Tony not being here,' Gilda said.

Charlie got up and stretched. 'I fink I'll slip out an' get the midday paper,' he announced.

The two women sat quietly, wrapped up in their thoughts, until after a while Gilda looked up at Linda. 'There's about seventy pounds left in the safe,' she told her, 'and the rent's due this week on the arch. I've a feeling it might be a good idea to pay for another month.'

The sound of a train passing overhead echoed through the empty arch and Linda shivered. 'That sound always reminds me of the war,' she said.

'Weren't you evacuated?' Gilda asked her.

'No, we stayed 'ere all frew the Blitz,' she replied. 'I remember when the doodlebugs came over. I was up on the roof o' the Buildin's in our street when one roared over. I was terrified; I thought it was gonna dive down on the block. I remember crouchin' down against the wall an' suddenly Charlie was there. 'E put 'is arm round me an' talked ter me all calm an' gentle. I fink that was when I first knew I loved 'im. I was only eleven at the time.'

Gilda smiled. 'You can consider yourself very lucky if your first love is the one you spend your life with. I married my first love and less than a year later I was widowed. I told you he died at Dunkirk.'

'I remember,' Linda said quietly. 'It must 'ave been terrible – I'm so sorry.'

Charlie came hurrying into the office. 'It's in 'ere,' he told them, holding up the midday *Star*. 'It ses Sam Colby was found late last night in Portman Street off the New Kent Road. 'E'd bin stabbed frew the 'eart.'

Chapter Thirty-Six

The two sisters sat in the quiet flat, united by grief but both secretly harbouring angry thoughts. Mandy still bore the marks of her beating: her nose was swollen and the area around both eyes was blackened. Her cracked ribs had been strapped up at the hospital and she sat upright on the divan with a cushion behind her back. Her sister Gwen sat in the armchair to one side of her, looking ashen and gaunt. She was dry-eyed and her head was bowed as she subconsciously wound her handkerchief around her fingers. Pale evening light filtered into the room and for a time the two women were silent. Mandy could feel no sorrow for her sister's husband: Sam Colby had been the cause of Billy's injuries as well as Nick Carter's death and he had paid the proper price.

Gwen was tortured by her loss. Sam had been a good husband and he had been content with his lot, working in the docks, until he got in with the Kerrigans – he had been a changed man from then on. Encountering the Carter brothers through the Kerrigans, he had come to detest them, especially after Tony Carter had insulted her in the pub that Saturday night. When Mandy became fond of Tony Carter and started an affair with him, Gwen had warned her that the man was no good but she wouldn't listen and had paid the price. Tony Carter was sick in the head; he got enjoyment from abusing women, whether running them down or beating them up, and it was natural for Sam to become angry. After all Mandy was his sister-in-law. The trouble was, Sam had always been hot-tempered, and he had let the hatred he felt for Carter simmer inside him until he wasn't capable of thinking clearly. Yes, it was wrong of him to deliberately set out to kill Tony Carter, and it was a tragedy that the wrong man had died, but none of this would have happened had Mandy heeded her words.

'I still fink you was wrong not tellin' the police what yer know,' Mandy said, breaking the silence.

'I've got ter live wiv the people round 'ere,' Gwen said sharply. ''Ow could I say it was Sam who put that bomb in the van?'

'Yer didn't 'ave ter mention that,' Mandy replied. 'Yer could 'ave said that Tony Carter an' Sam were old enemies.'

'I couldn't do that,' Gwen said, 'not wivout puttin' ideas in their 'eads.'

'Tommy Kerrigan'll fix that evil git Carter,' Mandy told her.

'I don't want 'im an' 'is bruvvers ter get involved,' Gwen retorted. 'There's Sam an' Nick Carter dead an' anuvver man badly injured. Don't you fink that's enough?'

'So what yer gonna do, let that bastard stay free?' Mandy replied, her voice rising.

'I dunno. I can't fink straight,' Gwen told her. 'I feel so empty inside.'

Mandy eased herself painfully out of the divan and went to her sister. 'I'm sorry, Gwen,' she said quietly, resting her hand on her shoulder. 'I'm bein' selfish. You must be goin' frew 'ell.'

'Sam was a good man, despite what 'e did,' Gwen sobbed.

'Yeah, I know,' Mandy said softly. 'That's right, you 'ave a good cry. 'I'll go an' make us a nice cup o' tea.'

Gwen held her handkerchief up to her eyes. 'Can I stay 'ere ternight?' she asked.

'Of course yer can,' her sister told her. 'You just rest. I won't be long.'

The kettle seemed to be taking forever to boil, Mandy thought irritably as she leaned against the dresser. Her ribs hurt and she found it hard to breathe through her damaged nose. Tony Carter had a lot to answer for. She would have no compunctions about adding him to the list of the dead herself. If he ever showed his face at her front door again, he would get a carving knife between his ribs.

The young folk had gathered up on the roof of Sunlight Buildings as the western sky changed from golden fire to a fading red afterglow. They looked out over the rooftops, along the City skyline, watching the dark shapes of purple night rising up, and as they stood in the deepening shadows they talked of many things, their hopes and fears, and desires for the future.

Jenny Jordan stood with Brendan, her short brown hair held back from her eyes with clips, and as she listened her eyes grew troubled.

'The firm managed to get a deferment for me but now I've passed my exams I'll have to go,' he explained.

'But they might send yer abroad an' I won't be able ter see yer at all,' she said sighing sadly.

Brendan laughed, his white teeth flashing in the dim light. 'I'm a trained accountant. They'll put me in the Pay Corps and I'll be stationed at Aldershot,' he told her. 'I'll most likely get a weekend pass nearly every week.'

'I bet yer'll look smart in yer uniform,' Jenny said, leaning her head on his shoulder. 'I'll feel very proud of yer too.'

Brendan slipped his arm around her waist. 'I was just thinking. Wouldn't it be nice if we got engaged before I got called up?' he said, looking down into her large brown eyes.

'Brendan, are you proposin' ter me?' she asked.

'Well, you do want to marry me one day, don't you?'

'Yer know I do.'

'Well, it's a proposal then.'

'I thought young men always got down on their knees,' Jenny said smiling coyly.

Brendan knelt down and took her hand in his. 'Jenny Jordan, will you marry me?' he said in a deep theatrical voice.

'Yes, I will,' she replied, her eyes fluttering dramatically in keeping with convention.

'I must see your parents soon,' Brendan remarked as he got to his feet. 'I'll need to ask your father for your hand in marriage to make it all formal.'

Jenny's heart suddenly felt heavy. Her mother would be very happy for her, but her father's reaction would be entirely different. When he was sober it was hard enough to talk with him, but when drunk he was impossible, and he was nearly always drunk. 'We could ask me mum instead,' she suggested.

'Why not your father?' he queried.

'I don't get on wiv me dad, none of us do,' she said quietly.

'You leave your dad to me,' Brendan told her firmly. 'If he says no then we'll ask your mum.'

'Mum's frightened of upsettin' 'im,' Jenny said, her eyes clouding.

'We'll ask them both anyway,' Brendan replied. 'In any case we could always get secretly engaged.'

'We could run away ter Gretna Green,' Jenny suggested, getting excited at the thought.

'Well, whatever happens, no one is going to prevent us getting married when the time comes,' Brendan said forcefully.

'I love you, Brendan,' she said softly.

'I love you too, Jenny,' he told her, kissing her gently.

In the deep shadows further along the roof the course of young love was not running quite so smoothly.

'I'm late.'

''Ow late?'

'Two days.'

'That's nuffink.'

'But I'm usually on time.'

'Well, it ain't my fault.'

'Whose bleedin' fault is it then?'

''Ere, I know. Why not 'ave a chat wiv Kate Selby?'

'Why 'er?'

'Peter Ridley told me she was late comin' on an' she got somefing from the chemist,' the young man said.

'I ain't takin' no bloody pills.'

'Well, it's up ter you.'

'You don't care, do yer?'

'Course I care.'

'What will yer do if I am pregnant?'

'I'll be round that barber shop quick as a flash fer me money back.'

'Yer should 'ave got 'em at the chemist.'

'I thought they'd be OK,' the young man said smiling. 'I knew they was second 'and, but the barber said they was all guaranteed not to 'ave more than one 'ole in 'em.'

'But that's terrible,' the young woman gasped. 'Second 'and! And anyway, they shouldn't 'ave any 'oles in 'em at all.'

'They've all gotta 'ave one 'ole in 'em, luv. 'Ow else is a feller expected ter get 'em on.'

'Very funny. Remind me ter laugh.'

'Look, I'm sure everyfing's all right,' he said quietly.

'S'posin' it's not?'

'Then I'll marry yer.'

'What about me mum?'

'She's already married, ain't she?'

'Be serious. She'll go mad.'

'Don't worry, I'll 'ave 'er certified.'

'Stop bein' silly an' give me a cuddle.'

The night closed in and a pale moon climbed in a black, starless sky. Its cold light shone through the open curtains into the large room and cast silvery shadows while melancholy music played on the radiogram. The woman sat in the window seat with her legs drawn up under her chin and stared down fixedly at the empty thoroughfare below. What terrible thing had she done in some previous life to be so severely punished, she asked herself. Was it not enough to have had her first love snuffed out like a candle in the wind, without losing the only other man who had ever made her truly happy?

The music finished and the constant click of the needle stuck in a groove finally compelled Gilda to move from the window. She replaced the arm and took the record off, wiping it on the sleeve of her dressing-robe before slipping it into its cover. She felt she could hear the silence, almost touch it as it closed around her, and she quickly put on the first record she laid her hands on. The 'Song of India' started up and Gilda slumped down into the divan. She had danced to that piece of music, teasing her lover, slowly drawing out the passion from him as she took off her clothes and then she had made love with him right here on the divan. Tears stung her eyes and the tight feeling in her chest grew, as though she were clamped in a steel band that would crack her bones. The music was softly killing her, but she could not bring herself to turn it off. She closed her eyes and sighed deeply, wishing the night would carry her away.

The soft touch on her arm suddenly roused her and she looked up into the large pallid face of her husband. 'Martin!' she cried out in surprise. 'You weren't due back yet.'

He sat down beside her on the divan and took her hands in his. 'I read about Nick Carter in the morning paper,' he told her quietly. 'I had to come home. I was so worried.'

Gilda noticed that he had drawn the curtains and lit the standard lamp. 'I'm all right, dear,' she said, forcing a smile.

Martin looked at her closely. 'You don't mind me coming back tonight? You didn't want to be alone, did you?'

'No, of course not,' she replied, leaning towards him.

He put his arms around her and held her tightly. 'You know I've been worried about you getting involved in that perfume business, but I didn't try to dissuade you. I just wanted you to be happy.'

'Yes I know, Martin,' she sighed. 'It's all finished now.'

'Do you want to talk about it?' he asked quietly.

'Tomorrow, dear,' she replied. 'I feel so drained. Will you hold me tonight?'

'Of course I will,' he said. 'Would you like a nightcap?'

Gilda smiled bravely. 'I don't know what you must be thinking,' she said, pulling her hands free. 'You've just got in after a long trip and you've having to wait on me. No, I'll get you something.'

'You stay right there,' Martin told her, loosening his tie as he got up. 'I'll mix you a brandy and port. It'll help give you a good night's sleep. We can talk tomorrow.'

Gilda watched him walk over to the drinks cabinet. His heavy frame and thick grey hair made him look older than his forty-five years. He was devoted to her, she knew, and so understanding. She didn't deserve him. 'Make it a large one, Martin,' she said.

Jack Thorp, the landlord of the Samson's Arms, had no idea why all the villains in south London had suddenly decided to grace his pub with their presence, but he had been in the trade long enough to know that it didn't do to get too curious. They obviously had business to attend to and they were thirsty customers.

'I've never seen it like this on a Tuesday night fer Gawd knows 'ow long,' his wife Rene remarked. 'They look a right 'andful, don't they?'

'That's Tommy Kerrigan over there. I know 'im,' Jack told her. 'Those two next to 'im are 'is bruvvers. An' see that bloke wiv the cigar 'angin' out of 'is mouth? That's Arfur Slade, Tommy's cousin. That's Derek Robey wiv the trilby on, an' the bloke chattin' to 'im is Tubby Dorkin.'

'I wonder what's goin' on,' she said.

'I dunno, an' I don't want to,' Jack replied.

Tommy Kerrigan had no delusions about why Sam Colby's murder had brought the rival gangs together. There was a lot of mutual suspicion and fear, and he knew that underneath their expensive-looking suits the members of each gang were heavily tooled up. He needed to get the leaders to one side, and to that end he moved around the bar, talking to the various groups. Finally a five-man party went over to a corner table and Tommy initiated proceedings.

'Gentlemen, I take it we're all aware of what 'appened ter Sam Colby last night,' he began.

'Yeah, there's a few bets bin laid on who put Sam's lights out,' Derek Robey replied.

'In case there's anyone 'ere bettin' on the Kerrigans, let me tell yer 'ere an' now that me an' my lads 'ad nuffink whatsoever ter do wiv it,' Tommy told them. 'Sam was one of us. As a matter o' fact 'e was drinkin' wiv us last night when 'e got a phone call. 'E went straight out an' that was the last we saw of 'im. We suspected that Sam put the bomb under the Carters' van. We knew 'e was after sortin' Boy-boy Carter out but I didn't fink 'e'd go ter that extreme. As a matter o' fact I fronted 'im about it but 'e was cagey. I was pressin' 'im fer a straight answer but the phone call interrupted us.'

'So yer'll never know fer sure,' Tubby Dorkin said.

'I fink we can find out,' Tommy went on. 'Sam was paranoid about gettin' Boy-boy an' I 'ad ter warn 'im that this was a private business between 'im an' Carter an' we didn't want a gang war startin' up. 'E seemed ter knuckle down an' accept it, an' then we noticed that 'e was gettin' very chatty wiv a no-good ponce who often drinks in our pub wiv a load o' Paddies. I got a feelin' this geezer put Sam in touch wiv a bombmaker. Anyway, we're gonna sort 'im out an' squeeze the trufe out of 'im.'

Tubby shook his head slowly. 'Sam goes to all that trouble an' ends up gettin' the wrong bruvver,' he remarked.

'Sam ends up on the slab, yer mean,' Robey cut in.

'I fink we can assume that Boy-boy Carter or one of 'is mob done Sam in,' Kerrigan said.

'I'd say that's where most o' the bettin' money is, on Boy-boy,' Tubby replied.

The other two men round the table had been listening intently. 'Sam Colby approached me last week, Tommy,' one said. ''E seemed ter fink we should get tergevver, form a syndicate an' take over south o' the river.'

Tommy Kerrigan looked him square in the eye. 'You were bein' conned, Jacko,' he replied. 'We all were. Sam Colby told me 'e'd got assurances from you lot that yer'd fall inter line. 'Is plan was fer all o' yer ter come in be'ind us, wiv 'im runnin' fings.'

'So there wasn't gonna be any syndicate?' the other man said.

'No, Dave, there wasn't,' Tommy told him. 'You was eivver gonna fall inter line or be put out o' business.'

'Did Sam actually say this ter yer face?' Tubby asked.

'Yeah, 'e did.'

'An' what was your response?'

'Unfortunately I never got the chance ter respond. Like I say 'e got called ter the phone an' that was the last I saw of 'im.'

'Well, yer got the chance now, Tommy,' Jacko Wilson said. 'What's your view?'

Kerrigan looked from one to another. 'Gentlemen, I fink we all run our respective patches pretty well,' he began. 'We get on wiv fings an' do our best not to encroach on each ovver. Us Kerrigans ain't interested in becomin' top dogs. There'd be needless bloodshed. If I 'ad ter make the choice between formin' one mob ter rule this side o' the river an' scratchin' a livin' on the docks, there'd be no contest: I'd choose the quayside, an' so would me bruvvers an' Arfur Slade.'

'That's all I wanted ter know,' Dave Buckman said quickly.

'That settles it fer me too,' Jacko added.

'What about you gentlemen?' Tommy asked Robey and Dorkin.

'I don't see the need fer any aggro,' Tubby replied.

'Nor me,' Derek Robey added.

'I fink we can take it that we all agree, gentlemen,' Tommy said, looking round at them all and smiling.

Tubby leaned forward over the table. 'You told Sam Colby that this business between 'im an' Carter was a private matter,' he said.

'That's right,' Tommy replied.

'So yer won't be goin' after whoever it was who stuck 'im.'

Tommy shook his head. 'If we find out fer sure that it was Colby who planted the bomb we can be pretty certain that it was Boy-boy who knifed 'im,' he said. 'The way I see it, it's a case of an eye fer an eye.'

'Well, I fink this 'as bin a very good get-tergevver,' Jacko Wilson remarked.

'Yeah, I fink we can dispense wiv the armoury now,' Tubby said grinning.

Jack Thorp noticed the smiles and general bonhomie when he looked over and he breathed a sigh of relief. 'I'd better put anuvver bottle o' Scotch on that optic, Rene,' he said. 'I fink we're gonna need it.'

Chapter Thirty-Seven

Linda had set two places at the table in the scullery on Wednesday evening, and while her brother James was washing his hands at the stone sink she served up the evening meal.

'Cor, meat pie,' he said, loudly sniffing in the aroma. 'My favourite.'

Linda put the hot food on the table and then placed a plate of thickly buttered bread in the middle. 'It'll be that on its own next week,' she joked, pointing to the bread. 'I'm out o' work.'

'That was a bit o' bad luck,' James remarked as he tucked into his food. 'Just one week there.'

'It was a terrible fing to 'appen,' she said.

James nodded. 'What yer gonna do now?' he asked her.

Linda shrugged her shoulders. 'I got a week's pay, so I'm all right fer the next few days, but I need ter get a start somewhere next Monday,' she told him.

He dipped a slice of bread in his gravy. 'Yer don't fancy the buildin' site, do yer?' he said smiling.

'I expect it's gonna be a factory job,' she replied, pulling a face. 'I fink Crosse an' Blackwell's are takin' women on.'

'You don't wanna work there,' James said sharply. 'I went out wiv a gel who worked there. She told me it was steamin' 'ot an' she was always feelin' sick wiv the cookin' smells.'

'Well, it's eivver that or the tin bashers,' Linda replied.

'Yer don't wanna work there neivver,' he said. 'Yer'll go permanently deaf wiv the noise.'

'Well, I don't know where else ter try.'

'Why don't yer see if they'll take yer back at the wine vaults?' he suggested.

''Ow can I go back there after only one week,' Linda said quickly. 'They'd all laugh at me.'

''Ere, I know. What about the clothes factory up near Tower Bridge? I saw a sign outside the ovver day sayin' they was takin' learners on.'

'The money's no good fer learners,' she said dismissively.

'Well, I dunno what ter suggest,' he sighed.

'Just get on wiv yer tea or it'll get cold,' Linda told him in an matronly voice.

James quickly finished his meal and leaned back in his chair. 'That was 'andsome,' he said, licking his lips.

'Want a piece of apple pie?' she asked.

'I fink I could manage it,' he replied.

Linda took the pie out of the hot oven with a teacloth and cut two slices. 'I was finkin' I might try one o' the tanneries in Grange Road,' she remarked.

James looked down at the apple pie she put in front of him before he glanced up at her. 'Linda, yer don't wanna go there,' he said with concern. 'That's bloody 'ard work. I know from experience. Remember I worked there before I went on the buildin' game.'

'Well, I gotta get somefing, an' quick,' she replied.

'Eat yer food before it gets cold,' he mimicked.

When they had finished, James got up. 'Stay there an' I'll make yer a nice cuppa,' he said, seeing her look of dejection.

Linda watched him busying himself at the gas stove. He was a quiet-natured young man and very caring, she thought. He was good-looking too and he would certainly break a few young women's hearts before he settled down.

'I've got a date wiv Josie Monagan,' he said casually. 'I'm takin' 'er up West ternight. I'll most likely be 'ome a bit late so don't wait up. I got me key.'

'I might be late meself,' Linda told him. 'Me an' Charlie are goin' out.'

'Where yer goin'?'

'Fer a drink somewhere.'

'Yer should try the Anchor at Bankside,' James suggested. 'It's right on the river an' it's one o' those old pubs. Yer can sit outside on a veranda overlookin' the Thames, if yer like. Me an Frankie used ter go there occasionally.'

'I wonder 'ow Frankie's gettin' on?' she said. 'We've not 'ad any more letters from 'im.'

'Give 'im a chance,' James replied quickly. 'Frankie can't stand writin' letters at the best o' times, an' besides, I don't reckon 'e's got much opportunity. The army ain't exactly a rest-'ome. Not when yer doin' yer trainin'.'

'I s'pose yer right,' Linda answered. 'I expect you're lookin' forward ter goin' in.'

'Yeah, but I'm gonna try fer the navy,' he told her.

'Why's that?'

'It's the uniform. All the nice gels love a sailor, didn't yer know?'

'Yer told me yer didn't go out wiv nice gels,' she said smiling.

''Ere, talkin' of which: what do nice gels get fer Christmas?'

'I dunno. What do they get?'

'Nuffink.'

'James, yer terrible,' she said, shaking her head.

'Well, I'd better start gettin' ready,' he told her. 'I'm meetin' 'er at seven.'

Linda looked at the battered alarm clock on the dresser and saw that it was ten minutes to. 'James, look at the time!'

'Yeah, it don't matter,' he said calmly. 'I told 'er I might be a bit late. She'll wait.'

'I wouldn't,' Linda said indignantly.

'Yeah, but you're not Josie Monagan,' he said, giving her a big wink as he hurried out of the scullery.

Boy-boy Carter had felt an urgent need to get away from London and he had spent two days at Brighton, trying to look up a young man he had become friends with in Borstal. The search had ended in disappointment when he finally discovered that his friend was currently serving five years for robbery. At a loss for what to do, Boy-boy travelled back to London on Wednesday evening and called at Mrs Samuels' house.

'The coppers called while I was doin' the cleanin',' she told him. 'I said you was out on business.'

'Plainclothes 'tecs?' he asked her.

'Yeah. One was fat an' goin' bald an' the ovver one looked more like a poxy doctor's clerk,' Aggie replied. ''E was tall an' 'e 'ad very bushy eyebrows.'

'The fat one sounds like Dan Sully,' Boy-boy said. 'Did they ask yer questions?'

'Nah, only where yer was.'

'Did they say if they was callin' again?'

'The fat one said 'e'd come back later. That was all.'

Boy-boy put a five-pound note into her hand. 'I dunno where I'm gonna be fer the next couple o' weeks so this'll take care o' yer money fer the time bein',' he told her.

Aggie Samuels shook her head sadly as she watched him go next door. 'That boy's gonna come to a sticky end, you mark my words,' she said to her elderly husband who sat slumped in an armchair.

Boy-boy let himself into his house and stood looking around the parlour. Everything was neat and tidy and he could smell fly spray. The cushions had been fluffed up and rearranged, and there were clean curtains hanging up. The kitchen range had been blackleaded and the hearth whitened, the tablecloth had been changed, and the few items of Nick's clothing that had been lying around were gone. For a while Boy-boy stood looking about the room with a sad expression on his face, then he went into the scullery to make a cup of tea.

The Anchor public house stood across the Thames from St Paul's Cathedral and was protected from the river by a narrow cobbled walkway and a four-foot-high concrete wall. The pub was noted for its association with Doctor Johnson and Samuel Boswell and it attracted visitors to London as well as local businessmen, market porters from the neighbouring Borough market and workers from the adjacent brewery. The bars had low oaken beams and studded leather seats, and old paintings and copper hunting horns were hung about the dusty walls.

Linda and Charlie sat in a secluded corner of the small bar sipping their drinks, intrigued by the rather loud conversation taking place at the counter.

'I was at Stratford for the season. I did *Troilus and Cressida* and *The Tempest*. Jolly taxing, if I may say so,' the ageing thespian said to his younger partner.

'I've been on location,' the other replied, brushing his thick fair hair back from his forehead.

'Really. Where, pray?'

'Scotland. We were up in the Highlands for two weeks and next Monday we begin work at the studio.'

'How terribly mundane that'll be, Greg. After all that heather and haggis.'

The young actor took a quick sip from his gin and tonic and leaned one arm on the counter. 'Actually, Robin, I'm rather looking forward to it,' he replied. 'They've got Nan Withers for the part of Flora Macdonald and Hector Ferris is playing Sir John Cope.'

'Good Lord, such talented company. You must be delighted,' the older man said, raising his eyebrows.

'Yes I am, Greg,' the film actor replied. 'There is a cloud on the horizon, however.'

'Oh?'

'They've engaged Wilf Norris.'

'Not that old queen,' Robin said, pulling a face. 'What for, may I ask?'

'He's playing the part of an English general.'

'I should have thought he'd be better playing Flora Macdonald.'

Linda and Charlie glanced at each other, smiling at the expression of disgust on the older actor's face. 'I've seen that old bloke in films but I can't fink of 'is name,' Charlie said.

Just then the door burst open and three men in overalls came in laughing noisily. They went to the counter to order their drinks, joking with the barmaid while she filled their glasses, then they brought their beers over to the table next to Linda and Charlie and began a loud conversation. At first Charlie was peeved at not being able to hear what Greg and Robin were saying up at the counter, but he quickly picked up on the discussion the newcomers were having.

'I tell yer it's Robin Oakland,' the biggest of the three said.

'Nah, that's not 'im,' the short one replied.

'I tell yer that's 'im. 'E's bin in loads o' films. As a matter o' fact 'e was in that war film about the navy. What was it called now?'

'*Convoy Alley*,' the third one told them.

'Yeah, that's right. I should remember the name of it 'cos I was in that film,' the big man said.

'Yeah, I should fink so,' his small friend replied scornfully.

'I tell yer I was.'

'Yeah, an' I was Maid Marian.'

The big man got up suddenly and sauntered over to the actors. 'I'm sorry ter trouble yer, sports, but we got a bet on,' he said. 'You are Robin Oakland, ain't yer?'

'Right first time,' the actor replied.

'I'm Len an' I'm pleased ter meet yer,' he said, holding out his hand. 'I'd like yer to 'ave a drink wiv me.'

'That's very kind of you but we're stocked up at the moment,' Robin replied, shaking hands. 'Thanks anyway.'

'Me an' my mates were just talkin' about that fantastic

film you was in. You know the one. *Convoy Alley*.'

'A very good film,' Greg cut in.

'Don't yer do any more actin', Robin?' the big man asked.

'I'm on the stage now, dear boy,' Robin told him.

'I was in that film *Convoy Alley*,' Len said.

'You were?'

'Yeah, I was. Straight up.'

'I'm afraid I don't remember you.'

'Nah, I don't s'pose yer would,' the worker told him. 'D'yer remember that bit when you was on the quayside an' you was talkin' ter the admiral? Well, just then an aircraft carrier comes past in the background. It was the *Newcastle* an' I was a killick stoker on it at the time.'

'Good Lord,' Robin replied. 'And what are you doing now, Len, resting?'

'Nah, we work nights in the brewery,' Len told him. 'We're just takin' our break.'

The smaller of his companions looked across at Linda and Charlie. ''E's so embarrassin' at times,' he said sighing. ''E talks to anyone.'

The pub was filling with brewery workers and the two young lovers decided to set off for home.

'You're quiet,' Charlie said after a while.

'I was just finkin' about all that's 'appened,' she replied.

'Well, we're back where we started, by the look of it,' he said, giving her a brief smile.

'You wasn't finkin' o' goin' back to diggin' ditches, was yer?' Linda asked.

Charlie shrugged his shoulders. 'I've got enough money ter see me frew this week,' he replied. 'I'll 'ave ter see what's doin' at the labour exchange next week. What about you?'

'It looks like Crosse an' Blackwell's or the tin bashers',' she told him.

'I fink we'd better make the most o' this week, Lin,' he said with a laugh.

The night was setting in as they walked back to Eagle Street. It was still very humid and people were standing at their doors chatting.

''Ello, Linda, 'ow's yer mum an' dad? 'Ave you 'eard from 'em?' Doris said as they walked along the little turning.

'Yeah, they sent a card. They're 'avin' a lovely time.'

Charlie noticed that Doris and her next-door neighbour were watching them intently as Linda slipped her key into the lock and let them into the house. 'Nosy ole bats,' he growled.

'Yeah, they just wanted me ter know that they know about Mum an' Dad bein' away,' Linda replied, slipping off her light cardigan.

'Is James out?' Charlie asked her.

Linda came up close to him and slipped her arms around his neck. 'James is takin' Josie Monagan out ternight an' 'e finks 'e's on a winner,' she told him. 'As a matter o' fact 'e said 'e'll be 'ome late. So what are yer gonna do about it, Charlie Bradley?'

'We could pass the time away playin' cards, I s'pose,' he replied, a smile appearing on his lips.

'Or we could play naughty games,' she said in a husky voice.

'That sounds good,' Charlie said, hugging her tightly round the waist. 'P'raps yer better show me.'

'No, you show me,' Linda whispered, pulling his head down for a kiss.

'What about James?' he asked. ''E might come in early an' surprise us.'

'No chance. I put the catch up when we came in,' she told him.

Charlie took her by the hand and led the way up the flight of stairs to Linda's bedroom. He pulled her to him and kissed her passionately on her open mouth, feeling the warm curves of her firm young body through the thin cotton dress.

'I've not stopped finkin' about last Saturday night,' Linda said breathlessly. 'Love me, Charlie. Love me good.'

He quickly undid the buttons of her dress and reached round to unclip her brassiere, and very soon she stood naked before him in the dark room. His hands were shaking with the desire coursing through him as he took off his shirt and unbuckled his belt. She felt his lips closing on her nipples and gasped with delight as he kissed her body, his mouth hot and wet on her flat belly. She leant her head back, arching up at the soft urgency of his tongue, and then she pulled him back down on to the cool bed and he came into her. She raised her hips beneath him, hardly able to get enough of his loving, and Charlie rose above her as he moved faster and faster. Her groan of ecstasy melted into his as they climaxed together, and he kissed her wet face as they rolled on to their sides, still entwined with love.

Outside, the moon was riding high in the velvet sky, and footsteps sounded and died away as Dick Conners walked home from the pub more steadily than he had for many a night.

Chapter Thirty-Eight

Maurice Crowley had always prided himself on the fact that he was a very good fixer. He often boasted to his few friends and many contacts that he could fix anything, at a price. Maurice had put villains in touch with a hard-up lorry driver and then subsequently read in the newspaper that a load had been hijacked. He had put another lorry driver in touch with a crooked wholesaler and Bermondsey was later swamped with black-market salmon. Another time Maurice had sat listening to an inebriated husband crying into his beer over his wife's infidelity and then put the man in touch with the Malandanes, who, for a few pounds and a round of drinks, put the unfortunate 'other man' in hospital.

Maurice Crowley had two phobias. One was dogs and he felt that every dog around was after taking a chunk out of him, so he avoided them like the plague. His other fear was physical toil of any description. Maurice would do anything to avoid soiling his hands. He pimped, set up meetings and put people in touch, and when he was down on his luck he scrounged drinks. The Irish navvies working on the sewers were always good for a touch, and he managed to ease himself into their company one night. They were a long way from home, earning good money doing a filthy, dangerous job, and they were a warm-hearted lot with a huge capacity for drink. It was through them that Maurice first found out about Patrick Foley.

Now, after reading that the Irishman had been found shot dead at his flat in Waterloo and hearing of Sam Colby's murder, Maurice was running scared. He felt that his latest bit of business was somehow jinxed and he was convinced that he was next on the list. He dared not go into the Rising Sun, at least until things had quietened down, and he was afraid of using the well-known pubs in the area in case he was spotted. He had to earn a living, though, and there was the small matter of two hundred cases of tinned fruit to be placed.

Maurice made a couple of phone calls, and when he had got a prospective buyer interested he arranged to meet him in a quiet pub behind Jamaica Road. The Ram was a watering-hole that people tended to avoid. The landlord was grumpy, the beer was never very bright, and the clientele were mainly older folk who used the establishment out of necessity rather than choice. People often wondered how the Ram managed to survive, but it did, and Maurice felt comparatively safe from detection when he walked in there on Thursday evening.

Among the few elderly customers in the pub that evening were Percival Enright and his wife Dolly. Percival was an ex-docker and still a trade-union official, and after collecting the men's subscriptions at the Labour Club in Rotherhithe every Thursday night he usually met his wife in the Ram for a relaxing drink. 'What's that whoreson doin' 'ere? he said, nodding over towards the far table.

'Who yer talkin' about?'

'Why, 'im over there,' he said sharply.

Dolly followed her husband's eyes. 'D'yer know 'im?' she asked.

'That's Maurice Crowley,' he told her. 'Our Tommy's lookin' fer 'im.'

'What for?'

'I dunno. Tommy was talkin' about 'im last night at the Risin' Sun,' Percival said. 'I fink they wanna ask 'im a few questions.'

'Why, what's 'e done?'

'I dunno. Tommy was just tellin' young Bernie an' Joe ter see if they could locate 'im.'

'P'raps you should go an' tell 'im Tommy wants ter see 'im,' Dolly suggested.

'If I did that yer wouldn't see 'is arse fer dust,' Percival told her. 'The way Tommy was talkin' it sounded a bit serious. The bloke could 'ave stitched 'em up or somefing.'

'Well, it's nuffink ter do wiv you,' Dolly remarked.

'Tommy's your nephew,' Percival retorted. 'Yer don't want anyone stitchin' your family up, do yer?'

'So what yer gonna do then?'

'I'm gonna slip outside an' use that corner phone, that's what,' he replied.

Maurice had made the deal and was pleased with his success. It had earned him a nice few bob, he thought as he looked down at the near-empty glasses. Never a generous spirit when it came to putting his hand in his pocket, he reluctantly went to the bar and ordered two large whiskies. He was out to impress, and it could pay dividends after all.

There was money to be earned and sometimes a man had to speculate to accumulate, he reminded himself.

Bernie and Joe Kerrigan arrived by taxi ten minutes later and when they entered the bar Maurice Crowley nearly died of fright.

''Ello, lads, what you doin' 'ere?' he gulped.

'Bruvver Tommy wants a chat, Maurice,' Bernie told him.

'I dunno if I can make it this evenin',' the fixer said, trying to impress his contact.

'I'm afraid yer got no choice,' Joe said, smiling coldly at him.

The young black marketeer did not know of the Kerrigans and he looked up at the brothers with disdain. 'Look, we're talkin' business,' he told them. 'Do yer mind?'

'Certainly not,' Joe replied. 'Now piss off, the meetin's finished.'

'Now, you listen 'ere,' the young racketeer began.

Bernie reached down and took the man by his coat lapels, yanking him out of his seat. 'I'm tellin' yer fer the last time ter piss off, or I'll chuck yer frew the bloody winder,' he growled, his face inches from the young man's.

The landlord had not witnessed any trouble in his pub since the night Granny Smith took her umbrella to him when he told her she had had enough to drink, and he stood open-mouthed as the well-dressed young man hurried out white-faced and badly shaken. He then watched in amazement as the two burly men picked up his customer by the arms and frogmarched him out to the waiting taxi.

'What's goin' on, fer Gawd sake?' he asked Percival.

'Dunno, mate,' the ex-docker replied. 'It's a mystery ter me.'

The landlord put his hands on his hips and tried to look important. 'I don't want too much o' that, it'll give the pub a bad name,' he said in a stern voice.

Mandy Davis had held her sister's arm tightly as she walked up the steps of the Borough Police Station earlier that day. 'I'd like ter see Chief Inspector Thomas,' she told the desk sergeant.

'If you'll just give me your name and address, madam,' he replied, looking at her inquisitively.

Mandy sighed irritably and rattled it off. 'I wanna see 'im right away,' she said sharply.

'Can you tell me what it's concerning?' the sergeant asked.

'No, I can't. Now do I see 'im or not?'

'I'll see if he's available.'

Mandy turned to Gwen Colby. 'Now listen, luv, there's nuffink ter be frightened of,' she told her. 'Just relax an' leave this ter me.'

A thick-set man with a mop of ginger hair came out of an adjoining office and looked over at the two women, immediately recognising the dark-haired one as Mrs Colby. 'It's all right, sergeant, let them come through,' he said.

The two women walked into the office and were given seats. Mandy smiled quickly at Gwen while the inspector settled himself at his desk.

'It's a bit of a surprise seeing you here, Mrs Colby,' he said. 'How can I help you?'

'I'm Mandy Davis, Gwen's sister, an' we've both got some information regardin' Sam Colby's murder,' Mandy told him.

The inspector looked from one to the other. 'Who'd like to start?' he asked.

Gwen Colby looked nervously at the policeman. 'I'm afraid I never told yer everyfing when yer come ter see me,' she began. 'Sam was my 'usband an' I was tryin' ter protect 'im, but I can't go on bottlin' all this up. As a matter o' fact, my 'usband was the one who put the bomb under the van in Abbey Street.'

'Did he tell you?' Thomas said quickly.

'Yeah. 'E said that when Boy-boy Carter went ter get the van out that mornin' 'e was gonna get a nasty surprise.'

' "Boy-boy" meaning Nick?' the policeman queried.

'No, Boy-boy Carter is Nick's younger bruvver, Tony,' Gwen explained. 'Everyone calls 'im Boy-boy. The bomb was meant fer 'im. There was a lot o' bad blood between my Sam an' Boy-boy.'

'This puts a different light on things,' Thomas remarked.

'Boy-boy Carter killed Sam,' Mandy told him.

'What makes you say that?' he asked.

'Because 'e came ter my flat earlier that night an' . . .'

'Hang on a minute,' the inspector cut in. 'You know Carter?'

'Yeah, 'e was my boyfriend once, but even after I got rid of 'im 'e still thought 'e owned me,' Mandy explained, disgust showing on her face.

'You were saying that he went to your flat.'

'Yeah, 'e wanted Sam's address, an' 'e wanted ter know where 'e'd most likely be at that time o' night.'

'And you refused to tell him?'

'Yeah, an' then 'e beat me up badly, didn't 'e, Gwen?'

'How did Boy-boy Carter find out it was Sam Colby who

406

planted the bomb?' the inspector asked.

''E said that Billy Nelson told 'im before 'e went unconscious,' Mandy replied.

'How does Billy Nelson fit into all this?' Thomas asked.

The two women looked at each other quickly. 'Billy used ter be wiv the Carters,' Gwen answered, 'but there was a bust-up between 'em over somefing that 'appened a long time ago. I dunno what it was. Anyway, I told Billy what Sam 'ad done as soon as I found out an' 'e tried ter warn Carter, but 'e was just that bit too late.'

'Would he have been all that concerned about what happened to Carter, considering they had recently had a bust-up?' Thomas asked her.

'You didn't know Billy Nelson,' Mandy cut in. ''E's a nice, gentle feller. There's not a bad bone in 'is body.'

The inspector's eyes widened slightly. 'Do you know him very well?' he asked.

'Well enough,' she replied defensively.

'Right, then, let's get back to when Boy-boy Carter beat you up,' he said. 'What happened then?'

'I was out cold on the floor an' the next fing I remember was the woman next door knockin',' Mandy went on. 'I managed ter let 'er in an' she told me she'd 'eard loud noises an' wondered if I was all right. She looked after me till I come round a bit more.'

'So Boy-boy had left by then?'

'Yeah.'

The inspector thumbed through a sheaf of papers he had taken out of the desk drawer, then he looked directly at Gwen. 'Thomas Kerrigan told us that he was drinking with your husband shortly before the murder and there was a phone call,' he said. 'Your husband took the call and then left immediately.'

'It's a certainty that Boy-boy made that phone call,' Mandy said quickly. 'I wouldn't tell 'im where Sam was so 'e must 'ave guessed that 'e was in the pub.'

'Would he have known what pub Sam was likely to be in?' the inspector asked her.

'Yeah, 'cos the Carters used the same pub till the Kerrigans chucked 'em out,' she replied.

'Are you going to make a formal complaint against Carter for assault?' Thomas asked.

Mandy shook her head. 'That no-good whoreson's gonna end up swingin' fer Sam's murder an' that'll be satisfaction enough fer me,' she told him.

'Well, thank you both for coming in,' Thomas told them. 'I'm going to need a signed statement. It shouldn't take long.'

Boy-boy Carter was deep in thought as he walked quickly through the quiet backstreets towards Guy's Hospital. He felt certain that no one had seen him knife Sam Colby, and anything that little whore Mandy Davis had to say to the police would only be circumstantial. He could counter her by saying that she was two-timing him and he beat her up to teach her a lesson. His main worry was that Billy Nelson might rally enough to tell the police who planted the bomb. They would know then why Colby was killed and he would be the prime suspect. Coupled with what Mandy Davis might say, it would put him in a tight spot.

The strong smell of hops from the nearby warehouse hung in the air as Boy-boy reached the hospital. It was after nine and as he walked up to the reception desk the duty nurse looked up with surprise. 'Can I help you?' she asked.

'I understand yer've got a patient in 'ere by the name of Billy Nelson,' Carter replied. ''E was the one who was in the bomb blast in Abbey Street. I'm Mr Toogood. I'm Billy's best mate but I've been away fer a few weeks an' I've only just got to 'ear of it. I understand 'e's on open order. Could I possibly see 'im?'

'Normally you would,' the nurse told him. 'Open-order patients can be seen round the clock, but in this case I'm afraid not.'

'Why's that?' he asked.

'There's a police guard round the clock and they would have to give you permission to visit,' the nurse replied.

'Couldn't I go up ter the ward an' see the policeman?' he suggested. 'Yer see I'm in the merchant navy an' I've gotta pick up me ship later ternight.'

'You might ask the ward sister,' the nurse said. 'She would still have to get permission from the police though.'

Boy-boy thought hard. He might be able to fool the sister with his story but the policeman would certainly want to see some proof that he was in the merchant service. He might recognise him too. His face was known to many of them.

He nodded compliantly. 'I see,' he said, putting on a sad expression. 'I s'pose I'll 'ave ter wait till I get back from me trip. I 'ope Billy's gonna pull frew. D'yer fink 'e will, nurse?'

His sad eyes and look of concern helped to sway the young woman and she picked up the phone. 'Look, I'm not on that ward but my friend is. She might be taking her break about now,' she told him with a sweet smile.

Boy-boy lowered his head and rubbed his forehead, playing his part well while she spoke on the phone.

'You're in luck,' she told him. 'If you'll just hold on a few minutes. Take a seat over there and I'll send the nurse over to you.'

The young man walked over to the long leather-covered bench and sat down, his eyes wandering about the large reception hall. Ten minutes later he saw a portly nurse hurry along to the desk and after a brief conversation with the younger receptionist she came over.

'Mr Toogood?'

'Yeah, that's me.'

'I'm sorry you can't see Mr Nelson, but I can tell you that he's very poorly. I'm very sorry.'

'Will 'e pull frew?' Boy-boy asked her.

The nurse shook her head slowly. 'No. It's only a matter of time, I'm afraid,' she said kindly. 'Mr Nelson suffered very bad head injuries and it's a miracle he's lasted this long. As a matter of fact, he did rally for a few moments earlier this evening and he mumbled a few words. I was there at the time.'

'Did yer 'ear what 'e said?'

'No, I'm afraid not,' the nurse replied. 'The policeman had to lean over the bed to catch his words.'

'Oh well, fanks fer yer time anyway, nurse,' Boy-boy said smiling.

As he walked out into the cool night Boy-boy could feel the net closing around him. The friendship he and Nick had enjoyed with Dan Sully would count for nothing now. Turning a blind eye to trading in counterfeit perfume was one thing. Murder was another.

Chapter Thirty-Nine

On Thursday evening in the Coombes' parlour Dick Conners stood upright while Ginny brushed his suit down.

'Yer look very smart,' she told him. 'I fink I done a good job wiv this suit o' yours, even if I say so meself.'

'Well, yer certainly got the dog shit off the turn-ups,' he remarked. 'An' I must say yer've put a nifty crease in the trouser leg.'

'Now look, Dick, don't go apologisin' to 'er fer the way you are, an' don't go runnin' yerself down,' Ginny went on. 'Yer too bloody honest fer yer own good at times. Don't ferget I know yer.'

'Yes, Ginny.'

'An' don't go rushin' fings. Take it nice an' easy.'

'Yes, Ginny.'

''Ere, while I fink of it, 'ave yer got yer key?'

'Yes, Ginny.'

'I don't wanna be gettin' up from a warm bed ter let you in,' she told him. 'Are yer sure yer got it?'

'Yes, Ginny.'

'By the way, 'ave yer got enough dosh on yer?'

'Yes, Ginny.'

411

'Turn round. Let me see that collar. It's a bit creased.'

'Yes, Ginny.'

'Who tied that tie for yer, Albert?'

'Yes, Ginny.'

'Is that all yer can say, "yes Ginny"?'

'I'm sorry, luv, I'm just finkin'.'

'What yer finkin' about?'

Dick sat down heavily in the chair. 'D'yer fink I'm wastin' me time?' he asked her, suddenly looking dejected.

Ginny's eyes flared and she leaned her head into the passageway. 'Albert,' she called loudly.

There was no response and she yelled out even louder. 'Albert, get yerself in 'ere, yer deaf ole sod.'

Albert walked into the scullery in his bare feet and looked irritably at his wife. 'What the bleedin' 'ell d'yer want?' he growled. 'Yer know I was tryin' ter cut me toenails.'

'Tell Dick what yer said ter me when yer see 'im tryin' that suit on this afternoon,' she shouted in his ear.

The elderly man winced as the shock waves from Ginny's voice rattled his eardrum. 'I said 'e looks a picture. I said 'e looks like an older version of Tyrone Power. I said . . .'

'Yeah, yeah, don't go overdoin' it,' Ginny told him, turning to Dick. 'Ter be honest, yer do look smart, an' that's the first time I've seen yer come down 'ere after a shave wivout an' 'alf-'undredweight o' fag papers stuck on yer dial. Eve Jeffreys is gonna feel proud to 'ave you 'oldin' 'er arm ternight. Just remember ter walk upright. There's no need ter slummack around like yer ninety-four.'

'Yes, Ginny.'

'Are you listenin' ter me, Dick?'

He nodded. 'I feel as nervous as a kitten,' he confessed.

Ginny's face took on a motherly look. 'The trouble wiv you is, yer've bin on yer own fer too long,' she said quietly. 'After a while yer'll be as cool, calm an' collected as yer like. Eve's not an ogre. In fact she's a very attractive lady, an' you know I'm not prone ter givin' out compliments. You play yer cards right an' yer'll be OK.'

Albert stood to one side trying to follow the conversation. ''Ere, Dick, d'yer wanna borrer me watch an' chain?' he asked him.

''N' where's 'e gonna stick it, round 'is bloody neck?' Ginny said disdainfully. ''E ain't wearin' a waistcoat.'

'I was only tryin' to 'elp,' Albert replied, looking downcast.

'Albert, that was a very nice gesture, seein' as 'ow yer treasure it,' Dick said smiling warmly.

'It's years old, that watch an' chain,' Albert said, leaning against the gas stove. 'I got it at Bennett's down in Dock'ead.'

Ginny sat down, knowing that her husband was about to go off on one of his extended tales. 'Mind Dick's time,' she warned him.

Albert went on regardless. 'Beginnin' o' the war it was, an' I was on nightwork at the glue factory down in Rovver'ive. I'd made an appointment to 'ave all me teef out. Well, me top lot anyway. I come straight off me night-shift, straight in the dentist's, an' I must 'ave bin sufferin' the effects o' the gas 'e gave me, 'cos I went straight in to Bennett's the pawnbrokers afterwards an' bunged a deposit down on this chain. Solid silver it is. Cost me a pretty penny in all. Anyway I used ter go in there every Friday mornin' after an' pay a few more bob on it.

413

Took me two years ter pay it up and then I come 'ome wiv it proud as punch.'

Ginny cut into the story. 'I remember sayin' to 'im at the time, what's the good of a chain wivout the watch, an' 'e said 'e'd wait till 'e saw a nice pocket-watch an' put a deposit down on it. I thought ter meself by the time 'e finishes payin' fer it 'e'll be too doddery ter tell the bleedin' time anyway, so I bought 'im the watch when it was our weddin' anniversary.'

'She bought me the watch fer me birfday,' Albert said.

'Weddin' anniversary, yer fergetful ole goat,' Ginny growled.

'Well, I'd better get goin',' Dick told them. 'Mustn't be late.'

The neighbours were at their front doors as the reformed character walked purposefully along the turning, nodding as he passed them. Doris and Phyllis were favoured with a grin and a cursory nod and they responded with reluctant smiles.

'Wonders'll never cease,' Doris remarked as he passed by.

'I bet that suit's just come out the pawnshop,' Phyllis replied. 'I could smell the mothballs on it.'

Doris was feeling a little charitable on that warm summer evening and she let the comment go. 'I 'ope this ain't a flash in the pan,' she said. 'It's nice ter see the change in the man. I bet Ginny Coombes is pleased too. It must 'ave bin a worry lately fer the poor ole cow. She's got enough on 'er plate as it is, what wiv 'er Albert, let alone 'avin' ter put up wiv a lodger comin' in every night pissed out of 'is brains.'

Phyllis nodded as she slipped her hands into the armholes of her clean pinafore. 'I was sayin' ter Lucy Perry only the ovver day, I dunno 'ow she's put up wiv it fer so long. I wouldn't.'

'Nor would I,' Doris replied.

Lights were burning late into the night in Dan Sully's office at Dockhead Police Station and fatigue showed on the faces of the two detectives as they sat sipping strong black coffee.

'Well, it all points one way now, Del,' Sully was saying. 'We've got a statement from Billy Nelson and it's backed up with your information. We'll pull Tony Carter in for questioning first thing tomorrow.'

Chief Inspector Derek Thomas nodded. 'You'll need to break him down, Dan,' he replied. 'All right, we've got a suspect with a good motive but there's no first-hand evidence to satisfy the department. A good defence brief would tear the case to pieces. A wronged woman's belief that Carter did the murder is about the strength of it. There are no witnesses to the actual killing, and no weapon's been found.'

'We'd need to dredge the Thames to find it, that's for sure,' Sully remarked as he ran his hand over his thinning hair.

'Do you know this Boy-boy Carter?' Thomas asked.

'Yeah, he's a young buck who fancies himself with the women,' Sully told him. 'He's been in trouble as a kid, did a year in Borstal as it happens, but no further record. He and his brother Nick were suspected of black marketeering and receiving but nothing has ever been substantiated. They recruited a team of hard men and ran the Tower Bridge Road area fairly tightly. Nick Carter was the number one and now he's gone it remains to be seen what'll happen with Boy-boy.'

'Will he be likely to take over?' Thomas asked.

Sully shook his head. 'No. Boy-boy hasn't got what it takes. He's too volatile.'

'Is he likely to scarper?'

'I don't think so,' Sully told him. 'Not until he finds out that Nelson's made a statement. That's why I've refused to give the press any more details although they were pestering me earlier this evening. One shrewd bastard even asked me about a possible link between the bomb blast and Colby's killing. They certainly do their homework.'

'Yeah, they seem to know more than we do at times,' Thomas replied wryly.

Dan Sully eased his heavy frame in the chair and drained his cup. 'I think we should call it a night, don't you, Del?' he said.

The moon had risen high in the night sky as the two detectives shook hands on the steps of the police station, and Dan Sully walked off towards the tram stop still turning things over in his mind. Despite all the security and care taken to keep people away from Billy Nelson, there was still a possibility that news might somehow leak out that he had talked. If that turned out to be the case then Boy-boy Carter was not going to hang around waiting to be pulled in for questioning, and they would have a manhunt on their hands.

Dick Conners met Eve Jeffreys at the buffet in Charing Cross Station and she gave him a warm smile as she shook his arm. They strolled through the evening crowds, chatting comfortably as they made their way to St Martin's Lane.

'I'm glad you said yes, Dick,' she remarked. 'Betty's a good soul but she does tend to go a bit.'

'Won't she fink yer've let 'er down?' he asked. 'She usually goes wiv yer ter plays, yer said.'

'Goodness me, no,' Eve replied. 'Betty knows about us. I've told her and she's pleased. To be honest I don't think she's all that keen on the theatre. I think she only came for my sake. She's a dear really.'

People were milling around at the stage door and Eve pointed to a tall, distinguished-looking gentleman with flowing grey hair who was trying to enter the theatre. 'Look, Dick, that's the main character, Jon Beswick,' she said excitedly.

Dick led her towards the actor who was gamely accommodating the ring of fans thrusting pencils and paper at him. 'Would yer do one fer anuvver ole reprobate?' he asked him.

The actor looked up quickly, fixing his eyes on Dick, then he smiled. 'Yes, of course,' he said.

'Quick, Eve, give the man somefing ter write on,' Dick told her.

While she was nervously fumbling in her handbag the reformed drunk put his hand on the actor's arm. 'Stick wiv it, pal, I am,' he told him.

Eve handed the actor an envelope and he took a pencil from an adoring fan with a charming smile then scribbled in a few words.

'That's champion, Jon,' Dick said smiling. 'Much obliged. We're lookin' forward ter seein' yer perform.'

'I hope you enjoy the play. It's earned an extended run,' the actor replied.

'I'm Dick Conners, an' this is Eve. She's a great fan o' yours,' Dick told him. 'She was dyin' ter meet yer.'

The thespian held out his hand. 'Very pleased to meet you,' he said in a deep voice.

'Stay wiv it, mate, we're right be'ind yer,' Dick said as the actor edged towards the door, in danger of being buried under his ardent admirers.

'Many thanks,' he replied. 'Look, perhaps you might like to come backstage for a few minutes after the show? Just see the theatre manager. Tell him I'm expecting you.'

As he struggled through the stage door Eve turned to her escort. 'Dick, you'd get where castor oil can't,' she said, shaking her head in disbelief. 'I'm amazed.'

The two entered the auditorium and were shown to their seats. Dick settled himself and then turned to Eve. 'I didn't say before but I like the way yer done yer 'air,' he told her.

'Why thank you,' she replied.

'Yer look very nice, an' yer smell pretty good too,' he went on.

Eve nudged him gently. 'You're an old charmer,' she said smiling coyly.

The lights went low and the audience became silent, waiting for the dramatic opening lines. Eve found Dick's hand and gripped it tightly. 'I love this play,' she whispered in his ear. 'I've seen it twice already.'

The booming voice filled the theatre and the crowd was immediately captivated. Jon Beswick strode the stage like a colossus, dominating and compelling, his timing impeccable, his melodious, resonant words delivered with masterly panache and clearly audible at the back of the grand circle.

Before the first act was more than a few minutes old he had everyone captive in the palm of his hand.

Dick sat enthralled. The whole atmosphere was something he could never have imagined, and at times he was emotionally moved. His hand was being gripped tightly and he could feel Eve's reaction, hear her nervous, interrupted breathing as she waited agog for the key lines to be uttered. The cast rose to the star's performance and complemented him magnificently.

When the first act ended and the curtains came together the applause was ecstatic. People were talking excitedly as they moved out to the bar, and as Dick took Eve by the elbow to assist her down the wide carpeted stairway he felt that he had witnessed a performance of rare quality.

'Just think, we'll actually be able to congratulate Jon Beswick in person,' Eve said excitedly when they had settled themselves on a leather-bound sofa in the bar. 'I still can't understand how you managed it.'

'Callin' 'im a reprobate did it,' Dick told her with a grin.

'What do you mean?'

'Well as a matter o' fact I saw a picture of 'im in the *Daily Telegraph* the ovver day, an' . . .' Dick began.

'I didn't know you read the *Telegraph*,' Eve said quickly.

'I don't as a rule,' Dick replied. 'As a matter o' fact it was wrapped round the cod an' chips I took 'ome. Anyway there was this photo o' Jon Beswick an' underneath there was a bit about 'is rivetin' performance in *The Wings of Love* at the Play'ouse. I knew that was the play you said we was gonna see so I read the article. It said Jon Beswick 'ad done wonders fightin' 'is drink problem an' 'e was now at the top of 'is profession. It also 'ad a little quote from the man 'imself. 'E said, "I'm a reprobate in the wilderness but like the Israelites I'm waitin' ter be led out".'

'How touching,' Eve sighed. 'I wonder what he meant by reprobate though.'

'Yeah, I wondered what 'e meant by it too,' Dick told her. 'So I went ter the library an' looked it up. It means someone who's bin cast out by God, 'ardened in sin.'

Eve nodded slowly. 'I see now why Jon responded to you,' she said quietly. 'You called yourself a reprobate too and he understood.'

The audience were beginning to leave the bar and Dick took Eve's arm as they climbed the stairs to the auditorium. 'Are you really enjoying this?' she asked him with concern.

'Eve, I've never enjoyed anyfing so much,' he replied passionately.

The final act got under way, and when the ageing lover appeared on stage to plead with the young heroine to marry him the whole theatre hung on her reply.

'I have watched with so much sorrow as you sank down into the soulless depths of Hades. I've seen your last vestige of pride and dignity borne away on the wind, and I have been helpless to prevent it, Grantley, but now I see you walking proud and tall, your eyes bright and your whole manner changed beyond all recognition. I see a miracle, and I could never begin to understand what in creation has prompted this transformation. I am charged to leave it there, in the cradle of the gods, and I give thanks that they have sent you back to me. You ask me to forgive you as they the gods have done, and who am I, a mere mortal, to challenge, to defy them as they sit with expectation in their astral palaces? You ask for forgiveness, and in one breath for my hand in marriage, and I am willed to say, yes, Grantley, and yes again.'

The final lines entranced the audience to such a degree that when the cast finally took their bows the applause was deafening. After several curtain calls the shouts of 'bravo' still filled the theatre, and when Eve and Dick walked out into the foyer the crowning climax of the play seemed more real than the world outside.

'I've been a theatregoer for a good few years now,' Eve said, 'but I honestly think that tonight we've witnessed a really great performance.'

'I was 'oldin' me breath in case she turned 'im down,' Dick told her.

Eve nudged her escort. 'Look, that chap looks like the manager,' she said quickly.

Dick walked over to him. 'Excuse me but we've bin invited backstage ter meet Jon Beswick,' he said with a winning smile.

The manager gave him a strange look which mellowed slightly as Eve joined them. 'If you'll follow me, please,' he said haughtily.

Jon Beswick got up as they entered his disorderly dressing-room. 'I'm glad you could make it,' he said smiling. 'If you'll just bear with me while I attempt to get this greasepaint off.'

Eve looked more than a little starstruck. 'I thought your performance was the best I've ever seen,' she told him.

'I'm humbled,' he replied with a slight bow as he applied a thick layer of cream to his made-up face.

'You got the gel, an' that was no mean feat,' Dick added.

421

The actor smiled knowingly. 'I think we both did,' he said, glancing quickly at Eve.

'The way you performed, 'ow could she possibly say no,' Dick remarked grinning widely.

'Us old reprobates will not be put down, dear boy.'

'We try our best,' Dick said, a serious note creeping into his voice.

'I hope we succeed, but it's a hard, uphill struggle, as we both know,' Jon replied.

'Have you any plans for another play when this one ends?' Eve asked him.

'I might think about doing a spell at the Old Vic,' he told her. 'I have been approached to do *Antony and Cleopatra* in the autumn but I really haven't allowed myself to look that far ahead.'

'Well, I'm gonna watch the papers,' Dick told him. 'I've got a feelin' that yer'll be there. An' if you are, I'm gonna be there too, Gawd willin'.'

Jon Beswick put down the pad and rubbed his face clean with a towel. 'You know something, Mr Conners, I believe we will.'

They stepped out into the cool, starlit night and Eve sighed with happiness as she slipped her arm through Dick's. 'I think this must be one of the best nights of my life,' she told him.

'I fink so too,' he replied.

They lapsed into silence as they wove their way through the traffic and theatre crowds, both savouring the evening, and when they reached Charing Cross Station Eve gently squeezed Dick's arm. 'I hope you won't take this the wrong way, but would you like to come home with me tonight,

Dick? I've got a spare bedroom and it's nice and cosy. I could do us some supper, then tomorrow you could escort me to work.'

'My dear lady, how could I possibly misunderstand your intentions?' Dick replied in a theatrical tone. 'Yes, I'd be delighted.'

Chapter Forty

Mrs Samuels had never been one for enjoying a lie-in. She was up early every day, taking her husband his morning cuppa before she got on with all the chores. She was a fastidious lady, and sitting around the house or chatting to neighbours did not come easily to her. Mrs Samuels believed sincerely that cleanliness was next to godliness and to that end she scrubbed and cleaned, polished and fussed until her long-suffering husband felt compelled to reprimand her.

'But yer did it yesterday,' he moaned.

'Yes, an' I'm gonna do it terday,' she told him firmly. 'There's bin feet trampin' over that doorstep since yesterday.'

'Who the bloody 'ell's bin in this gaff 'cept you an' me?' he asked peevishly.

'I went out fer me paper an' you went out fer yer pint, that's enough ter make the step dirty,' she replied.

'You should take it a bit easy, woman,' he chided her. 'Neivver of us is gettin' any younger.'

'I got plenty o' time ter rest when I'm in me box,' Aggie declared. 'Anyway work never killed anyone.'

'It did ole Jack Bromley,' he replied. 'A set o' bacon fell out of a crane an' landed on 'is crust. Killed 'im stone dead.'

Aggie tutted. 'I got no time ter listen ter yer stories. I gotta clean next door.'

'But it's not eight o'clock yet,' he moaned.

'The sooner I start, the sooner I'm done,' she told him.

With an air of stiff-necked dignity, Aggie went next door and began sweeping out the parlour. The loud rat-tat on the front door made her jump, and when she opened it she was surprised to see two uniformed policemen standing there.

'Mr Tony Carter?'

'No, I'm Mrs Samuels.'

'We wanna talk ter Mr Carter. Can we come in?'

'No yer can't, 'cos 'e ain't 'ere.'

'We'd like ter make sure.'

'Yer can't come in unless yer got one o' them there search warrants.'

'There it is, now would yer mind?'

'Looks like I got no choice.'

The two policemen went from room to room and then as they came hurrying down the stairs one of them turned to Aggie. 'D'you 'appen ter know where 'e is?' he asked.

'Look, young man, I'm only the cleaner. I don't ask Mr Carter where 'e's likely ter be durin' the day an' 'e don't ask me neivver,' she told him sharply. ''E might be back terday, an' then on the ovver 'and 'e might not.'

'Well fanks fer yer 'elp, missus,' the policeman replied sarcastically.

'It's no trouble,' Aggie retorted in the same vein.

426

★ ★ ★

Linda was up early on Friday morning, mindful that her family would be coming home the following day and the house had to be thoroughly cleaned. She made a pot of tea and then roused James, who was his usual bright self.

'Will yer be doin' any overtime?' she asked him as he sat sipping his tea.

'Shouldn't fink so.'

'I expect they'll be 'ome early termorrer.'

'Yeah, I expect so.'

'I bet they've all got a nice colour.'

James was slowly pulling himself together. ''Ave yer got fixed up wiv a job yet?' he asked.

Linda shook her head. 'I'm goin' down the labour exchange later,' she told him.

He glanced up at the alarm clock on the dresser and was suddenly galvanised into action. 'Bloody 'ell, that clock's stopped,' he growled.

Linda watched as he grabbed for his coat, gulped a mouthful of tea and made for the door. 'See yer ternight,' she said.

Her younger brother nodded quickly. 'I 'ope yer get fixed up all right,' he called out as he left the house.

Linda smiled to herself. James was not the most demonstrative of people but he would be worrying about her, she had no doubt.

The postman walked into Eagle Street and dropped two letters into number 6. The first one was addressed in Frankie's unmistakable scrawl but the second letter intrigued Linda. The small pink envelope had a Bermondsey postmark and the address had been neatly written with a violet-coloured ink. She tore it open and read the short message.

Dear Linda,

Hoping all is well with you and Charlie. I am bearing up, with Martin's support. He has been absolutely wonderful, which brings me to the request. Can you and Charlie call round this evening? (Friday). I have something I would like to discuss with you both. Seven o'clock would suit fine. I hope you can manage it.

Love,
Gilda.

The letter from Frankie was in his usual terse style, and as she read it Linda smiled to herself. He said that he was fit and well, had made a few friends and was looking forward to coming home on leave in a couple of weeks. He also added that he was expecting to be posted overseas in the near future. Linda put the letter on the mantelshelf next to the clock and then picked up the letter from Gilda once more. What did it mean? What was it that Gilda wanted to discuss, she wondered.

Eagle Street was gradually coming alive. Children were out playing and the rag-and-bone man pushed his barrow into the turning. Doris was getting ready to call on her next-door neighbour and Phyllis had a pot of tea keeping hot under the cosy. Maggie Gainsford was boiling the copper ready for yet another family wash, while Lucy Perry darted about the house flicking imaginary dust from her spotless parlour in case anyone decided to pop in on her that day. Freda Colton at number 4 was busy blackleading the grate, and at the last house in the street Liz Selby was carefully applying face powder from a small silver compact, wanting to look presentable for her daily trip to the market. At number 5 Mary Walburton eased her considerable bulk into a chair and searched the *Daily Mirror* for her horoscope, before writing her bet out, and at number 9 Ginny Coombes sat worrying, much to Albert's amusement.

'I dunno what yer gettin' so worked up about,' he told her. 'Dick's most likely 'avin' a nice plate of egg, bacon an' fried bread right this minute, fer services rendered.'

'Don't be so dirty-minded,' Ginny growled at him. 'Eve Jeffreys is a respectable woman. She wouldn't let a man into 'er bed just like that.'

'You did, an' you're respectable,' he reminded her.

'That was different,' Ginny said quickly.

Albert picked up the morning paper and grinned to himself behind the pages. If Dick Conners was getting his end away good luck to him, he thought. Eve Jeffreys was a respectable woman, it was true, but she had been on her own for a number of years and would no doubt welcome some attention from a hot-blooded man, not that Dick Conners came into that category. He was probably too far gone now to raise a gallop.

'Are yer gonna sit there chucklin' ter yerself all day or are yer gonna put that kettle on?' Ginny shouted at him.

'All right, woman, there's no need ter yell,' he replied sharply.

Dan Sully received the news early that morning and, after arranging to have Tony Carter brought in for questioning, he spoke to the newspapermen who were converging on the police station. 'I can tell you that the man injured in the bomb blast at Abbey Street died in hospital during the night,' he informed them.

'Have you got anyone for it yet?' he was asked.

'Can you tell us if the Colby killing was a revenge murder?' another of the reporters pressed him.

'My job is to ascertain the facts, not to speculate,' Sully replied quickly. 'We are questioning a number of people and we hope to make an arrest in the near future. That's all I can say for the moment, gentlemen.'

Another reporter pushed his way to the front. 'Would you like to comment on the rise in gangsterism in Bermondsey, inspector, and the possibility that these recent killings are the start of a gang war?'

'I see no reason to believe that any such thing is about to happen,' he replied curtly. 'I also refute your claim that there is a rise of gangsterism, as you put it, in the area. This is not Chicago, nor the roaring twenties for that matter. On the contrary, I feel that Bermondsey is a decent and safe place to live. I would also say emphatically that the local police are prompt to identify and deal with any groups of young men who band together in gangs to defy the law of the land. Our record over the past five years bears that out.'

The scribes hurried away to write up their reports and Dan Sully retired to his office to think about the jobs in hand. Nick Carter's body would now be released for burial and he would have to establish a next of kin in Boy-boy's absence. Gilda Lowndes would be the one to approach, he decided.

★ ★ ★

Charlie Bradley walked on to the building site at Dockhead only to find that the construction of the block of flats was well under way.

'I'm afraid there's nothing available at the moment,' the site manager told him. 'We've got some work starting in Rother-hithe in the next few weeks, and there's some shuttering work going on at the Royal Docks. You could try there, I suppose.'

Charlie had no idea what shuttering work was and he decided that he was wasting his time. He would have to get a factory job, at least for the time being, he told himself as he made his way back home.

May Bradley was busy ironing when Charlie walked into the flat. ''Ow d'yer get on?' she asked him.

'They're not takin' anyone on, Ma,' he told her.

'So what yer gonna do?'

'I dunno. Get a factory job, I s'pose.'

'I just can't understand yer,' May said, sighing with exas-peration. 'I wouldn't mind if you was a bit fick in the 'ead, but yer not. There's a good job in the shippin' office waitin' for yer if yer'd just pull yerself tergevver. Yer a bloody worry ter me. It's the army what's done it. It's made yer too big fer yer boots. I can't take much more of it. I got enough on me plate as it is, what wiv yer sister.'

'What's the matter wiv me sister?' Charlie said quickly.

'She's carryin' again, that's what,' May replied.

'I thought yer'd be pleased,' Charlie said frowning.

'I would, if it wasn't fer Cedric.'

'Why, what's the matter wiv Cedric?'

'It's 'is back. It's gone again. Sara 'as ter do everyfing for 'im.'

'What about the business?'

'Sara said Cedric manages ter get in ter work, but the pain seems ter get worse at night. She 'as ter prop 'im up in the armchair.'

Charlie gave his mother a dark look. 'Cedric's a pain in the arse, if you ask me,' he growled. 'I fink 'e's just a lazy git. Pity 'e didn't pass 'is army medical. They'd 'ave 'ardened 'im up a bit.'

'It done you a lot o' good, I must say,' May replied derisively. 'You ain't bin able ter fink straight since yer bin out. I 'ope that Linda Weston ain't bin eggin' you on.'

'Talk sense, Ma,' Charlie said angrily. 'I know what I'm after an' I mean ter get it.'

'I'm sure yer will, workin' on a buildin' site an' sellin' dodgy scent,' she retorted.

'That's just a means to an end,' he told her. 'There's money ter be made out there, an' I'm gonna stake a claim.'

'I expect the Carter boys thought the same as you, an' look what's 'appened ter them,' May reminded him. 'One dead an' the ovver on the run.'

'Who said Boy-boy's on the run?' Charlie asked her quickly.

'It's common knowledge down the market. Everyone's talkin' about it,' she replied. 'Yer gotta remember the Carters are well known in the area. They're sayin' Boy-boy was the one who murdered that bloke in the New Kent Road 'cos 'e was one o' the Kerrigans. Everyone's sayin' that the Carters an' the Kerrigans were at each ovver's froats fer ages.'

'It's only rumour,' Charlie replied, knowing full well that his mother was right.

'Well, we'll 'ave ter wait an' see, won't we?' May told him. 'It'll all come out soon enough.'

Charlie could tell by his mother's tone of voice that it would be useless to talk any further. 'I'd better be goin'. I got anuvver job ter look up,' he told her.

The young man hurried out of the Buildings and crossed the street, feeling dejected by his mother's attitude. She was never going to understand how he felt, never going to see that working in an office was not for him. He knocked on Linda's front door and the sight of her immediately lifted his spirits.

'Now, don't you laugh at me, Charlie Bradley, or I'll not let yer in,' she warned him.

'I wouldn't dream of it,' he said grinning, 'but yer do look a bit like Doris or Phyllis wiv that turban on.'

'I'm busy gettin' the place straight fer termorrer,' she replied sternly. 'Well don't just stand there, come in.'

Charlie walked into the immaculate parlour and sat down in the armchair. 'I've just 'ad words wiv me muvver,' he told her. 'She keeps on about me goin' back in that bloody shippin' office.'

'Never mind, you put the kettle on while I finish upstairs an' then we'll 'ave a nice cuppa,' Linda said cheerfully.

'Are yer goin' down the labour exchange terday?' Charlie asked.

'I was finkin' of goin' this afternoon,' she replied.

'I fink I'll come wiv yer. They might 'ave somefing fer me too.'

Linda picked up the letter beside the clock. 'This came terday,' she said. 'Read it.'

Charlie glanced through it quickly and handed it back to

her with a puzzled look. 'I wonder what it's all about?' he remarked.

'She's certainly got somefing up 'er sleeve,' Linda replied.

She hurried upstairs to finish changing the bed linen and Charlie walked out into the scullery to make the tea. He could see that she had been busy. The stone floor had been scrubbed and the wooden draining-board was scoured white; there were fresh lace curtains up at the window and everything looked in place. There was a smell of lysol in the air and Charlie saw that all the odd bits and pieces had been cleared from the dresser. He smiled to himself as he filled the kettle and lit the gas under it, and as he waited he found himself thinking about the letter from Gilda. He was still dwelling on it when Linda came hurrying down the stairs.

'Are yer gonna let that kettle boil away?' she asked him, smiling indulgently.

'Sorry, I was just finkin' about that letter,' he told her as he poured the water over the tea leaves.

Linda came up to him and slipped her arms round his neck as he put the kettle down. 'Yer fink too much,' she said softly. 'Just give me a kiss.'

'I don't fraternise wiv the 'ired 'elp,' he said with mock severity.

'But I love the master,' she said in a squeaky voice.

'To the attic, girl, and stay there until you are summoned,' Charlie said in a booming voice.

Linda giggled and quickly kissed him on the mouth. 'I love you, Charlie,' she said.

'I love you too, Linda. Now what about that cuppa?'

434

★ ★ ★

Tony Carter had crossed the river late on Thursday night and booked into a working men's hostel in Shoreditch. He had been given a bowl of watery soup and a hunk of rye bread for his supper and then shown to his cubicle. The bedding was clean, and knowing that he was comparatively safe there he slept soundly. Breakfast consisted of two pieces of crispy bacon and an over-fried egg. There was bread on the table and tea available in a large copper urn. Boy-boy filled his mug with the strong brew and sat down to eat his breakfast.

'I know you,' a voice said.

Boy-boy looked up quickly at the old man sitting opposite him. 'I'm sorry but yer got me mixed up wiv somebody else,' he told him.

'You're Mrs Guggenheim's boy,' the old man went on regardless. 'You lot are all the same. Peas in a pod. Tell yer a mile away, I can. It's the barnet what does it. Seven kids she's got an' they're all blondies. Funny fing, she ain't a blonde 'erself, though yer couldn't call 'er dark, but she's married to Abe Guggenheim an' 'e's as dark as they come. Nice bloke. One o' yer orfodox Jew boys. Very strict, 'e is.'

Boy-boy lowered his head and got on with his breakfast, but it did not deter the old man.

'Me an' my ole dutch used ter laugh about it. She reckoned someone 'ad it in fer ole Guggenheim. I mean ter say, seven kids an' they're all blondies. It makes yer fink.'

'My name's Jones. Fred Jones,' Boy-boy told him sharply.

'My Sadie used ter clean out the ashes an' lay the fires fer

435

the Guggenheims on the sabbath,' the old man went on. ''Ow is ole Betsy these days? I ain't seen 'er fer years. Last time I saw 'er she was at Petticoat Lane one Sunday mornin'. Didn't get chance ter talk much, mind yer. She was tellin' me though that she was pregnant again. It could 'ave bin you.'

'Yeah, it might 'ave bin,' Boy-boy replied, realising that it was useless trying to shut him up. The old man was obviously out of his mind.

'Is she still around?'

'Yeah, she's ninety-two an' still does 'er own washin',' Boy-boy told 'im.

'Not on the sabbath, I 'ope.'

'Nah, not on the sabbath.'

'What about Abe?'

'Yeah, 'e's still knockin' about.'

The old man drained his mug. 'You'd be the youngest,' he remarked.

'Yeah, that's right.'

'What's yer moniker, son?'

'Fred.'

The ancient got up and walked wearily over to the tea urn to fill his mug, and when he returned he looked at Boy-boy with glassy eyes. 'Is this seat taken?' he asked him.

'No. Sit yerself down.'

'Don't I know yer from somewhere?' he asked, sipping his tea noisily.

Boy-boy wiped his plate clean with a slice of bread. 'I'm Fred Guggenheim,' he replied, a ghost of a smile on his face.

'Nah, the name's not familiar,' the old man replied.

Boy-boy hurried out into the morning sunshine, feeling as though he had just escaped from a lunatic asylum. He knew that he had to put some miles between him and London and he set off quickly towards Fenchurch Street Station. It had been a couple of years now, he thought, but Annie Scroggins might still be a good port in a storm.

Chapter Forty-One

Charlie held Linda's hand as they walked up the steps to Gilda's house and rang the bell. 'Well, we'll soon find out what it's all about,' he remarked.

Gilda was wrapped in a flower-patterned dressing-gown when she answered the door. 'Come in, you two,' she said cheerfully. 'I was hoping you could make it.'

Linda smelt the familiar aroma of Elegance and she looked inquiringly at their hostess.

Gilda smiled. 'Yeah, I know. I've just poured what was left of the oil down the drain,' she told her. 'I only wish I'd done it a couple of weeks ago.'

The two young people followed her into a smartly furnished lounge and looked around approvingly.

'This room is lovely,' Linda remarked.

'I must show you round later,' Gilda said. 'But first a drink. What would you like? Whisky? Gin?'

'Whisky'll do fine,' Charlie answered.

'What about you, Linda? Aren't you drinking?' Gilda queried.

Linda looked a little confused. 'Er, could I 'ave a port or a sherry, if yer've got one?' she replied.

'Port with lemon?'

'That'll be nice.'

'Right then, make yourselves comfortable.'

Charlie and Linda sat together on the large divan and watched as Gilda prepared the drinks. They glanced around the room at the decor and the beautiful paintings and drapes and were very impressed by the tastefulness and refinement of it all. Charlie nudged Linda and nodded his head towards a tall figurine of a crusader which had been sculpted in bronze and mounted on a polished oak plinth. 'I bet that cost a packet,' he whispered.

Gilda came over with the drinks and then sat herself down in the wide armchair facing them. 'I bet you've been wondering what this is all about, so I'll put you both in the picture,' she began. 'First though, I must tell you that Inspector Sully came to see me this morning. He said that Bill Nelson died during the night.'

Linda lowered her eyes and Charlie shook his head sadly. 'Did 'e say if Billy said anyfing before 'e died?' he asked.

'Yes he did, as a matter of fact,' Gilda replied. 'Billy rallied long enough to tell the policeman at his bedside that Sam Colby planted the bomb and that he was trying to warn Nick when he caught the blast. Sully also told me that the police are releasing Nick's body for burial and he wanted to know if I would be responsible for the funeral arrangements. He seemed to feel that Tony Carter would be well away from London by now.'

'There'll be a country-wide search fer Boy-boy now, I should fink,' Charlie remarked.

'Anyway I told him I'd make the arrangements for the funeral. It's the least I can do,' Gilda said quietly.

Charlie sipped his drink, studying her as she spoke. She looked very pale and drawn but her eyes were bright and she seemed to be in full control of herself. 'Is there anyfing we can do?' he asked.

'You're a dear, but I can manage all right,' she replied. 'So now let me tell you the reason I asked you both here tonight, if you'll bear with me. When my husband Martin read about Nick's murder he came home immediately. I was absolutely distraught, but he was so kind and considerate, and I was feeling so guilty, I just broke down and sobbed my heart out. Martin wouldn't leave me, and slowly he made me realise that I owed it to him to carry on. You might find this hard to understand, but Martin knew of my affair with Nick. He'd known since it first started, but we have a special relation-ship with each other. He loves me and I love him, in our own ways. You have to know to understand. Our love is not a physical one. Martin is impotent, you see, but we have built up a very warm relationship regardless, and he understands my needs. We lead our own separate lives but we also share a life together. Can you understand what I'm saying?'

They both nodded their heads, surprised at Gilda's frankness.

'Martin has been the lifeline I clung to and it was he who suggested the way forward,' she went on. 'He knows only too well that I'm career-motivated so he asked me to consider accepting a franchise to produce specialised leather goods at the arch in Abbey Street. The goods would bear his firm's trade mark and be marketed through his company. Our job would be to make them and dispatch them off to wholesalers nominated by him. I say our job, because I would like to involve you two. I believe you both deserve another chance after what's happened, and besides, I need you to help me get established.'

Linda and Charlie both looked shocked. 'I dunno what ter say,' Charlie muttered.

'Let me explain a bit more about it,' Gilda said. 'Martin's business is in full production and this product we'll be making to begin with is a woman's vanity case. We'll be financed partly by Martin and partly by a bank loan covered by his company. We'll get our raw materials through him and he's promised to provide a stitcher, a leather-cutter and a riveting-machine. Once we have the expertise and the experience we can branch out independently. I have to admit that at first I felt I was being offered charity but Martin soon put me straight. He explained that with our low overheads we could produce the vanity case as cheaply as his firm could, without the expense of bigger premises that he would need if he were to take on this order himself. This is a stopgap for him, and a heaven-sent opportunity for us. I wanted to find out as soon as possible what your reaction would be. That's why I asked you both here tonight. Another thing. I'd need you to start right away. Next Monday to be exact. We can discuss a salary, with a view to you becoming equal partners if and when we become successful enough to branch out independently. In the meantime you would both learn the trade and the running of the business. I'd say we need two years of very hard work to get the company off the ground. Can you commit yourselves for two years?'

Charlie's face broke into a grin as he glanced quickly at Linda. 'As a matter o' fact we both went down the labour exchange this afternoon and got fixed up wiv jobs,' he told her, and seeing the look of disappointment on Gilda's face he quickly added, 'I'm s'posed ter start work in a glue factory.'

'An' I'm due ter start work packin' custard powder,' Linda added.

'I reckon we'll 'ave ter reconsider it in the light o' what yer've just told us,' the young man said, his smile widening. 'What say you, Lin?'

'Too true. I was dreadin' comin' 'ome streaked in yellow powder,' she replied, laughing aloud.

Gilda got up and took their near-empty glasses. 'This calls for a celebration,' she said smiling. 'Same again?'

In a relaxed atmosphere, fortified with more drinks, Charlie and Linda both began plying Gilda with questions.

'Neivver of us know anyfing about the trade,' Charlie said.

'That's no problem,' Gilda replied, a crafty smile on her lips. 'You'll be meeting Stanley Beamish on Monday morning. Stanley worked for Martin for over fifteen years and he's been in the trade all his life. He retired last year and he's jumped at the chance to get back in harness. What Stanley doesn't know about the leather trade you could write on the back of a postage stamp. He's a strong character and you'll be certain to pick things up very quickly with him at your elbow, believe me. I'm also going to ask George Morrison to come back to work, and I've already talked to Alice. You remember Alice, don't you? We need four women to start with. They can soon learn to work the machines and assemble the vanity cases. Linda, I'd like you to take up where you left off, in the office. You'll have quite a lot to do, but I know you'll cope.'

'What about the arch?' Linda asked. 'Isn't it rented under the Carters' name?'

'I had to make a decision,' Gilda replied. 'The way things are, Tony Carter won't be in a position to carry on paying the rent, so I had a word with British Railways. They agreed to change the name on the rent book. As from now the arch is rented to Elegant Leather Goods Ltd.'

'Do yer fink Boy-boy is likely ter cut up rough about you takin' over the arch?' Charlie asked her.

'To be honest, I think his days of freedom are numbered,' she said quietly. 'I know it's sad, but we can't be expected to wait indefinitely. Life has to go on. It's something I've come to accept over the years, believe me.'

Charlie drained his glass. 'Talkin' about bringin' George Morrison back, 'ave yer seen anyfing of 'im since Monday?' he asked.

Gilda shook her head. 'That's where you might be able to help, Charlie,' she said getting up. 'I've got his address here in my notebook. He lives somewhere in Dockhead. Yes, here it is: 24 Grove Buildings, Herring Grove, Dockhead. Maybe you could pop round there and tell him I'd like to see him at the arch some time next week.'

Charlie took the slip of paper from her. 'Leave it ter me. I'll see 'im soon as possible.'

'Well, you two, what's it going to be?' Gilda asked, smiling at them. 'Are you going to be making glue and packing custard powder for a living? Or are you both going to try your hand at the leather trade?'

Linda turned briefly to Charlie and caught a sparkle in his eye. 'We're comin' in wiv you, Gilda,' she said firmly.

Eve Jeffreys sank down thankfully into her comfortable armchair and leaned her head back against the cushion. It was late and soft, dreamy music drifted through the cool room. Since she had been on her own she had cleaned and polished her little terraced house, kept it in good repair, and tried to carry on in the way she had always done when Joe was alive. It had been very hard, and there had been times when she thought of going down to live in Brighton with her elder sister. Cicely had asked her often enough, she recalled. There were her memories though, too many just to pack up and move away from all she had grown used to: her friends and neighbours, and the surroundings she had been brought up in. It would have been different had she met someone else who could offer her a new life of love and happiness, but no one had come along, until now.

Eve closed her eyes, dwelling on the momentous changes of the past few weeks. She had got to the stage where she had looked at herself very carefully and become depressed by what she saw: a middle-aged woman alone, slipping into a comfortable, humdrum way of life, with only the prospect of dotage ahead of her. There was nothing to excite or stimulate her, nothing to challenge her, and she had begun to look around for the answer. She found it in the shuffling, good-natured wreck of a man from Eagle Street. He had had an exciting army career and then become a respected and admired air-raid warden during the Blitz, but, as with so many people, life had dealt Dick Conners a tragic card and he had sought solace in the bottle. From respectability to ridicule, from self-assurance to self-abasement; and like her, only misery seemed to be ahead.

Eve sighed deeply and let the gentle music soothe the stirrings of her heart. She had been warmed by the decency and shy dignity of the man and felt that she could be his salvation, but instead she had become a millstone around his neck. He could have run from her, and no doubt had been tempted to, but his innate goodness had won through. Not wanting to hurt her, he had opened his heart to her and, with all pretence gone, she had unburdened herself to him, confessing her stupidity and high-minded selfishness. He could have walked away from any further commitment and they would have remained honest friends, but he had not. He had come to her of his own accord, willingly, and they had spent a glorious evening together. They had talked and laughed, enjoyed the play and strolled afterwards under a starlit sky, and in the dead of night she had gone to his bed, timorous and needful. He had taken her in his arms, stroked her back and run his hand gently over her hair, like a parent soothing a frightened child, and she had fallen asleep, happy and safe. There had been no burning passion, no urgent desire for physical love, only the desperate need to feel his arms around her.

The music had faded and now, as Eve's eyelids became leaden, she heard on the radio the solemn voice of a minister reading the epilogue from the Book of Ruth.

> 'Entreat me not to leave thee,
> Or to return from following after thee:
> For whither thou goest,
> I will go;
> And where thou lodgest,
> I will lodge.'

Up on the roof the two old men sat on the wooden bench, smoking their pipes as they reminisced.

'There'll be a large block o' modern buildin's over this place afore long,' Jack remarked after a while.

'Not in our lifetime, though,' Bill replied.

'I dunno. Look at the changes round 'ere this last few years,' Jack said, tapping his pipe on the heel of his boot.

'Yeah, but that was the war,' Bill told him. 'It forced changes. They're startin' ter fill the gaps in, put up new 'ouses, but they won't pull the likes o' these places down. They'll most likely fall down of their own accord before then.'

'I s'pose yer could liken it ter the old London at the time o' the great fire,' Jack said, unzipping his tobacco pouch. 'That came just in time ter wipe out the plague an' then they built a new city out o' the ashes.'

'Well, once they build this new London they're all talkin' about it'll be goodbye to all those pigeon lofts,' Bill remarked. 'It stands ter reason, yer can't keep pigeons on slopin' roofs.'

'Perish the thought,' Jack mumbled as he drew hard on his refilled pipe. 'It'll be goodbye ter those rabbit 'utches an' outside carseys too.'

'I was never one fer rabbits,' Bill said, scratching the tip of his nose.

'Me neivver,' Jack replied.

A light breeze stirred the cloud of tobacco smoke above their heads and Bill rolled his shoulders. 'I fink I'll turn in,' he said. 'It's gettin' cooler.'

'Yeah, me too,' Jack answered. 'It's bin a long week.'

Chapter Forty-Two

John Weston leaned back in his favourite chair and clasped his hands across his middle. 'It was a lovely 'oliday,' he said. 'The place we stayed at was nice an' clean an' the food was good, but it's good ter be 'ome none the less,' he said smiling at Linda and Charlie.

'Yer look really brown, all of yer,' Linda remarked. 'It's certainly done yer good.'

'We got a present for yer,' Pamela butted in.

'It's in the case. Yer'll 'ave ter wait till I unpack it,' Dora told her.

'Me an' Tommy got presents for yer too,' Ben said, sidling up to Linda.

'I can't wait,' she replied, putting her arm around the lad.

'It was a glorious week,' Dora told them. 'We went on the beach every day.'

'I was a bit worried about ringin' yer, but I'm glad I did,' Linda said.

'Yeah, when we 'eard about what 'appened we were comin' 'ome straight away,' Dora replied. 'Wasn't it terrible?'

John looked at the children. 'Why don't you kids go

outside an' play,' he said. 'Yer muvver'll call yer in when she's sorted the presents out.'

'We wanna give 'em out,' Ben said quickly.

'So yer shall. Now off yer go,' John told them.

As soon as the children were out of the room Linda went over the events of the week with her parents listening intently.

'God Almighty, it could 'ave bin one o' you near that van when it went up,' Dora said, holding her hand up to her face.

'D'yer fink Boy-boy Carter killed this Colby bloke?' John asked.

Charlie nodded. 'I don't fink there's any doubt,' he told him. ''E went stormin' out o' the arch like a lunatic just after the blast. I couldn't stop 'im, an' we've not seen 'im since. I imagine 'e's well out o' London.'

'Is there any more about it in the papers?' Dora asked.

'I dunno,' Charlie replied. 'I've not seen this mornin's yet.'

Linda picked up the *Daily Mirror* from the table and quickly riffled through it. 'They're still talkin' about Billy Nelson dyin',' she said.

Charlie took the paper from her. 'It ses 'ere the police are questionin' people. I wonder if they've got Boy-boy.'

'I don't like you two bein' mixed up in all this,' Dora declared anxiously.

'We're not in any danger, Mrs Weston,' Charlie said reassuringly. 'All that perfume malarkey is finished an' done wiv. This new business is entirely different. It's all above board, an' there's a real good opportunity fer both of us. The way Gilda was talkin' I fink she wants us ter go in wiv 'er as partners once the company gets established. In any case we'll both be earnin' more than we'd get workin' in a factory.'

'Well, it certainly sounds good, from what yer've told us,' John remarked. 'The way I see it, anyfing's better than factory work, an' I should know. Just as long as it's all above board. We don't want you gettin' involved in anyfing dodgy, Linda, nor you, Charlie.'

The young woman went to him and slipped her arm around his shoulders. 'Now don't you concern yerself, Dad. There's nuffink ter worry about, really.'

Outside in the little street women went to and from the market and children played their usual games. Maggie Gainsford's two eldest boys were engaged in the time-honoured escapade of running the gauntlet in Sunlight Buildings. They crept up the flights of stairs and peeped out on to the roof to make sure the coast was clear before going over to the balustrade and waving down to the less daring children below. Ronnie Gainsford was eight years old and felt that it was an easy dare, but Bob, his six-year-old brother, was less confident and he looked around the roof area furtively. 'Come on, Ron, let's go down again, in case the caretaker comes,' he fretted.

'I ain't frightened of 'im,' Ronnie said. ''E can't run very fast anyway.'

On this particular Saturday, Eric Adams the caretaker arrived to sweep the roof after being told the previous day in no uncertain terms by Bill Simpson that the place was 'beginnin' ter look like a shit 'ole an' you should get yer finger out.' Eric was all for a quiet life and he had reluctantly delayed his visit to the Beehive for Bill's benefit.

Bob Gainsford looked over to the stairway and his eyes

bulged out of his head as he saw the caretaker leaning on his broom. He grabbed his older brother by the arm. 'Quick, Ron, run!' he gasped.

Ronnie was not too rattled as the caretaker walked over to them and he stood his ground.

'Now, what you two doin' up 'ere?' Eric asked them crossly. 'Yer don't live 'ere.'

'We was lookin' fer our ball,' Ronnie told him.

'Yer don't mean ter tell me that one of yer kicked it all the way up 'ere?' Eric said, looking sternly at the lad.

'Yeah, Kipper French kicked it up,' Ronnie replied. ''E's the best footballer in our school.'

'I've a good mind ter turn you two over ter the copper when 'e comes round,' Eric told them. 'I should fink they'll put yer in Borstal fer six months fer trespassin'.'

Bob started to get tearful. 'We ain't done nuffink, honest, mister,' he moaned.

'Don't start cryin' 'cos of 'im,' Ronnie told him, putting his arm around his young brother's shoulder before turning to glare at the caretaker. 'If yer give us ter the coppers my dad'll sort you out.'

'Don't you be so cheeky,' the man replied sharply. 'Anyway, I ain't frightened o' your dad.'

'Come on, Bob, let's get goin',' Ronnie said.

'Oh no, you don't,' the caretaker replied quickly. 'I ain't decided what ter do wiv yer yet.'

'Don't give us ter the copper, mister,' Bob urged him, his face flushing up.

Eric stroked his chin for a few moments. 'I tell yer what,' he said, looking directly at Bob. 'If you collect all the bits o' paper an' rubbish up an' put 'em in this sack then I'll let yer go. As fer you,' turning to Ronnie, 'you can do the sweepin' up. I wanna see a good job done, mind.'

The young lad glared at the caretaker for a few moments then he nodded. 'Yeah, OK,' he told him.

Eric sat down on the bench round the other side and smiled to himself as he rolled a cigarette. The sun was beating down and it felt pleasant on his face. He leaned his head back against the stairway wall and closed his eyes as he exhaled a jet of tobacco smoke. This was the life, he thought. A few more minutes and then he would see how the two kids were getting on with the cleaning-up.

'Oi! What's your game?' a voice said angrily.

The caretaker opened his eyes to see Bill Simpson standing over him.

'Wassa matter?' he replied quickly.

'I'll give yer wassa matter,' Bill growled at him. 'I come out me front door just now an' nearly fell arse over tit over yer bloody broom, that's what. There's also loads o' bloody paper all over me landin'.'

'All right, Bill, I'll shift it right away,' Eric told him.

'Bloody lazy git,' Bill muttered as he walked away.

The caretaker hurried off to retrieve his broom and saw the mess on the landing. 'I'll murder those bloody Gainsford kids,' he scowled.

The two hawks stood chatting together in the warm sunshine and Doris nudged her friend as the Gainsford boys came running out of the Buildings. 'They've bin up ter no good, yer can bet yer life,' she remarked.

'Bangin' on people's doors, I should fink,' Phyllis replied. 'Maggie should keep 'em under control.'

''Er ole man should,' Doris told her. 'I always maintain it's a man's duty ter chastise 'is kids. The woman's got enough ter do, what wiv the 'ousework.'

'The trouble wiv 'er ole man is, 'e's never in,' Phyllis snorted. 'If 'e's not workin', 'e's up the pub. Lives up there, 'e does. I dunno 'ow she puts up wiv it. I wouldn't.'

'Nor me,' Doris replied, pursing her lips and drawing in her chin.

Phyllis brushed her hands down the front of her pinafore. 'I wonder when they're gonna let the 'ouse next door,' she said. 'It's bin empty fer nearly four months now.'

'Yeah, it makes yer wonder if they ever will,' Doris replied. 'There's bin a lot o' talk about movin' us all out soon.'

'Gawd ferbid,' Phyllis said quickly. 'I wouldn't fancy one o' those council flats. I mean ter say, yer dunno who yer gonna get livin' next ter yer.'

'An' over'ead too,' Doris reminded her.

'That's all I'd need, 'alf a dozen noisy kids stompin' about over me 'ead,' Phyllis groaned. 'I'd end up in the loony bin.'

'They moan about these little 'ouses, but yer can't beat 'em as far as I'm concerned,' Doris remarked. 'Besides, we're all neighbourly in this little turnin'. Yer don't get that in those bloody great blocks o' flats.'

'It makes me ill ter fink about it,' Phyllis replied, shaking her head slowly.

'I shouldn't worry, luv. It might take years yet. We could still be 'ere when we're in our nineties,' Doris said smiling.

The balmy day wore on, and up at the market the stalls slowly became depleted. Children were called in for their tea and the two hawks retired to rest their weary tongues. Up on the roof of Sunlight Buildings, Bill Simpson let his pigeons out for their evening flight and Jack Marchant watched as Monty the earth-bound member of the flock strutted around by their feet. Alice Toomey collected her washing and gave Jack a lecherous smile, and he hurried off to seek sanctuary with his old friend who had walked round to the other side of the roof.

The sun dipped lower in the sky and the children were out again briefly before bedtime, their ears cocked for the sound of the toffee-apple man's bell. Doris and Phyllis appeared again, amply fortified with cups of sweet tea, and Wally Gainsford strolled by, on his way to place a bet on the greyhounds. Lucy Perry adjusted her cushions and straightened the ornaments, while her long-suffering husband raised his eyebrows to the ceiling and buried his head in the evening paper.

Along the street Dick Conners was getting himself ready to meet Eve and he winced as he heard Ginny berating Albert for forgetting about the accumulator.

'If there's one fing I like ter listen to it's Saturday Night Theatre,' she shouted at him. 'Surely that's not too much to ask.'

Albert looked crestfallen. 'I'm sorry, luv, but I 'ad fings on me mind,' he told her.

'What mind?' she growled at him. 'You ain't got a bloody mind.'

'Why don't yer see if Maggie'll let yer go in 'er place ter listen to it?' he suggested.

'I bloody well will,' Ginny went on. 'I ain't sittin' 'ere all night listenin' ter you snorin' yer bleedin' 'ead off.'

Dick came down into the parlour and brushed an imaginary speck of dust from his lapel. 'I'm off now,' he announced. 'Don't wait up, I got me key.'

Ginny gave him a knowing smile. 'You mind 'ow yer go ternight,' she warned him. 'You ain't as young as yer was.'

'We're goin' ter the pictures,' he told her. 'Eve wants ter see some musical or ovver, so I thought I'd take 'er.'

'Where yer goin?' Albert asked.

'Pictures,' Dick shouted at him.

'Ain't bin ter the pictures fer years,' Albert replied. 'We used ter like the pictures, didn't we, gel?'

'Last time 'e took me ter the pictures we saw this bleedin' 'orror film,' Ginny said. 'Bela Lugosi an' Boris Karloff. Frightened the bleedin' life out o' me, it did. I 'ad nightmares fer weeks after.'

'There's a good picture up the Trocette this week,' Albert cut in. '*Frankenstein meets the Wolf Man*. I used ter like those pictures.'

''E ain't finkin' o' takin' 'er up there, yer silly git,' Ginny carped.

'Cheap place the Trocette,' Albert went on. 'Mind yer, those wooden seats ain't all that comfortable, but yer could always go up the circle, I s'pose. We used ter go up there on Saturday nights, didn't we, gel?'

'Yeah, an' now I sit in an' listen ter Saturday Night Theatre, when the bloody accumulator's charged up,' Ginny said, giving him a blinding look.

'Well, I'd better be off,' Dick told them. 'Mustn't be late.'

'Don't ferget the Trocette. It's a good film,' Albert reminded him.

Charlie slipped his arm round Linda's waist as they stood at the balustrade looking out over the rooftops. Night was falling and a breath of breeze ruffled the young woman's fair hair.

'I was just finkin' o' the time the Carter boys were tormentin' yer an' I came ter the rescue,' Charlie said.

'That was when I knew yer loved me,' Linda replied, a smile on her lips.

'What about you? Did you fall in love wiv me then?' he asked, smiling.

'I loved yer before then,' she told him, resting her head on his shoulder.

Charlie sighed as he stared out at the distant lights. 'It's strange 'ow fings turn out,' he said quietly.

Linda looked up into his dark eyes. 'Yer'll never stop lovin' me, will yer, Charlie?' she asked him in a soft voice.

'Never ever.'

'Promise?'

'I promise. An' ter show yer I mean it, I've come prepared.'

Linda's forehead puckered in a frown as Charlie slipped his hand into his trouser pocket and drew out a penknife.

'You remembered,' she said, smiling.

'Come on, let's finish the job,' he said, grabbing her hand.

They walked across the roof and Linda leaned against the stairway wall while Charlie set to work on the wooden post. For a few minutes he whittled away busily, then he stood back and grunted in satisfaction.

'There we are,' he said, snapping the knife shut. 'Your initial's in the love 'eart wiv mine now.'

Linda went to him and put her arms around his neck. 'You can't leave me now, Charlie,' she whispered.

Charlie pulled her close to him. 'Sealed wiv a lovin' kiss,' he said, his lips finding hers.

Chapter Forty-Three

Linda and Charlie arrived at the arch early on Monday morning to find Gilda already sitting at the desk going through a sheaf of papers. 'As you can see, I'm making a start,' she said, giving them a welcoming smile. 'There's tea in the pot, help yourselves.'

Charlie put down the bundle he was carrying. 'I brought me overalls. I've a feelin' I'm gonna need 'em,' he said grinning.

Gilda passed her empty teacup to Linda. 'I've made the arrangements for Nick's funeral,' she said, looking at each of them in turn. 'It's next Monday. Ten o'clock. There's something else too. Just before you arrived I got a phone call from Tony Carter. He wanted to know what was happening about Nick.'

'Did yer tell 'im about the funeral?' Charlie asked.

Gilda nodded. 'He said he'll be going.'

'Surely 'e wouldn't chance it,' Charlie said incredulously. 'The police'll be there fer sure.'

She shrugged her shoulders. 'That's what I told him, but he started shouting over the phone. He said no one would prevent him going to his own brother's funeral.'

Linda handed out the mugs of tea. 'I can understand 'is feelin's but 'e must be mad,' she remarked. 'The police'll pick 'im up fer certain.'

Gilda sipped her tea thoughtfully. 'Well, there's nothing we can do about that,' she sighed. 'Tony knows the risks and it's his lookout.'

'By the way, I saw George Morrison yesterday,' Charlie said. ''E's callin' in some time this mornin' ter see yer.'

Gilda's face brightened. 'How is he?' she asked.

'Well, ter be honest 'e wasn't in when I called round but 'is wife told me where ter find 'im,' Charlie replied. 'Apparently 'e's taken ter sittin' in the park fer hours on end every day. 'Is wife was sayin' 'ow upset 'e still is over Nick. Anyway I finally found 'im sittin' near the bandstand, an' when I told 'im that yer'd like ter see 'im about comin' back ter work 'is face was a picture. 'E was full o' questions but I said you'd explain everyfing when yer saw 'im.'

'I am glad,' Gilda said smiling. 'George is one of the best. He really worshipped Nick, and Nick thought the world of him too.'

Charlie nodded. 'Yeah, George is as straight as a die.'

The bell rang and Gilda glanced quickly at her wristwatch. 'That'll be Stanley,' she said. 'Let him in, will you, Charlie.'

The young man opened the front door and saw a short, wiry-looking character standing with his feet apart and his hands stuffed down into his trouser pockets He was wearing a sports jacket, which looked about three sizes too large, and a checkered cap. 'Beamish is the name Stanley Beamish,' he announced, holding out his hand

Charlie felt the strong grip as he shook hands 'Come on in,' he told him.

460

The dapper little man stepped into the arch and looked around for a few moments with his hands on his hips. 'Hmm. There's a lot ter be done 'ere, I can see,' he said incisively.

Charlie led him into the office and Gilda jumped up with a big smile on her face. 'Hello, Stanley. It's so nice to see you again,' she said, planting a kiss on his cheek. 'This is Linda, our secretary, an' this is Charlie. He'll be helping you get this place sorted out.'

Stanley nodded briefly to Linda and looked Charlie up and down. 'Well, we'll soon get a few muscles on you, me lad, eh?' he said, sitting on a chair in the middle of the room. 'It's nice ter be invited back ter work, Gilda. I've missed it, believe me. Anyway I can see I'm gonna be needed. There's a lot o' work in front of us. After all, it's a bit of a tip, ain't it?'

'All right, I know it's only an arch, but we've got gas, water and electricity laid on, and there's plenty of room,' Gilda told him.

'I can see that, but just look at the place,' he replied quickly. 'It's dingy, dark an' depressin'. We'll need ter sort that out fer starters.'

'Well, that's your department,' Gilda said, smiling at him. 'That's why Martin got in touch with you.'

'Right then,' Stanley said, crossing his legs and folding his arms. 'First fing ter do is whitewash the 'ole bloody lot. Get a bit o' light in 'ere. We'll need extra lightin' over the benches an' better surfaces. Yer can't do leavverwork on bad surfaces, take it from me.'

'You should know,' Gilda remarked, still smiling at him.

An august look appeared on his face as he raised his chin proudly. 'I'm sixty-six in a few weeks' time, Gawd willin', an'

I've spent fifty-one o' those years in the leavver business,' he replied, 'so I should know what I'm talkin' about. No danger of a cup o' tea, is there?'

Gilda laughed. 'Yeah, would you like one?'

'I would, but make it snappy, I ain't got time ter waste,' he said firmly.

Gilda and Linda exchanged amused glances and Charlie hid a smile as he reached down for his overalls. 'I'd better get these on,' he remarked.

Stanley gave him a dubious look and turned to Gilda. 'We'll need about six gallons o' whitewash ter start wiv, an' a couple o' large brushes,' he told her. 'Better order a quart o' white gloss paint too, an' a couple o' small brushes. This office looks like it could do wiv sprucin' up a bit as well. Always good to 'ave a smart office. Yer dunno who's gonna pop in on yer. First impressions count, yer know.'

'Have you got that, Linda?' Gilda asked her. 'We'll have to order it over the phone and get them to deliver.'

'Won't we need ter scrounge a ladder?' Charlie asked.

Stanley shook his head animatedly. 'No no no no. I noticed there's a small bench out there. We'll use that ter stand on. We only need ter paint up to about eight feet.'

'Any other requests?' Gilda said cheerfully.

'D'yer know a good electrician?' he asked.

'Martin might be able to let us borrow his firm's electrician,' she suggested.

'Right then, get on the blower,' Stanley said quickly. 'We need two more lights in the middle o' the arch, suspended down over those two large benches.'

The two women exchanged another furtive smile and then Gilda gave Stanley an old-fashioned look, hands on her hips. 'Is there anything else you'd like before I get on the phone?' she asked him.

The old man shook his head abruptly and turned to Charlie. 'What you like at whitewashin', son?' he asked.

'I dunno, I never done any,' Charlie replied.

'Well, we'll soon find out,' he said, getting up.

The hot dry week in July saw a transformation take place at the Abbey Street arch, and the willing workers were kept hard at it as the dynamic character led by example. While Charlie reached up with his brush to paint the top half of the walls Stanley set to work on the lower half, occasionally pausing to roll a cigarette or inspect the office painting, which Linda and Gilda were tackling. His energy seemed boundless and he constantly nagged and cajoled his underlings. 'Don't let that paint run. Spread it evenly. When's that bloody electrician comin'?' And so it went on all week. George Morrison started work on Tuesday morning and was immediately ordered on to the whitewashing. The big, friendly character seemed to strike up a rapport with Stanley Beamish and there was a constant banter between them.

Charlie worked willingly but was coaxed to still greater efforts. 'We're gonna 'ave ter put a spurt on,' Stanley told him. 'There's those back walls ter do yet an' we've gotta be finished by Thursday.' Even Gilda did not escape the wiry little character's criticism. 'It's very patchy. Yer'll need anuvver coat on them frames an' the door,' he remarked.

Charlie grinned to himself as he thought how good their taskmaster would have been as a building site foreman, but he could see what he was aiming for. The arch was beginning to look bright and cheerful, and when large sheets of linoleum were fitted on to the benches and the extra lighting put in, the place was hardly recognisable as the drab, dingy hole in the wall where perfume had once been bottled and packaged.

On the Thursday afternoon of that hectic week the machinery was installed. Stanley supervised the setting up of a riveter and a stitcher, and he managed to get the services of a gas fitter who put in two large rings for boiling up the casein glue.

'I'll show yer what we need it for as we go along,' Stanley explained to his bemused workers. 'In the meantime there's anuvver job you two can get ter work on. I'll need wooden foot racks put round these benches fer the women ter stand on. It's not good fer 'em standin' on concrete all day long.'

Both Charlie and George looked puzzled until the old man drew a diagram on a slip of paper. 'All yer need is some slats o' wood, some nails, an 'ammer an' a saw. There's a timber yard in Dock'ead. Just tell 'em what yer want an' they'll cut it all up for yer. That shouldn't be too difficult, not even fer you, George,' he chuckled.

On Friday morning Gilda opened up the arch and sighed with satisfaction as she looked around. Everything was in place ready to start production. A supply of thin leather sheets was being delivered that afternoon as well as all the other sundry items necessary to make the vanity cases. Stanley had studied the design drawings and nodded confidently. 'I'll be doin' the cuttin' out,' he had told her, 'an' once the women get the 'ang o' the stitcher an' the riveter we'll be turnin' 'em out by the fousand.'

Gilda walked up to the long bench and ran her hand over the smooth linoleum surface. The arch was quiet, except for the faint sound of traffic on the main road, and she sighed sadly. There was the funeral to face on Monday and she prayed that she would be able to get through it without breaking down. She had to stay strong for Martin, who had been so supportive, and for everyone else who had come to know her as a friend and look up to her.

The young woman glanced up quickly as George Morrison came into the arch. His wide battered face took on a pleased look as he glanced around. 'Well, it's just about ready now, Gilda,' he remarked.

She nodded and mustered a smile. 'The women are starting on Monday, George,' she said. 'Stanley's going to show them what needs to be done and he seems to feel they'll have it off pat in a couple of days. In any case we'll be starting full production by the following week.'

'So it's fingers crossed,' he said.

'I'll see Stanley on Monday before the funeral,' she told him. 'Just to make sure everything's all right.'

George looked suddenly downcast. 'I'll be glad when that's over,' he said quietly.

'Yeah, me too,' Gilda replied. 'I just hope there's no trouble if Tony shows up.'

'I don't fink 'e'll be that stupid,' George remarked. 'The rozzers are sure ter grab 'im if 'e does show.'

'You know Charlie and Linda are coming?'

He nodded. 'I expected they would.'

Gilda looked at his sad face. 'You and Nick were very close, weren't you, George?' she said quietly.

The big man hunched his broad shoulders and stared down at his feet for a few moments. 'I know there were a lot o' bad fings said about 'im, Gilda, but 'e was a good friend ter me,' he replied, looking into her candid eyes. 'I remember one day I was in the gym an' they got this new younger fighter in. Everyone said 'e was goin' places an' they put me in ter spar wiv 'im. Normally boxers in trainin' take it easy wiv their sparrin' partners but there were a few reporters there at the time an' this young buck put on a show fer 'em. I only done a few rounds wiv 'im but I got a right good pastin'. As it 'appens Nick was there that day an' 'e came over ter me afterwards. I knew 'im fairly well 'cos 'e was always poppin' in ter watch. Anyway, 'e convinced me that I should turn it all in an' go an' work fer 'im. 'E 'ad the yard up the road at the time. I told 'im I'd fink about it an' 'e stuck a fiver in me 'and. Just like that. It was 'is way o' lettin' me know I'd earn more workin' fer 'im than gettin' me brains scrambled in the ring. Anyway, I went in ter see 'im the next day an' I bin wiv 'im ever since. It was a terrible fing what 'appened to 'im.'

Gilda nodded, feeling a lump rising up in her throat as she saw a tear run down the ex-boxer's cheek. 'I know you loved him, George. So did I. You knew that, didn't you?'

'Yeah,' he replied, swallowing hard. 'It was obvious, ter me at any rate.'

The young woman patted his arm gently. 'Come on, George, let's get to work,' she said, giving him an encouraging smile.

Dan Sully looked up as the two detective constables came into his office. 'The Carter funeral cortège is leaving the house in Abbey Street at ten o'clock on Monday,' he told them. 'It'll be going to Streatham Cemetery and I'll want you two on the main gates. You know Tony Carter by sight so there'll be no mix-up. If he does show up, the obvious thing would be for him to slip in at the back of the chapel after everyone else has gone in. I'll be there myself with DS Cranley. We'll wait outside the house until the cortège pulls away and then follow in a car. We'll join the mourners at the chapel and then go with them to the graveside in case Boy-boy decides to wait there instead of attending the service. There'll also be a patrol car skirting the cemetery with an officer inside who knows Carter by sight. Any questions?'

'What about other entrances?' one of the officers asked.

'As I just said, there'll be a patrol car on the lookout, but you have to remember that if Carter does decide to turn up he could try to get in anywhere,' Sully reminded him. 'Whatever he does, we'll be on hand to nab him.'

'Do you think he will attempt it, sir?' the other detective asked.

'The two brothers were very close,' Sully replied, 'and Tony Carter seems to act impulsively, judging by the way he went straight after Sam Colby without thinking it over. My own personal view is that he will. He might be thinking, wrongly, that we won't approach him until the funeral is over. He may feel that he can outrun us and it follows that he might decide to case the cemetery to look for boltholes before the funeral. I've been on to the Streatham police and they've agreed to put two officers on constant patrol there until it's all over. I think we've got it nice and tight. Can either of you think of anything we've missed?'

'If we nick him at the main gate, do we hold him there or take him down to the chapel?' the first officer asked.

'Come on, Patterson, we're not that unfeeling, or at least I hope we're not,' Sully said, raising one eyebrow. 'If you do apprehend him you'll handcuff him and let him attend the service.'

After the detectives had left the office, Dan Sully took a bottle of whisky and a glass out of the drawer and poured himself his first drink of the day. There could be no foul-ups on this one, he reflected. Boy-boy Carter was the prime suspect in the Sam Colby killing and he had to be brought in for questioning. And knowing the man as he did, there was no doubt in the inspector's mind that he would make an appearance, even if all the police in London were arrayed against him.

Chapter Forty-Four

Mrs Samuels was up earlier than usual on Monday morning and for the first time in a long while she felt that her daily cleaning of next door was worthwhile. When Nick was alive he had hardly ever used the house and his younger brother used it even less. They never seemed to notice if the sheets had been changed or the carpets beaten. Today was different though. People were coming to the funeral and they would notice. The women would anyway, and they'd be quick to comment if everything wasn't spotless.

Aggie Samuels did a thorough job of cleaning that morning and she found a fresh linen cloth for the parlour table. Fish-paste sandwiches and rock cakes would have to do, she told herself. What else could they expect, rationing being the way it was? Maybe she could run to a few biscuits as well. That skimpy teapot wouldn't be any use. She had better bring her large one in. Better bring the biscuit barrel too. It would look a bit more dignified than serving them from the packet.

How many sandwiches should she make, Aggie wondered? The woman who had called to tell her about the funeral had said there would be her and three of Nick's workmates. Then there would be those two maiden aunts who showed up that time when Tony Carter went down with influenza. That was six. Counting herself, seven. Who else was there? The woman said there would be eight people going in all. Ah yes. Mrs Collier from Compton Row, that was it. She was the one the brothers had lodged with for a time. Strange how people seemed to turn up for weddings and funerals. Pity they hadn't called round once in a while when Nick was alive.

Aggie made the sandwiches and then laid them out neatly on the two cake-stands she had brought in, along with the batch of rock cakes she had baked the previous day. She covered them over with a clean cloth before filling the kettle. Her husband was not used to doing much about the place and it would be just like him to light the gas under an empty kettle if she didn't fill it. As long as he remembered when they were due to return; she had impressed on him that it would be about one o'clock but she had better leave a note, just to be on the safe side.

Aggie finished her chores by nine o'clock, just as the flowers started to arrive. There was a wreath from the Abbey Street neighbours, one from Mrs Collier and a spray of carnations from the Walsh sisters, whom Aggie took to be the maiden aunts. Another wreath was delivered from Charlie and Linda and a spray of red roses from Gilda, along with wreaths from George Morrison, Don Jacobs and Con Ashley.

After she had laid the flowers along the front wall, Aggie went back into her house to get ready. It would be a nice change to get out of Bermondsey for a couple of hours or so, she thought, even though it was for a funeral. She was to go in the second car, along with the maiden aunts and Mrs Collier. Just as well that Mrs Collier was going; she'd have nothing in common with those other two scatty mares.

When she walked down the stairs wearing her wide black bonnet her husband pulled a face. 'Ain't yer got anyfing else ter put on yer bonce?' he sniggered. 'Yer look like Kate Carney in that bloody fing.'

'I got anuvver one but I can't very well wear it, now can I?' she growled at him.

'Why not?' he asked.

''Cos it's a pink one, yer dozy git.'

'Sorry I spoke,' he mumbled.

'I'm goin' next door to open up, they'll be arrivin' soon,' she told him. 'Now, yer gonna remember to 'ave the kettle boilin' by the time we get back, ain't yer?'

'Yeah. What time are yer due back?' he asked.

'Bloody blimey, if I told yer once I've told yer fifty times,' Aggie sighed in exasperation. 'One o'clock. If yer ferget just look at the note I've left on the dresser in the scullery.'

'All right, I won't ferget,' he said.

'Wanna bet?' Aggie muttered.

At nine-thirty Mrs Collier turned up and the elderly woman sat talking with Aggie until the maiden aunts arrived.

'Terrible fing. Just terrible,' Felicity Walsh remarked, dabbing at her eyes.

'Just terrible,' her sister Constance echoed.

'Would yer like a cuppa?' Aggie asked them.

'I don't s'pose yer've got a drop o' tiddly in the 'ouse, 'ave yer?' Felicity enquired.

471

'There's 'alf a bottle o' whisky in the sideboard, an' I fink there's a drop o' gin left,' Aggie told her, giving Mrs Collier a brief look of disgust.

'The gin'll do,' Felicity replied. 'I usually take a drop o' gin ter steady me nerves.'

'What about you?' Aggie asked Constance as she went over to the sideboard.

'Whisky'll be fine,' she replied. 'Not too much, though.'

Aggie poured out the gin and handed it to Felicity, who looked at the small measure with disappointment before swallowing it in one gulp.

As she poured out the whisky Constance watched her eagle-eyed. 'Eh, just a drop more, luv,' she said.

Aggie decided that the two sisters were most probably alcoholics and the prospect of sharing the funeral car with them all the way to Streatham filled her with horror.

'Are you Nick's aunts?' Mrs Collier asked them.

'Well, not really,' Constance replied. 'We're what yer would call second cousins on the farvver's side. It's a bit too complicated to explain really, so we just call ourselves Nick's aunties. That's what Nick used ter call us anyway.'

Aggie felt her head beginning to pound merely being in their company and she went to the front door for some air. It was a bright clear day, and already very warm. Not at all the day for a funeral. Trust Nick to be awkward, she thought.

'Eh, excuse me, but are those sandwiches fer now or later?'

Aggie turned round to see Constance standing behind her. 'They're fer later,' she said firmly.

Just then a car pulled up outside the house and a tall man

in a dark suit got out carrying a wreath. Without saying a word he placed it with the rest and then drove off. Aggie read the inscription which said: 'From the Kerrigan family'. A few minutes later Gilda arrived, holding on to George Morrison's arm, and behind her were Linda and Charlie. The hearse turned into the street watched by neighbours who stood at their front doors with sombre expressions on their faces.

Dan Sully and DS Cranley sat in the police car across the turning and watched as the flowers were placed on the coffin and on top of the cars. They then saw the mourners come out of the house and get into the two shiny black limousines. 'Well there's no sign of Boy-boy,' Sully said, starting up the car.

The cortège drove along Abbey Street very slowly, led by the undertaker who walked stiffly with his shoulders thrown back. At the end of the turning he jumped into the hearse and it moved off at a faster speed.

Dan Sully eased the car into position behind the procession and drummed on the steering wheel, watchful for anyone who might suddenly climb into one of the limousines when they slowed down for traffic.

The journey through the Old Kent Road and Albany Road to Camberwell was nonstop and Dan Sully began to relax. Maybe he had misjudged the situation. Boy-boy would know that he was going to be arrested if he showed his face and had decided to stay clear, although it must have hurt him terribly. As they progressed through Brixton and into Streatham the cortège was forced to stop a few times for the traffic lights and both detectives became alert, but nothing happened. The procession finally turned into the cemetery and Dan Sully waved to the two plain-clothes men who stood by the gates.

The hearse stopped outside a white stone chapel that was bathed in sunlight and surrounded by flowering bushes. The sky above was cloudless and the hot sun made the limousines shimmer.

'What a day for a funeral,' Cranley said, shaking his head slowly.

Dan Sully ignored the remark as he climbed out of the car and went to the chapel entrance. A member of the clergy stood holding a Bible, smiling respectfully at the mourners as they congregated around the door. The undertaker's men slid the coffin out and hoisted it on to their shoulders, walking in step into the tiny chapel behind the clergyman as he read aloud from the Scriptures, and the mourners followed. Gilda wept unashamedly, supported by the strong figure of George Morrison. Linda and Charlie both held their heads low as they followed behind, and along with the rest of the mourners they took their places on the hard bench seats.

The pallbearers went back to the limousines and Dan Sully looked around the cemetery garden before going to stand with Cranley by the chapel door. Hymn music drifted out into the sunshine, and timorous voices were shyly signing, 'Oh, God Our Help In Ages Past'.

Sully tried to relax, but his instincts told him that it was not wise. Tony Carter was a dangerous man, and it was sensible not to underestimate him.

The music ceased and then the solemn voice of the vicar echoed through the silence as he read the lesson. The pallbearers went back into the chapel and carried the coffin back out to the hearse, followed by the mourners. Gilda was dry eyed now, biting on her lip and holding George's arm in a vice-like grip as she struggled valiantly to keep control of herself. The big man's jaw muscles were tensing and knotting as he too struggled with his grief.

The cars wound their way up a long gravelled drive and stopped on the crest of a rise. The coffin was taken from the hearse once more and carried to the burial spot, and after it was lowered into the ground the bearers went back to the cars, leaving the mourners gathered around the grave. Dan Sully and Cranley stepped from their car and walked up slowly, keeping a respectful distance behind the clergyman as he chanted the valedictory words, 'Ashes to ashes, dust to dust.' The inspector looked around him; it was an isolated spot, and impossible for anyone to sneak up on the grave without being noticed. Boy-boy had obviously decided not to chance it.

The detectives trailed behind the mourners as they made their way back to the limousines and Sully glanced at his fellow officer as they got back into the police car. 'Well, we had to be sure,' he said.

Cranley smiled smugly. 'I was pretty certain Boy-boy wouldn't dare show his face. Still, as you say, we had to make sure.'

Sully gave him a hard look. 'All right, I was wrong,' he said curtly, 'but in the twenty-five years I've been in plain clothes I've met a few people like Carter, and I know what's going on in his mind. He's given his woman a good kicking, stabbed Colby to death without hesitation, and now when his brother's being buried, the one person who meant anything to him and instilled some order in his life, he can't come and pay his last respects. How do you think that makes him feel? Nick Carter was the shaper and mover, the only one who could ever tell Boy-boy what to do, and I tell you one thing: he'll think he's letting his brother down by not being here, just as if he was leaving him in his hour of need. If I know Boy-boy, deep down inside he'll never come to terms with his brother's death. He'll be clinging to him as if he were still alive, still there to tell him what to do.'

Cranley nodded his head vigorously in an effort to appease his superior, but inside he was seething at the man's patronising attitude. The last thing he wanted was a lecture on the criminal mind. Sully had been proved wrong and it irked him.

The limousines moved up the gravel drive to an area where it widened out, allowing them to make a complete turn, and as they came back past the police car Sully suddenly stiffened. 'Jesus Christ!' he cried out.

Cranley sat rigid in his seat as his superior officer swung the car out quickly behind them, and when the drive widened again by the chapel Sully overtook the cortège and braked, forcing it to a halt. He jumped out and ran back to the first limousine behind the hearse. 'Where's your man?' he asked him sharply.

The driver looked at him blankly. ''E 'ad ter go somewhere,' he said.

'What's wrong, sir?'

Sully turned to see the undertaker standing behind him. 'Police,' he said quickly. 'I want to know who else was in the front of this car with the driver.'

'Mr Watson,' the undertaker replied.

'And why isn't he travelling back with you?' Sully asked him.

'I allowed him to go,' he replied. 'He's got some business to attend to in Streatham.'

'I'll be calling on you later, and I'll want to see this Mr Watson,' Sully growled.

'Will that be all, officer?' the undertaker said stiffly.

'For now,' the detective told him.

When Bertram Knox had opened up his funeral parlour early on Monday morning he was aware that it was going to be a very busy day. When he admitted his first customers a few minutes later he quickly realised that it was also going to be a very unusual day.

'Do you wish to make funeral arrangements?' he asked the heavily built man with the broken nose.

'We might do, if yer give us any trouble,' Con Ashley replied.

'I beg your pardon?' Bertram said quickly.

'Yer've got a funeral this mornin',' Don Jacobs cut in.

'Look, would you mind telling me what this is all about?' the undertaker said, looking from one to the other.

'When are yer men due in?' Don asked him.

'Any moment now,' Bertram replied. 'Why?'

'Let's just sit nice an' quiet an' wait fer 'em, shall we?'

'I'm not putting up with this. Would you mind leaving.'

'Shut up and sit down,' Don growled.

The menace in his eyes was not lost on the undertaker and he slumped down at his desk.

As the drivers and bearers arrived they were hustled into the office and made to stand against the wall.

'We can do this all civilised or the ovver way. You please yerselves,' Con Ashley told them.

The burly appearance of the two visitors was enough to convince the staff that it should be the civilised way and they looked enquiringly at the undertaker.

'Now gentlemen, let me explain,' Con began. 'Someone'll be callin' in very soon an' 'e'll be takin' the place of one o' yer. The man whose place 'e takes is gonna stay wiv us until we get a phone call. After that 'e'll be free ter leave. OK?'

The men nodded dumbly, but Bertram Knox rounded on Ashley. 'I see it now,' he said quickly. 'This man. It's Tony Carter, isn't it?'

'You seem very well informed,' Don Jacobs remarked.

'I keep abreast of things,' Bertram said spiritedly.

'Well then, yer'll know it's best not ter try anyfing, because if yer do the man we'll be 'oldin' is gonna get 'urt – bad. Is that clear?'

Bertram swallowed hard and nodded. 'It's clear.'

At nine-thirty Boy-boy Carter walked into the funeral parlour and nodded to his two accomplices. 'Everyfing OK?'

''Andsome,' Don Jacobs replied.

Carter looked at the men standing against the wall. 'Who's the bearers?' he asked quickly.

Three of the men raised their hands and Boy-boy looked them over. 'Right, you'll do,' he said, pointing to the slimly built man. 'You can go wiv my two pals.'

The man looked nervous as he stepped forward and was grabbed by the arms.

'Yer've got nuffink ter worry about, provided your guv'nor don't try anyfing stupid,' Boy-boy told him. 'Right then, let's get goin'.'

★ ★ ★

The midday sun felt hot on Boy-boy's back as he helped lower his brother's coffin down into the grave, and he stepped back with the other pallbearers and mouthed a silent goodbye as the mourners gathered round. He held his head low as he walked slowly back to the limousines and with a quick nod to the undertaker he moved away down the path, straying on to the grass between the gravestones to keep the cars between him and the funeral party. He walked slowly, glancing at the carved inscriptions as though he were the relative of some long-departed soul; then when he felt safe he hurried off towards the cemetery perimeter. He thought about climbing the railings, but realised that it would attract the attention of any policeman who might happen to be watching. Better if he relied on his disguise and went out through the back gate, he decided.

As he walked out of the cemetery on to the wide thoroughfare Boy-boy saw a bus slowing down at a stop and he broke into a run. He had some ground to cover and he prayed that he wouldn't lose his wig and thick moustache as he sped along. The bus started to pull away from the stop and he leapt for the rail.

'Tryin' ter break yer neck, are yer?' the solemn-looking conductor asked him.

Boy-boy stared at him as he steadied himself on the platform. 'Brixton,' he said breathlessly, diving into his trouser pocket.

'We're only goin' ter the garage,' the conductor informed him.

'That'll do,' Boy-boy said, suddenly spotting a police car cruising by on the other side of the road.

The conductor flipped a ticket from his clip and slipped it into the machine strapped to his middle. 'That'll be fourpence,' he said.

Boy-boy grabbed the ticket and climbed to the upper deck. There were only two other passengers and he sat down at the back, taking a deep breath and puffing heavily. He had beaten them, but he felt no sense of victory. Nick was dead, and it was because of him.

The hot sunlight through the glass scorched Boy-boy's face and he began to feel sick. He tried to think about what lay ahead, what the future would be, but there was nothing there. Fear and anger had burnt a dark hole in him, and as he sat there on the seat, empty and alone, a black panic ate away at his stomach, a silent scream of pain and endless rage.

The phone rang and Don Jacobs picked it up quickly. 'Yeah. Right. We're well pleased, Tony. OK then, be careful. Yeah, will do.'

''E made it then,' Con said smiling.

Don nodded and turned to the man who sat slumped in the armchair. 'Come on, pal, time ter go.'

Norman Watson got up and made for the door, only to be grabbed by the arm.

'One last word, pal,' Don said, eyeing him sternly. 'Yer never seen us before, 'ave yer?'

'Certainly not. You're a couple of complete strangers,' Norman replied, grinning.

Chapter Forty-Five

Gilda let herself into the arch early on Tuesday morning and she was followed in shortly after by George Morrison. 'You shouldn't 'ave ter get in so early,' he told her. 'I can open up in the mornin's. I'm always up early anyway.'

'Are yer sure yer wouldn't mind, George?' she asked.

'Nah, course not,' he replied. 'I got in early ter get the glue goin'. It takes quite a while, so Stanley said.'

Gilda pulled a face. 'He's quite the old bossy boots, isn't he?' she remarked smiling.

'I find 'im ter be a nice bloke, ter tell yer the trufe,' George replied. ''E certainly knows the business.'

Gilda sat down at the desk and studied him as he ambled over to put the kettle on. 'Thanks for taking care of me yesterday,' she said. 'I needed a good strong arm to lean on.'

George gave her a lopsided grin. 'That's all right,' he said quietly. 'Anyway it's over now. We gotta look ter the future.'

'We certainly have, George,' she replied.

The big man stood by the gas ring looking abstracted and Gilda watched him, wondering what was going through his mind. 'Penny for your thoughts,' she said suddenly.

'I was just finkin' about yesterday,' he told her.

Gilda nodded. 'When we were standing at the graveside I expected to look up and see Tony Carter standing there. I had a strange feeling that he was there all the time. It was really creepy.'

''E was there, as a matter o' fact,' George replied, looking over at her.

'I don't understand,' the young woman said, frowning at him.

''E was one o' the pallbearers,' George told her. 'E was wearin' a dark wig an' a moustache. It was clever really: who takes any notice of a pallbearer at a funeral?'

Gilda shook her head slowly. 'I knew it. I just had that weird feeling.'

George's face relaxed into a smile. 'Con Ashley an' Don Jacobs looked after the undertaker's man till they got the phone call ter say they could let 'im go.'

'So Tony took his place.'

'That's about the strength of it.'

Gilda looked at George closely. 'What would have happened if Tony had got caught?' she asked.

'I dread ter fink,' he replied.

'They wouldn't have harmed the undertaker's man, would they?'

'Nah, I don't fink so.'

Gilda looked down at her clasped hands. 'Do you know, George, Tony Carter has always frightened me,' she said. 'It's something about his eyes. They often seem so cold and menacing.'

'Yeah, I know what yer mean,' George replied. 'I've seen the look, many a time.'

The arrival of Stanley Beamish interrupted the quiet

conversation and Gilda hid a smile as the dapper man took off his sports jacket and slipped on a fawn factory coat. 'I dug this out from under the stairs,' he told her. 'Do I look the part?'

'Unquestionably,' Gilda told him.

Jack Marchant was feeling worried as he watched the pigeons circle the buildings. He turned back to stare at his old friend, acutely aware that something was wrong. It wasn't like Bill to sit there on that bench when the birds were in flight, he thought. As they swooped down he would invariably raise his arms to send them soaring back up in the sky, but today he was ignoring them. Jack stroked his chin pensively. Maybe there was something troubling him. Perhaps he had said something out of turn that had upset Bill. No, it was more than that.

The flight returned to the loft and Bill got up slowly as Monty strutted by.

'All right, Bill, I'll shut it up,' Jack offered.

'Wassa matter, don't yer fink I'm capable?' Bill replied sharply.

'Suit yerself,' Jack said, going over to sit on the bench.

Bill came over and sat down heavily. 'It's bin four weeks now,' he mumbled.

'I beg yer pardon?'

'I said it's bin four weeks.'

''As it?'

'I usually get a letter before this.'

Jack became more concerned. 'Never mind,' he said quietly.

''E knows 'ow me an' 'is muvver worry.'

Jack's heart sank as he realised that his old friend's mind had started wandering. 'If you can make it down the stairs I'll buy yer a pint,' he said kindly. 'Come on, it'll cheer yer up.'

Bill shook his head. 'They're sinkin' fousands o' tons every week. That's what it said on the wireless. It's human lives they're talkin' about. When a ship goes down men go down wiv it. Why don't they say 'ow many lives are lost instead of 'ow many tons? It's 'cos they're not bothered, that's why. They're more concerned about their bloody ships.'

'Come on, Bill, let's go downstairs an' get a pint,' Jack said, now becoming frightened.

'You go. I ain't feelin' up to it,' Bill told him.

'No, I'm not neivver, come ter fink of it,' Jack replied. 'I'll just sit 'ere wiv yer, if yer don't mind.'

'Mind? Why should I mind?' Bill said sharply.

'I just thought . . .'

'If yer'd sooner go fer a pint why don't yer piss orf, instead o' pesterin' me,' Bill said angrily. 'I don't care if yer sit 'ere or not. It's no skin orf my nose.'

'I was only finkin' o' keepin' yer company,' Jack said quietly.

'I don't need yer bloody company,' Bill growled. 'You only sit there moanin' at the best o' times. Go on. Why don't yer piss orf?'

'All right, I will,' Jack said, getting up.

'Who needs yer?' Bill called out to him as Jack walked away sadly.

Eve Jeffreys strolled through the market holding on to Dick's arm. 'I must be back by one o'clock sharp or they'll think I'm taking liberties,' she told him.

Dick smiled. 'Yer know somefing, Eve?' he said. 'Yer look a picture.'

'Go on, you're just teasing me,' she said coyly.

'They say the sun always shines on the righteous,' he went on. 'It's certainly shinin' on you.'

'I'm far from righteous,' she replied. 'In fact I think I've become a bit of a harlot, after last night.'

'I fink you're a very lovely lady,' Dick told her with an intimate smile. 'You're warm an' cuddly, an' yer know just what pleases a man.'

'Not any man,' Eve retorted. 'My man.'

'Are yer really glad I called in the shop that day?'

'Which day? You call in every day.'

'You know the day.'

'Of course I do.'

'Well? Are yer glad?'

'Yes, I am glad. You made me feel young again.'

'Yer've given me a new lease o' life, Eve.'

She squeezed his arm. 'I'd love to just walk the afternoon away, but I must get back, Dick.'

They stopped on the corner of Eagle Street. 'Until ternight, Eve.'

'Until tonight, my love.'

Stanley Beamish was gratified by the progress everyone was making, and he stood back while Charlie ran a sharp knife around the plywood disc that he was pressing down on to a sheet of leather.

'That's right, but watch the knife don't slip,' he warned. 'If

485

yer careful yer'll get four pieces out o' one sheet. Just remember, we can't afford waste; leavver's expensive.'

Charlie concentrated on the next cut and Stanley nodded appreciatively. 'That's good, but don't stick yer bleedin' tongue out when yer cuttin'. It makes yer look like a novice.'

'Well, I am a novice,' Charlie said grinning.

'Not when I've done wiv yer,' Stanley told him.

Alice was taking very well to the stitcher and when Stanley inspected her efforts he was pleased. ''Ave you ever done any leavver stitchin' before?' he asked her.

She shook her head. 'Is it all right?'

'Very good. I fink yer got it off pat now,' he said, giving her a wink. 'See me after class an' I'll show yer 'ow ter put the bobbins in.'

One of the other women was responsible for gluing in the satin lining and another was busy cutting strips which would be riveted on to the inside of the case to hold the contents. The last of the four was becoming familiar with the riveter and she smiled as Stanley approached her.

'That's right, yer got the knack now,' he said. 'Just make sure yer get the rivet centred or it'll look cheap an' nasty.'

'It's taken me a while ter get used to it,' she replied, looking up at him. 'The rivet kept on slippin' off.'

'Yeah, not ter worry,' Stanley said, stretching his chin up and tugging at the collar of his shirt. 'It's finicky work. Mind you, I got enough practice doin' all the sewin' fer my two gels. The missus never did it 'erself, scatty mare. I s'pect you're too young to 'ave 'ad all that, ain't yer, Josie?'

'Carole,' she replied. 'I'm forty-four years old; I've got two grown-up sons, an' me daughter's just left school.'

'Nah, you're 'avin' me on,' Stanley told her, a mischievous

twinkle in his eye. 'Yer don't look a day past twenty-nine an' a 'alf.'

'Get away wiv yer,' Carole replied. 'I wish me 'usband said that ter me once in a while.'

'Oh, yer got an 'usband too,' he said, affecting a hurt look.

'Yeah, 'e works on the tugs.'

Stanley rolled his shoulders like a boxer. 'Is 'e big?'

Jack Marchant walked into the Beehive and ordered a pint of bitter.

''Ello, mate. I ain't seen anyfing of yer lately,' Bert Warner remarked. 'I was only sayin' the same yesterday ter Wally Gainsford.'

'I ain't bin in the mood fer drinkin' lately,' Jack told him.

'But yer feelin' better now?'

'I'm feelin' worse.'

''Ow comes?'

'Me an' ole Bill Simpson 'ave bin the best o' pals fer donkey's years,' Jack said with a sigh. 'I used ter get 'is baccy an' take 'im up a bottle o' beer or two when 'e was ill in bed that time, an' I've always bin ready fer a chat. Now I've bin told ter piss orf out of it.'

'Bill told yer that? I don't believe it,' Bert said, leaning on the counter.

'S'right, strike me dead if it ain't,' Jack replied.

'Why should 'e say a fing like that?' Bert asked him.

'Gawd knows.'

''E must be ill.'

'I dunno about that,' Jack replied, 'but 'e's certainly wanderin'. 'E was on about 'is boy not writin'. The lad's bin dead fer ten years.'

'That's what I mean,' Bert said. 'The man's ill. I shouldn't take it to 'eart what 'e said ter yer. What you 'ave ter remember is, when people get like that they take it out on the ones closest to 'em.'

Jack stared down at his drink for a while. 'Eighty-five next month 'e'll be, or is it eighty-four?'

'It's a nice ole age, whatever,' Bert replied.

'It wasn't very nice what 'e said ter me, though.'

'I shouldn't let it get yer down. Bill knows what a brick yer've bin,' Bert told him. 'I bet 'e's sittin' in that flat of 'is right now, worryin' 'imself sick about upsettin' yer.'

'D'yer fink so?' Jack asked.

'I know so.'

''Ere, gis a bottle o' sweet stout, Bert, will yer?'

'Comin' up.'

Jack handed over a florin. ''E likes a sweet stout.'

Wally Gainsford was standing nearby and had heard the conversation. 'Bloody shame,' he said as Jack Marchant hurried out of the pub.

Bert shook his head slowly. 'I've seen 'em like that many a time since I've bin in this trade,' he remarked. ''Ere, Wally, yer wouldn't like ter pop over the Buildin's an' make sure they're all right, would yer?'

'Consider it done,' the large man replied, quickly swigging down what was left in his glass.

Jack Marchant climbed the stairs, resting halfway, and he was out of breath when he finally knocked on Bill Simpson's door. There was no reply, and his forehead wrinkled in a puzzled frown. Bill wouldn't still be on the roof, surely, he thought.

Jack climbed the short flight of stairs and looked around. It all seemed quiet. He walked away from the stairway to the far side of the roof and there he saw Bill Simpson slumped down on the floor with his back against the stone balustrade. His eyes were closed and his breathing was coming in short gasps. 'Christ!' Jack cried out as he hurried over. He shook his friend but got no response, then he tried tapping his face. 'Come on, ole mate, it's Jack. Yer know me,' he said loudly. 'I'm yer ole pal.'

Bill groaned and his eyes flickered. 'Jack,' he said hoarsely.

'I'm 'ere, Bill, never you worry.'

'Get me down ter me bed, mate.'

'I will. You leave it ter yer ole pal. Look, I've got yer a sweet stout. Yer like sweet stout, I know yer do. I told Bert Warner yer like sweet stout.'

''Elp me up, Jack.'

Jack slipped his arms under Bill's shoulders and heaved. 'Yer'll 'ave to 'elp me,' he gasped.

Just then Wally Gainsford arrived and he gently eased Jack to one side. 'Leave 'im ter me,' he said quietly.

Jack stood back and watched while Wally picked the old man up as though he were a baby. 'Lead the way, Jack,' he told him.

Downstairs in the flat Wally carefully laid Bill down on the bed. 'Stay wiv 'im, mate,' he said. 'I'll go over the pub an' get Bert ter phone fer a doctor. Who is 'is doctor, by the way?'

'The same as mine. Doctor Sweeney,' Bert replied.

'Leave it ter me,' Wally said, hurrying out of the flat.

Bill's eyes flickered again and he reached out a gnarled hand. 'Are yer still there, Jack?' he asked in a faint voice.

'I'm 'ere, ole pal.'

'I remember bein' short wiv yer.'

'Nah, yer wasn't.'

'I told yer ter piss orf. I remember.'

'Well, it don't matter.'

'Oh yes, it does. I upset me best pal.'

'I got yer a stout, Bill.'

'I'll drink it later, mate.'

Jack felt a lump rising in his throat. 'You ain't gonna leave me, are yer, Bill?' he gulped.

'Course not. I just feel very tired.'

'Keep yer eyes open, Bill. Just till the doctor gets 'ere.'

'Too tired, ole mate.'

Jack Marchant's eyes filled with tears as he looked down at the sleeping figure of his old friend. He could see his chest rising and falling and hear the laboured breathing. 'Stay alive, Bill. Stay alive, yer miserable ole goat,' he croaked, lowering his head down on to the bed beside him.

Chapter Forty-Six

Very little happened in Eagle Street without the two hawks getting to hear about it, and on Wednesday morning Doris stood on her doorstep with her arms crossed, discussing the Bill Simpson affair with Phyllis.

'Well, apparently 'e's 'oldin' 'is own,' Doris was going on. 'Trouble is, at that age yer can't tell. They're up one minute an' down the next.'

'I 'eard that 'e collapsed on the roof an' Wally Gainsford found 'im,' Phyllis said.

'What the bloody 'ell was 'e doin' up on the roof?' Doris asked her.

''Im out the pub asked Wally ter go an' see if the ole boy was all right,' she replied. ''E'd bin goin' a bit funny, by all accounts.'

'A bit funny?'

'Talkin' to 'imself an' wanderin' a bit.'

'Goin' orf 'is 'ead, yer mean?'

'Yeah, that's right.'

Doris leaned against the wall and crossed one foot over the other. 'It's 'is age, I expect,' she said knowingly. ''E must be well over eighty.'

Freda Colton came walking up to them carrying a laden shopping bag. ''Ow's ole Bill Simpson, 'ave you 'eard?' she asked.

Doris shook her head slowly. 'I don't old out much 'ope,' she told her. ''E's started rantin' an' ravin'.'

Freda put her shopping bag down and massaged her numb fingers. 'What was it, a stroke?' she enquired.

'Just 'is age, I should fink,' Phyllis cut in.

''E's well into 'is eighties,' Doris added.

'I bet it's upset ole Jack Marchant,' Freda remarked. 'They've bin mates fer years. They was always in the Bee'ive tergevver at one time, but I fink the stairs was gettin' too much fer Bill.'

'Mrs Brown was turned eighty an' she still managed ter get up the pub,' Phyllis said argumentatively.

Freda decided that it was her cue to leave and she picked up her shopping bag. 'Well, I'd better get goin',' she told them.

When she was a few yards down the street Doris glanced at Phyllis. 'She's a funny woman at times,' she remarked. 'One day she stops an' talks an' anuvver day she ain't got five minutes ter spare.'

'I fink she's got a bit of a life wiv 'er ole man, if you ask me,' Phyllis replied. 'She was tellin' me the ovver day 'e expects 'is tea on the table soon as 'e walks in.'

'I'd soon tell 'im where ter get orf if it was me,' Doris said firmly.

Lucy Perry came up to the two viragos. 'I just bin talkin' ter Maggie Gainsford down the market,' she told them. 'She said the doctor's bin in again ter see old Bill Simpson an' 'e sounded 'is 'eart, so Jack Marchant told 'er.'

'I should 'ave thought they'd 'ave took 'im in the 'ospital if it was 'is 'eart,' Doris remarked, glancing at Phyllis for support.

'That's what I would 'ave thought,' Phyllis responded.

'They don't put yer in 'ospital when it's just old age, though,' Doris went on. 'That's all it is wiv 'im, if you ask me.'

'Maggie Gainsford told me that the old boy was fightin' fer 'is breath when Wally picked 'im up,' Lucy said.

'Well, the doctor told Jack Marchant it was just 'is age,' Doris replied firmly.

'The nurse is comin' in every day though,' Phyllis said, scratching her elbow.

'I don't fink the man's bin lookin' after 'imself properly,' Doris remarked.

'They don't when they're on their own, do they?' Lucy said. 'Bill Simpson's bin on 'is own fer some time now.'

'Since 'forty-two,' Doris informed her with a supercilious look. 'That was when Tessie Simpson died. I remember 'cos it was durin' that terrible winter. Double pneumonia was what packed 'er off.'

Lucy Perry had the sudden urge to take Doris Harriman by the throat and give her a good shaking. 'A lot o' people round 'ere said she died of a broken 'eart,' she replied. 'What wiv losin' 'er son the previous year when 'is ship went down. I thought she was a lovely woman. She always 'ad a kind word fer everybody.'

Phyllis and Doris looked surprised by their neighbour's sudden homily. 'Ter tell yer the trufe, I thought ole Bill was gonna follow 'er soon afterwards,' Phyllis said, licking her fingers and rubbing her itching elbow again.

'I fink most people did,' Doris added. 'I fink it was those pigeons of 'is what kept 'im goin'. Always up on that roof, 'e was. Mind you though, there was a few people expected 'im ter chuck 'imself off the top one day, just like ole Mrs Brown tried ter do.'

Waited for it with bated breath more like, Lucy thought.

''Ow is she, by the way?' she asked.

'Doin' very well, accordin' ter Mrs Gaylor who lives opposite 'er,' Doris replied. 'She goes in the 'ome ter see 'er every week. She said yer wouldn't reco'nise the ole gel. Got fat as butter, she 'as.'

'Mind you, Doris, yer can't take too much notice o' what Frannie Gaylor ses. She does incline ter pile it on a bit,' Phyllis told her.

'Well, I'd better get 'ome before my ole man gets in,' Lucy said. 'See yers later.'

The two hawks watched as their neighbour hurried off. 'It's a stone bonkers certainty she won't get as fat as butter, the way she rushes around,' Doris remarked.

Phyllis snorted. 'Scatty cow.'

At the arch Stanley Beamish ran his finger over the gold-leaf lettering and nodded with satisfaction. 'Well, that's the first Flair vanity case we've produced,' he said to Gilda. 'I gotta admit, it does look impressive.'

The young woman held the small case in her hands and unzipped it. It was lined with a light-brown satin and had a three-inch square mirror fitted into the lid. Two cylindrical stainless steel containers were held in with looped leather strips and there was space for other items. Martin's company trademark 'Flair' was embossed into the leather on one corner of the lid, and when closed the case looked very compact.

'The first of thousands, I hope,' Gilda said, zipping up the case.

'A couple more days an' we'll be ready ter go,' Stanley told her. 'I just need ter get the women used to all the machines, then they can swop about. It'll be 'andy too if any of 'em are off sick.'

'Stanley, you've done wonders,' Gilda said, beaming at him.

The dapper old man returned her smile. 'My only reservation is about that bonus system you were talkin' about,' he told her.

'Oh?'

'I don't like it.'

Gilda gave him a quizzical look. 'What's wrong with it, Stanley?' she asked.

He picked up the case and unzipped it. 'Just look at the precision work there,' he said. 'That zip fer a start. It 'as ter be set in very carefully. Then there's the rivetin'. It's all skilled craftwork. Pay the women a bonus an' they'll be more concerned wiv quantity than quality.'

'But we've got to produce a hundred of these a week to break even,' Gilda pointed out.

'We can double that figure in two weeks, once the women are all familiar wiv the machines,' Stanley replied. 'I'd suggest yer pay 'em a monthly bonus on sales, not output. That way they know that any bad workmanship means the item gets backed an' their bonus suffers accordin'ly.'

Gilda nodded thoughtfully. 'That sounds like a good idea, Stanley. I was talking to Martin last night and he said that he can market these vanity cases countrywide. He feels he can handle three, four hundred a week, once the outlets are established.'

'Yer'll need to employ more women fer those sort o' figures,' he remarked.

Gilda smiled at him. 'I'll be happy producing two hundred a week to start with,' she said.

'We'll manage it,' Stanley replied. 'Well, I'd better get back an' see what those women are up to. We can't allow 'em ter slack.'

A few minutes later Linda returned to the office with the women's insurance stamps. 'Sorry if I've bin a long while,' she said. 'I 'ad ter wait at the post office.'

Gilda shook her head. 'You've just missed Stanley,' she said smiling. 'I do believe he fancies one of those women.'

'What makes yer say that?' Linda asked her.

'Well, he was wearing a snazzy shirt and he reeked of aftershave,' Gilda chuckled.

The rays of the setting sun penetrated the dusty window and cast eerie light over the room. The two detectives sat facing each other, both aware that the higher echelons were becoming impatient for results.

Dan Sully poured himself another drink and handed the bottle to Chief Inspector Derek Thomas. 'We have to give him credit,' he said. 'He certainly fooled us.'

Thomas shook his head slowly. 'That's a new one for me,' he replied.

'Do you know, I must have been no more than two feet away from him at one time,' Sully went on. 'He was obviously wearing a wig or that blond hair of his would have stood out. If I remember rightly all the pallbearers were dark-haired, nondescript. It's strange how things work out. Not only did Boy-boy attend the funeral, he even carried his own brother's coffin to the graveside.'

'Well, that episode's done and finished with,' Thomas replied. 'How do you read things now?'

Sully pinched his chin thoughtfully. 'I'd make a guess that Tony Carter's slipped out of the area, for the time being,' he answered. 'He'll be back soon though, I'd bet on it. The Carters were small-time villains but they were big fish in a little pond on this manor. Boy-boy won't be able to survive on his own outside. He's crafty and devious, as we know to our cost, but he'll always be too arrogant to knuckle down and start somewhere else. Besides, he hasn't got enough vision. No, he'll be back. A dog always returns to its own vomit. I just wish I had the manpower to put out on the streets.'

'Don't we all,' Chief Inspector Thomas said, shifting his bulk in the chair and running his fingers through his thick ginger hair. 'I've had to double the patrols in one of the streets on my patch. I've been plagued by Carter's ex-ladyfriend. She seems to feel that he's out to kill her.'

The two policemen finished their drinks as the sun sank below the horizon and the room became dark. Dan Sully put the bottle of whisky back in the drawer and turned to his associate. 'Come on, Derek, let's have a pint at the Crown,' he said. 'We may get a whisper there.'

Up on the roof of Sunlight Buildings the pigeons cooed and settled themselves, while young people stood about in the deepening shadows. Around them night was closing in and stars shone in a cloudless sky.

'I told yer there was nuffink ter worry about,' he said lightly.

'If you was me, you'd 'ave worried,' she told him.

'If I was you, I wouldn't 'ave needed to.'

''Ow come?'

'Well, I couldn't 'ave got meself inter trouble.'

'Can't you ever be serious?'

'Only when Good Friday falls on Christmas Day.'

'You're stupid.'

'You're very desirable.'

'Now, don't start that again.'

'I fink this is where we come in.'

'Don't. People might see us.'

'Do us a favour. Take 'em off.'

'No, I won't.'

'Go on, take 'em off. Just fer me.'

'Don't keep on, yer know I can't see wivout me glasses.'

Across the roof Jenny Jordan nestled against Brendan and sighed. 'I was so proud of yer,' she whispered.

Brendan hugged her tightly. 'I told you your father wouldn't be any trouble. After two pints he started to come round and then when I gave him that double whisky he was putty in my hands.'

'You're so masterful, Brendan.'

'And you're so vulnerable, Jenny.'

'Why are yer smilin', Brendan?'

'It was something your dad said.'

'What was it?'

'Well, I told him that we had considered going to Gretna Green to get married and he said it was best to get married this side of London.'

In the deep shadows further along the roof, Kate Selby looked down at her hand and caught the sparkle of her new engagement ring. 'I'm so happy,' she sighed.

Peter Ridley smiled weakly as he stood holding her. 'So am I,' he replied.

'Mum said loose-fittin' weddin' dresses are all the go now,' Kate told him.

'Yer won't show anyway, will yer?' Peter asked her.

'I shouldn't fink so,' she replied. 'Didn't Mum take it well?'

'Yeah, she did.'

'It'll be nice livin' above Mum.'

'Yeah.'

'Try ter sound enthusiastic, Peter.'

'I am.'

'Well, it don't seem like it.'

'I'd really prefer a place on our own.'

'Livin over Mum'll be a godsend when the baby comes.'

'Yeah, I know.'

'Well, let's just fink ourselves lucky.'

'Yeah.'

On the far corner of the roof Jack Marchant sat in solitude, puffing on his pipe and staring up into the night sky. On clear nights like this his old friend would lean against the balustrade and pick out the stars, planets and constellations and explain their movements across the heavens. Jack smiled sadly to himself as he recalled such nights when he had been enthralled, listening like a child while Bill told him of his early journeyings to the far corners of the earth in the old coal burners, as he called them. Now his old friend was lying near to death, and in his sorrow Jack remembered what Bill had told him. Death was nothing to worry about; it was just another journey, a sort of homecoming, he had said, quoting Robert Louis Stevenson's 'Requiem':

> Under the wide and starry sky,
> Dig the grave and let me lie.
> Glad did I live and gladly die,
> And I laid me down with a will.
>
> This be the verse you grave for me:
> 'Here he lies where he longed to be;
> Home is the sailor, home from the sea,
> And the hunter home from the hill.'

Jack Marchant tapped the bowl of his pipe on his boot, affording himself a wistful smile. Bill had recited that poem often enough for him to have learnt the words, though at the time he had hardly realised that he was listening.

Chapter Forty-Seven

Late on Thursday evening Gilda sat back in the divan and watched as Martin poured out the drinks. 'Do you have to go off tomorrow, dear?' she asked him.

'I must. Things have been piling up lately,' he told her. 'I'll try to get back as soon as I can. If all goes well I'll be home on Saturday evening.'

'It's all my fault,' she said quietly. 'I really am sorry.'

'I don't want you to give it another thought,' he replied. 'I couldn't possibly leave you the way you were. Remember I'm your husband, and I love you, Gilda.'

'I love you too, Martin, and I'm going to miss you,' she told him. 'You don't know how much you've helped me these last two weeks.'

He came over and handed her a tall glass. 'There we are,' he said, avoiding her eyes.

'What's wrong, darling?' she asked.

'It's nothing. Really.'

'There is. I can tell,' she persisted.

'How long have we been together?' he asked.

'Years and years,' she said lightheartedly.

'Well, in all those years and years I've never once heard

501

you say you'll miss me,' he replied. 'Oh, I know you tell me to be careful and come back soon, but I've never heard you actually say that you'll miss me.'

Gilda put down her drink and took his hands in hers, gently pulling him down on to the divan beside her. 'Martin, you know how much I love you,' she said softly. 'I've always loved you, in my own way, but these last two weeks I've seen the real man. The man who cares, despite everything. I've seen the man who props his wife up and instils into her a new vitality, a fresh sense of living, and I've suddenly real-ised that I've come to depend on you. Yes – me, the strong, independent Gilda. I'm lost without you, Martin, and every minute you're away I'll think about you, wonder where you are, what you're doing. The past has gone. It's over, but the future's ours. Ours together. Do you understand what I'm trying to say?'

He nodded, lowering his eyes as if he were gazing on her beauty for the first time. 'I'd like to try again, Gilda,' he said quietly. 'I'd like to try and love you in the way a man should love his wife.'

She leant closer and his arms went around her. She could feel his heart beating and the warmth of his hands as he gently stroked her back. 'We'll try, darling, and we'll make it work, you'll see.'

Charlie held Linda's hand as they went into the Buildings and climbed the stairs to the roof. A cool breeze was rising and traces of moonlit cloud drifted high in the heavens.

'What a lovely night,' Linda remarked as they walked over to the stone balustrade.

Charlie nodded, focusing his eyes on the City glow that

rose up like a dome of golden haze. 'We're gonna miss this place when these ole buildin's come down,' he said.

'So will a lot o' the young people round 'ere,' Linda replied.

Charlie turned to face her, his eyes searching her face. 'I bet there's bin a few proposals made up on this roof,' he remarked.

Linda smiled as she looked into his large dark eyes. 'Yeah, I'd imagine so. It is romantic up 'ere, though,' she sighed. 'This was where we first met, wasn't it?'

'Well, I do remember seein' this leggy little gel runnin' around Eagle Street,' Charlie said grinning.

'I remember this scruffy lad a bit older than me who used ter pull me pigtails,' Linda replied, 'but it was up 'ere on the roof when we first really met.'

Charlie nodded as he slipped his hand into his trouser pocket. 'Little did I know then that one day you an' I would be standin' up 'ere an' I'd say ter yer: Linda, will you marry me?'

The young woman caught her breath as she saw the ring in his hand. 'Charlie, it's beautiful,' she gasped.

He smiled. 'Well? Will yer marry me?'

In answer she threw her arms around him. 'Oh darling! Of course I will,' she replied, kissing his mouth again and again.

'That means we're engaged, so yer'd better try it on,' he told her matter-of-factly.

Linda held out her left hand and Charlie slipped the engagement ring on to her finger.

'It's a perfect fit,' she said. ''Ow did yer know the size?'

He grinned. 'That part was easy. I asked yer mum. She remembered from when she bought yer that signet ring on yer eighteenth birfday. The 'ard part was gettin' round to askin' yer dad fer 'is permission.'

Linda stared down at the five-stoned ring. 'I can't get over it,' she said excitedly. 'It's absolutely beautiful.'

'It's fer a beautiful gel,' Charlie said smiling at her.

It was late into the night when Bill Simpson opened his eyes and saw Jack Marchant sitting by his bedside. 'What are you doin' 'ere?' he asked, looking puzzled.

Jack grinned. 'Yer bin very sickly, you ole fraud.'

'I got a dry mouth,' Bill said, pulling a face.

'I'll make yer a nice cuppa,' Jack offered.

'Nah, I feel like a cold drink. Water'll do.'

''Ere, I know what,' Jack said, fishing down beside the bed.

'Bloody blimey. Where did that come from?' Bill asked, staring at the bottle of stout.

'I got it for yer when yer were taken bad,' Jack told him.

'What time is it, mate?' Bill asked, struggling to raise himself up in the bed.

'It's just after two,' Jack replied, helping him sit up and propping a pillow behind his back.

'In the afternoon?'

'Nah, in the mornin', yer silly ole sod.'

''Ow long 'ave I bin out?'

'Well, it's 'ard ter say,' Jack told him, stroking his chin. 'Yer bin in an' out fer the past couple o' days. Yer kept openin' yer eyes, then droppin' off ter sleep again.'

'I could do wiv that stout.'

'Comin' up.'

Bill watched his friend pour the frothy drink and he licked

his lips in anticipation. 'You're a good sort, Jack,' he remarked. 'I've often wondered why yer never got married, but I never asked yer. I thought it was none o' my business anyway. As it 'appens yer'd 'ave made some woman very 'appy, I'm sure.'

Jack smiled indulgently. 'It's a long story, yer wouldn't be interested,' he replied.

'Yes, I would,' Bill prompted.

Jack handed over the glass of stout and then sat down on the edge of the bed. 'There was a big family of us, seven kids, an' I was the youngest,' he began. 'Me farvver died when I was five so I don't remember much about 'im, but I remember the 'ard times we 'ad. We used ter live in this big 'ouse in Grange Road. Me muvver took in washin' an' skivvied fer the well-ter-do. She got ter be an ole woman before 'er time. Me two eldest sisters went inter service an' then Benjamin joined the army an' went out to India. Sammy an' Marfa both died wiv the fever when they were very young an' there was just me an' me sister Rosie left at 'ome. By this time me muvver was consumptive. Me an' Rosie nursed 'er fer years. We never considered marriage. I knew that if I met a nice lady an' got spliced, poor ole Rosie would bear the full burden o' lookin' after our muvver. She felt the same way about me, so I s'pose we accepted our role in life an' carried on nursin' the old lady till the day she died.'

'That's bloody sad,' Bill remarked.

Jack nodded his head slowly, staring into the empty grate. 'When the ole lady passed away, me an' Rosie were in our forties,' he went on. 'The 'ouse we lived in was much too big fer just us so we left there an' went inter service, both of us at the same place. It was a big residence

505

just outside o' Canterbury, owned by Lord Bassett. Rosie was employed as an 'ousemaid an' I was a footman. There were s'posed ter be related ter Royalty, as it 'appened. Anyway, it all come to an end in nineteen thirty-one. The family lost a lot o' money in the depression an' we got put off. We come back ter Bermondsey an' moved inter these Buildin's. Rosie managed ter get a job at the bagwash in Long Lane an' I used ter sell shoelaces an' collar studs out of a suitcase in the markets. Bloody 'ard it was, but like everyone else we managed ter survive. We were set in our ways, both lookin' out fer each ovver. Then Rosie got ill. It turned out ter be consumption, but there were clinics openin' by then an' I managed ter get 'er in a sanatorium down in Sussex. Five years she spent in that place before she died. I used ter go there every week ter see 'er. I 'ad ter scrape up the fares an' a few coppers fer somefing ter take 'er. So yer see, there was never any inclination on my part, nor the time, come ter that, ter go courtin'.'

Bill's face was sad as he stared at his old friend. 'Me an' Tessie moved in the Buildin's in the summer o' thirty-six. I remember, you was on yer own then, wasn't yer?'

Jack nodded. 'That was the year Rosie died.'

Bill Simpson took a swig from his glass. ''Adn't yer better get back ter yer flat an' get some sleep? I'll be all right now.'

'There's no rush,' Jack told him. 'I ain't bin sleepin' well anyway.'

''Ow's the pigeons?'

'They're fine.'

'What about Monty?'

'Yeah, 'im too.'

'I ain't stoppin' in bed termorrer if I can 'elp it,' Bill said firmly.

'Yer'll 'ave ter wait an' see what the doctor ses,' Jack replied. ''E's comin' termorrer mornin'.'

Bill sipped his beer gratefully. 'I 'ad a strange dream ternight,' he said, his forehead wrinkling as he struggled to recall it clearly. 'I was on board this clipper ship an' we was full sail wiv the wind at our backs. She was movin' very fast frew the water. "Up aloft, Simpson," the captain shouts out. So up I goes, right up the riggin' terwards the crow's nest. The wind was takin' me breath an' I was strugglin' ter keep from fallin' down on ter the deck. Anyway I finally managed ter get inter the barrel at the mast-'ead an' then I saw it.'

'Saw what?' Jack asked, his eyes open wide.

'I saw this crop o' jagged rocks. Right there in front of us, an' there we are, smack bang in the middle o' the roarin' forties.'

'What's the roarin' forties?' Jack asked.

'Well yer see, when sailin' ships come round Cape 'Orn inter the Atlantic Ocean they rely on the roarin' forties ter get 'em 'ome,' Bill explained.

'So they're winds.'

'You got it. They're winds that blow ter the north, an' if yer lucky yer pick 'em up when yer round the Cape an' they speed yer 'ome.'

'Go on then.'

Bill took another sip of beer. 'I was terrified when I saw those jagged rocks, an' I shouts down, "Rocks ahoy! Two points on the starboard bow!" Well, the captain can't believe it. 'E finks I've gone orf me 'ead. "Rocks ahoy!" I shouts again an' then before yer could say Jack Robinson we was on top of 'em. Tore the bottom right out o' the ship, they did. Now there was I, still up in the crow's nest an' the ship's goin' down beneath me. I was really scared, an' I closed me eyes an' said me prayers. I really thought I was a gonner. Then after a while I could feel this floatin' sensation so I opened me eyes again, an' what d'yer fink?'

'I dunno,' Jack said quickly.

'I saw you sittin' by me bed,' Bill told him.

Chapter Forty-Eight

Boy-boy Carter stood up in the low-ceilinged caravan on the outskirts of Barking and breathed out heavily through his teeth. 'I need a drink,' he said flatly.

Rubin Scroggins rolled his fat, aged bulk over on the battered divan and coughed. 'Don't go down the Pheasant,' he told him between splutters. 'Us lot don't use that gaff anymore. We ain't welcome.'

'Nah, they don't know me,' Boy-boy replied.

'The locals know yer live wiv us,' Rubin said quickly. 'They make it their business ter know. Pikers they call us. You go down there an' yer'll end up wiv five or six of 'em on yer. I got a drop o' special stashed away 'ere. Annie don't like me drinkin' spirits, so we'll 'ave ter go over the ovver side o' the yard. It'll do yer more good than that flat piss at the pub.'

Boy-boy followed him out of the old trailer and over to the far hedge, where the old man reached down inside the rusty wreck of a smashed Bedford van. 'There yer go,' Rubin said, groaning as he straightened up. "Ave a snort o' that.'

Carter leaned back against the van and folded his arms, staring out into the gathering darkness as the fiery whisky warmed his belly. The old breaker's yard was menacing in the gloom, the wrecked chassis of cars silhouetted like dead bones in the half-light amongst grey puddles of diesel. Blackened metal drums stood out amongst the debris like burnt sentinels, and piles of cogs and broken gearboxes had fallen into a mire of lumpy leaden sludge.

Rubin looked askance at Boy-boy and saw the cold dead cast of his eye. He had been like this since returning from his brother's funeral, and the old man's wife Annie had noticed it too. She had watched him working in the yard, and grown nervous at the hateful rage in him as he swung the heavy sledgehammer with all his weight behind it. His fair hair had become unkempt and he had not shaved for days. Gone was the smart, well-dressed man they had once known, and, as Annie said wryly, he could easily be taken for a Scroggins now.

Boy-boy took the bottle again without a word and had a long swig. 'Well, this place ain't changed much,' he said finally with a gasp. 'It really don't seem like all them years ago now. Me an' Mickey 'angin' about the caravan waitin' fer you ter go out so's we could nick yer bottles o' barley wine.'

Rubin's old face creased in a painful grimace at the mention of his dead son, and he shifted his boot in the dirt. The old Scroggins temper had been strongest in Mickey, the firstborn, and had been his undoing at an early age. Battering a local lad over the head with a tyre lever had got him eighteen months in Borstal, where Boy-boy became good friends with him. It was while Boy-boy was staying that last time, hiding from a mob of aggravators south of the river, that it happened. How could the old man ever forget that black Sunday? Mickey had got stupid drunk on gin, and after a nasty argument he stormed off in the old Morris. An hour later the police were banging on the flimsy door of the caravan. The mad tyke had tried to break in through the skylight of a warehouse, but being so drunk he had slipped down the sloping roof and fallen over the edge like a stone, breaking his neck.

'Annie don't seem 'er usual bright self lately,' Boy-boy remarked, still staring ahead. 'I 'ope she ain't got too much on 'er mind.'

Rubin looked at him and smiled crookedly. 'Nah, don't worry about 'er,' he replied. 'She's a bit fed up wiv Gerry an' Danny's kids runnin' round 'er all day.'

Boy-boy did not say anything. The old man's two remaining sons made it pretty clear that they resented him being around, and the feeling was mutual. Family meals in the dilapidated caravan had become a grinding ordeal. Hardly a word was spoken as mutton stews swimming in fat, or burnt sausages, mashed potatoes and watery cabbage were slopped up on cracked plates with hunks of hard dry bread. No one else seemed too bothered and they always scraped their plates clean, but the greasy dull slurry turned Boy-boy's stomach.

''Ere, it was a laugh, weren't it?' Rubin said suddenly. 'D'you remember when those two were little? Annie'd be goin' on at 'em an' givin' 'em a larrupin', then they'd start bawlin' the place down, an' there's you, me an' Mickey, 'idin' up the ovver end wiv a couple o' bottles pissin' ourselves.'

Boy-boy burped and tasted the fat from his stodgy dinner. He remembered several times when Rubin was sprawled on the steps of the caravan after drinking all morning, shouting at a couple of kids to go and play outside their own home.

His wife had had to remind him in her most sarcastic voice that this was the kids' home, and she was their long-suffering mother, the stupidest mother in the world for having stayed around so long.

Rubin was shaking his head slowly, and Boy-boy realised that the usual old yarn was coming. 'Nah, the poor cow never got over the day she clapped eyes on this yard,' the old man remarked. 'Place we lived in in Bermon'sey weren't much better, mind. Well, it was a decent 'ouse really, but the neighbours got the 'ump wiv us over somefing or the ovver. Just sort o' built up, I s'pose. There must o' bin a bit of a racket, what wiv me bein' in the scrap game then. The backyard was always overflowin' wiv bits of iron an' rags, an' we 'ad bundles of old newspapers piled up in the passage. Course Annie ended up chuckin' a fit an' she was gonna piss orf out of it if I didn't find somewhere wiv a bit more space. She took a lot, mind. Cookin', cleaning' – when she could get round the junk – mendin' clothes an' that, an' she 'elped me sort the rags an' smash up old wringers an' cartwheels an' bits o' machinery. She could use a cold chisel, strip wire an' wield a sledge'ammer like a good 'un. Anyway, she'd finally done 'er nut, an' as fate would 'ave it, that very Saturday on the pub beano ter Southend I got pissed out me brains an' the charabanc sodded off an' left me while I was 'avin' a slash. Right over there, it was.'

Boy-boy puffed in irritation and looked over to where the old man was pointing, at a thick clump of nettles by a drainage ditch. He wanted to get hold of the old man's head and smash it against the side of the van until he shut his drivelling mouth up for good.

'Yeah, yer should've seen the look on 'er face,' Rubin went

on. 'I thought she was gonna drop down stone bloody dead right there wiv an 'eart attack or somefing. She'd bin kiddin' 'erself a lot though, an' I never said nuffink. Goin' on about livin' in the country, growin' vegetables an' taters, an' the kids growin' up rosy-cheeked like yokels. I should 'a' told 'er it ain't that easy. I'd just slapped down a month's rent an' still 'ad change in me pocket. Yer get what yer pay for, I always reckon. Course it's got worse since then, what wiv the smells from the factories an' the bloody caravan rattlin' all night wiv the lorries goin' to an' from the gravel pits.'

He suddenly kicked out at a scrounging cat and it scuttered away. 'I bloody 'ate cats. I know they keep the rats down, but I can't abide 'em.' He took a stiff swig from the whisky. 'When we was kids we used ter shoot 'em wiv catapults. Yer gotta use the little sharp stones, they really 'urt. I shot one right in the eye once.'

Boy-boy remembered the cat Nick had when they were young, a small black and white stray he found in the backyard one morning. It always seemed to follow him everywhere, and when two big kids threw stones at it over the yard wall he chased them halfway down the Tower Bridge Road and ended up giving them both a right good spanking.

He leaned across to the old man. 'Gis that bottle 'ere, Rubin, fer Chrissake. Yer gonna marry it or what?'

When the last drop of whisky had been drained, Rubin staggered over to the caravan, eager for his bed. Tony Carter remained where he was, staring into the dark.

Annie was nodding off in the chair and she woke up with a start as Boy-boy came over to her. She blinked and quickly noticed that he had washed and combed his hair, and shaved for the first time in days. He was wearing his reefer jacket and carrying a small bag. 'So yer leavin' us, Tony,' she remarked.

'I gotta move on,' he said simply.

'Come an' see us again, when fings are better,' she said.

'I will,' he replied. 'Look after yerself, Annie. Fanks fer everyfing.'

'Rubin's in bed,' she told him.

'Tell 'im I said goodbye,' Boy-boy replied, turning on his heel and walking quickly out of the caravan.

Annie Scroggins shook her head sadly, her rheumy eyes staring after him. As with the Scroggins', there's only one direction for that bloke, she thought, and that's down.

The parlour light was burning late in the last house but one in Eagle Street and Ginny eased herself in her favourite armchair. 'It's bin a few years now, Dick,' she reminded him.

Dick Conners nodded. 'I owe yer a lot, Ginny,' he said quietly. 'In fact I wouldn't be 'ere now if it wasn't fer you.'

'That's nonsense,' she replied.

'No, it's not,' he said, both hands clasped round his mug of tea. 'Before you said yer'd take me in, I was lookin' ter spend the rest o' me days in some lodgin'-'ouse. Nobody else would take the chance, not round 'ere anyway.'

'I was always a soft touch,' Ginny replied. 'Even Albert tells me that.'

''E's right, yer know,' Dick said. ''E's got you taped.'

'The crafty ole git 'ad me taped the first day 'e met me,' Ginny told him. 'Still, 'e's a good 'un is Albert. I could 'ave done a lot worse.'

'Yer should go a bit easier on 'im, yer know,' Dick urged her. ''E can't 'elp bein' deaf.'

'The crafty ole sod 'ears me more than 'e lets on,' she replied. 'It suits 'im ter be mutton jeff at times. Take yesterday. I asked 'im if 'e'd clean me front winders. I don't normally get 'im ter do 'em but me back was playin' me up somefing shockin'. Anyway 'e nods, an' I went up fer a lie down. Two hours later I comes down an' there's bloody Albert fast asleep in the armchair. I could see the winders 'adn't bin done so I wakes 'im up. "Oi you, why ain't yer done me winders," ' I asks 'im. "Yer never said yer wanted me ter do the winders," 'e ses. Anyway I goes rantin' off at 'im. "I asked yer afore I went up fer a lie down an' you nodded," I told 'im. "I thought yer said clear out the cinders," he replied. So I looks at the grate an' the cinders are still there. "You ain't even done that, yer lazy ole goat," I shouts at 'im. "There was nowhere ter put 'em," 'e ses. "The dustbin's full." I tell yer, Dick, that man's got an answer fer everyfing.'

'Never mind, Ginny, 'is 'eart's in the right place.'

'Yeah, I s'pose so,' she replied, affording herself a smile. ''E's gonna miss yer when yer go.'

'I shouldn't say anyfing to 'im just yet awhile,' Dick advised her. 'Like I said, it won't be fer a good few weeks yet.'

'I 'ope yer'll call round an' see us from time ter time,' Ginny told him. 'After all, it's only Catford.'

'Yeah, course I will,' he replied.

She shook her head slowly. 'Who'd 'a' thought it? Wait till those two ole cows at the end o' the street find out. They'll 'ave a field day.'

'I bet they'll be glad ter see the back o' me,' Dick remarked.

'I still can't believe it,' Ginny said. 'Dick Conners gettin' married.'

He grinned sheepishly. 'Eve's a very respectable woman, Gin. She said she wouldn't like people ter fink we was livin' in sin.'

'Well, you are, ain't yer?'

'If yer put it like that, I s'pose we are, but it was all very proper. It wasn't a bit of 'ow's-yer-farvver on the first night. I slept in the spare bedroom as a matter o' fact.'

'Well, yer got yer feet under 'er table an' yer shoes under 'er bed, so it's only right yer do the right fing by 'er, if yer serious about it. That's my way o' finkin',' Ginny declared firmly.

'I make yer right, Ginny,' he told her. 'Ter be honest, I can't see me life wivout 'er now. We seem ter like the same fings, an' she's not a naggin' bitch.'

'Like some you could name,' Ginny said quickly.

'You've never nagged me; well, not much anyway,' he said smiling. 'When yer did I needed it.'

'Yer'll 'ave ter bring 'er round one night,' she told him. 'It'd be nice to 'ave a chat. P'raps we could lock Albert in 'is room.'

'Better if we send 'im up the Bee'ive fer a few pints,' Dick replied grinning. ''E said 'e likes that barmaid wiv the big knockers.'

'She's more woman than 'e can 'andle,' Ginny remarked. 'In fact, any woman's more than 'e can 'andle these days.'

Dick yawned widely and put down his empty mug. 'Well, I'd better be off ter bed,' he said. 'I need ter be at me best termorrer if I'm gonna land that job.'

'Yer'll get it,' she replied encouragingly. 'After all, it ain't everyone's cup o' tea bein' a bus conductor.'

Gilda eased her arm out gently from under him and sat up. In the dim light from the curtains she could just make out two-thirty on the bedside clock, and she glanced down at Martin as she ran her fingers through her hair and stretched leisurely. He was breathing slowly and evenly, curled like a baby in the sheets, and she drew her knees up to her chin and gazed around the bedroom. The vague shapes of the furniture seemed vibrant in the dark, infused with an energy of their own and suddenly unfamiliar. She hugged her shoulders and smiled, warm and happy, like a stranger to herself.

The previous evening they had gone to bed early. He had fondled her in that gentle way of his, but then she had taken the initiative and climbed above him, her legs straddling his hips, her body arched as she provocatively pulled her cotton nightdress over her head and exposed her full breasts. She had taken his hands and pressed them over her nipples, slowly moving against his limp manhood, smiling down at him, her eyes half closed, moistening her red lips with the tip of her tongue. Beads of sweat stood out on his forehead and his face was flushed but she ignored his anxiety, and with the sensual caresses of her lithe body she used him, daringly and wickedly, indulging her own desire, her own selfish needs. His breathing grew faster as he lay beneath her, and when her lips glided over his chest and belly and she stroked him with the tips of her fingers he groaned with pleasure. She rose up, slowly riding him again, and then she felt the swelling of his passion under her and he pulled her down to him . . .

Gilda stared at the shadows that clustered round the dressing-table and wardrobe, and in the faint light they seemed to move, as if the wooden surfaces were sprouting branches, breaking out with new life and returning to their source. She was like a wild animal in the forest, naked and open, the smell of growth and danger about her and the breath of her lover on her flanks.

She lay back down next to Martin, savouring the heat of his body as she pulled the covers over them, and as she slipped her arm over his chest he mumbled a few words in his sleep and snuggled against her.

For the first time in a long, long time, she felt at home.

Chapter Forty-Nine

Before the sun was up, the clatter of feet sounded on the pavements as people made their way to the wharves, tanneries and food factories of Bermondsey. Workers streamed through Abbey Street on their way to the tin-box factory and the council depot, and men hopeful of a call-on as casual road sweepers gathered outside the council yard or, if they were early, in the cafes and coffee shops nearby. Trains carrying workers from the suburbs rattled over the Abbey Street arch on the way to London Bridge Station, and in Toby's cafe in Abbey Street the proprietor and his assistants were kept busy dispensing large mugs of tea and slices of thick new bread coated with beef dripping. The man on a bench seat next to the window sat sipping his sweet tea, his eyes never leaving the arch opposite.

At five minutes to eight George Morrison walked briskly along the turning, unlocked the arch and stepped inside. His first job was to get the glue pots over the gas, ready for when the women arrived at eight-thirty. There would be time enough then to have a sweep-up and clear the benches, he thought.

George did not hear the man from the cafe enter the arch

but he sensed a presence, and as he turned he already knew somehow who would be there. 'Bloody 'ell, yer give me a turn,' he said quickly. 'What you doin' 'ere? It's a bit risky, ain't it?'

Boy-boy smiled. 'I'm as safe in 'ere as anywhere,' he replied. 'I was curious ter see just what was goin' on 'ere. Don Jacobs told me that Gilda 'ad started up in the leavver business.'

George grabbed hold of the broom. 'Yeah, that's right. We've only bin goin' a week.'

Boy-boy stepped to one side as George set about the sweeping. 'We, yer say? It sounds very cosy,' he remarked sarcastically.

George eyed him with suspicion. 'What yer want, Tony? There's nuffink 'ere fer you.'

'I fink that's fer Gilda ter say,' he replied. 'I pay the rent on this arch. I don't fink she'll wanna row me out.'

'This is legit, not like the perfume game,' George said quietly.

'Well, well. Fings do change,' Carter said, smiling scornfully. 'What time's Gilda due in?'

'Any minute now,' George told him. 'She likes ter get in before the women.'

'So yer've got women workin' for yer too. It gets better an' better.'

The big ex-boxer put down his broom and walked up to the younger man. 'Look, Tony, don't give Gilda any grief. She's done wonders gettin' this business goin' an' she can do wivout you pesterin' 'er.'

'What's it ter you? Are you 'er minder?' Carter growled.

'If yer put it that way,' George said firmly.

Just then Gilda stepped into the arch, her eyes widening with surprise as she saw Boy-boy. 'What are you doing here, Tony?' she asked.

'It's funny you should say that,' Carter replied. 'George asked me the same question. Like I told 'im, I've called in ter see this new business yer settin' up.'

'This is my venture,' Gilda said quickly. 'It's all above board.'

'That's nice ter know,' Boy-boy smirked. 'I fink we should 'ave a little chat about this.'

'You'd better come in the office,' the young woman told him.

Carter followed her into the small room and looked around. 'I see yer bin busy tartin' the place up,' he said.

'Take a seat,' she bade him.

'I prefer ter stand,' he replied. 'Yer said this was your venture. Don't yer mean *our* venture?'

Gilda looked him full in the eye. 'Listen, Tony. When you ran off there was almost a month outstanding on the rent and the railway were going to evict us. I persuaded them to let me take over the rent book, and after a lot of wrangling they agreed. The backing for this business is partly from Martin's company and partly from the bank. You don't fit into this.'

Boy-boy's face darkened with anger. 'You listen, Gilda,' he snarled. 'You was Nick's woman. 'E took yer inter the perfume business wiv my agreement an' you earned out of it. I'm Nick's bruvver. 'E wouldn't want yer ter row me out.'

'I'm sorry, Tony, but there's no room here for you,' Gilda said quickly. 'If it was solely my money I'd say yes, but it's not. The bank has issued guidelines that I've got to abide by.'

'Yer've not got the message yet, 'ave yer?' Boy-boy said. 'I've got 'alf the coppers in London on the lookout fer me. I don't want in, I want out. A pay-off. One tidy sum, an' the business is yours, lock stock an' barrel.'

'I've got no money of my own, Tony,' she replied.

'There's gotta be some of the firm's money in that safe,' he retorted. 'That'll do.'

'I think you'd better leave right now, or I'll call George in,' she said, shaking with anger.

Boy-boy suddenly grabbed her by the throat, his hands tightening over her windpipe, and as Gilda struggled she heard an ominous click and found herself looking at the cold steel blade of a flick knife.

'One peep out o' you an' I'll slit yer throat, believe me,' he hissed.

Gilda went stiff with fright as she stared at the notched edge of the blade and she felt herself being pulled across the room.

'Call George in,' he said, his wide staring eyes boring into her. 'Try anyfing an' I'll cut yer bad.'

Gilda opened the door a couple of inches, feeling the knife blade pressed to her throat. 'George, have you got a minute?' she called out, hardly recognising her own voice.

Boy-boy shoved Gilda away just as the big man pushed open the door, and before George knew anything Carter smashed a length of lead piping down hard on the side of his head. George dropped on to his knees, stunned by the force of the blow, and another quick blow laid him out cold.

Gilda brought her hands up to her face. 'You've killed him, you bastard!' she cried out.

Boy-boy looked down at the prone figure and saw the

trickle of blood beginning to stain the lino. He grabbed Gilda and pushed her into a chair. 'Stay there,' he ordered her, moving over to the safe.

Gilda watched as he twirled the combination lock and pulled down on the handle, and when the door resisted he swore. 'Yer've changed the combination,' he snarled. 'Open it!'

'I can't,' she replied, her heart pounding.

He grabbed her by the hair and yanked her out of the chair. 'Open it or I'll open you,' he hissed, pressing the knife to her throat as he pushed her on to her knees.

Gilda turned the dial back and forth and then leaned back while Boy-boy opened the heavy door.

'This is more like it,' he said quickly as he pulled out the two large wads of notes. 'What time do those women o' yours get in?'

'Half past eight,' she said.

Boy-boy looked up at the wall clock and saw that it was seven minutes past. 'Right, I want yer ter phone me a cab,' he told her, pocketing the money. 'It should only take about ten minutes ter get 'ere. I'll be out of it before they arrive.'

Gilda knew Charlie would be in at any minute and she agonised about what to do. If she warned Boy-boy he would jump him the way he had poor George, but if she kept quiet there might just be a chance of Charlie surprising him and overpowering him.

'Did you 'ear what I said? Pick that phone up,' Carter growled.

Gilda heard the front door go, and as Boy-boy made a grab for her she eluded him and moved round the desk. 'Charlie! Quick!' she screamed.

As the young man came hurrying into the office, Boy-boy swung the lead pipe at his head but Charlie slipped over George's body and the blow caught him on the shoulder. He cried out in pain, twisting round to see Boy-boy slowly coming towards him brandishing the knife in one hand and the piping in the other. Gilda grabbed the phone to call the police but Carter was too quick for her. He yanked it out of her hand with such force that the connecting wire came away from the wall socket. Charlie suddenly dived at him, grabbing his wrists. They fell in a heap by the door, blocking Gilda in and she stood petrified as Charlie fought for his life. It was then that she saw George Morrison stirring.

Charlie was lying under Boy-boy but he had a good grip on his wrists and he summoned every ounce of his energy to keep the knife away from his face. His arm was beginning to go numb from the blow to his shoulder and he knew that he could not hold out much longer. They rolled over away from the door and Charlie struggled to get on top but Boy-boy seemed to have the strength of two men. He slowly lowered the knife as Charlie's trembling arm began to succumb with the exertion and now the blade was only an inch from his throat. The young man felt then that he was going to die and with one last effort he managed to twist his head to one side. Boy-boy countered by suddenly pulling back and he managed to free Charlie's grip on his wrist. With a maniacal cry he raised the knife over his head, preparing to drive it home. The office door sprang open and Boy-boy hardly managed a glance at the newcomer before a heavy gluepot came down on the top of his head. He dropped sideways, the knife falling from his grasp, and quick as a flash Stanley Beamish retrieved it.

Charlie hauled himself up, one arm hanging uselessly at his side. Boy-boy staggered up too, his lips parted over clenched teeth as he rushed at him. No one had noticed George climb to his feet and as Boy-boy grabbed Charlie and grappled with him, the big man's hands went round the fugitive's throat from behind.

Gilda could see that Boy-boy's face was turning blue and his eyes were almost popping out of his head. 'No, George!' she cried out, tugging on the big man's arms as he tightened his grip.

He looked at her, his face set hard, then suddenly he let go. Boy-boy collapsed in a heap, fighting for breath.

'There's been enough killing, George,' Gilda said quietly. 'We don't want any blood on our hands.'

Stanley was still holding on to the gluepot. 'I'll phone the police,' he said, picking up the phone from the floor, then he spotted the broken cord. 'The man's a bloody lunatic. I'll 'ave ter use their phone next door.'

'Wait, Stanley,' Gilda said quickly. 'George, Carter's got the money from the safe in his pocket.'

The ex-boxer dragged Boy-boy to his feet and leaned him against the wall while he took the money back. 'What do we do wiv 'im?' he asked her.

Gilda counted some notes from one of the wads and folded them in half. She looked at Charlie who sat white-faced on the desk, at Stanley, and then back at the big man. 'Put this in his pocket and show him the door, George,' she said quietly. 'Even an animal like that deserves a chance to get away.'

Five minutes later the women arrived and Stanley was waiting, dabbing at his brow with a large red handkerchief.

'I'm afraid we've had a bit of a kerfuffle, ladies,' he said. 'Nuffink I wasn't able ter sort out, but it means we'll be startin' a bit later. Take yer coats off an' I'll tell yer the full story, or maybe it should be the tale o' the old iron pot, ter be more precise.'

Linda came into the office a few minutes later and saw Gilda fixing a make-do sling on Charlie's arm. 'Oh my God!' she cried out. 'Whatever's 'appened?'

'I fink I've busted me collarbone,' Charlie told her, trying to force a smile.

'Perhaps you could go over to Guy's with him,' Gilda suggested. 'I'm sure Charlie'll tell you all about it.'

Tony Carter dragged himself along Abbey Street and out into Dockhead, his head pounding from the blow he had taken. He knew that the police would be alerted and there was no time to lose. He crossed the Tower Bridge Road and hurried through the arch into Crucifix Lane. People were going about their business and he slowed his pace a little, trying not to look conspicuous. He climbed the long flight of steps to the forecourt of London Bridge Station and bought a one-way ticket to Brighton. The train was waiting and as he hurried on to the platform he began to breathe easier. He found an empty carriage and pulled open the door.

'I don't think so,' a voice said.

Boy-boy spun round and saw Dan Sully facing him, and for an instant his body tensed, then he sighed in resignation and his shoulders sagged. The policeman took him by the arm. 'You're not going to give me any grief, are you, Tony?' he said quietly. 'I don't want to put the cuffs on.'

'I gave yer a run for yer money, didn't I?' Boy-boy said.

'You certainly did.'

''Ow did yer get on ter me?' he asked.

'We got a tip-off from the cafe you used this morning,' Sully replied. 'You walked out without paying for your tea and toast. You were seen going in the arch and the beat bobby was alerted. He phoned me and I was waiting for you.'

'Why did yer let me get this far?' Boy-boy asked him.

'Let me tell you something,' Sully said quietly. 'I've been on this manor a few years now and I've known quite a few desperate characters who ended it all by diving off platforms under the wheels of trains. You could have attempted that now, couldn't you?'

'I'm not that desperate,' Boy-boy retorted.

'Yeah, but supposing you were, and I put in my report that I pursued you as far as the station then I grabbed you just in time to prevent you throwing yourself under a train,' Sully said, smiling.

'Bloody nice,' the fugitive growled as they turned and walked down the platform. 'You get a commendation an' I get ter swing on the end of a rope.'

'Think about it, Tony,' the detective said quietly. 'It's a question of state of mind. You killed Sam Colby out of revenge. No premeditation there. Then after living a life of hell on the run, and being filled with remorse for taking a man's life, albeit the man who killed your brother, you decide to purge yourself by taking your own life. I should think a good barrister would have the jury weeping into their handkerchiefs, what say you?'

'Would it wash?' Carter asked him.

Sully nodded. 'A stone certainty, I should think. There'll be a recommendation for mercy.'

'I wonder what Nick would 'ave done if 'e'd bin in my shoes,' Tony Carter said as they left the station.

'I think you know the answer to that one,' Dan Sully replied.

Frankie Weston clipped his webbing belt on and looked in the mirror as he adjusted his tie. He did not feel happy about the short haircut, but that was the lot of trainees unfortunately, he told himself. Anyway the uniform fitted well and he had put on a few pounds. The lads would be out in force tonight and he could spin them a few yarns. Maybe there would be a party to go to. James would know. He seemed to be able to row himself into most of the weekend jollifications in the area.

Frankie walked along the turning and saw the two hawks chatting together.

''Ello, son. 'Ome on leave?' Doris asked.

Frankie nodded. 'Embarkation,' he told them.

'Where yer goin', any idea?' Phyllis cut in.

'Korea,' he replied.

'Oh my good Gawd! Yer muvver must be worried sick,' Doris remarked.

'I dunno why. It ain't 'er goin' out there,' Frankie said with a cheeky grin.

Jack Marchant sat up on the roof and watched the pigeons swoop down low as they made their first circuit. He raised his arms the way Bill did and the birds climbed back high into the summer sky. Monty strutted along by his feet and then fluttered up on to the balustrade and settled down to await the flock's return.

The old man leaned against the stairway wall and watched the birds' progress. How sad it was that Bill was too ill to be here today, he thought. The flight was moving in tight formation and it seemed almost musical in its rhythm. Maybe there was a verse or two to fit the sight of birds on the wing. Bill would certainly know. Maybe his old friend would rally soon. He missed their rooftop chats.

Jack Marchant tapped the bowl of his pipe against his boot and got up from the bench. Monty was still perched on the balustrade although the rest of the pigeons had returned to their roost. Jack scratched his head and frowned. It was strange, he thought as he walked over to shoo the bird back to the loft. Suddenly Monty flexed his wings and took off. He flew straight, climbing even higher in the sky. Jack watched as the bird became a dot, and still he flew on, until he disappeared into the blue and was gone.

The realisation hit him like a flash of cold fire in his belly and throat and he felt like crying, but it was strange, there was no despair in his heart. He hurried down to the flat below and the visiting nurse met him at the door. 'Mr Marchant, I'm afraid Bill Simpson's just . . .'

'I know,' he said. 'I know. Monty told me.'

Epilogue

Kate Selby sighed wearily as she entered the clinic and looked around her. Young mothers and expectant women were sitting chatting together while small children played noisily with an array of well-used toys. The day was hot and she felt uncomfortable as she walked over to a vacant seat and sat down thankfully. The young woman opposite smiled and Kate gave her a tired smile in response. The woman got up with an effort and came over. 'Don't yer remember me?' she asked.

Kate's eyes narrowed. 'Jenny Jordan?'

'That's right,' she said, holding her hand to the side of her bulge. 'You too?'

Kate Selby nodded. 'This is me first visit,' she replied. 'I didn't reco'nise yer at first. It's yer 'air. Yer've gone blonde.'

Jenny laughed aloud. 'Yeah, I'm told it suits me,' she said, touching it. 'Where yer livin' now?'

'Tower Estate.'

'I moved ter St John's Estate near Tower Bridge,' Jenny told her. 'Me mum an' dad live there too. They've got a ground-floor flat.'

'Is this yer first baby?' Kate asked.

She nodded. 'What about you?'

'Third,' Kate replied, sighing. 'I've got two gels, the eldest is almost four an' the ovver one's two. Me mum's lookin' after 'em.'

Jenny sat down puffing loudly. 'I'm expectin' any day now,' she said. 'I've gone a week over. Brendan's really worried.'

'I wish Peter was,' Kate remarked. ''E takes it all in 'is stride.'

'If I remember rightly 'e wanted four kids, didn't 'e?' Jenny said smiling.

Kate Selby pulled a face. 'I told 'im 'e'll 'ave ter make do wiv three,' she replied. 'I'm certainly not goin' frew this again. 'Ere, d'you remember Linda Weston? She's got two kids now.'

Jenny looked surprised. 'I 'aven't seen anyfing o' the ole crowd since I moved,' she said. 'Do 'er an' Charlie still work at the leavver place?'

Kate shook her head. 'Nah, it all folded up. Linda told me that the woman who owned it 'ad ter sell it off on the cheap. 'Er 'usband 'ad a stroke an' she 'ad ter go an' look after 'im. They moved inter the country by all accounts.'

'That's sad,' Jenny replied, shaking her head.

'Yer remember ole Dick Conners who was always drunk?' Kate went on. 'Well, 'e married the woman out o' the baker's shop. They live in Catford, but 'e comes ter visit ole Ginny Coombes quite a lot. Yer wouldn't reco'nise 'im if yer saw 'im. Dead smart 'e is. Always wears a collar an' tie an' a nice suit. Ginny an' Albert Coombes managed ter get a ground-floor flat on our estate and so did Maggie Gainsford.

Mrs Colton an' the Perrys moved ter Dock'ead, an' yer remember those two old busybodies, Doris an' Phyllis?'

'Yeah.'

'Well, they stuck out fer ages fer ground-floor flats on that new estate off Long Lane. They got 'em too. Right next door to each ovver, would yer believe?'

Jenny smiled. 'I pity their neighbours.'

'I miss the old Eagle Street,' Kate said sadly. 'Remember 'ow we used ter go up on the roof o' Sunlight Buildin's?'

''Ow could I ever ferget,' Jenny replied. 'I 'eard old Jack Marchant died, though.'

'They found 'im dead in 'is bed,' Kate told her. ''E died in 'is sleep, by all accounts.'

'Remember that summer when Nick Carter got killed?' Jenny said.

'Do I,' Kate replied with a frown. 'I fink everybody was surprised when they commuted Boy-boy's sentence ter life. We all expected 'im ter swing fer killin' that Colby bloke.'

A nurse appeared and called out Jenny's name. The young woman got up with a sigh and smiled at Kate. 'I'll most likely see yer back 'ere wiv the next one,' she remarked with a saucy grin.

'No fear,' Kate replied sharply. ''E'll 'ave ter tie a knot in it from now on.'

Charlie Bradley held his four-year-old son David's hand as they strolled through Abbey Street beside Linda, who carried eighteen-month-old Sally in her arms. The warm summer day was tempered by a cool breeze, and high above them traces of cloud drifted smoothly across a blue sky. Charlie smiled at Linda and nodded towards the arch which had the sign above the entrance: 'Bennett's Motor Repairs'. 'I see it's changed 'ands again,' he remarked.

'It's bin almost three years now,' Linda replied sadly. 'It was good while it lasted though, wasn't it?'

Charlie glanced over to the derelict yard opposite as they walked on. 'I don't fink we'll ever ferget that summer,' he said nostalgically. 'We 'ad big ideas, big plans. It's strange the way fings turn out.'

'You are 'appy, ain't yer, Charlie?' she asked him, anxiety appearing in her eyes.

'Of course I am,' he told her with a reassuring smile. 'I've got you, an' these two little perishers. What more could a man want?'

Linda still seemed a little concerned as she glanced at him. 'I remember those summer nights we spent up on that roof in Eagle Street,' she said. 'We did make a lot o' plans, didn't we?'

Charlie nodded. 'We're still young enough ter dream a few more up, darlin',' he replied. 'Anyway it ain't too bad workin' fer the electricity board. At least it's in the open air, an' there's a chance ter get upgraded, once I've done the courses.'

They crossed the Tower Bridge Road and walked through the Saturday afternoon market, stopping to buy both children a hot, jam-filled doughnut before turning right at the Beehive into the newly built Tower Estate. Children played in the grounds and people stood out on balconies, leaning on the railings as they watched the activity below. Dora and John Weston waved down to them and Charlie bent down to point them out to David, whose face lit up as he spotted his grandparents.

Linda smiled up at them. They seemed happy enough, she thought. Their flat was modern, with a bathroom and an airy kitchen, much like Charlie's and her flat in Dockhead. It was cool in summer, damp-free and warm in winter, but in her heart the young mother knew that her parents would often recall and no doubt yearn for the old days in Eagle Street. They would remember the draughty house with its outside toilet and tiny rooms, and the backyard, where the wringer stood, the tin bath was kept, and the washing stretched from wall to wall. They would remember the fresh lace curtains, whitened doorsteps and blackleaded grates, and the ever-open front doors where neighbours chatted together, and they would see in their mind's eye the ancient Sunlight Buildings, with its creaking, gaslit stairs and rotting woodwork, and the flat roof where pigeons swooped and soared.

Charlie took the baby from her as they crossed the courtyard and she clasped young David's hand as they climbed the stone stairs which had been freshly scrubbed and smelt of carbolic. They reached the landing and David ran to receive a hug from his grandparents. Linda looked down over the balcony and wondered if there was any place on this new estate to watch the glorious sunsets and weave those special dreams, as there once had been, atop those old Buildings, that summer in Eagle Street.

PEDLAR'S ROW

HARRY BOWLING

In 1946, Pedlar's Row in Bermondsey is home
to a close-knit community counting its blessings
to have survived the war intact – and full of
curiosity about the new family moving into
number three. And the Priors' move into the
Row is not without incident.

Laura Prior, who's unmarried, having had to
care for her invalid father, enjoys the excitement
of her new home – not least because of her
growing attraction to docker Billy Cassidy. But
her sister Lucy finds life harder; with rationing,
a shortage of homes, having to contend with a
husband who's emotionally scarred from his
internment in a Japanese POW camp, and her
guilt about a war-time affair, it isn't easy to
settle down to normal married life. So the
situation isn't helped when Lucy finds herself
and her family embroiled in local villain Archie
Westlake's shady dealings. And when a body is
discovered on a bombsite behind the Row, no
one is beyond suspicion of murder.

'What makes Harry's novels work is their warmth
and authenticity. Their spirit comes from the author
himself and his abiding memories of family life as it
was once lived in the slums of southeast London'
Today

FICTION / SAGA 0 7472 4520 7

More Enchanting Fiction from Headline

The Farrans of Fellmonger Street

FROM THE BESTSELLING KING OF COCKNEY SAGAS

HARRY BOWLING

When widowed Ida Farran runs off with a bus inspector in 1949, she leaves her five children to fend for themselves. Preoccupied with the day-to-day task of earning enough money to keep the family together, eighteen-year-old Rose battles bravely on, thankful for the mysterious benefactor who pays the rent on their flat in Imperial Buildings on Fellmonger Street, a little backwater off the Tower Bridge Road.

Life isn't easy but between them Rose and her younger brother Don just about manage to make ends meet – though the welfare would soon put the three young ones into foster homes if they believed Rose couldn't cope. Recently, however, Don has become rather too friendly with the Morgan boys. Everyone knows the small-time Bermondsey villains are a bad lot and Rose is desperately worried Don might end up in trouble. But even this concern pales into insignificance when Rose finds herself pregnant. Now it'll need a miracle to keep the Farrans of Fellmonger Street together.

FICTION / SAGA 0 7472 4795 1

A selection of bestsellers from Headline